DUST

Sharbari Zohra Ahmed was born in Dhaka, Bangladesh. Her family moved to the United States when she was three weeks old. She is a playwright and screenwriter, and also writes fiction. She barely graduated high school but now teaches creative writing in the MFA program in Manhattanville College, and is Artist in Residence in Sacred Heart University's graduate Film and Television Program. She lives in Darien, Connecticut.

This is her first novel.

Advance Praise for *Dust Under Her Feet*

Dust Under Her Feet knits together themes of war, politics, sisterhood, and love, all energised by Sharbari Zohra Ahmed's atmospheric prose, bringing to life not only wartime Calcutta but also the beautifully complex, tender-yet-steely voice of her fascinating protagonist, nightclub owner Yasmine Khan.

–Tahmima Anam, award-winning author

Dust Under Her Feet is an exquisite debut novel. Sharbari Zohra Ahmed immerses the reader in WWII Calcutta and assuredly peels back the layers of racism and classism in India, England and America, and all the connections between Empire and colonialism. Ahmed beautifully creates the tender yet no nonsense atmosphere of the nightclub, Bombay Duck, where the charming and complicated courtesans leap off the page as they struggle through friendships, sisterhood, betrayals and first loves. Ahmed deftly writes her male characters too… A topical and endearing tale of morality, decency and the many nuances of being human.

–Soniah Kamal, author of *Unmarriageable: Pride and Prejudice in Pakistan* and *An Isolated Incident*

Full of heart, wit, and glamour, *Dust Under Her Feet* honours and subverts old Hollywood war movies and British Raj nostalgia. Yasmine is a whip-smart heroine, observing and narrating the absurd inequities of the coloniser and the colonised, and everything in between. You will love this novel.

–Chaitali Sen, author of *The Pathless Sky*

SHARBARI ZOHRA AHMED

DUST UNDER HER FEET

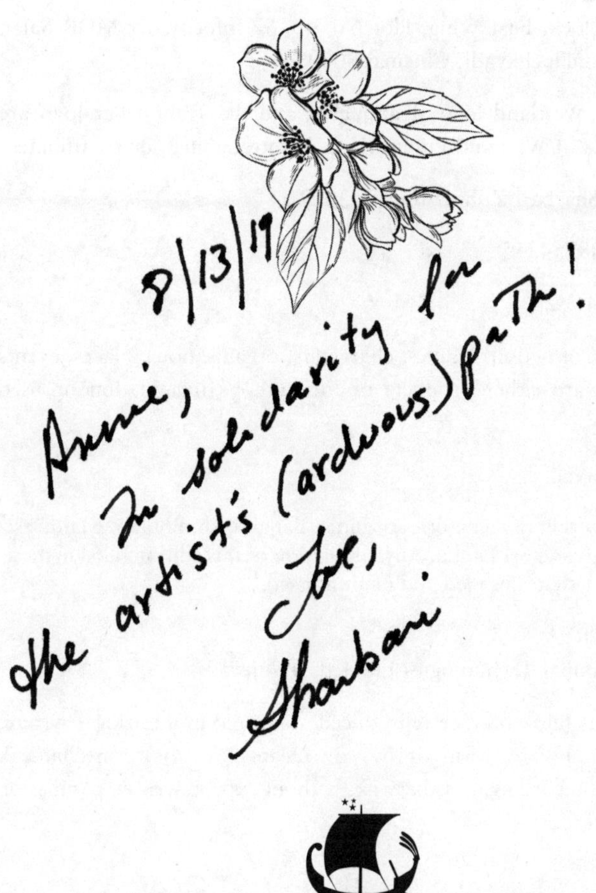

First published by Tranquebar, an imprint of Westland Publications Private Limited, in 2019

1st Floor, A Block, East Wing, Plot No. 40, SP Infocity, Dr MGR Salai, Perungudi, Kandanchavadi, Chennai 600096

Westland, the Westland logo, Tranquebar and the Tranquebar logo are the trademarks of Westland Publications Private Limited, or its affiliates.

ISBN: 9789388754255

10 9 8 7 6 5 4 3 2 1

This is a work of fiction. Names, characters, organisations, places, events and incidents are either products of the author's imagination or used fictitiously.

Typeset by SÜRYA

Printed at Manipal Technologies Limited, Manipal

For my mother and father, Anowara and Manzoor Ahmed,
and my son, the original AAK

Let us go forth, the tellers of tales, and seize whatever prey the heart long for, and have no fear. Everything exists, everything is true, and the earth is only a little dust under our feet.

–William Butler Yeats
'The Teller of Tales', *Celtic Twilight*

Jiboner dhon kichui jabena fela –
Dhula-ey tader jotoi houk obohela.

Nothing of life's nuggets is ever lost –
However much hidden in neglect under the dust.

–Rabindranath Tagore

PART ONE

OF ALL THE GIN JOINTS...

Drink if you like. You should have as good a time here as is commensurate with your duties. Do, however, keep your Indian liquor separated from its two quarrelsome partners, woman and song.

–*The Calcutta Key*, 1945
'Helpful Hints for American Military
Personnel in India'

1

Akash Alexander Khan '61
Hayden Hall
Mt Hermon School for Boys
Gill, MA
10 October 1959

My dearest Akash,

You asked, so I am telling you. But I must warn you: this is a love story. I will tell it in my way. In fits and starts because that is the nature of love stories that happen during wars. With delays, disruptions and sudden diversions. I will also keep in mind how much you disliked all that sappy stuff when we used to go to the Lighthouse to watch the picture shows. When Gable kissed Vivien, everyone sighed and you groaned and sunk deeper into your seat. You only paid attention during the battle scenes. I know that makes you a normal boy but I am so relieved that you never had to experience war first-hand. I suspect you would not be so enthusiastic about torpedoes if you were staring down the business end of one. Nonetheless, I will do my best to provide a battle or a skirmish for you, which, as you will learn, often accompany a story of love.

This story, mine, yours, began a long time ago. It actually began before I was even born. Even before my grandmother was born. It began in 1757, near a small Bengali village called

Plassey, where the British Raj was officially born. We Bengalis consider ourselves the artists and intellectuals of India and pride ourselves on being visionaries. A wise Indian nationalist leader (I shudder to think what you haven't been taught about your history), Gopal Krishna Gokhale, said, 'What Bengal thinks today, India will think tomorrow.' So, initially we had no problem with the British—by all accounts they were like wide-eyed children let loose in a candy store, and they wanted to partake of everything. But since that first battle in Plassey, we were agitating to get them out as soon as possible. They got greedy you see, and then of course, some religious types showed up and demanded they cease and desist feeling good at once, and to that end sent them pinched-faced English women, who 'tamed' them. As soon as the memsahibs alighted the ships in their crinoline and corsets, the party was over.

Two hundred years later, the agitation reached a fevered pitch, and we pinned all our hopes on one man. He seemed to be the only one who knew how to get under their skin. He did it by doing nothing. He sat quietly, received people, peered at them over his too-small spectacles and showered them with love, wove cloth, starved himself and irritated Winston Churchill to the point of dementia—an added benefit. I know people don't want to imagine this, but Gandhi was no saint himself. He had odd proclivities that you are too young to understand. Great leaders don't have to be saints, however, as you will someday see.

When they first arrived in the 1600s to set up a trading post, the Ingrez embraced everything about India. They donned Indian clothing, ate with their fingers from communal platters and learned to speak the various languages fluently. They seemed to draw no distinction between themselves and the natives. Most importantly, they married Indian women; they didn't just take them as mistresses. Unlike now, of course.

It's amazing how backward modern civilisation can be. If the opportunists hadn't arrived with their frigid, corseted wives, things might have been very different for us.

I know I told you that this was a love story, but it is through no machination of mine. Even my own father was impervious to my charms. He never came back, did he? Men sometimes have to be convinced into loving a woman. I can convince a fishmonger to charge ten cents less for a pound of koi but that's about it. Being pretty is not enough; even being beautiful is not enough. My strength lay in my ability to, as the Americans say, make a buck. I wasn't suited for the family business. Your grandmother realised quickly that my tone deafness and my indifference towards men in general were not ideal for a life of courtesan-ship.

Speaking of Americans, I have to say they are a most paradoxical and peculiar group of people. They are not as stuffy and formal as the British. When they were in India, they treated all the Indians they encountered with warmth and innocent curiosity. I noticed they loved to laugh and were generally sentimental and optimistic, yet they segregated their coloured soldiers and treated their Jewish soldiers with suspicion and contempt.

Well, this is my legacy to you—among other things, not quite so delightful. I knew someday you were going to want to know where you came from, and my life before you. I knew you would want to know why your eyes are green, a wholly unexpected trait, or why the sun doesn't have quite the same effect on your skin as it does on mine. I know you want to know what kind of a man your father was.

I fear, though, that some of the story may have suffered from too many nights at The Lighthouse Cinema. I do love a good war-torn love story, despite my reputation for being aloof and dispassionate. Speaking of love: I love you. This is my story, this is your story—but only the bits you choose to claim. Use it, discard it, whatever you want. What I want you to know is that your karma doesn't have to be tied into your father's or mine. So please try not be burdened by it.

Your mother,
Yasmine

2

The girls of Bombay Duck arose by noon, washed and hung their precious few silk stockings to dry, hummed, smoked, and gave one another massages. Yasmine, the owner and boss, was awake well before. She needed the silence. Once everyone was up, they would all be tugging on her. Sometimes she loathed the sound of her own name; it usually meant there was something that needed sorting out. She did enjoy hearing the girls trade stories about the previous night's events: who had to fend off that lecherous adjutant from Pinner; whose rancorous wife had come along to keep an eye on her husband and glare at Patience, the main singer, and the prettiest one; who got the low tipper; who felt they sang off key. At 5 p.m. sharp, the performers and the staff all took their meal together in the main room, which was cleared early in the morning, aired of the stale smoke, sweat and liquor, tables pushed to the side, chairs neatly stacked, floor swept, and bar wiped down. The cleaning staff grumbled that the room would once again be smelly and in disarray within a few hours, so why did Yasmine insist that every nook and cranny be swept? Yasmine believed that the club came alive every night, as if for the first time. It was reborn, with new energy, new patrons, and new stories. No two nights were the same, and it required a blank slate. She also insisted that the evening meal before the doors opened was taken together so everyone could sit down and listen to one another. She felt creating a hierarchy of caste and religion would only cause problems for her later. At the Duck, she said to everyone individually their first day, there was no 'India' as they knew it; that, in fact, this was not India.

'Yes,' Patience, her closest confidante and oldest friend, would quip. 'You have entered Yasministan, where there is no caste, no god is held higher than any other, the sexes are equal, but the Rupee, above all, reigns supreme.'

Yasmine made sure the lighter-skinned girls were not treated better, nor were the men—such as Pharaoh and his bandmates, or the cook-cum-manager Adil Baboo—considered superior to the women. This sat well with everyone. The youngest performer, Radhika, was a sixteen-year-old Dalit; Madhu, another one of the performers, was a strict vegetarian, and possibly a Brahmin, though she never talked about it, but did not object to eating next to anyone consuming meat and did not insist her food be prepared separately. The one exception was Asma, the Parsi. She was educated and pernickety by nature. She held herself above everyone at the Duck. Even Yasmine. One got the impression she would find fault with King George's table manners if she were dining with him. At Yasmine's table, Muslims broke bread with Hindus, a reformed Catholic and at least one agnostic—Yasmine herself. On the 'outside', beyond the Duck's doors, where Calcutta sweltered and grew increasingly restless, this would not be possible.

Yasmine arbitrated who performed on stage first to last. But when it came to meals, even the lowliest peon, who cleaned the water closet, took the laundry down to the dhobi ghats and ran errands, was served the same food and the same amount, though they ate after serving the girls and the band.

It was not that Yasmine was making a political or social point. It was that it was impractical to be divisive. It was bad for business. She did not believe in dividing and conquering, though, as she and everyone around her would find out a few years later, the British most certainly did.

The meals were a raucous affair, with much arguing and laughter and good-natured teasing. It was everyone's way of getting ready for the night's inevitable intensity. Yasmine also used the time to observe how everyone was doing and feeling, to watch the girls interact in case there was simmering resentments or ruffled feathers that required soothing. They worked the club as one entity, trawling the room and creating the necessary energy needed for the soldiers to keep spending money, and if the girls' chemistry was off, then Yasmine noticed a substantial dip in the night's take. These men were facing death, or had faced it, and they came to Bombay Duck to forget that for a time. Feminine squabbles and malcontent undermined the fantasy. Her mother, a savvy businesswoman descended from a long, noble line of courtesans from the Nawab of Lucknow's court, had warned her, 'A man leaves his wife's side to come to us and pretend he is still young, still relevant, still virile. She represents his lost youth and sometimes his failures. It's in her recriminating glances, her sighs of disappointment. We are here to the create the illusion that she is not correct in her assessment of him.' It took Yasmine a few years to understand that her mother also thought they were doing the wife a favour.

That evening they sat around, lingering over their meagre dinner of some watery daal, a fistful's worth of previously verminous rice, and two scrawny chickens that Adil Baboo had to trade a bottle of black market whiskey for. He boiled the worms out of the rice but joked they were pure protein and would have been a much welcome delicacy if one were starving in a Burmese jungle. Up until then, they had not eaten meat in two weeks because all that they received as rations was served to the customers. The Muslims were dismayed by the forced vegetarianism. The government had also started rationing rice more actively, claiming there was a shortage and it was needed for the troops. Yasmine's black-market connections had not been able to provide her with anything substantial in a while. What she could find, she had to pay top dollar for, and had barely broken even as there had been several nights when the American GIs did not spend as much as usual.

It was 1942, everything was in flux. Yasmine wanted to keep up with the opportunities that the war presented, and not drown in panic, but it was daunting. She saw more and more Americans arriving in the city, which was good for business, but it meant the war was getting bigger—and closer. Early on, Yasmine had tried to ban any deep discussions on the war, in case it proved demoralising or led to hysteria. As time went on, even she could not resist speculating and weighing in. The shifts in the world were too great to ignore, and watching a new type of white person, the odd, seemingly friendly American, slowly taking over their beloved, scrappy city, bore discussion. Everyone had their opinions. Yasmine was vigilant to keep people from each other's throats, though sometimes that proved futile. Her preoccupation was this new non-Indian element, the American; Asma's was in supporting Britain. Others still did not know what to make of Hitler and the Axis. The conversations rarely focused on one aspect of the war. The lack of focus was how Yasmine wanted it. She wanted to maintain dispassion. In order to maintain control.

'Did you see the latest they are sending over to Burma?' Yasmine said, referring to the Americans who would be deployed soon. 'It is mostly coloured men and very young soldiers, with some older engineers who will be building a road between India and China.'

'England is the only safe place in the world,' Asma said wistfully. She longed to go live somewhere on a stormy moor, in a stone house with a draughty chimney, pining after a chaste love. 'It's Germany, France and Poland that are not.'

'It's not really safe back home. The Germans keep bombing it,' Patience said. She always referred to England as 'home', even though she had never been there and had been born in Calcutta. Many Anglo-Indians thought of England as their real home, and felt they had ended up in India by some cruel mistake.

'We're safer here,' Madhu agreed. 'The Japs won't bother bombing Calcutta,' she added. 'What's in it for them?'

This was met with a thoughtful silence.

'I heard a terrible thing a few days ago. I am sure it can't be true. It's too evil,' Adil Baboo said into the quiet. He rarely gave his opinion, so he had everyone's attention. 'I heard that Hitler has built these camps, these places where they're herding all the Jews in Europe and killing them, slaughtering them like cattle. They even take them in cattle cars to these places.'

'Children as well?' Asma asked. Adil Baboo nodded. Asma shuddered.

'No, it must be a rumour,' Yasmine said.

'He wants them all out forever,' Madhu said.

Yasmine was doubtful. 'If Hitler is trying to take over the world, why would he bother with a few Jews?'

Madhu shrugged. 'Who knows? But if Hitler wins, he will want to rid India of her Jews as well. All five of them.'

Everyone laughed and Yasmine was relieved—she couldn't have everyone becoming morose so close to show time.

'We're not blonde and blue-eyed either,' Asma said. 'He'll probably rid India of Indians.'

'A few less Indians wouldn't hurt anybody,' Patience said. She smiled wickedly. 'We reproduce like cockroaches. At least there would be more room on the street cars.'

'Actually, he must like us,' Madhu said. 'It's the swastika after all. He only hates Jews.'

'He's probably just going to get rid of everybody. He'll be so lonely he's going to have to kill himself,' Patience said.

'Well that's one way to solve the world's problems,' Asma said.

'His right-hand man, what's his name?' someone asked.

'Goebbels,' Asma said.

'He looks like an undertaker,' Patience said. 'Have you seen him, his face is so pale and thin. Perfect!'

Everyone laughed again, this time a bit more heartily. Rahul, the young peon, started clearing the dishes.

Asma gathered all the silverware together and piled them on to a dish and handed it to him. Everyone watched as Rahul kept adding more dishes and silverware on his tray. He kept glancing at Radhika and nearly dropped a fork.

'Arrey Rahul,' Yasmine said. 'You do this every time, and every time you break something.'

Rahul gave her a gummy grin and kept grabbing things off the table.

'Look at how much I can balance,' he said, again glancing at Radhika, who stared down at her plate and did not seem to be aware of what was happening around her.

Patience snatched a glass out of his hand before he placed it on the top of the precarious pile of dishes.

'If you break anything, I'm taking it out of your wages,' Yasmine said, shaking her head and stifling a smile.

'I don't care if he is doing that!' Radhika cried out in Hindi. This startled Rahul, causing him to drop a plate, shattering it. He managed to steady the tray, saving the rest of the plates, and a month's wages. Everyone stared at Radhika in bewildered silence.

'What am I doing?' Rahul said after a moment.

'He hates the Ingrez. He wants to destroy them! Anyone who fights the English is my friend,' the girl continued. It took a second or two before it dawned on anyone that Radhika was talking about Hitler and not Rahul.

Radhika's was not an unusual sentiment. Many Indians supported Hitler because he was fighting the British. A distant Chittagongian relation of Yasmine's even named her sons Hitler and, paradoxically, the other one, Stalin—or Hitoo and Staloo as they were known affectionately.

The general notion was if Hitler was going to stand up to the British, then bully for him. Yasmine, on the other hand, did not trust Hitler. He was European, and seemed more obsessed with class and race than anyone. There was no evidence he would be a just ruler, but, she ventured at times, he would be better than Hirohito, and somehow less foreign.

Until this outburst, Radhika had been quiet all through the meal, but that was normal for her. She saved all her energy for her dancing, it seemed. No one tried to engage her in small talk anymore. She had picked at her food though, and that was not normal, as she usually gulped it down like it would be snatched from her at any moment. She was moody, however, and unpredictable.

'Why are you always so cranky?' Asma asked the girl in Hindi.

'Speak English,' Yasmine said. 'Or she won't learn.'

'She's sixteen,' Madhu said, and patted Radhika on the arm.

'Rahul is sixteen; look how happy he is all the time,' Asma said.

The group looked at Rahul, who grinned and quickly walked out with the tray before Yasmine remembered he had broken a plate.

'Rahul is a boy. Radhika is a—' Madhu was about to say Dalit, but stopped herself. '...a girl in India.'

Patience shuddered. 'Egad! Thankless, to be sure.'

Everyone, including Radhika, smiled at the mock horror on Patience's face.

'All right, time to get ready,' Yasmine said firmly, clapping her hands twice. 'Adil Baboo wants to do a sound check on one of the mikes, Patience. Will you help him? And listen, everyone,' Yasmine continued, 'a new batch of Americans have come in just a few days ago. They will be homesick, confused and in need of libation—'

'And us!' Patience chimed in. She gave a high kick, revealing too much leg, but it broke the tension from Radhika's outburst.

'Most likely some of them will come in tonight. Keep an eye out for the new ones. Make them forget home,' Yasmine said.

'You won't be able to miss them,' Patience said to the others. 'They'll be walking around in a daze at the heat and wall-to-wall wogs.'

'Patience! That's awful,' Asma said.

'Yet, true,' Patience replied.

'What is a wog?' Radhika asked softly.

'Never mind that,' Yasmine said, and briskly ushered the girl up the stairs.

For Yasmine, Radhika's anti-English rant was worrisome. There was a great deal of paranoia in the air because of the agitation to end the Raj. 'The stultifying air in Calcutta,' a drunken and disgruntled English customer once said to Yasmine, 'smells of burning trash and treason.'

Yasmine herself noticed that more and more posters around town admonished, 'Loose Lips Sink Ships', while others showed images of luridly grinning, slant-eyed, and oddly fanged Japanese soldiers brandishing bayonets and threatening cherubic, white babies. Yet another one depicted a comely blonde temptress holding court with a gaggle of adoring men. 'Keep mum, she's not so dumb', it warned.

She remembered this suddenly, and it made her more anxious. She would have to watch Radhika.

The bandleader, Pharaoh, and his musicians wandered in wearing white jackets and loosened black bowties. They all made their way to the stage to set up. The microphone gave off a screech, breaking into Yasmine's reverie. The club slowly came to life. Lights were switched on; chairs were set upright. The musicians tuned their instruments and laughed amongst themselves and smoked cigarettes.

Upstairs in their rooms, the girls helped each other dress and put on makeup. Radhika chose to get ready by herself, as always. Yasmine decided it would be a good time to have a chat with the girl. She walked into the small room and watched her for a while, wondering what she could say that would send a clear message that Radhika was not to utter anything traitorous again, but without upsetting her so much that her performance was affected.

Radhika silently tied bells around her ankles and fastened the hooks around the fitted bottoms of her pants. She did not acknowledge her boss at first but then handed her strands of fragrant beli phool and asked her to plait them into her hair.

Yasmine silently tied the flowers into Radhika's thick hair. The girl sat still, but she was nervous. She knew Yasmine was displeased. She assumed it meant her pay would be cut, as that was how Yasmine meted out most of her punishments.

'There are posters and pamphlets around town that say "careless talk costs lives". I know you have seen them,' Yasmine began.

'I have, didi. But I can't read,' the girl replied.

Yasmine turned the girl's head around to see if she was being cheeky. Radhika blinked at her, a blank look on her face.

'Mind your tongue, or I will send you out into the street with less than what you came in with. Tonight there will be more English officers than usual—you will dance for them and make them believe you love them. Even if it kills you. Do you understand?'

Radhika nodded silently.

'And you cannot utter words like the ones you did downstairs again, understand?'

'But…'

'What?'

'Don't you want them out?'

'I am telling you that what you say might mean the difference between life and death.'

'But Gandhi-ji speaks his mind always.'

Yasmine stared at her, incredulous. 'You are the furthest thing from Gandhi-ji,' she said. 'And besides, Gandhi-ji doesn't have a house full of mouths to feed or debt collectors breathing down his neck. He's living in a dream world. Though I wish you lot would go on a hunger strike once in a while. It would save me money.'

Radhika clapped a hand over her mouth in horror at Yasmine's words. To her that was far more traitorous talk than anything she could have said against the British. Yasmine scowled at her.

'Uff-oh!' she said in exasperation at the look on Radhika's face. One would think Yasmine had insulted Lord Shiva himself. 'It was a joke.'

'At least Gandhi-ji doesn't see me as a shudra,' Radhika said, tears welling up in her eyes. 'Or a prostitute.'

'Neither do I,' Yasmine said. She meant it, but to the girl it sounded hollow.

'You do!' she cried and flung herself onto her lumpy bed.

'Your life is very different from his. He is a politician, and you, a mere girl. You cannot afford to be a revolutionary right now.'

'I am not a child,' she sniffed, even as she wiped her nose with the back of her hand and shuddered from her tears. Yasmine almost smiled. The girl was so young.

'You're from Chittagong,' Radhika said.

'So?'

'Pritilata was not much older than me when she took over the armoury and shot a Britisher.'

Yasmine sighed. Growing up, all she ever heard about was how a twenty-one-year-old girl and a rag tag group of schoolboys had thrown over the British Raj for a few days, ten years ago, in Chittagong. It was impressive to be sure, but Yasmine, ever the pragmatist, felt it was a monumental failure as the British appeared to have recovered quite heartily from this aberrant jolt to their colonial presence. It barely registered in the rest of India, and in the end, the British hanged or tortured to death almost every one of the main agitators. Pritilata (who was anything but pretty, Patience often said) killed herself before she was caught. It was a story, a legend Yasmine took for granted, as it was so much a part of her growing-up years and had ceased to have meaning. But she knew some people—Bengalis especially—felt very differently. There were a few things Bengalis were unabashedly biased about: the Chittagong uprising, their activist past, Rabindranath Tagore, and their language. They all believed there was nothing more mellifluous than Bangla, the 'French of the East'.

'Had they succeeded, I would have been more impressed,' Yasmine said, smiling at the fresh look of horror on Radhika's face. 'And it goes to show, children have no business being revolutionaries.'

'How can you say that?' Radhika said. A new feeling crept into Yasmine then. One she had not experienced very often in her short life—guilt. She was looking at the mottled face of a sobbing child, but she was going to send this child downstairs to dance enticingly for a room full of ogling men who would fantasise about her later while they abused themselves or someone else. Yasmine would make money from this, and this was her legacy.

Her mother had warned her against having too active a conscience. 'You must decide how rich you want to be,' she said, 'and adjust your conscience accordingly.'

The girl was not having sex with anyone, she managed to keep wandering hands at bay when she was on stage, yet it still seemed wrong to be asking her to dance when she was so emotional. This was precisely what Yasmine wanted to avoid, these pangs of attachment. She simply could not afford them.

'Get a hold of yourself, young lady!' Yasmine barked. 'Stop, Radhika,' she pleaded more gently when the girl kept sobbing. She handed her a cloth. 'Here, wipe your face.' Radhika took the cloth and dabbed at her cheeks. Yasmine knew if Patience had been there, she would have hugged the girl. All Yasmine could manage was what she hoped was a reassuring pat on the shoulder. She left Radhika standing alone, staring at herself in the mirror.

Yasmine paused when she reached the main floor of the club and took in the scene. She needed to gather herself before the night began in earnest. She had been tending to Radhika for forty-five minutes. There were only a handful of customers. But that changed quickly. Within two hours the Duck was filled with GIs hollering and engaging in good-natured verbal sparring with their British allies.

Sorry we had to kick you out of Massachusetts!

Can you explain cricket to me? Why does the poor son of a bitch run back and forth? And what the hell is a googly?

At least he doesn't run in a circle like a rabid dog, mate!

'I was almost hoping for a slow night,' Yasmine said to Adil Baboo later, but she was happy.

Yasmine liked the Americans—purely for business reasons. Americans were bottomless beer drinkers who seemed to get rowdier as the night grew longer and more willing to spend money. They were also much less formal than the English patrons and did not treat the Indian waiters like inferiors. This served to incite the ire of the British men, who were resentful of the Yankee presence in their beloved Raj. They were loath to admit that they needed American help to fight off the Japanese. According to them, the Yanks were arrogant buffoons, who were upsetting the delicate social balance that was colonial India.

American treatment of Indians was so confoundedly friendly, yet it was not lost on Yasmine that there was not a single coloured soldier in sight. Patience, who had been to the American base, had told her that the Negro soldiers ate and slept in separate facilities and were not allowed to mix with the white soldiers. They had been brought to India to serve white officers. This was *their* caste system.

At half past ten, in the midst of the rowdiness, there was a moment of thunderstruck silence as Patience and Asma began to sing the Yankee national anthem in lilting Indian accents. The girls did not know all the words to the song, but the Americans soon helped them out. Some of the English sat and listened with dour expressions on their faces, annoyed at the way the Yanks had of barrelling into places and taking over. But other Brits just shook their heads and smiled. They were allies, after all. The rowdiness resumed with a rousing rendition of *Don't Sit Under the Apple Tree*, which everyone sang in a round. All in all, it was shaping into a happy night.

'Yasmine, you have to open some windows in here,' Adil Baboo complained. 'Those firangis keep smoking and what not!' He nodded towards the Americans. Adil Baboo made no bones about the fact that he was wary of white men, but if he were hard pressed to choose which he could tolerate, it would be Americans. But there were times that even he found them excessive.

'This is a club, Adil Baboo,' Yasmine said.

'Please! It's so bad for Patience and Asma's voices!'

This was true. Yasmine walked to the entrance and asked the darwan to open the doors and let some of the smoke out. She decided to step out for some fresh air herself, if one could call the densely humid Calcutta night, fresh.

A thunderstorm was on its way. The thought of this made Yasmine happy. When the rains came, it seemed as if the sky was going to burst at any moment, filling every depression with water. Like most Bengalis, Yasmine loved the rain. At night, she fell asleep easily to the sound of water running off the tin roofs. To Yasmine, the rains always brought with them a hint of some great excitement. Thunderstorms could wreak havoc, but there was promise in the rains, too. Afterwards, everything was in Hollywood Technicolor. The trees were greener, the bougainvillea more vividly hot pink and orange. The air smelled fresher—not a mean feat in Calcutta. She believed that being surrounded by fertility and growth made people more romantic. It reflected the Bengali nature: lugubrious, but still hopeful, and inclined towards poetry. It was one of the few times Yasmine felt at home in the place where she was born.

Maybe that was why the vision of a man walking towards her in the damp air made her feel like a heroine in a movie. It was like she was waiting for her lover to arrive, and he finally had. She didn't see his face at first; she saw his form, and that was enough to make her keep watching. He was tall and broad-shouldered, and had an easy gait. He was dressed in his officer's uniform. When he came closer, she saw from his uniform that he was American. One hand was in a pocket; the other held an almost finished cigarette and a slip of paper that he peered at under the street lamp. He wore glasses. When he loosened his tie, looked up and saw Yasmine standing under the sign, his handsome, boyish face broke into a smile.

His voice was deep.

'Salaam waleikum,' he said. 'Or namaste.'

'A simple hello will suffice,' Yasmine said. The Americans always tried a bit too hard.

'Phew! English. My name is Edward.' He held out his hand. 'Hello!'

'Hello yourself,' she replied. His hand was warm and dry, something she would always remember. It was hard to come by a dry hand in such a moist place, she would think later. 'I'm Yasmine.'

'That's a nice name. Jasmine.'

'Uh, no—*Yas*mine. Same difference, I suppose.'

'Funnily, I know the Bengali word for jasmine,' Edward said after a moment. He paused again, as if unsure he should continue.

'Well, go on then,' Yasmine said.

'Belly full,' he said, and smiled at her winningly. 'It was one of the first words I learned because my wife loves gardening and I wanted to tell her about it; plus, it was easy to remember. Belly full, like a full tummy,' he added, rubbing his stomach to demonstrate.

Yasmine heard the word 'wife' and was disappointed.

'It's more like belly fool,' she said softly.

'Would you happen to know why there is a fish hanging in front of a club that is called Bombay Duck?' he asked after she offered nothing more.

'Bombay Duck is a kind of fish,' she said.

'Ah! I kept looking for a duck.' He glanced at his watch.

'Am I keeping you from something?'

'Not at all,' he said. 'I was supposed to meet my pal here, and I'm a little late because I got confused. About the duck and fish. It's one of those Indian things, I guess. I must have passed this place six times.'

'Yes, foreigners always think that India is a great paradox,' Yasmine said. 'When really it's just like any place else, just a bit more so.'

'A bit more so what?' he asked.

'A bit more so everything. Loud, hot, smelly, crowded. I have never been anywhere else, so I am just assuming. But from what I see in the movies and the newsreels, other places seem very different,' Yasmine said. 'Cleaner.'

'I haven't travelled that much either,' he said. 'But yes, Calcutta is very different from Norwich, Connecticut. Dustier. Everything here is covered in a thin layer of dust. That's where I'm from, Norwich,' he added after a moment.

'I should go inside,' Yasmine said. She did not want to go back in. She wanted to stand outside in the thick night and keep talking to the American, even though beads of sweat were forming under her breasts and above her lip. And he had a wife back home who knew the Bengali equivalent of her name.

'Yes, you shouldn't keep your date waiting,' Edward said. 'I'm sure he's wondering where you are.'

Yasmine smiled. 'You're the one who's late ... and I don't have a date.'

He was still smiling at her, but his expression had changed.

'Oh, of course not,' he said.

'I beg your pardon?'

'Oh boy! What I meant was, of course no respectable unmarried Bengali woman would be outside a nightclub, smoking with me. What I mean is, you should not keep your husband waiting.'

Men had the same misplaced propriety, be they American or Indian, and the urgent need to put a woman in a neat category that they could then cope with while bedding them.

She was either someone's whore or someone's wife, there was no in between, Yasmine reflected. She decided then and there, she was not going to make it easy for him. She looked at him, challenging him. Go on, then, she said silently, try and figure out which one I am. Whore or wife.

Edward took off his hat and wiped his brow. 'You know, the *Calcutta Key* never talked about this.'

'What's that?' Yasmine asked.

'A manual on how to discreetly navigate the Indian female mind.' He chuckled.

Yasmine raised her eyebrows. 'Not even Indian men know how to do that.'

'Well, you're a native, and a woman. That's what we call a double whammy back home.' He grinned at her.

'I have to go in now,' she said.

'I guess you don't like to flirt much, huh?'

'Is that what you were doing?'

'Ouch,' Edward said, and shook his head.

The door opened; two officers, English, walked out, tipped their hats to Yasmine and did not give Edward a passing glance as they proceeded down the street. Music wafted outside as neither made a move to go in. It was Patience singing *Smoke Gets in Your Eyes*.

'Looks like a hopping club,' Edward said. 'My buddy raves about this place,' he added when Yasmine remained silent. She turned around and walked back into the club, leaving Edward standing outside, holding his hat in hand, puzzled by what had just occurred.

3

Yasmine reached the bar just as Edward entered the main room. He saw her talking to the bartender and she could feel him watching her as she made her way around the tables and patrons. She smiled at everyone but did not touch a single man. Once in a while, she would lay a hand on the arm of a woman. She leaned over people, but did not crowd them. This was what Patience called 'the soft sell'. Yasmine chatted easily with the Europeans in the room.

She made sure that when Edward reached the bar, a drink was already awaiting him. If he was surprised, he didn't show it. She knew he had blurted out the remark about flirting without meaning to. He had flushed pink the moment he said it. She made him nervous, and that gave her satisfaction.

Yasmine watched him for a moment and then walked up to the bar. He was still alone, scanning the room for his friend.

'You work here then?' he smiled at her pleasantly. But his demeanour had changed. Now he's judging me, she thought.

'Yes, I do, actually—'

'Another one?' Ghosh, the bartender, enquired. Yasmine frowned at him for interrupting as Edward polished off his drink.

He shook his head no to Ghosh, but then thought better of it.

'I usually don't drink this much back home,' he said to Yasmine. 'How much?' he asked, reaching for his billfold.

'On the house, sahib,' Ghosh said.

'Really. Who—?'

'The owner, sahib.'

Ghosh glanced at Yasmine. She shook her head slightly, and he went back to wiping the bar.

'Wow, that's service for ya,' Edward said. 'This beats the Black Goose back home. I have to remember to thank the owner when I see him.'

He leaned back against the bar and looked at Yasmine. 'Except I don't know what he looks like.'

'I'll introduce you,' Yasmine said. 'Someday.'

'Funny. I just realised. At home, my watering hole is the Goose and here it's the Duck. If I become a regular that is,' he said.

'I hope you do. We appreciate your sacrifice,' Yasmine said in the voice she reserved for servicemen. 'And the owner likes Americans ... for the most part.'

'Pardon me for saying so, but you speak English awfully well,' Edward said as she started to leave, to stop her. The scotch had loosened him up. He felt warm and took off his jacket and rolled up his sleeves.

Normally, Yasmine would have been irritated by his presumption but he was smiling at her almost diffidently.

'I was taught by nuns,' she said, as if that really explained anything.

'Okay,' he said, surprised. 'Well, we have been ordered to be good guests, if you know what I mean?'

She shook her head.

'The brass made it clear that we should be on our best behaviour.' He grinned at her. 'I can imagine that doesn't always happen here.'

Another American walked up to the bar and ordered a drink. He was smiling broadly, though at no one in particular.

Why do Americans smile so much, Yasmine wondered. And in the middle of a bloody war too.

'Go easy on that soldier,' Edward said. The startled young man saluted quickly. 'At ease,' Edward said. They shook hands, and the younger American added a hearty pat on the back for Edward; it was inappropriate, but he let it pass.

'I'm Corporal Rob Mckimmey, sir. I'd like to buy you a drink, sir.'

'That's not necessary.'

'I think it absolutely is, sir.'

Mckimmey put up one finger, and Ghosh, who was at the other end of the bar, slid a tumbler with a finger's worth of scotch down to Edward. They each held up their glass.

'What're we toasting?' the private asked.

'It's up to you.'

'I have to go into the Big Green tomorrow,' he said quietly. 'I've only been in India for a month and volunteered to join General Stilwell and work on the Ledo Road. I hear it rains for months straight and the skin falls off your feet from jungle rot. You get the *National Geographic*, sir?' he asked, suddenly switching topics.

'Not regularly,' Edward replied.

'I used to look at the pictures as a kid and wished I could travel to all those crazy places. Anything was better than Scranton, you know what I mean?'

'I think so. I always dreamt of going to Europe.'

'When do you think you'll make it out to Burma, sir?'

Edward hesitated and frowned slightly before he said, 'Eventually, I assume.' He held up his glass. 'To you, then.'

'Nah, you don't have to do that.'

'Yes, Private, I absolutely do.'

Both men looked towards the stage in the front of the room. They momentarily forgot to toast. The private swayed on his feet and sat down on a barstool and almost missed it. He chuckled, slightly embarrassed. 'I usually hold my liquor better than this.'

Radhika had taken up her position on stage. A spotlight shone on her bowed head. The mirrorwork on her dupatta glittered. The music started, and she began to dance. The room was silent. A Kathak performance always started off slowly, building its way to a dramatic climax of twirling that made onlookers dizzy. Radhika's feet fell to the rhythm of the tabla. She wore bells on her ankles. Her feet and hands were stained with henna. She flirted with the audience freely as she danced. She gave them half smiles and averted her eyes from their gaze at perfectly timed intervals. The Americans were especially enthusiastic when she smiled at them. They whistled at her. One stocky, barrel-chested soldier, an officer, tried to grab her skirt, but she deftly sidestepped him and kept dancing. He was not to be deterred, however, and jumped on to the stage. Seemingly out of nowhere, two large men—the largest Sikhs Yasmine could find—materialised, Adil Baboo in their wake, took him by the arms and led him offstage. It was done gently. Radhika danced on. She finished to thunderous applause.

Rob Mckimmey put his drink down and clapped his hands energetically. He whistled and took up the toast again.

'That's some mesmerising stuff right there,' he said, his hand on his heart. 'I haven't seen anything like that in Scranton.'

Yasmine could not help but smile at the young man's awe.

'It is somewhat different from the watoosie,' she said, not unkindly.

She felt Edward's eyes on her and cleared her throat. She looked at him after a moment. His face was flushed, surprising Yasmine. Had Radhika's performance moved him that much? He cleared his throat twice and took a healthy gulp of his drink. He seemed almost—*embarrassed*. He looked at Yasmine.

'The muscle in this place—the ones who took that guy off the stage, they're not going to rough him up, are they? Louis is sharp around the edges, but he means well.'

'That was your friend?' Yasmine said, unimpressed, which was plain.

Edward nodded. 'He's from New Jersey. Can you tell the owner?'

'That your friend is from New Jersey?' Yasmine asked, genuinely baffled.

Edward chuckled. 'No, that he's not a bad guy, just kind of rough.'

'They won't hurt him,' Yasmine said. 'But he won't be allowed back in, I'm afraid. At least not tonight.'

'Yeah,' Private Mckimmey said, earnestly shaking his head. 'You can't touch the girls, even in Scranton.'

Edward sighed. 'Thank you, Private,' he said, annoyed that the young man had inserted himself into the conversation.

'I should probably go and see if he's all right,' Edward said, though he didn't move.

'Stay, have another drink. I'll let the owner know about your friend,' Yasmine said in what she hoped was a reassuring tone. She leaned over and whispered something in Bengali to Ghosh, who nodded and left the bar. 'He'll be fine,' she said to Edward. 'Do you want another one? I'm the bartender at the moment.'

He smiled at her, and she found herself smiling back. His green eyes were bright. Yasmine searched around for something else to say, but his gaze suddenly wandered elsewhere. Patience had taken the stage, to the loud appreciation of the audience. She looks particularly charming tonight, Yasmine thought. Edward was staring at Patience and Yasmine found she was disappointed, though resigned. Of course, once he saw Patience, she, Yasmine, would be forgotten. Why would anything be different from when they were girls?

'There are some pretty girls here,' Mckimmey said to Edward and smiled at Yasmine. 'Not like the ones we got back home, but pretty all the same.'

'How about we toast the Indian woman?' Edward said. His eyes were no longer on Patience, but Yasmine had already withdrawn.

'To the women of India!'

'Hear, hear,' Edward said. They raised their glasses to Yasmine, and she acknowledged the toast with a quick nod.

'The Brits are always complaining about how terrible everything is around here. It's too dirty, the natives are too backward … but I love it here!' Mckimmey said. 'I'm going to miss it! You can stretch a buck here, let me tell you! I never had it so good. I'm one of ten kids. My dad works in a coal mine. When I tell them back home how I got this guy, I mean an actual servant who changes my sheets every day, they're floored. I gotta tell you, my mother could use ol' Rajiv around the house in Scranton. You know he cooks too? He can cook anything—*anything*. Mashed potatoes, pot roast, 'course it's more like goat roast with the holy cow thing and all. It took me a month to get him to stop using cumin in every goddamn thing. You should come over to our basha sometime, and ol' Rajiv can whip up some Indian food, like daal and stuff. I have to admit my stomach can't get used to all the spices.'

The soldier stopped for a moment and looked down at his empty glass. 'Course you can't come over. I won't be there. Hey, maybe you can come visit me in Scranton sometime, sir. You know where that is?'

'I can find it,' Edward replied gently. The soldier was very young. Barely nineteen. He had spoken too freely with a superior officer, Yasmine noted. But Edward did not seem to mind. India was not Europe. Maybe it was the heat, but things must seem more lax here to them, and the boy was clearly anxious about leaving the next day.

Mckimmey put down his glass and saluted. 'I should join my buddies,' he said.

'Thanks for the drink,' Edward said. 'I'll buy you one in Scranton.'

'It's a deal.'

They watched him walk back to his table where he was greeted with backslapping and laughter.

'That was very nice of you,' Yasmine said. She had been pretending not to listen as she watched the performances on stage.

'Well, think about what he's going into,' Edward said. 'That green hell.'

When Yasmine didn't say anything, he added, 'That's what we call Burma.'

She nodded.

'Don't talk much, huh?'

'Well, what is there to say?' she said. 'I don't flirt, remember?'

'I'm sorry about that. It wasn't meant as an insult.'

Ghosh had returned. He nodded slightly, indicating that he had done as she asked—which was to get Edward's friend a gharry back to the base. She took a tray of drinks she had made off the bar, passing them on to a waiter who stood waiting, and smiled at Edward. 'Well, it wasn't a compliment either. Enjoy yourself … what should I call you?'

'Edward.'

'What is your rank? I can never remember the military lingo.'

'Lieutenant. But please just call me Edward.'

~

At midnight, two hours until closing, Patience sang *I'll Be Seeing You* for those who were shipping out to Burma later that day. The atmosphere became more subdued. Some of the men sang with her, their arms around each other's shoulders. They swayed unsteadily to the music. Yasmine stood at the front, looking over the reservations list. Edward had long since left. He had said goodbye to her and politely asked her to thank the owner for the drinks. She still didn't tell him who she was; instead, she had nodded, said he was most welcome and gone back to staring at the book at the front desk. Edward stood looking at her uncertainly and then realised he had been dismissed when she did not look up again.

Yasmine had observed him furtively all night. He had met some friends and sat and talked with them awhile. The other men seemed to respect him. He had an air that commanded respect. Restrained, a bit aloof. He was an observer, just like she was. The English wives flirted with him, but he did not pay them much attention. They were all well-kept, sleek and moody. Their resentment of the girls was plain. Yasmine felt him watching her whenever she passed near him. Once she caught his eye and he held up his glass to her. She nodded but did not approach him. He was clearly a gentleman's son, and therefore made no overtures towards her. His gaze made her feel warm, but she knew it was pointless. He was going to the jungle eventually and would most likely die there. If he survived, he would return to his wife.

The band had started one of the last sets of the night. Yasmine heard Patience singing *It Had to Be You*. There were cries of approval and scattered applause.

The clock on the wall behind her showed a quarter past twelve. People were still coming in. They were almost all Americans. She had not known there were so many of them in the city. This night, the American officers were looking the other way when the enlisted men came in and had one too many. This could very well be the last night any of them heard a note of music or saw a beautiful girl dance.

Adil Baboo gently tapped Yasmine on the shoulder.

'What is it?' she said as she sighed.

'There are some customers who wish to come in,' he said, still very quiet. His face, as usual, was impassive.

'So, let them in,' Yasmine said, annoyed.

'Have I ever disturbed you if it was not necessary?'

'No, I suppose not.'

'Please come to the back.'

Three American soldiers stood in the alley, smoking. One said something and the other two laughed loudly. Now Asma was singing *Stormy Weather*, and they stopped to listen, their heads bowed, as if praying. Yasmine watched them listen.

'Not bad,' one of them said.

'Almost like home,' another added wistfully.

'Almost,' the third one said. They turned to see Yasmine and Adil Baboo watching them. All three immediately took off their caps. Two of them stubbed their cigarettes out under their feet.

'Namaste, ma'am,' the first one who had spoken said. He was the tallest of the three. He looked Yasmine over in open appreciation and broke into a wide smile, displaying a row of gleaming white if somewhat crooked teeth. As if in support of his friend's opinion, one of the other men whistled softly. The third man, who looked younger than his companions and was lighter skinned—almost white; and like Patience could have passed for white—was quiet. He finished his cigarette and looked away. Yasmine saw his jaw tighten. She thought suddenly that it must almost be harder for him, being so obviously from both worlds and with only, as the horrible expression went, a touch of the tar brush. But that was considered enough to be viewed as 'kalo' forever.

Yasmine's heart beat a little faster. Their faces were so hopeful.

'We were wondering if it would be possible to sneak us in and let us sit in the back. We're engineers, ma'am—'

'We have money!' another one interrupted. He held out a handful of rupees.

'It is not about that,' she said very softly. There was a burst of laughter from inside the club as the band started up a new number. Yasmine hated turning people away for no good reason.

'No one would notice us, ma'am,' the first one said.

Yasmine looked at Adil Baboo. 'Why shouldn't they come in?' she said to him in Bengali. 'They are paying customers.'

'You know why,' Adil Baboo replied. He looked over her shoulder at the young men who were politely looking away.

'Adil Baboo, there is nothing separating us from them,' she said.

'You think I don't know that?' he said. 'It is ridiculous, but it's the law. I am doing this tonight, tomorrow while I am walking down the street I will have to step aside if an Ingrez walks close to me.'

Yasmine looked at the young men again. She could tell that the light-skinned one was proud, and that somehow made it worse. He had made no eye contact with anyone. He looked down the alley as his friends pleaded to be let in.

'You cannot come in,' she said finally. 'But you can stay and listen, and we will serve you. Leave this door open, Adil Baboo, and send Rahul to take their orders.'

'Yasmine—' Adil Baboo began.

'They can stay,' she said firmly. 'But you have to sit here,' she told the men, 'where no one can see you. We will bring you chairs and drinks and food and whatever you need ... on the house.'

'Thank you!' one of them called after Yasmine as she walked away.

She could hear them talking.

'Man, Tommy did you see that piano? What you wouldn't give to just get hold of that piano. Did you see it?'

'Yeah, I saw it.'

'Maybe if she hears you play—'

'Shut your mouth, boy!'

'Better than nothing.'

'I'd rather take nothing.'

'Oh, come on now, Tommy. It's not bad. We can hear the music and she said, "on the house".'

'Sitting in the alley like a stray ass dog.'

'You said it yourself, all the comforts of home.'

Yasmine stopped to listen at the laughter. How could they laugh, she wondered. How often they must be humiliated like this.

'I'm paying. I don't care about "on the house".'

'Suit yourself.'

'She's beautiful.'

'She's as coloured as me.'

'Quiet, Tom! Come on now!'

Inside, Yasmine gestured to Radhika to come to her.

'Go to the kitchen. Adil Baboo will hand you a tray of food and drinks. If it's too much, get Rahul to help you.'

Radhika nodded.

'Take the tray to the alley. But don't walk through the club. Exit from the kitchen and go to the back. Yes, I think Rahul will have to help you.'

Radhika nodded again, puzzled. Yasmine waited for her to ask a question and was grateful when she didn't. She liked this about Radhika; the girl wasn't inquisitive, even when confused.

'There are three American servicemen in the alley awaiting food and drink. After you give them the tray, make sure the back door is left ajar so they can hear the music, but not enough so that they can see anyone ... or anyone can see them. I'll meet you there in a moment. Don't talk to them. Do you understand?'

The girl nodded and left to fetch the tray.

Yasmine forgot to meet Radhika and Rahul in the alley. Two distracting things happened. She was swept into a conversation with an English officer and his drunkenly hostile wife about Darjeeling vs. Assamese tea, and every time she attempted to extricate herself from the conversation, she was prevented from leaving and could only do so when they started to bicker amongst themselves after the wife posited that he loved Assamese tea chiefly because he had an Assamese mistress. Yasmine felt she could escape then, only to be faced with a disgruntled Asma, who was refusing to go back on stage because Patience had said she sounded flat during the last set.

'Why must you torment her?' Yasmine demanded of Patience.

Patience shrugged one perfectly golden shoulder and said, 'I have no idea what you're on about. I just said she must be coming down with cold because she sounded a bit creaky.'

'No, you said flat,' Asma said. 'Flat. I've never been flat in my life.'

Patience's eyes moved down to Asma's arguably flat chest and she smiled. Asma gasped and crossed her arms over her chest and said, to Yasmine, 'I am retiring for the evening.'

'You are doing no such thing, Queen Victoria,' Yasmine said. 'I can replace you.' She looked at Patience. 'I can replace both of you.'

'That's not true, ducky, and you know it,' Patience said after Asma reluctantly took to the stage. She kissed Yasmine on the cheek.

'I know,' Yasmine said, 'but Asma doesn't.'

Madhu, who had been onstage right before, came down, wiping the sweat off her neck.

'Why is Asma so upset? What did you do, Patience?' she said, frowning.

'Why are you always so concerned about her,' Patience said.

'That's enough,' Yasmine said, sensing a growing tension between Patience and Madhu, who were both stubborn, though Madhu was more reserved and would never rise to any bait Patience set out for her. However, Yasmine observed, where Asma was concerned, Madhu responded with more vigour. She was protective.

'Madhu, I think you're done for the evening. Patience can take your next set,' Yasmine said.

Patience turned to Yasmine. 'Am I being punished?'

'You both are,' Yasmine said. 'Because neither of you are being discreet, and paying customers are looking over here.'

Yasmine went into her office and collapsed into a chair, suddenly exhausted. She glanced at her watch. The evening was far from over. Adil Baboo walked in, holding a cup of tea. He placed it on the desk in front of her.

'Drink,' he said.

She took a sip. Yasmine, unlike the majority of India, did not love tea and could imagine her life without it. 'It's not bad. Thank you, Adil Baboo. What is it?'

'Assam blend, I think. Who knows these days?'

Yasmine smiled, remembering the inane debate about tea she had been forced to join moments before.

'The girls need a day out,' Adil Baboo said. 'We have been open every day for the past three months. If we don't go out at least for one day, there will be a world war three.'

Yasmine nodded. She knew what he said was true, even though she loathed the loss of revenue for that one day.

'We can plan an outing for tomorrow, I think,' Yasmine said. 'Tuesday is normally our slowest night.'

'I don't think we should open at all that night,' Adil Baboo said. Yasmine began to argue with him when Rahul knocked on the door.

'We have delivered the tray and chairs to the kalos,' he said. For a moment, Yasmine did not understand what he was telling her and then remembered.

'I forgot to supervise this,' Yasmine said to Adil Baboo.

'I will go,' Adil Baboo offered, but Yasmine stopped him. She was curious to see that young man, Tommy's, reaction. His disapproval and pride made her curious about him.

Rahul walked with her to the alley.

'They were fresh with Radhika,' he said. 'Why did she allow that?'

'Radhika is a flirt,' Yasmine said, yawning. She resisted the urge to rub her eyes because all the kohl would get smeared. This evening could not end soon enough.

'She is not. She is friendly. But they should not be fresh with her,' he said. Yasmine looked at him. She took his arm and stopped him from walking.

'Radhika is anything but friendly. What she is doing is her job,' she said to the boy, whose eyes slid to his feet. 'Look at me when I speak to you,' Yasmine said. 'She despises the Americans.' But she was nonplussed. She had made it plain to Radhika that she was not to talk to them. She didn't even speak English. What could she have said?

'These ones are different,' Rahul said. Yasmine sighed, impatient at the petulance in his voice and resentful she was being forced to play nursemaid to a love-struck teenager.

She took his chin in her hand. 'Mind your own business and let Radhika do her job,' she said. Rahul nodded.

Radhika was still in the alley when Yasmine and Rahul arrived. She was dancing for the Americans, to the music that was playing in the club, *Night and Day*. She moved gracefully in the cramped, filthy alley, twirling so her silk tunic flared up. Her ankle bells jingled. The bottoms of her salwar were grimy from the dust in the alley. Everyone could smell the jasmine still braided in her hair. It helped cut the odour of trash and wet earth. Yasmine looked at the men's faces, lit up in smiles. Even Tommy was smiling, though not as widely as his friends, one of whom suddenly stood up and approached the girl, his arms out. Radhika stopped, startled.

'My name is Campbell,' he said. 'Would you dance with me?'

Radhika looked at Yasmine. Yasmine smiled and nodded slightly, signalling to Radhika that it was all right. It went against her previous order, but she could see it made the men happy and her guilt at leaving them in the alley was heavier than she realised. Besides, she would stand watch. Nothing untoward would happen. Radhika walked slowly into the soldier's outstretched arms. Campbell smiled at her and took her hand, placing his free arm around her waist, only to draw back when she gasped at this unfamiliar sensation. Yasmine could feel Rahul's agitation behind her, so she demanded that he tend to his duties in the kitchen. The boy left reluctantly, and Yasmine nodded again to Radhika to allow herself to be held. She wasn't fully aware of why she did this. Later, she would be ashamed of herself for allowing it. Was it because she could demand it? Was it her arrogance at knowing the girl was under her control and she wanted to show them that? Did she want to show Tommy that? She was aware of his gaze on her. She touched the back of her neck when he looked at her, because it was tingling. She didn't meet his gaze. They started to dance.

At first, it was stiff. Radhika kept looking down at her feet, trying to keep count. The soldier, who towered over her, stopped and said, 'Let me lead, miss.' Radhika looked up at him, confused.

'Let him show you,' Yasmine said in Bangla to Radhika. 'Let him lead you in the dance.'

This was a bizarre concept to the girl, Yasmine knew, but she also knew Radhika was a born dancer and would learn quickly. Soon enough, as the music inside picked up tempo, Radhika's partner was twirling her around the alley and they danced in step almost perfectly. It was the first time Yasmine had heard Radhika laugh.

'Rogers and Astaire,' Tommy's other friend said as he clapped along to the music. 'Look at that now.'

The music ended, and Radhika was out of breath. She put her hands together in a namaste to her dance partner, who did the same. With eyes downcast, Radhika walked back into the club, to the audible disappointment of Tommy and his friends. When the music struck up again, one of them said to Yasmine, 'You wouldn't mind dancing with me, ma'am, would you?'

Before Yasmine could reply, Tommy stood up and took her in his arms. He held her close and did not move her energetically around the narrow alley like his friend had with Radhika. Yasmine could only feel his open palm on her lower back, which was exposed, and his breath on her neck. Everything else fell away. The music ended, too quickly, and he let her go. Yasmine cleared her throat and asked them if they needed anything else. She had never been this physically close to a customer.

'No, thank you,' Tommy said. 'This evening turned out a lot better than I expected.'

He took out his billfold, but Yasmine stopped him.

'This time it's on the house,' she said, surprising herself for meaning it when she said it the first time.

'This time?' Tommy said. 'Will we be in the alley the next time?'

'Tom, you fool, why you got to be like that?' Campbell said.

Tommy's gaze was fixed on Yasmine.

'I hope not,' Yasmine said. 'But it's not always up to me.'

'Ma'am, it's not up to any of us,' Campbell said. 'It's up to them.'

Yasmine nodded. 'That is very true.'

4

Adil Baboo had finally turned out the last customer at 1.45 a.m.

'Well, that was a peaceful night in the end,' Yasmine said. She longed for her bed and the cool sheets she had laid out fresh the night before.

'Are you sure?' Adil Baboo asked. He stood behind Yasmine as she slid the four bolts in and padlocked the door. She was overly cautious, but it made for a good night's rest. She did not turn around immediately. She wondered if somehow Adil Baboo knew about Edward and how they had spoken to one another, or Tommy and how they had danced.

Even if he did, it should not matter. It was all so innocent, she thought. But she felt self-conscious all the same.

'You don't think so?'

'What about the three soldiers we served in the alley. You don't feel that was unusual?'

'Well, yes, but not in a bad way.'

'Hmm.'

Yasmine turned around to face him. 'You're becoming as superstitious as Patience,' she said. 'Frankly, I would have liked to have served them in the building. It's a crime what we had to do.'

'Yes, it is,' Adil Baboo agreed.

'To bed,' Yasmine said brightly, and yawned.

'Aren't you going to count the night's take?' Adil Baboo asked.

'Not tonight,' she replied. 'I'll do it first thing.'

He frowned. 'But you always do it the night of. Why not tonight?'

'I don't see why it matters,' she said, taken aback. She was not used to being questioned about how she ran her business.

'Yasmine, in all the months I have been here, you have always counted the night's business as soon as the doors were bolted. Why is tonight different?'

'Uff-oh! What bloody difference does it make?'

'I don't know, but I feel an uncertainty that I cannot explain,' Adil Baboo said.

'It's the war, I'm telling you,' she said. 'It's closer now, with all the Yankee soldiers on the trams and taking pictures at Sealdah Station.'

'Yes, they are changing everything, the balance of things,' he said. 'It's different from the English; they are more polite, but strange.'

Yasmine fingered the edge of her sari and looked down at her feet. 'They are not all bad,' she said.

'No, of course, not all of them are bad. But they will always stay amongst themselves.'

Yasmine looked up quickly. 'Of course, I know that!'

'Have you given any more thought to the outing?' Adil Baboo asked. 'I think it is important.'

From the corner of her eye she saw Rahul looking up, watching Radhika walk to her room as he swept the floor. She still had on her anklets. For a moment, she listened to the musical footfalls as Radhika walked into her room and closed the door.

'Yes, but it should be just for the girls,' she said.

'That doesn't seem fair,' Adil Baboo said. 'Everyone needs a day out.'

Yasmine was too exhausted to argue so she merely nodded and bid Adil Baboo goodnight.

She watched him disappear into the dark kitchen. She had offered him a room upstairs, ignoring propriety, but he declined, not wanting to make the girls uneasy. She never really knew what he was thinking. He had no demands and offered nothing about his life before the Duck. She knew not to pry.

She endured a fitful night's sleep and was up with the muezzin's call to dawn prayer.

She wrapped herself in a shawl and looked out her small window as she listened to the call. From her room, she could see the drowsy bustle of Park Street and the vendors slowly readying for the day. She watched as baskets of fruit were uncovered, oxen were nudged to their feet and a man squatted down and urinated discreetly onto a low wall.

She decided to ask Radhika to join her for breakfast before the others were awake so she could have some time alone with her. The girl had danced wonderfully the night before. More than one patron had come up to Yasmine to express their admiration, men and women. Yasmine wanted to tell Radhika how proud she was of her. Or try to. Yasmine often found herself unable to share her feelings with the girl because Radhika was so impassive. Any expression of affection or praise was met with silence.

She knocked softly on Radhika's door. There was no answer. After knocking louder two more times and not receiving a response, Yasmine tried the door knob, expecting it to be locked, and was surprised when it was not. She slowly opened the door, startling a mouse that scampered under the almirah. Yasmine sighed. No matter how hard they tried, the Duck was never rid of them. Radhika's charpoy was made. Yasmine's eyes went to the girl's tushok, rolled up neatly on the floor next to it. Sometimes Radhika slept on the cement floor on the thin cotton mattress. The mice and roaches did not bother her.

Perhaps the girl had risen earlier than usual and was in the kitchen, Yasmine thought as she went downstairs for tea and a cigarette. The club was so peaceful when everyone was asleep. As she entered the kitchen, she saw Rahul slip out into the back alley. It felt secretive.

When she opened the back door and thrust her head through to confront him, she found the alley empty. She saw Rahul further ahead, on the street, watching for something or someone.

She called to him. He walked up to her and kicked at the dirt sheepishly.

'What are you doing?' Yasmine said.

'Nothing,' Rahul mumbled.

'If you lie to me one more time, I will release you. I am asking again, what were you doing?'

'If I tell you, you will be cross with Radhika.'

'Never mind that. Tell me at once.'

'I was looking for her.'

'Why?'

'Because I love her.'

'Oh dear lord. What do you know about love?'

'Plenty.'

'Has she been gone all night?' Yasmine asked, a mixture of alarm and irritation starting to rise up in her.

'I'm not sure,' Rahul said.

Yasmine searched his young face. He seemed sincere.

'Spying on a girl will not make her love you,' she said.

'Are you not worried about where she is, didi?' Rahul said.

Yasmine *was* worried but did not want Rahul to see that.

'Go, look for her,' she said to Rahul, who nodded and ran down the alley as fast as his chappals could take him.

~

Later in the morning, Yasmine gathered her employees and told them they would be closed as it was Tuesday, a slow night, and an outing had been planned. This was met with much enthusiasm. As expected, no one could agree to a location for the outing. Asma wanted to go to Freeschool Street to browse all the open-air book stalls, Patience to Outram Ghat to walk along the river and flirt with officers, Madhu wanted to picnic at Eden Gardens and smoke and nap under a large tree.

Radhika had not returned, but Yasmine tried not to worry. Had the girl finally run off, she wondered. Unlike the others, she did not appear to have any fealty to either Yasmine or the Duck.

A consensus was finally reached that there was no need for everyone to be together. It was simply a day off for people to do what they liked. Adil Baboo suggested that every Tuesday be such a day and perhaps the group not being together would work in everyone's favour. Yasmine agreed reluctantly.

'What will you do with your day?' Patience asked Yasmine, as she put on lipstick and perused her closet.

'I'm not sure, but I assume yours involves a GI of some sort?'

'Surprisingly, no. I'm spending it with Mum. She wants to shop. I'll buy her a few fripperies.'

Patience was devoted to her mother, Daisy, who was, in Yasmine and her own mother Shirin's estimation, not a very pleasant woman.

'Every time you spend the day with your mother, you come back peevish,' Yasmine said.

'Not true,' Patience said, as she adjusted her curls.

'Yes, it's very true, and you're quite impossible to manage for at least a week because Daisy tells you how you are not being paid enough—'

'Well, I'm not.'

'—or that you should be running the club.'

'Well, I should be a partner at least.'

'Or that you are the star.'

Patience turned to look at her friend then.

'Well, I *am* the star,' she said, her hands on her hips. She winked at Yasmine, who giggled in spite of herself.

'Radhika is giving you a run for your money,' Yasmine said, and gave her an exaggerated wink back.

Patience flopped down on the bed. 'This is only too true. But she's sixteen. I'm old enough to be her mother. Naturally she's besting me.'

'I think a nine-year-old mother is a tragic thing. Not to mention criminal.'

Patience lay on her side and faced Yasmine. 'I'm almost twenty-six,' she said. 'I'm a granny. Still no husband and no baby.'

'You still think you can achieve those things?' Yasmine said.

'Yes, yes, I am an Anglo, kalo singer in a nightclub, the daughter of a courtesan, etc., etc. Who would want me?'

'Every man wants you, Patience. But who will marry you or any of us?'

'I want a baby more than I want a husband. Babies are easier to raise.'

Yasmine shook her head, marvelling at Patience's acute lack of ambition.

'Do you want to meet me later?' Patience said. 'We can get ice cream at Flury's.'

'Will Daisy be there?' Yasmine asked, but regretted it immediately. Patience was hurt, and Yasmine could see this.

'I'm sorry.'

'It's fine. She hates you too. I wish you two could try to like one another. You're my family, after all.'

Yasmine nodded and managed a smile. She would never like the small-minded, braggart Daisy.

'All right,' Patience said. 'I'll tell Mum to bugger off after shopping. If I buy her enough glass bangles, she'll be happy.'

'I'll meet you at Flury's. What do I care if you want to spend all your money on ice cream?'

'Who says I'm treating?'

Yasmine walked into Flury's four hours later, trying not to appear uneasy. She was conscious of all the Europeans looking at her. There were hardly any other Indians in the restaurant. The wait staff watched as Patience waved her over to the table where she sat. Seated opposite her was the American from the night before—Edward, the bespectacled lieutenant.

'Yassu, meet my new friend, Eddie, from Ipswich Connecticut,' she said. 'It turns out my day involves a GI after all.'

'It's Norwich, actually,' Yasmine said without thinking, a move she regretted intensely and immediately when Patience broke into a wide, knowing grin. Edward had stood up when Yasmine approached and was still standing because Yasmine had not yet sat down.

'I'm surprised you remember,' Edward said.

Yasmine mumbled something unintelligible.

Patience looked at them both.

'Are you going to let the poor man sit down?' she finally said to Yasmine.

'Of course.' Yasmine sat next to Patience, even though Edward had moved to the side, making a space next to him. For a moment everyone was silent. A waiter approached and looked at Edward for guidance.

'Well, give her a menu, you dolt!' Patience said to the waiter, an elderly man who fetched one at once. He handed Yasmine the menu.

'What precisely are you gawking at?' Patience asked the waiter in Bangla.

'I should not have come—' Yasmine started to say.

'That's bollocks,' Patience said. 'So, how do you two know each other?'

'The club, naturally,' Yasmine said. She knew she was blushing. It was frustrating. She could feel Edward's quizzical gaze on her.

'We met last night,' Edward said.

'Did you have a good time?' Yasmine asked. She felt her throat tighten and beads of sweat break out on her brow. It was suddenly warm in the dining room.

'I had a great time. I had to tuck my pal Louis into bed, but other than that, it was almost like being back home.'

'Oh, that's brilliant!' Patience said. 'That's exactly what Yasmine wants with the club.'

Edward smiled, confused. 'What Yasmine wants?'

'Yes,' Patience said. 'When Yassu opened the club she said, "Patience, this has to be like any old place back home for these men. So they can forget for a bit what they are facing".'

'The owner likes Americans, huh?' Edward said to Yasmine, who shrugged.

'For the most part,' she replied. 'Your friend is fine then?'

Edward nodded. 'Just hungover, I think. And a little embarrassed.' He gazed at Yasmine, whom he found even more fascinating than when she walked in. What an odd, intriguing woman, he thought.

'I have no idea what you two are talking about, but Yassu, Edward has so graciously invited us to the ARC for dinner. Well, he asked me, but I said I am not going without my friend.'

Yasmine opened the menu and pretended to read it. 'I don't want to intrude on your date,' she said.

'What nonsense,' Patience said, studying Yasmine closely. 'Eddie's a married man, Yassu. He's going with some other officers, who I hope are not married.'

'Only Deccico—Louis is married,' Edward replied. 'The rest are free as birds. Please come,' he said to Yasmine. 'The Red Cross always puts out a good spread. I bet you guys haven't had roast beef and mashed potatoes in a long time.'

'I've actually never had that,' Yasmine said. 'It sounds a little bland.'

'Yassu,' Patience said, shocked at her rudeness. 'Just slather it in jhaal morich,' she advised and nudged Yasmine under the table. 'We'd love to come,' she said to Edward. 'We accept.'

Yasmine knew that was not a possibility for her. She was having a hard enough time bearing the curious glances of the customers and wait staff there, at Flury's, where Indians were allowed, though not encouraged to frequent. 'No. Thank you for your invitation, Lt Lafaver,' Yasmine said. 'But it's well known natives do not go to the ARC. We are not welcome there. Patience will be able to get away with it. As you can see, I will not.'

'Yas—'

'Enough, Patience!' Yasmine said in Bangla, a bit more forcefully than she would have liked. 'This is not a child's game. I'll see you back home later.'

Yasmine got up and walked out as quickly as she could. She did not look at anyone.

~

Yasmine waited up for Patience until she could not keep her eyes open. Everyone else had come home by nine that night, but at midnight, Patience's and Radhika's rooms still remained empty. The girl had now been gone for nearly twenty-four hours. Another day and Yasmine would tell the others Radhika had most probably run away.

One hour after Yasmine had finally locked the doors and gone to sleep, Rahul came bounding upstairs, where he was not allowed, his voice hoarse with panic.

'Yasmine didi, Yasmine didi!'

Patience was the first to step out into the hallway. She had her hair net on, and her face was slathered with Hazeline Snow cream.

'Uff Rahul,' she said. 'Stop yelling! Didi is asleep. Where's the fire?'

Minutes later, Patience quietly slipped into Yasmine's room. Yasmine had left the shutters open and moonlight streamed onto the plain, wooden floorboards. She was sleeping peacefully. Patience regretted having to wake her friend up. She shook her gently so as not to startle her.

'Yassu?' she whispered.

It took a few shakes and Yasmine opened one eye.

'I don't know how you do it, but you manage to glare with one eye,' she said to her childhood friend with affection. Yasmine sat up slowly and looked at Patience's face, still beautiful despite being slathered with oily night cream.

'When did you get home?'

'Just now.'

'Have fun, did you?'

'Yes, but we have a problem.'

Yasmine sat up. She recognised the tone in Patience's voice.

'Patience, how bad is it?' she said. The normally vain girl would never be wandering around at night in this state if it weren't bad.

'Firstly, it's not your fault,' Patience began.

'Oh dear lord.'

'She is an odd one, you know that. Remember, I said I thought she was a bit haunted?'

'How bad, for crikey's sake?'

'Bad.'

'Give me a scale. One to ten.'

'Oh god! I always forget, which is the worse end of the scale?'

'Dhoor!' Yasmine cried, exasperated. She quickly put on her robe.

'Sorry! Okay. If ten is bad, then this is an eleven,' Patience said, as Yasmine reached the door. Yasmine paused with her hand on the doorknob and looked at Patience. Somehow, she knew.

'Radhika?'

'Poor lamb.'

'Oh god, you were right, everything has been off kilter of late.'

Patience nodded. 'I know.'

'Is she dead?'

'Not sure. Probably. Or worse.'

'What could possibly be worse?' Yasmine said, throwing up her hands.

Patience sighed. 'Come now, Yassu, you know what could be worse for a little girl.'

Yasmine swung the door open, a little frightened now. Asma and Madhu were gathered behind Rahul, hugging their wraps around them.

'What is it, Rahul?'

'Radhika,' he said, his voice breaking. 'She is in trouble. I think the Amrikans have arrested her.'

'How do you know this?' Yasmine asked, trying not to let the panic overtake her. Everyone was watching her.

'That's what my friends said. They said they saw her walking with some American soldiers.'

Yasmine looked at Madhu, whose room was adjoining the girl's. 'Can you check her room?' she asked. 'I checked earlier, but maybe—' Madhu went to look, while Yasmine tried to calm the boy down. He was out of breath.

'This will all be cleared up in a moment,' she said, patting Rahul's sweaty back. 'Your goonda friends might be wrong.'

Madhu returned and shook her head. 'Still not slept in,' she said.

'All right,' Yasmine replied. 'But there is nothing I can do until sunrise, and I cannot go to the base and demand answers.'

'Why not?' Patience said. 'They can't go around arresting innocent little girls—'

'Innocent, hah!' Asma snorted. 'I told you, I told you,' she said and wagged her finger in Yasmine's face.

Yasmine pushed Asma's hand away. 'What did you tell me? We don't know what happened.'

Yasmine then started quietly and methodically issuing instructions. Everyone was asked to get dressed in case the police came knocking. Rahul was sent to talk to his friends, all of whom were known loiterers, and goondas, and always appeared to know what salacious thing was happening in the area.

'They're not goondas!' the boy protested, and only shut up when Yasmine gave him a withering look.

Yasmine turned to Patience. 'Don't you have an old friend who was a barrister? Who works on the governor's staff?'

Patience nodded, 'William Darrow. But he and I did not part well—'

'How badly? So badly he would not see you?'

'Hmm, well I threw him over for a Whiteaway Laidlaw hosiery salesman I met that summer. Angus McDonough.'

Despite the knot in her stomach, Yasmine chuckled. She remembered that solemn young man, newly arrived from

Glasgow, who gave himself airs of refinement and resented his store's nickname, 'Right Away and Paid For', as they catered mostly to junior officers and accepted only cash not credit. He was besotted with Patience, who Yasmine was quite sure had deflowered and promptly discarded him. She had received silk stockings that lasted well over one year for her exertions.

'Did you ever speak to him again—Darrow, that is?'

Patience shook her head.

'Do you think you could cast a Patience Goodwin spell and enlist his help?' Yasmine asked.

Patience grinned. 'But of course.'

'What does he like?'

'Chess, single malt, and me, served on a platter.'

'Was he rough?'

Yasmine remembered one night tending to a cut above Patience's lip when she was seeing this Darrow. Patience did not offer an explanation and Yasmine did not ask.

Patience shrugged. 'Sometimes. But nothing too horrid.'

Yasmine sighed. 'All right. Tell Ghosh to choose a bottle of something. Single malt might as well be the Kohinoor diamond. How is your chess these days?'

'Been a while, but the night I left him, I had back rank check-mated his king.'

'That sounds a bit painful. Is that bad or good?'

'Well his king was pinned by his pawns because I had moved my rook into his first rank. So, bad for his ego. I don't give an arse.'

'Oh dear. You do know you have to let them win once in a while?'

'It's all right,' Patience said, as Asma listened in horror at this casual exchange about seduction and chess. 'I'll let him check my queen this time.' She winked at Asma.

Asma gasped. She was not sure why this sounded vulgar, but it decidedly did. Yasmine and Patience spoke in a sort of shorthand that was hard to follow and reminded her of the way women talked in the movies. At least Barbara Stanwyck was subtle and not so blatantly tarty. Even in *Stella Dallas*, Asma thought. Also, they seemed so nonchalant about Radhika's absence and possible arrest.

'Is he married?' Yasmine called over her shoulder as she walked into her room and started dressing.

'She's back home, lucky cow,' Patience said. 'Something about the climate in India being just too too.'

'She might be here now, you know,' Yasmine said, as she expertly folded the pleats of her cotton sari and tucked them into her petticoat waistband.

'The wives come back sometimes and suddenly get pregnant,' she added. 'It's insurance, I suppose, to keep them in place.' She pinned her hair at the nape of her slender neck and checked in the mirror for flyaway hairs. 'Make sure she is not around.'

Patience nodded. 'You know, Yassu, not all babies are mere man traps,' she said, smiling.

'I agree. It's the woman who serves the life sentence,' Yasmine said.

Asma was aghast at Yasmine's cynicism. Yasmine noticed. 'What are you gaping at?' she said. 'You were an ayah, you know.'

'I know,' Asma said. 'But how can you talk so carelessly about seducing a married man and having babies? Radhika could be in jail!'

Patience and Yasmine looked at each other and smiled.

'We are going to get her out of jail,' Yasmine said. 'That is precisely what we are discussing, how to execute this plan.'

'And if this barrister's wife is back?' Asma asked.

'Well then we will work around her, like we always do,' Patience said.

'Marriage vows are sacred,' Asma muttered.

'Yes,' Yasmine said. 'That is why men maintain their mistresses and wives separately. To spare feelings and keep their vows.'

'You are all so cold!' Asma cried.

'And you are naïve,' Patience said. She patted Asma on the head.

'Get dressed and head to the governor's offices as soon as possible,' Yasmine said to Patience. 'Wear that jaunty hat with the red feathers. And red lipstick. The Max Factor one that Yank gave you.'

'Yes, mon capitaine!' Patience saluted Yasmine and left to dress, after sticking her tongue out at a thoroughly scandalised Asma.

'What can I do?' Asma asked after she had recovered, though she was afraid of the answer. 'You're not going to dispatch me to some junior police officer for flirting and information extraction, are you?'

Yasmine stopped smoothing her hair and eyed Asma. She almost chuckled at how anxious Asma was.

'I feel your talents would be better used here, Madam Mata Hari. Just stay with me and receive the police if they come. Try to hide your disdain for me and Bombay Duck,' Yasmine said cheerfully, and patted Asma's arm.

'I don't care for Radhika too much, you know. I don't trust her. But she is just a girl,' Asma said.

'I know,' Yasmine said. 'We will get her out.'

~

All that day and well into the evening, Radhika did not return, and Rahul was not able to find out what had happened to her. Not even the goondas knew. The girl had vanished. The guards at the American base were not helpful. They shrugged and said they didn't understand what Rahul was trying to say. He came back exhausted and frantic. Yasmine sent him out again after feeding him some rice and a small piece of fish. This time, Adil Baboo went with him. The club was opened but customers were scant, and Yasmine told everyone they would close early. Adil Baboo suggested that they shut shop for a few days until the situation was under control. Yasmine reluctantly agreed, though she hated losing the business. If news got out that one of the Bombay Duck girls had been arrested, it would affect her reputation.

There was no dancing or singing that night as the other girls took on their hostess and waitress duties. Madhu flirted as usual, as did Patience, though less obviously. She had returned from a fruitless visit with William Darrow, who had been cool and slightly contemptuous, as she described it. When he got a little rough, she fled. She didn't have the stomach for any of that.

'The fact is, if the Yanks have her, they have her. Darrow seemed very ill disposed, if you know what I mean,' Patience told Yasmine.

'No, I don't,' Yasmine said.

'Everyone feels the Yanks have free rein here, and this is British India, nah? Not American India. But some deals have been struck, some treaties or something, what do I know? That gives the Yanks jurisdiction over Tollygunge and what happens with their men. Short of murder, and even then, who knows? They decide how to deal with their men, no one else. They have taken over the Hindustan Building. That has everyone in high dudgeon in the clubs. It houses everything the Americans need to run their operations, from air and rail bookings, post exchange, to officers' quarters and radio station.'

'But that building is the pride of the Ingrez. They have no say?'

'Not in this case. So it has become a bit of a pissing contest,' Patience chuckled. 'Little boys and their cocks. Well, what do you expect? They cannot beat the Japs on their own so they have prostituted themselves and let loose Uncle Sam.'

Yasmine smiled at Patience's assessment.

'I cannot believe it,' she said. 'A former colony is humbling them. Maybe Radhika was right. Maybe their time here is over.' Yasmine said the last in a whisper, the thought of being treacherous ever present.

'Uh, not yet, but everyone has a price.' Patience was not keen on the Raj ending and Yasmine knew it. What that would mean for the scores of half-caste Indians was very uncertain. 'We will find her, Yassu,' Patience said after a moment.

'Yes ... Get back to work now. I should not distract you. We will close soon.'

'What time?'

Yasmine looked at her watch. 'How about eleven?'

'Yes! Please. I want this day to end.'

Patience looked out on to the floor at the few customers, most of whom were already drunk. She sighed.

'What is it?' Yasmine said.

'Nothing ... it's just that sometimes I wonder what a normal life would be like, babies and nappies, and holidays near the ocean.'

Yasmine shrugged. 'We don't have that option.'

'No, I suppose not. Oh, bloody hell! Asma just smacked someone.'

'You better get out there then,' Yasmine said.

5

Lt Edward Lafaver had awoken as he did every morning, to the drone of a mosquito buzzing in his ear, sweating, and abruptly. He never remembered his dreams, but he knew he'd had one because he was breathing heavily when he woke up. It was not uncommon to have night terrors in extreme heat or cold. He often heard his basha mate, Louis, call out unintelligible things in the middle of the night.

He was late getting to the latrines, and by 7.30, it was already backed up, spreading its foul odour almost down to the Mess hall. The heat and humidity would naturally make it worse.

He had lost ninety rupees in an ill-fated poker game the previous night.

Like he had so many times before, Edward decided to swear off poker forever. He hated losing the money. He had written his wife, Maggie, asking her for some novels and back issues of the *Hartford Courant*, *The Norwich Bulletin* and *Life* magazine. Thus far, he had received only three packages. He told himself that, as long as he had reading material, he would avoid the poker games, so he pressed his wife to keep sending him books.

He brushed his teeth and shaved, trying to breathe through his mouth the entire time. After breakfast, he went to the hospital for his first class. The army brass had decided that his

BA in clinical psychology would come in handy for treating shell-shocked and mentally ill Allied troops. He was assigned halfway around the world to the 142nd General Hospital in Calcutta, India, of all places. His job there was to conduct group therapy classes daily. His main job, he soon found out, was to root out all the frauds who had declared themselves mentally unfit to serve, and even those who had been declared unfit by the army itself. But as far as he could tell, Washington, DC seemed to have forgotten about these men and maybe even all their men in Burma and India. They were assuredly not a priority, along with the Ledo Road itself.

There was little sympathy among the enlisted men and their officers for the men who attended Edward's group therapy sessions. Louis called them all 'yellow-livered cowards'. At first, Edward felt a real sympathy for these men, some of whom were legitimately traumatised from their time in Burma. This day, however, he had his worst group, the ones who were thought of as mentally deviant. One GI kept having dreams about raping his mother. After much discussion and private sessions, Edward determined that, in fact, this young man from Mesa, Arizona, had engaged in sexual intercourse with his mother but that it happened when he was very young and most certainly without his complete assent.

'It's enough to make you lose hope in humanity,' he had written to his wife Maggie, who was waiting for him in Norwich, 'The Rose of New England', a once-booming mill town where General George Washington had stopped in and spent the night at a local tavern on his way to the front and where they had both been born and raised.

'I thought the war was designed to do that,' Maggie had written back. 'Come back to me, my only love,' she added. 'I want you back, even minus hope.'

Edward carefully wiped his glasses as his group sat silently, watching him. He did not make eye contact with them. They knew the drill. One of them would have to start. There were six in all. Most of them, he decided, were either very stupid or very smart or at least adept at deception. There was one GI in particular whom he knew to be neurotic. He was at the nurse's station every day with some ache or discomfort that required immediate attention or medication, but Edward had not been able to sign off on his release from the army because he had no diagnosable illness that would prevent him from engaging in combat. His lack of focus and constant avoidance of mandated chores did not instil in Edward the confidence that he could be trusted on the battlefield, something he had tried on numerous occasions to explain to the soldier's commanding officer.

Finally, one of them volunteered to speak.

'They are saying six months at the outset,' the patient said. He had strawberry blond hair and freckles. His voice was thin. He had been admitted after attacking his CO—commanding officer—with a machete. The only thing between him and a court martial was Edward saying he was mentally unfit.

'Now, Phil, you know we're not here to talk about the war,' Edward admonished. Even as he said it, he knew it was ridiculous. There was nothing else but the war. The unit was always rampant with rumours. In fact, it was one of the trademarks of the war, and the speculation actually kept morale high. When he looked back on his time in India, Edward wrote his wife, he would remember the interminable waiting for action and the rumours. They always seemed based in some intractable truth that could never be confirmed, and shouldn't be for that matter, as it could give the enemy an advantage. Like most of his fellow soldiers, Edward allowed himself to believe all the good news.

Phil fell silent, and the sullen silence remained for the rest of the session. Edward ended the session on time and left the patients sitting in a circle. He stalked out in frustration. It had been six weeks of these sessions that seemed to yield nothing. He had been assigned to the group the moment he arrived in Calcutta, before he could even adjust to being in India. He headed straight to the officer's club, where he ordered a beer and sulked until lunch. The menu at the Mess advertised Vienna sausages that he likened to earthworms and he lost his appetite. He went back to the hospital administrator's office and started to fill out the necessary reports for the day.

Sadie Howe, the twenty-year-old tow-headed Anglo-Indian secretary, barely acknowledged his presence and kept smoking incessantly so that Edward had to finally ask her to open a window or desist at once. She threw him a resentful glance, lit another cigarette with the one she was already smoking, and pried open a window. All Edward knew about her was her name and that she lived near the Lighthouse movie theatre, which was air-conditioned. Edward saw her there nearly every Saturday. He disliked most of the movies shown there, but it was a welcome respite from the wet heat. Sometimes she nodded at him, but mostly she didn't. Edward found her to be truculent in the extreme and resented having to share the typewriter with her. He knew she deliberately took her time when he needed it.

Edward waited patiently for fifteen minutes as she pecked at the typewriter with long painted fingernails and then asked her when she thought she would be finished. She looked up at him with a bored, insolent expression and continued typing.

'Ms Howe, I am in a hurry here—'

'You Americans are always in a hurry,' she replied, without looking up. The ash on the end of her cigarette was too long. Edward watched the tip fall off and onto the report he had neatly handwritten and left next to the typewriter to be typed up later.

'Okay, that's it,' he said, red faced.

'What's it?' she asked innocently.

'Lt Lafaver?' a male voice said behind them, just as Edward was getting ready to light into her.

Both Sadie and Edward turned around to see a military police officer standing behind them. He seemed tense.

'Yes?' Edward said.

'Ooh, what did you do, Lt Lafaver?' Sadie smirked. Her teeth were yellow. Edward grimaced.

'He didn't do anything, ma'am,' the MP replied. 'Sir, we have a situation and we need your assistance.'

Sadie shrugged, disappointed, and went back to pecking at the typewriter.

~

Outside the examination room sat a light-skinned black soldier, his head in his hands. He looked up as Edward walked by, locking eyes with him. His face was young and smooth. He looked barely twenty, but his eyes seemed old. Edward had seen him in the Mess. He sometimes served him or bussed his table. They had never spoken. He didn't know what the soldier's voice sounded like. Edward nodded at him in greeting as he walked past him. The soldier stood up, saluted, then returned to holding his head the moment Edward passed by. The MP led Edward to an examination room where a young girl, barely sixteen years old, sat huddled in a corner on the floor. Her dupatta was wrapped around her head, covering her mouth, and her kurta was grimy and torn. There were drops of dried blood on the bodice, and the bottom of her garment was almost soaked in blood. She looked vaguely familiar, but Edward could not place her. Kneeling down next to her was another young Bengali woman, the interpreter. She was dressed in a crisp, blue cotton sari, with a red shawl around her shoulders. She appeared almost as distraught. Though she was saying what Edward assumed to be comforting things to the girl, he noticed she would not touch her.

'What's this?' Edward asked the MP.

The MP removed his helmet and placed it under his arm. 'She needs to be examined, sir. She's claiming rape at the hands of two coloured GIs.'

'Was that one of them outside?' Edward asked.

'No, sir. He was the one who brought her in. His story keeps changing, of course. He's trying to protect his pals, I guess. First he says he found her in some back street somewhere and felt an obligation to bring her here, then when this lady shows up and starts translating what the girl is saying, he claims that he found her in a room—' here the MP paused to read from a notebook, '—in Karnani Mansions, where she had entertained them, dancing and such, and that they paid her and left. He claims she was fine when they left.'

'And why did he go back?' Edward asked, kneeling down beside the girl, who shrunk back.

The MP sighed. 'That's where it gets murky. He says that halfway back to base, he realised he forgot his hat and went back to get it and found her, beat up on the floor, barely conscious.'

'Do you believe him?' Edward went to stand next to the MP. He saw that he was scaring the girl.

The MP snorted. 'Would *you* believe a Negro who got a chance to taste some native pussy—sorry sir—would pass it up?' he whispered so the interpreter wouldn't hear.

Edward hesitated. 'No, I guess I wouldn't,' he said.

'Problem is the victim claims that the boy outside had nothing to do with it, but his friends did.' The MP shrugged. 'So that's that.'

The girl was shaking. 'She's going into shock,' Edward said. 'She needs to be covered. Can you give her your shawl?' Edward asked the interpreter. The woman hesitated.

'Would it be possible to find a blanket,' she said, giving Edward a small smile.

'Sure,' he replied, 'but before she dies of shock, let's get that shawl around her.'

'My mother gave me this shawl as a gift. If I give it to the girl, I can't have it back,' she said, tears welling up in her eyes.

The half-empty examination room began to echo with the sound of the girl's chattering teeth.

'I'm sure you'll get it back. We'll even have it laundered for you. Courtesy of Uncle Sam, okay?' Edward said, holding out his hand.

'She's of a different caste,' the interpreter insisted. 'Laundering won't help.'

Both the MP and Edward stared at the translator slack-jawed.

'This fucking country,' the MP muttered, after a moment. 'What, you have cards saying, "Hello! My name is so and so and I'm a Brahmin"? How could you tell?'

The translator's voice shook. 'We just can,' she said.

The girl's shivering had become worse, and Edward ran out of the room in search of a blanket.

'What is it, sir? Is she all right?' The soldier was still outside the room.

'Can you find a blanket?' Edward asked. 'The girl is in shock.'

The soldier nodded and ran down the hallway.

'Try the nurse's station,' Edward called after him.

After what seemed like more than the six minutes it took to find a blanket, Edward wrapped it around the girl. When her shaking ebbed a bit, he glared at the interpreter and then asked the MP, 'When did the assault take place?' He glanced at the girl, who was now looking down at her dirty bare feet. Edward squatted down again so he could be at eye level with her. He wanted to reach out and reassure her, but he knew he should not touch her.

'She first met them at the restaurant Bombay Duck on Monday night and then later at Karnani Mansions. I'm going to say the assault took place early Tuesday morning,' the MP said.

'Why was she only brought in now?' Edward asked. At the mention of Bombay Duck, Edward eyed her more closely, thinking about how he had been with the steely owner, Yasmine, the day before at Flury's. She had left abruptly. Her friend, the singer, had been more pleasant.

The wounded girl now stared back at Edward. Her soft brown eyes were wide and frightened. It was the dancer that he and a young private from Scranton had been mesmerised by two nights before. The one Louis tried to touch when she was on stage.

'According to Private First Class Thomas Faison Jr. out there, he only just remembered his hat this morning. I'm calling bullshit on that one, since he wouldn't have passed inspection, but she's saying it's not him and she doesn't seem scared of him,' the MP said. 'We have to go by what she's claiming.'

'Okay. Let me call the nurse in. I am not sure which doctor is on duty. I need a moment.'

As the morning went on, the girl was able to tell them more. She claimed they took her to a back alley nearby, where they assaulted her. She offered nothing more than that American soldiers had hurt her. 'Kalos?' the interpreter had asked again, but this time the girl collapsed before answering. Though Edward did notice the hesitation when the girl was asked the question.

~

Yasmine stepped out into the narrow alley where the Negro GIs had been two nights before and lit up a cigarette. She was now allowing herself to worry. Neither Rahul nor Adil Baboo had returned.

So lost was she in the wilderness of her worries that she did not see the soldier waiting in the shadows between two buildings. He stepped out, startling Yasmine.

'Ma'am?' he said in a hushed voice.

She jumped even though he was so quiet.

'I didn't mean to scare you,' he said. It was one of the young Negro soldiers Radhika had danced for, the almost white one who was arrogant and did not want anything on the house ... Tommy. Yasmine could not remember his name at once. She remembered she had felt particularly embarrassed for him.

'No,' Yasmine said, even though she was shaken. 'I am not scared.' She smiled wanly at him, her hand to her pounding heart as she tried to still it. She was actually happy to be able to let him in, as there were hardly any customers in the place and the ones who were there were so drunk they would mistake him for a white soldier.

'You can come in,' she said. 'We are closing soon and there is no singing tonight, but you can come in and have a drink. I'll even let you pay for it this time,' she said, smiling.

'No, thank you, ma'am,' he said politely. He was abashed, as she had unwittingly reminded him of his previous arrogance. He removed his cap quickly and turned it over in his hands. He seemed skittish and started at the sound of a car horn going off.

'Ma'am, it's about your girl, the dancer...' Tommy started and then trailed off.

'Radhika?' Yasmine said. 'Do you know where she is?' she asked, urgently.

Tommy nodded. 'I ... I found her. Beaten up so badly. I couldn't leave her there so I took her to the base, where the doctors could patch her up. I did this, knowing they would think I hurt her. I did tell a lie, ma'am. I said I found her in a back street somewhere early today. But I found her yesterday, right after it happened—at about three in the morning. I said I remembered I had left something in the room. They seemed to believe me. Later, when I went to ask about her, they said it was none of my concern but that I should be prepared to tell them exactly what my friends did to her. It seems she told them that they hurt her. I don't know why she said that.'

Yasmine stepped closer to him. He smelled of tobacco and soap.

'What room? Why were you alone with her?' she asked sharply.

'It was all in good fun, ma'am, I promise!' he said. 'She took us to her room in Karnani Mansions, on this here street. We had to sneak in. When we left, she was fine. I mean, she was okay, you know? We even gave her some money, and we left her in the room. And the next we know, the MPs are pulling us away from the Mess, that's where we all work, in the kitchens there, and dragging us in to ask questions because the girl is beat up. Bad. And she is saying it's us who did that to her, well really my pals, who are in the brig—jail now, ma'am. And I swear to you, on God, Jesus, my mama's head, it was not, ma'am. When we left her in the room she was fine. Not a mark on her—' he stopped suddenly, stricken, his jaw tightening. Yasmine watched him. He was anxious before, but now he seemed fearful.

'My biggest regret is that I didn't take her to the infirmary immediately.'

'Why didn't you?' Yasmine demanded. 'You said she was so badly injured—'

'Campbell stopped me; he said we would be blamed for this. None of us could agree on what to do. He said to bring her back here and I didn't want to. She seemed fine at first, just bruised really, but then she started bleeding. I took care of her as best I could. We had been trained in first aid. But when I went to touch her, she was terrified. I thought she would die, so I took her to the infirmary before it was too late.'

Yasmine was shocked. It was too much to take in at once. Radhika was apparently terribly injured, maybe on the verge of death. She had taken the men to a room that Madhu rented sometimes, so she could be alone, away from the constant bustle of the club. Though Yasmine suspected it was also so she could meet her lovers there, people Yasmine would never meet. She did not feel the need to pry into Madhu's reasons for having a room away from the Duck, because it had never affected Madhu's work at the club.

How could she not have known that Madhu had given Radhika permission to use her room? She prided herself on being aware of what was happening around her—her success and survival depended on it. Asma had said to her repeatedly that Radhika was no innocent.

'Ma'am, look,' he said, when Yasmine remained silent. 'You have to know how it is for us here. My pals and I, we keep our heads down and do what we are told. We got no place here. We came to fight, we are willing to die, and they stick us in the kitchen or cleaning up white boy shit, pardon my French, ma'am. What they get away with, we can't even think about, you know? If a white soldier did this, then maybe he'll get latrine duty for a few days, what we do anyway. If we do it, it's court martial and dishonourable discharge and that's if we are lucky, okay? Some of us came here to get away from all that shi—stuff. Why would we want to do anything that could mean my mama visiting me in a military jail?'

'And what of the risk of going to a room with a local girl?' she said.

He smiled at her sadly. 'We're human after all, ma'am. And she is a pretty girl, and she wanted to dance for us. We didn't see the harm,' he said.

'My girls are not prostitutes,' she said, angry.

'No ma'am, they are not. We know that,' he said.

'They're like courtesans,' Yasmine said to protect Radhika's honour in some small way.

'I do not know what that is, ma'am, but I will assume it has to do with being a lady,' he said. 'Because she sure acted like one. She wasn't even going to take money, but we gave her it anyway.'

Radhika not take money? That did not sound like her at all. But there was something in the man's voice and demeanour that made her think he was telling the truth.

Before Yasmine could fully process what Tommy had told her, a jeep pulled up in front of the club, blocking their way out of the alley. The American was anxious. His hands shook as he lit another cigarette. She cupped her hands around his to still them while he lit his cigarette. She did this automatically, without thinking. His hands were calloused and warm. He looked at her, and she dropped her hands quickly and stepped back from him.

'Be calm. Please wait here,' Yasmine said, 'let me see what they want.'

'Yes, ma'am.'

The jeep was driven by two sullen MP officers, wearing black armbands. Adil Baboo was in the back, with Radhika and Rahul, who was holding Radhika's head in his lap. Radhika's right cheek was bruised and she had an open cut on her forehead. It was fresh. Yasmine's eyes flashed with anger. She glared at the MPs in the front seat. They both looked at one another and then at her, surprised at how boldly she met their gazes.

'Did you do this to her?' Yasmine demanded.

'No, ma'am,' one of them said. 'She came to us like this. Our nurses tended to her.'

'They did a shoddy job of it then,' Yasmine said. She could barely conceal her anger.

'Yasmine,' she heard Adil Baboo say softly, bringing her back to the problem at hand.

'You can't bring her through the front,' Yasmine said. 'We are open.'

'Okay, ma'am,' one of the MPs said. 'How about the back? Do you have a back entrance?'

Both MPs peered into the alley where Tommy was presumably still hiding.

'Yes—' Yasmine said and hesitated. She looked at Adil Baboo. 'One of the Negro soldiers from the other night is there,' she said to him in Bengali. 'He will get into trouble if they see him.'

She took out a handkerchief tucked in her bodice and wiped the sweat from her upper lip. She knew she had incited their suspicion by speaking to Adil Baboo in Bengali. It was obvious she had something to hide.

'Accha, leave it to me,' Adil Baboo said.

To the MPs, he said, 'Boss, yes, we can take her through the back, but let me move the things that are there.'

One of the MPs got out of the jeep. 'Sure, let me help.'

'No, no need, please,' Adil Baboo said. 'It is not clean…' he trailed off and looked at Yasmine for help.

'Yes! That is where we throw out the trash and such,' she said. 'Adil Baboo will remove the bins for you.'

Adil Baboo walked quickly into the alley as Yasmine engaged the MPs in small talk. He saw the soldier but turned his back to him and started moving the garbage bins around. He said, over his shoulder, 'Please stay here and don't move until I say so, when I do, just walk into the club and go to the bar and order a drink.'

'But—' the soldier started to say.

'It is not a problem tonight,' Adil Baboo said. 'Bartender's name is Ghosh, please tell that Madame Yasmine sent you.'

'Thank you!' the soldier said. 'My name is Tommy, Tom—'

'Yes sir, very good,' Adil Baboo said urgently but not wanting to be impolite. 'Later, we shall tell names.'

Adil Baboo looked towards the jeep and saw the MPs engaged in conversation with Yasmine. Tommy understood. He gestured for Tommy to go inside, which he did, with one nervous glance towards the MPs.

When he was safely inside, Adil Baboo beckoned the MPs and Yasmine directed the men towards the back stairs. The MPs were large, burly men. They remained grim-faced and serious as one of them carried the girl up the stairs and the other followed closely behind. Radhika looked tiny in the MP's arms. Her kurta was torn and bloodied. They lay her gently on her bed. She was still unconscious. The more stoic MP—he had not joined in the conversation at all when Yasmine had tried to talk to them—silently handed her a neatly typed up report in a manila folder, then both men saluted her and left without a word.

Yasmine parted the curtains and looked down into the alley. She saw the soldier, Tommy, walk out the back door and duck onto the street. Yasmine sighed and turned back to Radhika.

Everyone had crowded into her cramped room. Adil Baboo took Radhika's wrist and felt for a pulse because she was so still.

'Surely she is still alive,' Asma said. 'They would not just dump her body here.'

She had a pulse but it was faint. 'She's alive,' Adil Baboo said.

'What's wrong with her?' Patience asked. She leaned down and peered closely at the girl's ashen face. 'She must be drunk.'

Yasmine handed Patience the report.

Patience started reading the report. 'This says nothing. It says she was roughed up a bit and fainted and made her way to the base—how the bloody hell did she do that?'

Yasmine remained quiet, unsure whether or not to reveal what Tommy had told her.

'But why is she so poorly?' Asma asked.

'Trauma, shock,' Patience suggested. 'Let me read the rest.'

At that moment, Yasmine realised that everyone was in Radhika's room and no one was downstairs, minding the floor.

'It's time to close down,' she said to Adil Baboo. 'Please put up the sign.'

Radhika's grey face was almost ghoulish by the light of a kerosene lamp. Adil Baboo entreated Yasmine to turn on the lights. Yasmine wanted to save money, so she usually kept the electric lights off above stairs. She shook her head now. 'If we are closed, even for a few days, then we certainly cannot afford these extra luxuries. Light the lamps, please.'

Radhika opened her eyes, but did not speak. Rahul brought in a basin of water with a towel. He avoided Radhika's eyes as he dunked the towel in the cool water, wrung it out and handed it to Madhu, who then applied it to Radhika's forehead. The girl had a high fever and shivered.

Asma was silent as she watched everyone bustle around, trying to help Radhika. Just three days back, she had been complaining about how long the girl took in the bath and how she never shared anything. Asma was guilt-stricken and kept muttering, 'For god's sake!'

Madhu and Patience, who both chain-smoked while Radhika's fever spiked, remained silent. It was not an unfamiliar sight to any of them, a girl who had been attacked with no recourse. Despite the fever, or maybe because of it, Radhika fell into a deep sleep. Madhu pulled the cotton quilt over her loosely. When her fever broke, she would need to toss it off.

Before dawn, the fever grew worse, and she began haemorrhaging from between her legs. She began to writhe and moan. Rahul, who had fallen asleep on the floor next to her, jumped up. 'What is happening?' he cried, as Yasmine and Patience ran into the room.

Patience gently lifted the girl's kurta and parted her legs.

'Oh lord,' she said softly and looked at Yasmine, who shook her head.

'This was not in the report,' she said.

'No, I would imagine not,' Patience said. 'I'll tell you though, whatever did this is not natural.'

'Uff! Please, Patience, stop! No supernatural talk,' Yasmine said. 'It was a man, a man did this. This is what they do, they rape!'

'I know, I know,' Patience said soothingly. 'I am saying she is cut up, look.'

There were small scratches on her inner thighs no one had noticed before, and she had possibly been wounded internally as blood had soaked her undergarments and the bottom of her kurta.

Frightened, Yasmine sent for a doctor. Neither she nor Patience trusted doctors who were educated in England or in the western traditions—especially when it came to female concerns—but Radhika was bleeding heavily, and Yasmine did not know how she could stop that. If they did not act quickly, the girl would be dead within the hour. She had seen this before when she was a young girl and one of the baijans miscarried or terminated a pregnancy.

'Let's make a poultice,' Patience said when Yasmine first suggested they call a doctor.

Yasmine shook her head. 'What kind of a poultice?'

'I don't know,' Patience said. 'I just know Mummy always made poultices. There must be something that will dam this up.'

'Why do you make light of everything?' Asma said. 'I'm nervous. Is there anything to eat?'

'I have some hard candy in my room,' Madhu said. 'Come.' She led Asma away with a backward glance at Yasmine. Her face said what Yasmine was feeling. Radhika was most likely going to die.

Yasmine sat next to Radhika and looked at the child's pale face. Her lips were white. 'Is she going to die?' Rahul asked behind her. 'That is too much blood.'

'No, she will live,' Yasmine said, with false certainty. She did not want to further upset Rahul.

'If I had found her earlier…' he began.

'No,' Yasmine said. 'You could not save her.'

Yasmine sent Rahul out of the room and placed a cotton rag against Radhika's vagina, but, as expected, the bleeding would not stop. The animal that had raped her had used more than his body to hurt her.

'I think something sharp was used to penetrate her,' she said to Patience. 'But I cannot look.'

Patience nodded. She lifted the now soaked kurta, pulling it over the girl's waist and parted her thighs again.

Yasmine closed her eyes and tried to remember Monday night's events, and Edward's face came to her. When she tried to piece together the various parts of the evening, she kept going back to when they first met outside the club. The way he looked up at her, standing on the top step. She had been self-conscious and self-assured at the same time. She remembered his smiling at something she had said, and sighed.

She shook her head, as if to shake the memory out of her. She always knew what was happening in her club. She always knew where the girls were. But she had allowed her mind to wander and focus on the American, and Radhika had been harmed.

'It's a mess down here,' Patience said. She began to gag. 'She's been cut, I think. He sliced her to her anus,' Patience said once she recovered.

Yasmine began to cry, though she did not know it. She took up a clean rag.

'Why didn't the sodding Americans do anything for her?' Patience said, also crying.

'Because she's not their problem,' Yasmine said.

Radhika stirred and opened her eyes. She looked down to see Yasmine pressing a cloth between her legs and closed her eyes again. She whispered something unintelligible. Yasmine leaned closer.

'Yes?' she said. 'Speak a little louder.'

'Let me die.'

Yasmine sat back. 'Nonsense!' she said, though she was shaken.

'I'm dirt,' Radhika whispered. 'I'm dirt now.'

'No Bombay Duck girl is dirt,' Yasmine whispered, and stroked the girl's head.

Radhika nodded weakly and slept.

~

When he finally arrived more than an hour later, the haughty doctor's opinion of everyone was plain. It was hard on him, Yasmine thought caustically, having to lower himself like that. But he did his job, and as far as everyone could see, he did it well. He went to work quickly, sewing her wounds up, and bandaging them with clean white cotton and a clotting agent. Then he sat back to see if the girl would last until the next day.

Standing outside Radhika's room, Yasmine scoured the report the MPs had handed to her. It had been signed off by one Doctor Sansom and a Lt Lafaver. She had missed that when she first glanced through it. Lt Lafaver. Edward. There was nothing indicating that the girl had been seriously injured and, according to the report, they had done a thorough examination.

'I say that you go straight to the governor!' Patience demanded.

'And he will tell me to go straight to the devil,' Yasmine said calmly. 'He has bigger concerns than a little girl who was brutalised,' she added. 'Especially a little Indian girl.'

'Go to Gandhi-ji then,' Madhu said. 'Someone can get a message to him.'

'In jail?' Yasmine said, shaking her head. 'His concerns are greater than one person.'

Adil Baboo had joined everyone outside Radhika's room. He sighed. 'I am sorry to say this, but we can only afford to remain closed for two days at the most,' he said.

'I know,' Yasmine said. She looked at Madhu biting her thumb nail. 'Madhu, how long have you allowed Radhika to use your room in Karnani?' Yasmine asked.

'This was the first time she had ever asked me,' Madhu said. 'I thought she wanted to be alone. You know how broody she is. We're all on top of one another here. I understood.'

Madhu was private and reserved but Yasmine had never had cause to think she was a liar. She gazed into Madhu's eyes for a moment. Madhu didn't flinch. Yasmine knew she had no reason to lie about this. She nodded. Madhu exhaled.

'Who will pay for what has been done to her?' Madhu asked, lighting a cigarette. 'I say we remain closed as a snub to these filthy goras.'

'They'll just flock to Firpos,' Patience said. 'No one has any real loyalty. And if we remain closed, how will we eat? Besides, it wasn't the goras who did this to her.'

'It wasn't one of our people,' Madhu protested.

'No,' Yasmine said. 'The report states that the suspects are two kalo soldiers I had allowed to sit in the side alley so they could listen to the music. Radhika met them again, outside the club.' Yasmine thought of the GI Tommy, who had been downstairs drinking her liquor. It was very possible she was protecting the person who had done this to Radhika. He had seemed sincere, but Yasmine was no longer sure she believed him.

Madhu shook her head. 'That cannot be.'

'It is in the report,' Patience said.

'Yes, but would they not want to protect their own men?' Madhu said.

'I do not think that they would risk anything for these men,' Adil Baboo said quietly. 'They all stick together.'

Radhika stirred then and they went back into the room. The disapproving doctor—he had emphasised several times how this was utterly beneath him and that he was most likely soiled for life—took her pulse and checked to see if the bleeding had stemmed.

He declared her out of danger but extremely weak and requiring strict bedrest for the next several weeks.

'And,' he added dispassionately as he packed up his bag, 'most likely, she cannot bear children. Whatever they used was dull and not too long.' He demonstrated the length by touching his thumb to the base of his index finger. His fingers were unusually long and delicate. 'Like a butter knife the Ingrez use when buttering their crumpets,' he continued. He was the only one who chuckled at his cruel joke.

Yasmine looked at him then. Brahmin or not—she doubted he was—he had the corrupt air of a back alley doctor. His tasteless joke was not lost on anyone, but everyone kept quiet as he had come to their aid so early in the morning. Radhika was nothing to him.

'Come, Doctor. I'll show you out,' Adil Baboo said. As he was leaving, Yasmine pressed some extra cash into his palm to buy his silence. The doctor took it silently and slipped it into his bag.

~

Alone in his basha, Edward wrote to his wife later that evening. He wrote to his wife every day and tried to describe his daily life to her in detail. Normally, there was nothing unusual to report, but though this news was certainly a departure from the ordinary, it was unsavoury. Finally, he decided to share the details with her.

Darling Mags,

...We located the soldiers in question immediately and they all claimed that they did not have intercourse with the girl. Three coloureds. I know them to be good boys—hardworking, respectful. (They're given a pretty raw deal if you ask me, aching to fight, but stuck cleaning up latrines and feeding us day after day.) But all claim it was consensual. I think it might be a case of a business deal gone awry. I'll bet the girl wanted more money. But, Mags, I have to say, I can't be totally sure. She was cut up pretty badly and had lost blood. Something doesn't feel on the up and up. The girl is a child really, and works out of what I thought was a swank establishment called Bombay Duck. The woman who runs it even puts on airs, barely tolerating having to talk to and fraternise with the white patrons. I had thought her very elegant and beautiful at first, but now see that she is nothing but a fancy madam. None of them holds a candle to you, sweetheart. That is the material point. I suppose desperation makes even the most beautiful woman ugly, however. Except for Sadie—she would be ugly under any circumstances! Please tell Mom that I was really

happy to receive the handkerchiefs and that she should expect a surprise in the next packet home. Okay, I will give you a hint. It's made of brass. Yes, more of that stuff. That's all they really have over here worth sending. I promise to pick out a nice sari, the kind you saw in Ali Baba, silk with gold thread medallions, on my next foray into the bazaar.

Love, always,
Me

Edward glanced at his watch. It read seven o'clock. He had not eaten dinner and time had flown. As he sealed the letter, he wondered why he had written the things he had about Yasmine. In fact, she had been pleasant to him and everyone else in the club. He suddenly felt guilty—was it that he was attracted to someone other than his wife and so decided to vilify the woman in question?

Just then, Louis and two other officers walked in and tried to lure Edward into a game of poker. Edward was firm he would not participate. When their cajoling didn't work, they suggested they all hit Bombay Duck to tie one on before they retired for the evening.

'I don't think we should go anywhere near there,' Edward said. 'They threw you out last time, if you recollect, Deccico.'

'It's still a great joint,' Louis protested. 'Have you seen the girls? Gorgeous! I promise I'll keep my hands to myself this time.' He gave a low whistle and elbowed Edward in the ribs. 'What better way to pay them back than by buying their overpriced hooch?'

'Yeah, the girls are very seductive,' Edward said.

'You can't get close to any of them, though,' Louis said. 'These Indian gals are locked up tight and protected.'

'Well, not all of them,' Edward said.

'Yeah? Like who? Sorry, whom?' Louis asked quickly.

Louis often spoke fast, and always seemed to be in a hurry, but this time, Edward noticed, his voice was not as confident, even though the 'whom' was a jab at him. Louis cleared his throat several times. Before Edward could respond, one of the other officers said, 'Not the ones down near the ghats.'

'How would you know, Pierce?' Louis said, laughing at him.

'I would advise you to stay away from the ghats and Bombay Duck,' Edward said caustically. 'You'd be surprised at how similar they really are.'

'What the hell are you on about, Lafaver?' Louis demanded. He removed his shoe and rubbed his big toe. Years of heavy drinking had left him with chronic gout. Somehow, he had managed to pass his physical.

'Jesus, Deccico, put that mess away!' Edward said.

Louis ignored him and continued to rub his inflamed toe. 'If it's about that little filly who charged those niggers, then forget about it. They won't be able to prove anything. Besides those boys are off to Burma in a day or two to clean up everyone else's shit there. I figure that's enough punishment for anyone,' he said.

Edward shook his head. 'The medical exam showed that she was assaulted.' He was not surprised Louis knew about the girl. It was difficult to keep anything private on the base.

'I bet it was all a misunderstanding,' Louis said, a bored look on his face. 'She doesn't even speak English, so she could have said no, but how would they know what she was saying? She could have been screaming stop and they thought she wanted it rougher. They don't speak Hindoo.'

'Bengali,' Edward said softly. 'How do you know she doesn't speak English?'

'None of them do. Bengali, Hindoo. It's all the same,' Louis said. 'I don't want to waste time talking about these sorry-ass people. Are you coming or not?'

'I'm going to call it a night.'

Louis shrugged, but he was puzzled. 'Suit yourself. Could be a good time.'

6

Three mornings after he had examined Radhika, Edward encountered Bombay Duck's young bearer, Rahul. The boy had been sent to the American base with a message to the officers that Bombay Duck was once again open for business but was finding it difficult to discharge his sternly directed duty. Distractions abounded. Edward watched as Rahul tried in vain to communicate with a somewhat hostile nurse who possessed a shelf-like bosom that the boy could not help but gawk at. It was only a matter of time before Nurse Winter either slapped him or reported him to the MPs, so Edward intervened. The boy was asking for his friend, Lance Corporal Craig Addison, whom he had met at the Duck not long before.

'I do not speak Hindi,' Nurse Winter said loudly to Rahul. She turned to Edward and said, 'I have no idea what he wants. Do you suppose he's an urchin?' She looked the boy up and down, taking in his dusty sandals and greasy hair. He looked unwashed.

'No, Nurse Winter. He is gainfully employed,' Edward replied.

The woman looked doubtful and walked off.

'Corporal Addison sahib?' Rahul persisted. He could barely form the word 'corporal'.

Edward smiled at the teenager. 'She's kind of chilly, huh? I guess her name fits. Winter.'

The boy didn't understand but put his palms together quickly. 'Namoskar,' he said, dejected.

'Do you remember me?'

Rahul shrugged—he did not understand what this man was saying. He recognised him but did not feel friendly towards him.

'Corporal Addison sahib,' the boy said again. 'Tell something to him. Also, you.' He paused, trying to remember exactly what Yasmine had taught him to say.

'We open now,' he said slowly. He made an 'opening the door' gesture. 'You come and—' he pantomimed drinking and then hopped around, waving his arms, in what Edward assumed was a demonstration of dancing.

'Oh,' Edward said, understanding. 'The club's open, is it? But you want to see Corporal Addison. Okay, well, let's see what we can do.'

He put his arm around the boy's bony shoulder and led him to where the enlisted men quartered. Rahul shrugged off his arm.

'Okay. We're not friends yet,' Edward said.

Corporal Addison was located after some confusion as to his whereabouts and seemed happy to see his pal Rahul, as was the boy to see him. Edward explained that the Duck had re-opened for business, much to the joy of the men. Rahul, relieved to have dispatched the message as instructed, made ready to leave but was stopped by the corporal.

'I think his boss needs him back,' Edward said. 'He might get into trouble.'

'Look at him, sir,' Addison pleaded. 'He's just a kid. When was the last time he had some fun? They work him to the bone.'

'That's the way it is here,' Edward said. 'We can't mess around with the way they do things, okay?'

'Aww, but look at him, sir! He's all scrawny and just a kid,' Addison insisted. 'Just an hour? What could it hurt?'

They all looked at Rahul then, who was happily drinking his first bottle of soda pop. His shirt was grimy and torn, and the straps of his sandals were held together by twine, having long since lost the buckles. Upon first glance, he was a pathetic sight to be sure. What the Americans did not know was that he had simply forgotten to send his laundry to the dhobi that week, so this worn old shirt was all he had that was clean, and that he had decided against wearing out his newer chappals and put on an old pair. The boy, unaware of the bedraggled picture he painted, was trying to concoct an excuse to tell Yasmine for his extended absence. He was frightened of Yasmine but was willing to incur her wrath if it meant he could bask in the GIs' affectionate company a bit longer.

'I see all those little guys, working the dumps and the streets, sir,' Addison continued. 'It kills me. There's this kid who works the ghats, where they burn the dead bodies. His job is to gather the kindling and stuff. He can't be more than eight. My sister's eight. It kills me,' he repeated. 'It's not right. There's a lot about this country that isn't right. Give me America any day.'

Edward looked over at the black soldiers cleaning up and bussing the tables. They were jovial—with one another—as they picked up after everyone. He thought about the two young black men languishing in the brig, accused of rape.

'I think this kid is pretty well taken care of, considering,' Edward said. He was defensive. He did not want the men to view Rahul's boss, Yasmine, as a slave driver. He was not sure why, but it bothered him. 'He gets three squares a day.'

Edward's defensiveness was apparent, and he was suddenly self-conscious when he saw the other men looking at him curiously. He cleared his throat.

'I guess it's okay. Just don't let him stay too long. They might need him back. We have to respect his boss's time. Our dealings with the native element have to be handled tactfully.'

'Okay, sure, sir, whatever you say,' Addison said. Edward was aware that he had become suddenly stiff. He smiled at Rahul, who did not smile back.

As soon as Edward left, a baseball game was immediately organised and lasted well into early evening, until it was hard to see the ball. By the end of it, Rahul was solidly the company pet and could pitch a decent curve ball. His inclination had been to pitch overhead, like they did in cricket, but the Americans showed him the 'right way' to throw a ball. The GIs ruffled his hair and referred to him as 'Southie' because he was left-handed. Through an interpreter, they insisted he join them when they watched the Calcutta Yankees play the Canada–US team, and told him he had to come play with them whenever games were on. So entranced was Rahul that he lost track of the time. He had completely forgotten that Yasmine had told him to return to the club as soon as he had delivered his message. They had much to do before the doors opened that evening.

When the dinner bell was rung, the soldiers started to make their way to the Mess. Corporal Addison invited Rahul along. The boy hesitated, caught between curiosity and starting to feel guilty that he had spent so much time in the company of Americans. He suddenly remembered Radhika, still so ill, lying alone in her dark room. But this was also the most exciting thing that had happened to him in his sixteen years. At the club, he never interacted with the English customers; they barely acknowledged him. He was invisible. But the Americans treated him as one of their own; the limits of language overcame that. Before he could protest, they had shuffled him into the Mess hall and onto the chow line. His eyes widened at the steaming trays filled with food, some of which he could not identify at once. It was more meat in one place than he had seen in months. As the delicious smell of roast beef and mashed potatoes filled his nostrils, his stomach growled, pushing the image of Yasmine's scowling face out of his mind.

~

Yasmine felt as if she were losing control over everything, with Radhika being so awfully harmed and now Rahul disappearing for the entire afternoon. She felt she could not protect anyone, and she felt an especial duty to Rahul and Radhika; they were both just children, really. She had taken care of Radhika all day; the girl was in and out of consciousness. The fever would abate and then return. Yasmine and the others took turns washing her hands and feet in cold water and mopping her forehead. The fever caused the girl's pulse to race, and she could not rest for long. When she finally fell asleep, Yasmine looked at Radhika's sweaty face and bloodless lips, and felt a powerful need to get outside and get some air.

'Has Rahul returned?' she asked Adil Baboo, while she fanned Radhika's face.

The older man shrugged. He silently took the fan from Yasmine.

'You should rest now,' he said. 'You look pale.'

'You don't think anything has happened to him too, do you?' Yasmine said, suddenly fearful.

'Yes,' Adil Baboo replied. 'The Amrikans happened to him. Why did you send him of all people? You know how easily distracted he gets.'

'We should go get him,' she said.

'Let me go,' Adil Baboo replied. 'I am not sure it's safe.'

They both looked at Radhika, who had started to shiver in her sleep, indicating the fever was back.

'No, it has to be me, so when he sees my face, it will strike fear into his heart,' Yasmine said, with more bravado than she felt.

In the hopes that the boy had left the base, Yasmine went to the various places Rahul had often been caught loitering before—a tea house on Harrison Street, where he played cards, and the alley behind the Tollygunge Golf Club, where a sign read 'No Natives or Dogs Allowed', to gape at the English memsahibs as they emerged from their freshly washed cars. Some of his chums, thugs in the making, Yasmine considered them, were aimlessly hanging about in front of the tea house when she went in search of him, but had not seen him. In fact, no one had seen him the entire day. Though she hated to, Yasmine knew she had to go visit the American camp. In the eighteen months since the base had been established, Yasmine had never ventured near it.

Her determined stride slowed down as she approached the first checkpoint. She hesitated. She had no curiosity about the Yanks, as Patience had started calling them. They made decent movies, some wrote decent novels. She liked Hemingway even though the nuns at Loreto told her he was, unfortunately, a misogynist. But she felt ultimately that they were no better than the British and in some ways worse, because they pretended to believe that all men were created equal—even had it written into their laws—and did nothing to uphold it. Yes, the American way was infinitely worse, Yasmine decided, because it was deceptive. Total bullshit, she said to herself resolutely, an American phrase Patience had been bandying around after learning it from an admirer from New York City. It had a satisfying ring to it. 'Better than bollocks,' Patience had said.

At least one knew where they stood with the English. No waffling or ambiguous platitudes there. One knew one's place, however lowly it may be.

Yasmine steeled herself for what she knew would be a humiliating experience. She was dressed tastefully and modestly in a navy blue cotton sari; the bodice was quarter sleeved with a high boat neck. She had even thrown a flowing beige chiffon scarf around her shoulders and covered her head with it for further modesty. She had left her hair down. She didn't know it or didn't care, but she looked fetching. Her intention had been to avoid looking like a common Calcutta whore.

There were two separate checkpoints she had to pass through before she could enter the base. She hoped that she would find the information she needed by questioning the guards at the checkpoints, so she would not have to run around the base aimlessly.

Two guards, who could not have been much older than Rahul, were stationed at the first checkpoint. One stood outside the guard box, holding a rifle across his chest. Under his helmet, his cheeks were pink from the heat. He had never seen an Indian woman up close, and found himself tongue-tied. He scowled at her and indicated that she should walk no further. He had been instructed that the natives were generally peaceful but one could never be too careful. They were capable of unpredictable bouts of mob violence, like the Negroes back home in West Virginia, but unlike the Negroes, the Indians were the majority.

She stopped at his behest, and he approached her. Yasmine looked warily at his gun. She seemed frightened and this made him immediately contrite. He slung the gun behind him and attempted to smile at her. She was pretty.

Yasmine watched the approaching soldier with growing anxiety—the gun was the least of it. She looked around and saw there was not a single native face in sight. It was truly as if she had landed in America itself, which she always imagined to be brimming with white people as far as the eye could see.

Still, it was so odd not to see at least one Indian face, not even a random mendicant, squatting on his haunches nearby, waiting for a handout, thought Yasmine. For the first time in her life, she missed the inevitable, madding crowd. At least it was familiar. She knew how to navigate the suffocating press of sweaty, smelly Indian bodies on the tram or on the street, but this wide, open space was intimidating and seemed dangerous. She had never been alone with two white men. In the club, Adil Baboo or the bartender Ghosh or the girls were always milling about. At the club, she was the boss and could have these men forcibly removed, guns or not, if they threatened her. Here, she was at their mercy, on their turf. If she turned and ran, they might shoot her, because it could very easily be deemed suspicious. She realised suddenly how frightened Radhika must have been when she was attacked by two huge American men. White or black, they were so bloody foreign and so much larger than the slightly built Indian men she was used to, and much better fed. Judging from the healthy glow of this young soldier, there was no rationing on the American base. They must have pinned the tiny girl down. Radhika didn't stand a chance, just like she, Yasmine, would not stand a chance. She had no weapon on her that could compete with a loaded rifle. This thought made her pulse race. She began to sweat. They could drag her behind the guard post and rape her at gunpoint, she thought, and there would be no recourse. Her remorse at not protecting Radhika surged.

When she finally located Rahul, she thought, she would make him pay dearly for putting her in such a horrendously vulnerable position.

She took a step back as the soldier drew nearer. Her fear was written plainly on her face, causing the young American to throw his hands in the air and say, 'See? I slung the gun behind me! Don't be scared.'

He attempted to smile at her, but he was just as tense and it came out as more of a grimace as he bared a set of uneven, nicotine-stained teeth.

He's approaching me like I'm a wild animal, she thought. He's just as scared of me as I am of him.

This thought gave her confidence. She set her shoulders back and stood her ground, allowing the soldier to walk up to her. If a Bengal Tigress is what he expected, then that is what he would get.

They faced one another. He kept smiling, his nostrils flaring a little. She said nothing.

'Hello!' he shouted. 'Do you speak English?'

Why do white people always think that shouting clarifies everything, she wondered. She was about to respond when the other guard yelled out, 'Jesus, Denny, she's not deaf.'

'I do speak English, actually,' Yasmine said. 'I studied Shakespeare in school.'

Yasmine had observed that the best way to confound (or impress) an American was to reference Shakespeare with some authority. And, indeed, both soldiers looked shocked. This information caused Denny to remove his helmet quickly, against regulations, and caused his companion to abandon his post.

'Sorry, ma'am,' Denny said, abashed. 'Wasn't sure is all.'

'It's perfectly fine,' Yasmine said, in what she hoped was an intimidating and haughty voice. 'I am used to being underestimated.'

Private Denny Henderson, age nineteen, of Coal City, West Virginia, population 897, gaped at Yasmine, slack-jawed. He had not completed high school by the time he enlisted and had only a fleeting idea of who Shakespeare was. He had seen *The Jungle Book* twice when he found out he was being sent to India, and attempted to read *Gunga Din*, but did not get past the third stanza. Nothing had quite prepared him for Yasmine Khan. He forgot to replace his helmet. His comrade-in-arms soon joined him in gaping at Yasmine up close. The three of them stood silently for several seconds, staring at one another. Everyone seemed at a loss for what to do next.

'How can we help you, ma'am?' Private Gordon Schiffer of Muncie, Indiana, finally asked. He had an intrinsic mistrust of anyone who was not white or Presbyterian but was not sure what to feel about this petite young woman whose posture was ramrod straight and who spoke correct English with a polished accent.

'I am trying to locate my employee, a young lad, about this high, who I think is on your base,' she said.

'Any more natives come in today, Henderson?' Private Schiffer asked, trying to sound official.

Yasmine winced slightly at the word 'natives' and looked away. She knew he had not meant it unkindly, but it smarted just the same.

Private Henderson didn't take his eyes off Yasmine. 'Just some of those hawkers selling that brass junk, and Southie.'

'Ma'am, are you talking about Southie?' Schiffer asked.

Yasmine shook her head. 'No, this boy's name is Rahul,' she said. 'He is skinny, with spindly legs and his hair is a bit oily and short, and sticks up. He doesn't speak English.'

Private Schiffer scratched his chin. 'Sounds like Southie,' he said.

'I don't know who this Southie is,' Yasmine replied. 'My boy's name is Rahul.'

'Well, anyone coming into the base has to sign in,' Private Schiffer said. He led Yasmine to the guard box and handed her a sheet and pen. 'So if he's on the base, then he would be on here.'

He looked down the list of people who had signed in that day.

'So he can't speak English?'

Yasmine shook her head.

'Can he read or write?'

She shook her head again.

'Okay, here he is. It's gotta be him,' Schiffer said and pointed to an 'X' that had signed in at two o'clock that afternoon next to the name 'Rahul', which someone had helpfully scrawled for him.

'You have to sign in too. You can just write your initials, if that is easier,' Schiffer said, trying to be helpful and succeeding in only being insulting. Yasmine scowled at him and signed her full name in both print and cursive, though the latter was not needed.

'When you get to the next checkpoint, just tell them you're looking for Southie, okay?'

'What kind of a nickname is that?' Yasmine asked. She was expecting it to be something wholly demeaning. Though she could not imagine what.

Private Schiffer scratched his sweaty head and grinned. 'Oh, because he pitches left-handed, ma'am, so we call him that.'

'Rahul is left-handed?' Yasmine was surprised she had not noticed that before.

'Yes, ma'am. He's real smart and a good pitcher.'

'Yes, he sure is. He struck Fuller out, remember that?' Private Henderson said.

'You lot play cricket?' Yasmine asked.

The two young men looked at one another and then burst into laughter, which Yasmine found off-putting. She did not like to be laughed at.

'Uh, no ma'am. We play baseball, a real sport,' Henderson said, snorting.

'Now, Henderson, that's rude,' Schiffer said.

'Oh, sorry! No offence meant,' Henderson said. His face had turned red. 'I just meant—'

'I am not bothered, either way,' Yasmine replied airily. 'I find both sports equally tiresome, though baseball seems more senseless.'

Not sure how to respond to what they considered to be an egregious declaration, the young men replaced their helmets and solemnly ushered Yasmine through the gate.

As luck would have it, the guards at the next checkpoint knew exactly where the boy was because more than one of them had participated in the impromptu baseball game that had seen the hapless Fuller struck out by Rahul. They spoke of the boy warmly, which only irritated Yasmine more. One eager young guard, who stammered when addressing her, led her to the Mess hall where Rahul was enjoying his first ever meatloaf and macaroni salad. He had just asked for seconds when she walked in.

'Uh oh, kid,' Corporal Addison said when he saw an irate Yasmine stalking towards them. Rahul turned around to see his boss glaring at him. He silently pushed away his plate and rose from his seat to meet his fate.

'Who's she, Southie, your mom?' one private enquired.

Yasmine shot him a sharp look. 'No,' she said, 'I am his employer.'

Her perfect English surprised the Americans, yet again.

'It's just a joke, ma'am,' the soldier said, grinning. 'No offence meant. You just look serious, like a mom.' Everyone chuckled, and Yasmine's face flushed.

Edward furtively watched Yasmine from his table on the other side of the Mess, where he sat with the officers. She had not noticed him. Seeing her again, and how pretty she was, was a jolt to his system and reminded him that he had been curious about her. A curiosity that he felt so guilty about he decided he would write Maggie again, confessing to it. He knew Maggie was practical, and she would be able to come up with a rational explanation for the fact that Edward had thought about Yasmine at least four times since he had met her. He had never thought about a woman who was not his wife so much. He had not been married long enough to be bored with his marriage. There was the occasional fantasising about dark-haired, full-lipped Dorothy Lamour in a clingy, wet, floral sarong, her nipples poking out underneath the thin fabric, while she was being lashed by waves brought on by a hurricane—but that was it. Yasmine did not look like Dorothy Lamour at all; well, not totally.

As Edward watched Yasmine trying to talk to the smirking soldiers, his emotions moving around inside him like restless mice, he imagined what Maggie would say: 'Well, of course you're curious about the Indian woman, sweetheart! You've always been curious, and you need to understand your surroundings, and this woman is a native to those surroundings. It's intellectual, hon. A purely intellectual pursuit. She's not your type.'

'Yes, this is an intellectual curiosity. It's natural, given the alien environment, to want to understand the natives,' he told himself.

'You okay, Lafaver?' one of his fellow officers said. 'You got a sudden case of flop sweat.'

Edward wiped his forehead, muttered something about feeling a bit unwell from the heat, and took a gulp of water.

~

Back in Norwich, there was a relatively small population of coloured people, and they all lived on one side of the town. There was a Chinese laundry, where they over-starched everything, run by the same family for twenty years, but that was it for Asians in town. The only Indians he had ever encountered were Mohegans like Greg Tantaquidgen, with whom he had gone to school, and most of them had blue eyes and blond hair.

The thought of his childhood friend gave him pause. Greg would not let Yasmine flounder. He would be a gentleman. He heard Yasmine sharply address Corporal Addison and now hoped no one would insult her or say something untoward. He would be forced to do something and decided that he (for the most part) was ready to intercede if something happened, unlike the unpleasant night when Louis jumped on the stage and had to be forcibly removed. He knew he should have immediately alerted his CO, but Louis had talked him out of it, arguing their CO might then make the club off limits, and there were so few places in Calcutta where they could go to blow off steam.

He could not hear what was being said, but he closely watched everyone's body language. Yasmine appeared confident. She stood with her hands on her hips and feet slightly apart. Rahul was hunched over his half-eaten meatloaf, and Addison sat easily, with his elbows on the table, grinning at Yasmine in a way that Edward instinctively knew she probably found offensive. She wouldn't suspect it was not insolence but just the way a kid from a small town in California's agricultural valley would behave. She would not know that his people were poor—almost as poor as some of those of who lived in the slums around Tollygunge—and were descended from 'Okies', who had lost everything in the Dust Bowl and had migrated to California to find a means of survival. However, not a single soldier had stood up when Yasmine approached their table. Most, if not all, would have stood up had a white woman or one of the nurses approached them. Edward hoped that slight was lost on her. But he also knew somehow that very little was lost on Yasmine Khan.

While Edward pondered if he should intercede and come to her rescue, Yasmine's heart was pounding, her self-possession ebbing. The hall was full of men. All of whom seemed focused on her. She smelled the sweat and the aftershave and the dust. She looked around for a friendly face. Her eyes alighted on the other women in the hall—the nurses, who were watching and whispering among themselves. Their expressions displayed no empathy. Now, everyone was looking at her. The cooks had stopped dishing out the grub to watch her chastise the soldiers for keeping Rahul from his duties. She looked for Tommy, but he was not there.

'The kid needed to have some fun,' Addison said in his own defence. 'You work him like a dog.'

'As opposed to how gently you would work him if he was your bearer,' Yasmine snapped. Her voice shook.

'Now, ma'am, I don't know what you're getting at,' Addison protested, 'but this kid has been treated like one of us, and I would give him days off if he worked for me.'

'Hah!' Yasmine said and took Rahul by the arm to lead him out. It was then that she felt Edward's eyes on her. For a fleeting moment her eyes lit up, until she saw his face was uninviting. He was looking at her the way the rest of the men were, with a bemused, slightly contemptuous curiosity. His impassive gaze made her feel small.

Yasmine pulled up Rahul roughly by an arm and marched him out of the room. His new friends looked at one another as she took the boy away.

They shook their heads. 'She's nasty,' someone said as they left, and they all agreed.

'Kinda pretty though,' someone else said, after a contemplative silence. 'I'd give her the high hard one.' They all chuckled, and a consensus was reached yet again as they watched her walk away, all eyes on her backside.

Edward watched the men ogle Yasmine and felt a pang of irritation. He quickly finished his dinner and got up, leaving his tray on the table to be bussed, which he never did. Louis always teased him about emptying his own tray and not giving the 'coloured boys something to do'.

The officers watched him rush out of the Mess, one calling out, 'Hey Lafaver, where's the fire?'

Edward ignored them and ran towards the entrance.

At the gate, the guard shook Rahul's hand and patted him on the head. Like a dog, Yasmine observed resentfully.

'How did you manage to become their pet?' she asked him.

'They like me, didi,' he said quietly.

'Yes, like you were a performing monkey—'

'No! That's not true!' Rahul had never raised his voice to her. Yasmine was too surprised to say anything. Everyone was right; the Americans seemed to upend everything, she thought. When she recovered, she cuffed Rahul on the back of the head and walked a little ahead of him.

'You know what it took for me to come here? No lady in her right mind would come here unaccompanied!' She stopped so suddenly that the boy ran into her back.

'I was coming home, Yasmine di, I was,' Rahul cried.

'Another boss would have done worse. You would have been beaten and then let go without this week's wages. I would have been well within my rights.'

'They're not like the Ingrez, didi,' Rahul said. 'They're kind. They don't look down on me.'

'You're a fool!' Yasmine snapped. 'You know nothing! And as long as you work for me, you are never to fraternise with them again, do you understand?'

'What does that mean?' the boy asked.

'We cannot be friends with them, Rahul, outside the club. It's impossible. That is what that means.'

'But they *are* my friends,' the boy protested. Yasmine shook her head.

'Rahul, this friendship of yours could hurt you,' she said. 'Now let's get home. We don't have much time to get ready.'

'Ms Khan?'

Yasmine turned around to find Edward. Unlike in the Mess hall, he seemed friendly. He took off his cap and smiled at her. Yasmine was glad he remembered her name.

'I wanted to enquire after the young lady from your … establishment. I was one of the doctors on duty the other day.'

'You're a doctor? You didn't mention that.'

Edward turned to look at the young guards, Henderson and Schiffer. Henderson had waved goodbye to Yasmine. They were watching him and Yasmine with curiosity.

'Privates, you got something to do besides gape at the young lady here?'

'They're fine,' Yasmine said. 'It's quite sweet, really, the way they are so baffled by me.'

'Baffled?' Edward said. 'I'm not sure that's what it is—more like awestruck, really.'

He cleared his throat in embarrassment and wondered where this thought had come from. 'What I suppose I mean is, well, they're small town boys, you know? And India is so strange…'

'And I am strange too?' Yasmine asked.

Edward found her lilting accent not altogether displeasing. In daylight, or in this case, twilight—the time of day that led poets like Hafiz to write about a woman's beauty—she looked charming. Fetching was the word that came to mind, if not astoundingly stunning. Sometimes Edward read poetry, a habit he had formed at Wesleyan. Before he came to India, he had stocked up on translated Urdu poetry, thinking it would give him added insight into the native mind. So far, it hadn't helped a great deal. If one was to go by the poetry, Indians were passionate but spent a great deal of time longing for their beloved from afar, like Petrarch. In general, Indians were very confusing; not two-faced exactly, but they definitely played it close to the vest. It was hard to know where one stood with them. Even when they nodded 'yes', it seemed like they were saying 'no', as their affirmative nod was side to side and not straight up and down.

Yasmine's arms were crossed but her eyes were soft.

This gave him courage. He wanted to tell her that he liked the Sufi poets and of course Tagore, the Bengali poet and thinker, but it was more the political, anarchic stuff, like Faiz Ahmed Faiz's poetry, that spoke to him. Of course, he would never tell any of his fellow Americans that, because Faiz Ahmed Faiz had a decidedly Socialist bent. It would probably be all right to share this with Yasmine, as all Bengalis seemed to have a Socialist bent, but he controlled himself and said nothing.

'You're from a large city, then?' Yasmine asked when he was silent. He seemed lost in his own thoughts. 'Norwich is large?'

'Shoot no!' Private Henderson cried behind them. 'He's from a mill town smaller than a minute. I'm from a coal town, in fact that's the name of it, Coal City, West Virginia, and he's from a mill town. Isn't that right, sir? That's what you said, sir. We're all small town boys.'

Edward glared at Private Henderson until the young soldier turned pink.

'Sorry, sir. Didn't mean to speak out of turn, sir,' he said, abashed.

Edward ignored him. 'As Private Henderson so helpfully offered, Norwich is a small town, yes, in eastern Connecticut on the Thames River.'

He shifted his weight and cleared his throat.

'You said you were a doctor?' Yasmine asked.

'I am a counsellor. I studied psychology in college,' he replied. 'I never actually finished. The war started ... but I have every intention of completing my degree when I get back,' Edward left off, wondering at himself and why he had shared this information with her. It would surely undermine him. He took off his glasses and busily wiped them with a handkerchief, though they were not dirty.

'Radhika is alive, but barely,' Yasmine said. She took another step back and looked at him. She had changed again. Her eyes were not soft anymore.

She's defensive, Edward thought. She doesn't really like me.

'What do you mean?' Edward said. 'When we released her, she was weak and tired, but it was more from shock.'

'Radhika was ... violated,' Yasmine said.

'Yes, I know there was assault,' Edward said carefully. 'But not life threatening.'

Yasmine allowed that to sink in for a moment. Edward's tone was clinical. She shook her head. 'Naturally that is what a man would say. She may be alive, but her life will never be the same.'

Edward's face flushed. 'Oh of course! I'm not implying that it's not serious. But she is alive. That's good news at least.'

'Is it? Some would say she is better off dead, given the shame that's been brought upon her. In India, a woman surviving an ordeal like this is not considered good news. Somehow, it will be her fault she was attacked and not the beast who did this to her. When a marauding army approached, women and girls would throw themselves into wells or off rooftops to avoid what soldiers would most likely do to them. It was preferable to living with the shame.'

Edward remained silent, knowing that anything he said would be inadequate. He slapped a mosquito on his neck.

Rahul, who had tried to remain inconspicuous the entire time, looked from Edward's face to Yasmine's in confusion because the energy had so swiftly changed. He stood near Private Schiffer, who playfully smacked him around the head and pretended to punch him in the stomach, while Rahul fended off his mock blows. Yasmine called the boy back over to where she was standing, telling him it was time to go.

Edward could see he had displeased her but found he was unable to say anything to mitigate this new tension. Instead, he stood staring into Yasmine's warm brown eyes, avoiding glancing at her full breasts, hoping she would not leave. His feelings were inexplicably intense.

Be courteous, maintain boundaries, he told himself. He shook her hand. She invited him to the club. He hesitated, which was not lost on her, and then nodded.

We are the guests in her country, Edward thought. He watched her until she was almost out of sight with Rahul trailing behind her.

'She was a pretty thing, huh, sir?' Private Henderson said to Edward. 'I liked looking at her. It made me feel good to just look at her.'

Edward shielded his eyes to look as Yasmine walked away. All three men watched silently.

'What fucking difference does it make?' Edward muttered under his breath after a moment.

'Sir?' Henderson asked.

'I'm never going to see her again anyway,' Edward replied. 'We'll all be shipped out any day now.'

'You think so, sir?' Schiffer, who was eager to see action, asked.

'One can only hope,' Edward said, knowing the irony and sarcasm would be lost on Schiffer.

'Yes, sir! That's true. I pray for the chance to kick some Jap ass!'

~

As she was walking away, Yasmine decided she found Edward insufferable. She could no longer remember what she saw in him. His glasses that she thought gave him a studious, thoughtful air now made him seem plain. And pompous. It highlighted a rather weak chin, she thought. Why didn't I notice his weak chin before? She felt immensely foolish for thinking he might have found her pretty. It was obvious he looked down on her. Just as one would expect a white man to do. This thought made her surly and she cuffed Rahul, the nearest victim, in the back of the head as they walked away to the main road.

'Ow!' Rahul cried. 'What did I do now?'

'Nothing,' Yasmine said. 'This is for the next time.'

After they had walked on a bit, she was tempted to look back at Edward to see what he was doing and, as she explained to herself, to give him a haughty, parting glare. But her pride prevented her. She asked Rahul to do it instead.

'Is that choot still standing there?' she asked, as casually as she could. Rahul had never heard her utter such foul language. It sounded unnatural coming from the normally elegant Yasmine's mouth. He looked back, squinting as he did so. He made a show of it, stopping and shading his eyes with his hand.

'Uff!' Yasmine said and started walking faster. 'Don't be so obvious. He'll think I asked you to look.'

'But you did,' Rahul said.

Yasmine shook her head and sighed.

'He is di.'

'He is what?'

'He is standing, di, and watching. They all are.'

Yasmine smiled. Maybe she had inherited something from her mother and grandmother after all, but then she did exactly what they would never have done. She turned and looked back.

PART TWO

STRAY DUCKLINGS

This is India! The land of dreams and romance, of fabulous wealth and fabulous poverty, of splendor and rags, of palaces and hovels, of famine and pestilence, of genii and giants and Aladdin lamps, of tigers and elephants, the cobra and the jungle, the country of a hundred nations and a hundred tongues, of a thousand religions and two million gods, cradle of the human race, birthplace of human speech, mother of history, grandmother of legend, great-grandmother of tradition, whose yesterdays bear date with the mouldering antiquities of the rest of the nations—the one sole country under the sun that is endowed with an imperishable interest for alien persons, for lettered and ignorant, wise and fool, rich and poor, bond and free, the one land that all men desire to see, and having seen once, by even a glimpse, would not give that glimpse for all the shows of all the rest of the globe combined.

–Mark Twain, *Following the Equator*

7

Akash Alexander Khan '61
Hayden Hall
Mt Hermon School for Boys
Gill, MA
5 December 1959

Dearest Akash,

You asked me again the other day about the Japanese bombs. As always, I love your curiosity, and I think you are now old enough to hear about the bombings. But first, I want to talk about the Japs. Well, these are a spectacularly tight-lipped people. They took the expression 'loose lips sink ships' quite literally. We knew very little about them when the Allies went to war with them—or rather when they declared war on America—and knew even less by the time the war ended. The way the Japanese were portrayed made them seem sinister and foreign. As cruel and bigoted as the English were, they were not foreign to us. Also, the notion of being ruled by other Asians was insupportable. This is part of that inferiority complex that the colonised suffer from, I suppose. If we had to be ruled by someone, it should be white people. Somehow, that made more perverse sense...

So many things changed, seemingly overnight, when the bombs started to drop. So many Japanese businesses closed, it seemed, like I said, overnight and became Anglo-Indian businesses. Patience and I used to have our hair cut at a Japanese salon near Dalhousie Square by a slight young man named Asagai, who knew how to recreate the latest Hollywood styles. It was a family-owned business that had been in Calcutta for over twenty years, and one day, it was gone. There was no sign on the door. Inside, the place looked the same, except some of the pictures on the wall had been removed—the Japanese-themed ones. We never saw Asagai again—after seeing him almost every other week for years. But that was war. When I stopped long enough to think about it, it bothered me a great deal.

On 20 December, in the cover of night, the Japs tried to shake us out of our stoicism. I remember it clearly. It was ear-splitting. First, there was stillness and then a whistle, like a teakettle, and then the explosion. It was the whistle that was for me the most terrifying, because you knew what was to follow and that could mean anything. If the whistle was heard directly overhead well, then, as the Brits would say, Bob's your uncle!

We survived, of course; actually, the city as a whole managed beautifully. This is what the chief minister had to say about it (I have included cuttings from *Anandabazar Patrika*, 21 December 1942, and translated them for you, in case you have lapsed in your Bangla):

We are all delighted to find Calcutta has taken its first experience of enemy night air attack with a stout heart, without the morale of the people being shaken in the least.

He practically shouted it from the rooftops. Well, I don't know whose stout hearts he was referring to, because it took me several days of repeated bombings to get used to it. I did not manage to maintain my calm courage or matter-of-fact coolness like the newspaper said we did. I was hysterical well through the New Year—which is another story.

The nearest bomb shelter was at the Metro picture hall—under the stairs. On 20 December, we all found ourselves huddled together there, being bossed about by pushy Anglo girls who had signed up to be in the Women's Auxiliary Corp.

I remember odd little details of that first onslaught. I saw a poster of Clark Gable leaning over Lana Turner light up as a bomb hit its mark across the street and blast a gash down the centre of it, shattering Das's storefront windows.

An hour into it, they gave the all-clear and we emerged from beneath the stairs, blinking and coughing at the dust the bombs had kicked up. I was never the first to emerge, as I never fully trusted that everything was, in fact, clear. I waited. Asma bolted out as fast as her plump body would allow. I worried that one day they would yell 'all clear!' and the girls would bolt out—and boom! All that remained of them would be their shoes, with wisps of smoke coming out of them, like in cartoons.

We walked home slowly, lost in our own thoughts. You would think that people would be in a hell fire rush to get home. I think everyone was dazed. Keep calm and carry on, the government told us, and that is what Calcutta did. Christmas was a few days away, but the Japs would continue bombing us well past New Year's. This time, there was only the one gash down the street, and it was not that deep, perhaps three feet long and only five feet wide. It looked as if someone had attempted to dig a trench and given up halfway through. Other than that and some dust, the street and other buildings were intact. We would later find out that only one soul had lost his life and that was because the bloody fool refused to leave his father's body down by the burning ghats. Well, now he had joined his father. The unlucky sod.

We had left the club in a hurry, overturning chairs and knocking over glasses. As hard-bitten and casual as some of us seemed, it was always in the back of our heads that this day might be the day the Japs hit their mark again and again, like the Luftwaffe did in London on a daily basis. This might be the day that the last thing I see is Gable's wide smile and Turner's heaving bosom from underneath the dirty marble stairs at the Metro; Asma whimpering on one side of me, Patience tossing her curls about in that studied Bette Davis way she tried to emulate when she was most afraid, and Radhika silent as usual. Afterwards, each day I lived through an air raid made me more confused as to God's plan for me, and this feeling of urgency crept up, like I was not living the way I should. I kept getting spared. Surely this meant something.

The news from Burma, where the Allies were barely holding the Japs back, was grim. I kept expecting to wake up to a Japanese voice telling us through a megaphone that we were now the subjects of Emperor Hirohito and would have to commit hara kiri if we resisted. Anything was possible.

I hope this is exciting enough for you. If I remember anything more, I will let you know. No one close to me died in the air raids. I do remember, however, the terror, and the feeling that the world was ending and that I had no control over anything, though that had been compounding with increasing frequency since someone under my employ and care, a girl really, the age you are now, had been attacked. Did I ever tell you what happened to Radhika? I cannot recollect.

Your mother,
Yasmine

8

As the months wore on, Radhika became more and more laconic, isolating herself and not taking her meals with the others. She had also stopped dancing. Every morning, Yasmine would ask her if she was ready to perform that evening and every morning the girl would shake her head, pull her dupatta lower to cover her face and skulk away.

'She's costing me money every day,' Yasmine complained to Adil Baboo.

'A little kindness, Yasmine,' he would say. 'She has no mother, be gentle.'

'Well, I'm not anyone's mother, Adil Baboo! I am a businesswoman.'

Yasmine had an image in her head of what Radhika's mother must have been like; a hardworking, lean woman who toiled in the rice paddies next to her husband, uncomplaining and stoic. This was one kind of Indian woman, of a certain class, nothing like the languid, almost laissez faire types Yasmine grew up with, who had honed gossip and 'adda', the distinctly Bengali style of conversation, into an art form, took long naps in the afternoon, and knew how to tell entire stories with their bodies, without uttering a word. Yasmine suspected Radhika's mother was so beaten down by life that she rarely showed her daughter affection. The girl was the youngest performer at the Duck, and Yasmine knew she should try to be more like an elder sister or even a maternal figure to her.

Why the men responded so well to Radhika, though—that was a question that puzzled everyone really. There were certain women that other women found beautiful but men did not. And then there were women, like Radhika, whose appeal was baffling to those of her own gender. Radhika's body was slim and supple, but she lacked radiance. Her dark skin had no lustre. Her eyes were her best feature, as it was with most dancers, and she used them to talk to the audience. And sometimes, when she danced, her braid came undone and rippled in waves underneath the dupatta. But she was not what could be described as beautiful. For instance, Patience, who was half-Irish, half-Indian, was considered a great beauty. Her skin was burnished gold. Her dark hair did not fall limply down her back as Radhika's sometimes did, but was bouncy and cut just above her shoulders with poufy bangs, like Betty Grable's, which was what Patience wanted. Patience sang skilfully and could perform a shimmy that elicited wolf whistles from many of her male fans. She was not a sonorous singer but could carry a tune and bantered easily with the audience and the musicians like any seasoned Broadway star. There was something vaguely American about Patience, and that was what Yasmine knew would make her money. It added just the right flavour to the club. She was a survivor and tender when she needed to be, tough when it called for it. Just like Bette Davis in *Now Voyager*, as Patience never failed to point out.

And yet, it was Radhika who packed them in every night.

What struck Yasmine was that Radhika was born a Dalit and therefore she, out of everyone, knew exactly where she stood in Indian society. She was born in a village near Noakhali, whose inhabitants believed implicitly in the caste system—at least the Brahmins did. The lower castes did not have the wherewithal to disagree. But there was one point with which all the castes were in agreement: nothing was lower than a Muslim, and Radhika had committed an egregious sin. She had shared a meal with a Muslim, a step below an untouchable, and was thus disowned by her family and banished from the village.

As Radhika told it, there was an enormous peepul tree about a kilometre outside the village. It had had time to grow since it was over three hundred years old, and was considered sacred by the villagers. It stood forty feet high and its trunk was nine feet around. For many years a man had lived in the lower branches, until one day he abruptly fell out of it, stone dead. The villagers had fed him, leaving food at the foot of the tree. The meaner children had sometimes mocked and tormented him by belting him with rocks and fruit. Usually he just climbed onto a higher branch, but once in a while he would let loose and urinate on them, hooting the whole time, and the children would run away, screaming.

After she was banished, Radhika decided to hang herself from that peepul tree. She fashioned a noose with her dupatta and wrapped it around her neck and hanged herself. Her bladder emptied and she lost consciousness. When she awoke she was on the ground, a dirty man with gnarled hair and in a white loincloth staring down at her. He squatted next to her with a concerned expression on his face.

When she opened her eyes he said, 'Not yet,' and walked away.

Radhika assumed it was the ghost of the old man who had lived in the tree—or as her Muslim friend, Farida, the one for whom she had been banished, thought, a kindly djinn who lived in the tree and saved many people from suicide attempts and dacoits. When Yasmine heard it, she loved this story. But she told Patience, 'God knows if it is true.'

'Who really cares? It's a delicious Indian tale,' Patience said. 'I always knew that Radhika was interesting. Maybe she's possessed by that djinn.'

Adil Baboo had said as much when he found the girl wandering the streets, dehydrated and in real danger of being abducted by goondas, and brought her in.

'She seems quite haunted,' he said. 'But that doesn't mean she cannot assist me in the kitchen.'

When Adil Baboo brought Radhika in, it seemed apparent that she was not meant to be much more than a maid. No one knew anything about the girl's history, and Radhika did not share any details about her life. Yasmine did not let that deter her. She always prided herself on being above things as petty as caste and race and constantly lamented how mired Indian society was in social strata. It was easy to blame the Brits for it, but they had not invented the caste system, after all.

Yasmine had inspected the girl carefully, noting her teeth (yellow, with two terrible cavities that made her breath stink) and pallor (ashen from lack of food). Her fingernails were bitten down and her toenails were long and dirty. Her heels were cracked, with dirt embedded in the cracks because she had no shoes. There was no indication that she could dance or even wanted to dance.

The first two days, the girl refused to sleep in a bed. It was too soft and gave her a sore back, she said. She rolled her thin cotton quilt out on the hard cement floor and slept on top of it, until Patience and Madhu coaxed her onto a string charpoy that was so sunken in the middle, her bum grazed the floor. All day, Radhika squatted in the kitchen doing whatever was required of her. Adil Baboo's assistant, Naila, protested at first, saying the kitchen was too small for three people to be moving around in it, but soon came around when she realised she could tell the girl what to do. Mostly, Radhika sliced fish and meat the old-fashioned way, on a scimitar-shaped blade that was mounted on a block of wood and set between her legs, and washed dishes in two large metal bins, one for soaking and one for rinsing. She did it uncomplainingly. She never smiled, never asked questions other than, how small do you want these pieces? Or, should I throw out the fish eggs? Adil Baboo, who was still the main cook in the club at the time, before he started assisting in the front and a grumpy Naila took over, figured out that she especially liked hilsa fish eggs. He would fry them in the sac for her with butter, a dash of turmeric and onions. She ate them with rice. She ate very little. She was accustomed to deprivation and expecting little from life.

Yasmine paid Radhika a small salary that she advised her to save, and provided her with room and board. Maintenance of her room and eventually, when she began to perform, costumes came out of her wages. When the girl started to dance, Yasmine paid for any purchases as long as they were meant to enhance Radhika's performance, such as baubles or make up. Radhika's diet was also strictly monitored so she could maintain her lithe dancer's body but still receive the proper nutrition, so Yasmine would share her milk rations with her.

At first, Radhika watched the others rehearse every day. She never spoke. She covered her mouth with her dupatta so no one would see her smile when Patience sang or Madhu danced. The dancing captured her attention the most. One afternoon, Yasmine lay down for a nap. She had just closed her eyes when she heard the distinct sound of rhythmic footfalls on the floor of the stage downstairs.

She opened her door as quietly as she could and peeked through the bannisters at the top of the stairs to see Radhika dancing. There was no music. She skipped around the stage and twirled in place, her arms spread out, like a dervish. Her hair was loose down her back. She imitated some of Madhu's steps perfectly, high kicks and pliés, dancing from memory. She stopped and looked at an imaginary spot in front of her and bent her arms at the elbow, her hands in front of her, knuckles touching, and spun once, quickly, shooting her right arm out as if to punch someone in front of her. She had executed a perfect Kathak turn, and did it over and over again without getting dizzy. In fact, Yasmine became dizzy watching her. She was gripping the bannister with both hands and smiling from ear to ear because she had witnessed something so pure and joyful. It filled her heart with inexplicable hope.

Radhika became breathless from spinning and fell in a heap on the ground, giggling. Yasmine cleared her throat loudly, and Radhika jumped up in alarm and stared up at where Yasmine stood at the top of the stairs. She twisted her dupatta and stammered, 'S-sorry, di.'

That was unexpected. Yasmine did not understand why she was apologising and carrying on as if she had done something wrong. In fact, Yasmine felt she was the one who should have been embarrassed because she was suddenly so emotional. She cleared her throat again, pretending she had a cough, and marched down the stairs.

'Please don't be cross, didi,' the girl said.

'I'm not,' Yasmine said. 'Why should I be?'

The girl nodded and gave her a half smile and darted into the kitchen. Yasmine sighed. The girl was so odd. She followed her and asked her point blank if she had any desire to dance professionally. Radhika did not understand the question at once.

'What do you mean?'

'Would you like to dance here?'

'Oh! I don't know,' she said. She looked confused, and then suddenly her face broke into a smile.

'Do you mean like Madhu di?'

'Well, yes, what else would I mean?'

'I want to dance Kathak only,' she said.

The bloody cheek! Here Yasmine was offering a chance to change her life, and she was laying down conditions. She was both taken aback and impressed.

'You will do as you're told,' Yasmine said sternly.

'Yes, didi,' she said, suddenly all meek. 'Will this mean a raise?'

Within three weeks, she was dancing only Kathak, after many attempts to coax a high kick out of her. She was a child, but she knew what her strengths were, and the customers were clear on what their preferences were.

Asma, out of everyone, took the news of Radhika's new role very badly. She entreated Yasmine to reconsider.

'On what grounds?' Yasmine asked.

'On the grounds that she is bad luck,' Asma said, pounding her fist on the bar for emphasis. 'She cavorts with djinns.'

'Nonsense,' Yasmine said. 'You don't even know what that means. Cavorts with djinns. Bollocks!'

'Why are you threatened?' Madhu asked Asma. 'She dances, you sing. 'Tis not your territory.'

It was Asma who first complained that, after the attack, Radhika was not doing much.

'We are all pulling our weight here! And she is allowed to just sit around,' she said.

'Yes, you are definitely pulling more weight than others,' Patience said. She grinned at Asma and looked pointedly at her rotund behind.

'Yes! I agree!' Asma began until she realised Patience was making fun of her.

Madhu lit a cigarette and glared at Asma.

'Why are you cross at me?' Asma said, stung by her expression. Madhu had always been in her corner when

Patience goaded her. Lately, though, she had noticed that Madhu defended Radhika more and her less.

'Radhika is just a girl, nah?' Madhu said. 'And she has had her insides torn out and everything stolen from her. You should be kinder and not whinge so much. Focus on singing.'

Madhu stalked outside, leaving Asma confused. After a moment, she started to follow Madhu, but Yasmine stopped her.

'Leave her be. When she gets like this she wants to be left alone,' Yasmine said. 'You know this better than anyone. Madhu is right. Focus on your work.'

Asma was the club's resident crooner. Customers called her The Nightingale, but when she got plump, Patience started calling her The Hen behind her back.

Asma came from an educated Parsi family that she had left somewhere in Sindh. Her father was dead from a heart attack, and her mother had sunk into a depression that rendered her incapable of taking care of her three girls. Asma was pale with a cherubic face and prone to melancholy. Yasmine had found her babysitting a pair of English brats as blond as they were demonic—the progeny of an English fabric exporter who overcharged his customers and underfed his servants.

When Yasmine met Asma, she was twenty pounds lighter with dark circles under her eyes. Yasmine was walking down a muddy, unpaved alley, and heard a woman singing. Every so often a child's whine drowned out the angelic voice that sang of lost love and longing. It was an old song, one that, Yasmine thought, her mother sang to her when she was a little girl, so naturally, she followed the voice to a bungalow with bright red bougainvillea snaking along its arabesque eaves. She looked through the wrought-iron gates and watched and listened as Asma gently lifted a wailing little boy who had fallen and cradled him in her arms and sang to him. His older sister sat nearby, building a mound of pebbles. From a distance, Asma could have been their mother—or older sister. Indeed, if it weren't for the faded yellow salwar she was wearing, one could not tell she was Indian.

The little boy allowed himself to be held for a moment, lulled by the sound of his nanny's lovely voice, and then yanked her hair. Yasmine watched as the children spat at Asma, taunted her, and generally refused to listen to anything she requested of them.

'Claire, please don't dirty your dress,' she said in perfect English. 'Your mother will be cross.'

Claire responded by picking up a handful of dust and rubbing it into her frock. Almost on cue, their mother, a slim, blonde woman dressed in a pink satin dressing gown, emerged from the house. There was a tumbler in her hand, filled with ice and what appeared to be water, but Yasmine knew better based on the way the woman was listing as she stood at the top of the stairs.

'Asma! Really! How many times have I told you not to let Claire do that? I can't have this sort of thing. Really, I am very cross!' With that she went back into the house, but came back out to say, 'And stop that racket. You know I can't stand your singing! God, I hate this blighted country!'

When Asma tried to shake the dust off the little girl's dress, she protested, slapped Asma across the face, and ran into the house. Yasmine cleared her throat to get Asma's attention. Asma walked up to the gate and watched as Yasmine extracted a slip of paper from her purse and wrote something on it.

'Can you read?' she asked, holding out the paper through the gate. Asma gave her a haughty glare and didn't answer. Her small blond charge trailed behind her. He clutched the edge of Asma's frayed kurta and sucked on the grimy fingers of his free hand. Yasmine scowled at him in disgust. Really, children were just so grotesque at times, she thought.

Asma took the proffered note, squinting as she read it. Months of malnutrition and reading by the light of an oil lamp had permanently damaged her eyesight. Yasmine saw that her eyes were green and that she was clearly near-sighted. She mentally calculated how much eyeglasses would cost her. She decided that she would not take them out of her wages.

'What is this?' Asma asked.

'It's my nightclub,' Yasmine said. 'We need a singer.'

'I am not a singer. And I do not frequent such places,' Asma said, holding the note out.

Yasmine lit a cigarette and smiled at Asma's indignation. When Yasmine didn't take the note back, Asma crumpled it up and tossed it into the gutter. She coughed delicately as Yasmine blew smoke through the gate. She pushed the small boy behind her protectively, but he had other ideas and slapped Asma's hand away. He peered up at Yasmine slack-jawed. She stuck her tongue out at him, and he retreated behind Asma again.

'I know what you mean by "singer",' Asma said, trying to sound gruff but only managing to sound curious.

'Really?' Yasmine said, amused. 'What do I mean, then?'

Asma batted away an imaginary mosquito to buy time and finally replied, 'I won't answer that.'

'I'm going to tell mummy on you,' a thin voice announced from behind Asma. He began to tug at Asma, dragging her back to the house.

Yasmine called after her, 'I can tell you come from a good family, however.'

'I do!' Asma said, surprised. 'Papa was a scholar.'

'Then why would you want to be someone's servant?' Yasmine yelled out, in English, in hopes that the mistress of the house would hear. It was something she could not have done before, but things were different now, since Gandhi-ji and Neta-ji had started agitating and demanding the British leave India. It gave her courage. Asma was on the steps now. The small boy's five-year-old instincts told him that it was necessary to get Asma away from the lady at the gate as soon as possible. He looked up at Asma, whom he probably actually loved more than anything, and saw that she had already left him.

Yasmine's loud voice had drawn the mother out again.

'What's all this?' the mother demanded. She saw Yasmine standing at the gate.

'What does she want?' she asked Asma. Before Asma could answer, the wan Englishwoman had walked unsteadily down the steps of the house. 'We don't need anything. No bangles, mangoes, papayas, nothing! Shoo!' she said to Yasmine, who raised her eyebrows at her. The Englishwoman took small steps in her high heels and made small sweeping motions with her hands like she was trying to herd chickens. Her robe fell open to reveal a flat chest. 'We don't want to buy anything.'

Yasmine threw down her cigarette. 'I'm not selling you anything,' she said.

This startled the woman. 'Oh,' she said. 'Then what—'

'I've come for Asma,' Yasmine replied smoothly. 'I'm her cousin, Tamina, from ... I'm Parsi too. Tamina Javan is my name. She has to come with me. Her mother is gravely ill.'

Yasmine almost smiled at the panicked look on Asma's face. But, as if in a trance, when she held out her hand to her, Asma walked up to her, took it and allowed Yasmine to lead her through the gate, while her dumbfounded English mistress stood there, opening and closing her mouth like a fish. Her little charge, the boy, started wailing almost immediately, and Asma hesitated, staring at Yasmine.

'Don't look back,' Yasmine whispered and squeezed her hand. Asma began to walk, but she stopped when the little boy called out her name.

'I'm all he's got,' she said.

'He has a mother,' Yasmine replied, tugging at her hand.

'You call that a mother?' she said, her eyes filling with tears.

'This is not your war,' Yasmine said.

'Maybe he's all I've got,' she said. She seemed to even startle herself with that admission.

Yasmine dropped her hand.

'Do what you will then,' she said. For Yasmine, the thought of returning the girl with the angelic voice to that dusty courtyard, with grimy white children and chicken droppings, was insupportable.

Asma backed away from Yasmine. The tears poured down her face.

'I'm sorry,' she said. 'He's sickly, you know?'

Yasmine peered behind her at the boy, who was clinging to the wrought iron gate, watching them through the bars. His chubby face was pink from crying.

'He looks the picture of health to me, but what do I know?' Yasmine said. She looked up at the sky. It threatened rain so she opened her umbrella.

'That's bad luck you know,' Asma said.

'Are you afraid?' Yasmine said.

Asma stopped, a confused look on her face. 'Of what?'

'Of being alone?'

Asma wiped her face with the back of her hand. Her wrists were so thin, one unkind yank and they could be snapped in half.

Yasmine sighed. They would starve her to death, slowly. Though her mistress was not exactly plump either. Perhaps it was just misery that made them both thin, Yasmine thought.

'I don't know,' Asma answered honestly.

'Well, you would not be alone. There are two other girls, Patience and Madhu. You would have three meals a day, clean sheets, new clothes, eyeglasses—'

'Eyeglasses?' She took two steps towards Yasmine.

'Yes, you seem to need them. Since you like to read so much—'

'How did you know I like to read?' she said.

''Sma!' a small voice called out insistently behind her, but she ignored it.

'Well, you are from a scholarly family,' Yasmine said.

'I read the classics, you know?' Asma stated, her haughtiness creeping back. 'Like Austen and the Brontës.'

'Emily or Charlotte?' Yasmine said, unable to help herself. 'I believe there was also a brother, but I always pictured him as somewhat of a eunuch.'

Asma looked scandalised and then irritated that Yasmine knew who the Brontës were.

'Asma, I really must insist you come back here at once, or, or I shall have to sack you,' the mistress of the house said. Though she did not sound at all certain.

Asma continued to look at Yasmine.

'There was a third sister as well, you know?' she said, sniffing.

'Yes. Anne,' Yasmine said. 'Do you fancy yourself Jane Eyre then?' she asked quickly before Asma could retort. 'Suffering behind the iron gates for some noble purpose. I doubt there is a Rochester behind those gates, to carry you away from all this. I am afraid I am the closest thing to Rochester you are going to get.'

'I don't understand,' Asma said. She was genuinely baffled. 'You have read the Brontës, seem educated but you are unmarried and run a nightclub. How is this possible?'

'I think if Austen taught you anything, it should have been that educated women of little means must make their own way in the world,' Yasmine said.

'Yes, I suppose that is true,' Asma conceded. Yasmine could tell this appealed to her immensely. 'What if you kick me out?' she said. 'What then? I cannot come back here.'

'I will try not to,' Yasmine replied.

'That doesn't instil confidence in me, let me tell you,' she said.

'Well, look at it this way,' Yasmine said. 'I wouldn't kick you out until I train you or at least until the end of the week, and by then you will have enough money to buy a rail ticket to wherever your family is. In other words, I will give you the money to clear out if it comes to that.'

'You promise?' she said.

'Yes, I do. This is not the most auspicious way to start a relationship, however,' Yasmine said. 'Already talking about what to do if it ends badly.'

'I have to think about what comes next,' Asma said. 'Because I have no one really to vouch for me.'

The truth of that stung Yasmine. A person needed that, someone to speak up and say, Look! I know her, she is real. She exists. This is her name, she prefers her tea with milk but no sugar. The scar above her left brow is from when she fell off the bed at the age of three. It helps a person to know that someone else knows these details and can attest to them. Not having someone to bear witness to one's life rendered one invisible in a way. India was teeming with invisible people.

'I should say goodbye to him,' Asma said, referring to her small charge.

'Do what you want, but my advice is to walk away and not look back,' Yasmine said. 'It will be more painful for both of you if you linger or let him even touch you.'

He called out again in his reedy little voice, and Asma's eyes once again filled with tears.

'He will survive,' Yasmine said. 'He is white and English. And at least he has a mother.'

~

As fastidious and exacting as Asma was, she did not haggle about wages—it was better than what she was being paid by her former employers, and she was grateful for the three meals a day and lodging. It was her puritanical, Victorian sense of propriety that made her difficult to live with at times. It became increasingly apparent that she, in fact, did fancy herself one of the Brontë sisters and actually relished the notion of whiling her life away as an austere, consumptive spinster who wore eyeglasses and deflected the opposite sex with grim admonitions and severe glares. When she sang, however, she transformed into someone altogether different, which disconcerted Asma. Her full hips swayed seductively to the song, whatever it was, a ghazal or *Night and Day*, and she became generous, opening her arms and heart to whoever was listening to her. It frightened Asma so much that she insisted on wearing her eyeglasses when she faced the crowd at the Duck.

'When I feel it on the bridge of my nose or pinching my head, I remember who I am—'

'That is precisely what I don't want you to do,' Yasmine said. 'When you forget that you are a nice Parsi girl from a nice Parsi family whose papa was a teacher—'

'Scholar.'

'Whatever. Then you become who you really are. A goddess like Parvati,' Yasmine suggested, knowing the effect it would have on Asma. Madhu and Patience burst out laughing at the look of horror on Asma's round face. 'Or Lana Turner,' she added to further agitate the young woman.

'There are worse things, darling,' Madhu said when Asma stood up to leave. It was only Madhu who could talk Asma down from a ledge. She was a woman, but with a man's sensibilities. She was feminine and rough and tumble as well. Madhu disliked men, almost as much as she disliked the English. She preferred the company of her female friends.

Madhu was not 'found', so to speak, as the others had been, or brought to the Duck by someone else. Madhu came to Bombay Duck of her own accord and enquired about work. She had heard there was a new spot in town and that it was run by a woman, which set tongues wagging and seemed to upset enough people so as to intrigue Madhu. She was reserved and private. Not secretive exactly, but not prone to gossip and small talk like Patience and Asma. Yasmine was not even sure she was literate. She had never seen her read anything or sign her name. Somehow, her mannishness did not bother the men who came to the Duck. But she never warmed to any particular customer or had favourites. Even Asma had a devoted admirer in the form of a shy, socially inept American sergeant named Andrew Sasoon, who sat right in the front whenever Asma was on stage and regaled her with stories about Bensonhurst, New York, where he was from. He was also very preoccupied with his rabbi's daughter, Rachel, who he said looked like Asma. He showed her a picture. Asma stared down at the grainy photo of a plump, dark-haired girl, holding a roast chicken in a pan, and was appalled that Sergeant Sasoon thought she bore a resemblance to her.

'Why do I remain fat when the rest of the world is starving,' she said one day. 'I really thought the rationing would cut my weight in half.'

'You hold on to everything,' Patience said. 'That's why. You don't like to share, so you hoard.'

'That makes no sense,' Asma cried. 'I will gladly share this roll around my middle with you! Here! It's yours!'

'It makes sense,' Patience said. 'You are afraid of losing anything. Including that arse of yours,' she giggled.

'I hardly think you are in a spot to say anything,' Asma said, eyeing Patience over her glasses and moving her gaze down to her belly. Patience looked down at her stomach and put a hand over it, almost protectively. This was not lost on Yasmine.

'If you've got something to say, spit it out, you big girl's blouse,' Patience snapped.

'Well, you're not so skinny anymore yourself,' Asma said. 'I've noticed a bit of a bump around your middle!'

Before anyone could stop her, Patience was out of her chair and grasping a handful of Asma's hair, giving it a tight yank. Yasmine nodded to Adil Baboo, who sighed and pulled Patience off Asma. Asma was on the floor by then. Yasmine helped her up and wiped Asma's tear-stained glasses on her sari.

'Why do you provoke Patience so?' she asked. 'You won't win, not in a game of fisticuffs or wit.'

'Was she always so monstrous?' Asma sniffed.

Yasmine smiled as she watched Adil Baboo admonish Patience.

'Well, yes, she was,' Yasmine said. 'Since we were girls.'

Yasmine watched Patience light another cigarette. Her eyes slid down to Patience's belly. When she looked up again, it was to Patience gazing steadily back at her. Patience threw her unfinished cigarette to the floor and stubbed it out. That was against the rules and she knew it.

'Is there something you want to tell me, Patience?' Yasmine asked.

Patience shrugged. 'Nothing comes to mind,' she said.

9

While the Burmese jungle—the Big Green, the Yanks called it—seethed, Calcutta continued to grit her teeth and cover her ears. She was stoic and resolute, even as the bombings increased. The viceroy made a grandiose speech after the bombings started, to boost morale. 'We are all prepared to face our fate with calm courage and robust optimism.' That was how Yasmine wanted to fashion herself. With calm courage and robust optimism. That was more easily said than done.

The fact was that the war had taken people away, scarred the face of the city, forced rations upon everyone, and spurred great, and ultimately unnecessary, deprivation. Eventually, it would bring a famine to Bengal, the likes of which would not be seen again in Yasmine's lifetime. The Bengal Famine started in 1943. It lasted three years. It killed millions.

The war was, at that moment, a livelihood for Yasmine and she felt that she too was a soldier, in a way. What she provided at the Duck was invaluable to the morale of the men sent to fight. The Duck was almost a holy place to some people, a sanctuary. People came there to pretend that everything was all right with the world and they were safe. And indeed, when one stepped through its doors, it was as if the war did not exist. She and the girls worked hard to create that environment for the men and women who paid to frequent it.

She had not seen Edward in many months. Many of his friends still frequented the club, but he was never seen. She thought about him only fleetingly. At the Duck, she kept herself aloof and continued to have what she would describe as peripheral contact with various people she encountered as hostess and proprietor. She was still congenial to her customers and never outwardly showed any curiosity about them. The war had brought together an odd assortment of characters and some of them ended up at the Duck. Like Adil Baboo. When she opened the club, she had not heeded advice about getting a male front man to make the club more 'respectable', largely because she had not found anyone she could trust would not steal from her. One day, Adil Baboo had appeared on her doorstep.

'Are you Shirin Khan's daughter?' he asked Yasmine politely in Bengali. His eyes searched her face. 'I think you were very small when we first met. Perhaps five or six. I was a young man myself. About twenty.'

Yasmine nodded, surprised. But then again, it was from her mother that she had inherited this ability to collect people. Growing up, the haveli had been a hodgepodge, as Patience described it, of these collected types, usually the ones most people would ignore or feared in some way, because they always stayed on the edges of things. He must have been one of those strays that her mother had taken in.

'Shirin-ji was very kind to me. She paid me a fair wage and never asked questions. A great lady.'

Yasmine smiled at Adil Baboo's shrewd way of laying out his terms. It was disconcerting, yet she liked him for it.

Yasmine surmised that her mother must have sent this peculiar man. She showed him around. He was silent as he inspected the small, poorly ventilated kitchen, but his eyes lit up at the sight of his sleeping quarters, which were also small but clean and private.

'So? Does it meet with your approval?' Yasmine asked.

'Yes, of course,' Adil Baboo replied. 'It would be an honour to work for Shirin-ji's daughter. I owe her a great deal. You come from a good family,' he added.

Yasmine was taken aback, and Patience snorted. No one had ever described her family as 'good'.

'Can you cook Chinese food?' she asked Adil Baboo.

'No, but I can learn,' Adil Baboo replied. 'I can cook anything with very little in front of me.'

'We are competing with Cathay,' Yasmine explained. Cathay was the most popular Chinese restaurant in town and was frequented by American troops.

'I think we will win this battle,' Adil Baboo said. His voice was soft and confident, and Yasmine felt a weight lifted off her, like she was not going to bear all the burdens alone.

Still, she said, 'I think we'll try you out, see how you manage.' It was the sensible thing to do, she felt; good business sense, and also to show she was not a soft touch.

Adil Baboo nodded, walked into the kitchen, tied an apron around his waist and became a fixture at the Duck until the day Yasmine closed its doors.

Yasmine was seeing brisk business. By 1942, more and more Americans were being deployed to Burma to build the road to China. Many of them spent the last few months in Calcutta, preparing for their arduous journey into the jungle. The girls at the Duck had gotten to know a few of them well. They were almost all fresh-faced farm boys from places with unlikely sounding names like Nowhere, and Sheboygan. There was also the odd boy from Hell's Kitchen—an obviously decrepit area of New York City, Yasmine explained to the girls, just by the name. This was the farthest some of them had ever travelled from their farmhouses and tenements. They often carried pictures of their sweethearts or mothers with them and showed them proudly to the girls. One boy showed Asma a picture of his dog, which he shed many a tear over. Some men, they had it on good authority, had been disciplinary headaches for their previous commanding officers. They had been asked to volunteer for a dangerous mission and displayed tremendous bravado when told about the harrowing conditions of a tropical jungle.

What's a little rain? Shoot, I lived through three tornadoes!

We got 'skeeters in Minnesota, some the size of a Buick. I can handle some Chinese bugs!

Most had never even heard of Burma.

It was December, nine months after Radhika's attack, and she was still not on stage. All the girls had taken turns looking after her, nursing, feeding, bathing her and even, on occasion, cleaning out her bed pan when she was too weak to walk to the water closet. But now she seemed fully healed, at least physically. Yasmine had no way of knowing what was going on in the girl's mind. After being silent for months, Asma tried once again to convince Yasmine to let Radhika go because her sullen presence was starting to grate on everyone and was bad for business. Patience challenged Asma, saying that the young dancer's appeal was undeniable.

'She used to rake it in for us,' Patience said. 'We have to be patient. Once she gets going, we can even take turns, right Yassu? We can be on a rotation and have nights off, like normal working stiffs.'

'Nights off?' Madhu said. 'Oh, how lovely!'

'Yes! The nights Radhika used to dance, she made as much on her own as we do combined!' Patience said, excitedly.

'That's not entirely true,' Yasmine said.

'Well, she makes enough for at least two of us, which means one of us can have a night off and then perform the following night,' Patience said. 'We just have to get her back on stage. Once she's back, she will be right as rain.'

'Why are you insisting on this?' Yasmine asked.

'Yes!' Asma chimed in. 'Why are you insisting?'

Patience sighed and seemed to deflate a little. 'It was just an idea,' she muttered. 'Good business sense.'

Asma's assertion that the girl was bad luck and that she had somehow brought that bad luck into the Duck irritated Yasmine. Asma described the girl as 'suspicious'. It was all superstitious nonsense to Yasmine.

'Suspicious how?' Yasmine asked. 'She is manipulative, yes, but she is a child. Most of it comes from being a baby and not knowing the world.'

'She is no baby!' Asma gasped. 'I see the way she looks at the Ingrezi officers,' she said. 'They order so much liquor and say those nasty things. Radhika looks at them as if, as if…'

'As if what?' Yasmine wanted to know.

'As if she is inviting them to her bed!'

'That means she is doing her job,' Yasmine said.

Asma groaned. 'You would think that after what happened to her, she would be more cautious, but if anything she is more brazen. I simply cannot be associated with something like this.'

Yasmine held her tongue and let Asma speak. She could have easily pointed out that, in fact, Asma had no other associations but the one she was currently in. Her mother had long since become utterly incapable of caring for anyone, and her sisters had married and actually seemed to stay away from Asma. They dropped by once, during Nowruz, and looked the place up and down. Her eldest sister, a reed thin, pale thing, delicately held a handkerchief to her nose the entire visit, except when she was offered a chair by Rahul and dusted the seat with it.

'Does she think we are contagious?' Yasmine whispered.

'Yes,' Patience had said. 'She might catch some personality.'

They were offered sweetmeats—which they refused—and something to drink, at which they looked shocked. Even though it was only orange squash. They peered over at the bar, where the few meagre bottles of gin, whiskey and scotch were displayed. It was painful for Yasmine to watch Asma trying to please her sisters and reassure them that she was not a fallen woman. She showed them the stage and gamely attempted to sing a song or two from her act. They were not impressed.

Asma loved children, but was not allowed to see her nephew and nieces. Therefore, it was too late, Yasmine wanted to point out, to save her reputation. It was already ruined in the quarters she fancied herself from, so she should stop complaining and make the best of it. But alas, this was futile and would only serve to upset Asma, and so Yasmine remained silent while Asma went down the laundry list of grievances about Radhika, ending with:

'Radhika doesn't like to eat with us,' Asma said. 'She's always been like that. I find it suspicious. It's not as if she is a Brahmin,' she added meanly.

'You're just annoyed because she eats more than you and never gains a kilo,' Patience said.

'I was skinny like that at seventeen too,' Asma huffed.

'We all were,' Patience said, patting her stomach. She did it without thinking and looked away when Yasmine frowned at her, puzzled.

'Uff! Forget about Patience's belly! I have to tell you something, Yassu!'

'Go on, what is it?' Yasmine said wearily.

'She sneaks out at night,' Asma said. 'Where does she go? I want to know.'

This was news to Yasmine, but she pretended she knew about it as it would not do for anyone to think that she was not aware of what was happening under her own roof. It was most assuredly worrisome.

'She attends school,' Yasmine said, realising too late that now Radhika would have to provide evidence of literacy.

'What kind of school?' Asma asked.

'Seductress school,' Madhu said, winking at Asma.

'This is not a whorehouse, no matter what people think,' Yasmine said, pointedly looking at Madhu and trying to change the subject. 'But this is also not a house where we merely sip tea and serve laddoos on silver platters and talk about the state of the roads. We are not a Jane Austen novel, we are a business, and Radhika seems to understand that. I never lied to you, memsahib,' she said to Asma. 'But I have never put pressure on you to sleep with any of the patrons, male or female—'

'Female!' Asma said, aghast.

'Haven't you read the *Kama Sutra*?' Madhu asked innocently.

'Absolutely not!' Asma replied. Everyone looked at her and laughed. Asma got up and marched out.

'I'll go and calm her down,' Madhu said, rubbing her hands together. 'What she needs is a good rub down.'

'Behave yourself!' Yasmine warned.

Madhu threw up her hands. 'Don't I always?'

Patience and Yasmine smiled at one another. They both enjoyed teasing Asma. They fell silent for a time, each lost in their own thoughts. Patience was always chatty but had learned from a young age that Yasmine rarely made small talk, so she was surprised when her friend said:

'Did you have one of your visions recently?'

Patience was known for her sudden premonitions. But they were not consistent. She was not what Yasmine would call a psychic. She had dreams and strong urges to share information at odd moments. It was not unusual for her to come down in the morning and say to someone, 'Look, I think you should stay in today, as I am pretty sure you will get hit by the Park Circus tram. You won't die, but it will be a nuisance.'

The occupants of the Duck had all learned the hard way to listen when she shared these premonitions. Once, Madhu had ignored Patience's warning to stay away from small children playing ball in the street for at least a week. She was walking back to the club after shopping in New Market, encountered some neighbourhood boys playing shaath chara—a game with stones and a ball—and decided to join in for a quick round, God knows why, probably to prove Patience wrong, and severely bruised the second toe on her left foot.

'No visions,' Patience said to Yasmine. 'Just dreams. About you.'

Yasmine chuckled.

'Really,' Patience said, and became silent.

'Well?' Yasmine said after a moment.

'It's all very unlikely.'

'So you dreamt that the Duck will someday turn a profit?' Yasmine said.

Patience looked at her.

'I don't know what it is,' she said. 'I mean I don't remember everything, but I think you were wearing a black sari with a silver border.'

Yasmine looked up.

'And standing on the steps, waiting for ... someone.'

'Oooh, does he look like Ashok Kumar?' Yasmine grinned, still not taking her seriously.

'No,' she shook her head. 'But he is very handsome.'

'Then why do you look so sad?' Yasmine asked.

'I don't know. I got a sad feeling suddenly.'

This often happened to Patience. She would be laughing and merry, then suddenly she would sit in a corner and become sombre or go into a trance. Yasmine's mother said that Patience was experiencing a collective sadness then, and there was an abundance of melancholy around them. These episodes were always short-lived, as Patience was far too happy a person to be down for long.

Yasmine took a drag of her cigarette. 'Men are a bother,' she said. 'The only things we can count on men for pregnancy and war. Right? And all the men are off fighting, and I am not pregnant, never have been. Thank goodness.'

Patience nodded.

'In fact, we are both so lucky we lasted this long without the bother, theek nah?' Yasmine added in Bangla. She appraised Patience as her friend reached out, indicating she wanted a drag of her cigarette. Yasmine handed it to her. 'Keep it,' she said when Patience started to hand it back.

'Yasmine, you would always tell me, nah? If you ever fell in love?'

'Well, yes,' she replied. 'Though that will never happen.'

'How do you know?'

Yasmine swept her arm around. 'Because of this. What man will be able to love a tavern owner?'

'Not an Indian man or even an European,' Patience said. 'But maybe an American? Don't you ever dream of love, Yassu? And a family?'

'No, never. That's not my lot in life. What happened to Hollywood?' she asked.

Patience shrugged. 'Yes, yes, that's still there,' she said.

Patience was beautiful enough to be a movie star, Yasmine believed. She was also talented and possessed that quality that drew people—namely men—to her easily. She was never contentious with them. Men loved that, Yasmine noted, especially English men. In the Hollywood movies, it seemed American men—chiefly Gable or Spencer Tracy—enjoyed banter and a challenge. All the leading ladies were brassy and bold. Katharine Hepburn, with her razor-sharp cheekbones, was frankly scary. She was Madhu's hero. There was nothing soft about Ms Hepburn, Patience would say; only a burly Irishman, such as Spencer Tracy, could handle her.

But Yasmine knew that as lovely as her girlhood friend was, Patience lacked the drive and passion needed to be in the pictures. She secretly felt that had she been as beautiful or talented—or pale—she would have been grasping the deed to a Mission-style mansion with a terra cotta tile roof in Beverly Hills by now. She had seen pictures of Joan Crawford posing in front of a house like that in *Life* magazine and thought, now this is what I need.

'You would tell me as well?' Yasmine said. 'If you fell in love ... or the family way?'

Patience closed her eyes and sighed as Yasmine's stomach lurched.

Yasmine watched as Patience sat on the club stage rocking back and forth, looking at her feet.

'How far along are you?' she asked her friend.

'Not too far.'

'But it will be too far soon, nah?'

Patience nodded.

'What will you do?' she asked Yasmine. 'Turn me out?'

'I can't think now. You want it, don't you?'

'Is there any way I can keep it and still work—?'

'No,' Yasmine said. 'How?'

'Our mothers did it, their mothers...'

'No,' Yasmine said. 'They had patrons, we have only ourselves, and you make the most money here. If you don't bring it in, we won't have enough for—it anyway.'

'If you give Radhika more shows?'

'So that's why you were insisting about Radhika? She's refusing to dance.'

Patience shrugged, and then, to Yasmine's alarm, began to cry.

She walked to her friend and patted her awkwardly on the head.

'I'm not a bloody Pekinese, Yassu!' Patience said. She wiped her nose with the back of her hand. Yasmine handed her a handkerchief she always had tucked in her sari bodice.

'You're always prepared, Yassu. But sometimes it's for the wrong things.' She blew her nose.

'You can't keep it, Patience,' Yasmine said.

'Here then,' Patience said, handing her back the handkerchief.

'I meant the baby.'

'I know what you meant.'

Yasmine hesitated. 'But let me think.'

Patience's face lit up. 'Yeah?'

Yasmine shook her head. 'It doesn't mean anything.'

Patience grabbed Yasmine's hands. 'Think all you want as long as you let me keep it and still work here.'

'Oh, why do you need a baby?' Yasmine cried, baffled. 'You have your whole life to have babies.'

Patience dropped Yasmine's hands. 'I don't want to be alone,' she said softly. 'There won't be a husband. So, I want someone of my own.'

'You might marry,' Yasmine said, though she did not believe it.

'Not here,' Patience said.

Yasmine sighed. This was true. 'This is a business, Patience, not a haveli. It's not like when our mothers had us. You know this. I cannot afford it. And if I let you, what will happen with the others? Asma adores babies. I can see her bringing home an urchin.'

'Just please ask your mother what she thinks,' Patience said.

Yasmine nodded. She had forgotten about her mother. Her greatest advisor.

Every other Saturday, Yasmine went to see her mother at her home in Burdwan, about half a day's journey by horse-drawn gharry, though as the club started turning a slight profit, Yasmine sometimes hired a car. Patience knew Yasmine's mother very well. What she did not know was that she lived with her lover there and had been for over a decade. This was information that her mother did not want getting into the hands of Daisy, Patience's malignant mother.

'She has a way of poisoning everything,' Yasmine's mother said. 'Her jealousy could seep into my peace of mind. Once I considered her a friend and even allowed her to read my fortune. Can you imagine?' she shuddered. 'This is like kissing a leper full on the mouth. I was a fool.'

Yasmine's mother believed in the concept of nazar, and Daisy had a darkness to her that was hard to combat at times. She was bitter and mired in schadenfreude and would have been beside herself if she knew that her old friend and imagined rival had found love at this late stage in life, though Shirin was hardly aged. At forty-two, she looked like Yasmine's sister.

In Shirin's opinion, people like Daisy brought misfortune with them, and their jealousy caused the evil eye to turn its gaze on a victim. This was what the family Sufi pir, back in Chittagong, had told Shirin, and advised her to stay away from Daisy. He gave her a tabiz locket with verses from the Koran inside, written out on tiny slips of paper, as protection.

Sometimes, Yasmine wondered if Radhika possessed the same sort of darkness or was victim to it.

Her mother's home was a respite for Yasmine: she was pampered (in between lectures on good business sense and admonitions against attachment) and fussed over. She ate to her heart's content. Her mother had cultivated a garden that was brimming with tomato and every kind of squash. She also had a cutting garden with a small fountain in the centre, where Yasmine would sit and watch the sunset or listen to her mother sing. Faruq mama, her mother's lover and the only father Yasmine had ever really known, doted on her as well. He had an entire family somewhere, complete with cherubic grandchildren, and a dog, but they never spoke of it. When Yasmine was there, she was his daughter. He was absentminded and jolly, always full of stories and gossip, and enjoyed their company thoroughly. He was nothing like her mother. She was slim, tall and elegant. He was short, rotund, balding and not even that cash rich. He had been wealthy at one point, Yasmine remembered, as there were always gifts and bills paid and extra cash slipped into her hands on Eid. Perhaps taking care of her mother, as well as his other family, had taken its toll on his personal coffers. But he never begrudged Yasmine or her mother anything. Now, Yasmine believed her mother was actually his patron and not the other way around. She felt that they looked out at the world with the same pair of eyes. She sometimes longed for that kind of contentment.

She told her mother as much one Saturday afternoon. She was sitting between her mother's knees on the grass, like she had when she was a small girl, while her mother oiled and braided her hair.

'Oh, that's simple,' she said to Yasmine. 'Don't fall in love.'

Yasmine shook her head.

'What?'

'You love Faruq mama!'

Her mother chuckled and yanked her hair back as she braided. 'Yes, but I am not attached to him. He is free to leave me, and I him, at any time. I have told him this almost every day … for ten years.'

'I don't believe that. If Faruq mama stopped coming to you one day, you would be very sad.'

'Yes, but not forever. We understand one another and that understanding is that he is mine at only certain times. He belongs to his wife and children at others.'

'How can you share him?'

'No one really belongs to anyone, Yasmine. Everything, and everyone, is here on short-term lease.'

Shirin raised an eyebrow when Yasmine's shoulders stiffened. She leaned down and looked her daughter in the eye. 'I hope you are not growing attached to anyone, dear,' she said thoughtfully.

The moment Shirin had uttered the words, the image of the American Edward inexplicably popped into Yasmine's head. She had not thought about him for weeks. The last time she had seen him was months earlier, during the Fourth of July celebration she had organised at Bombay Duck, wilfully ignoring the irony of celebrating America's independence from Great Britain. British officers looked on balefully as Patience sang *Yankee Doodle Dandee*, but business had been good that night.

Edward had briefly enquired after her health and made no attempt to strike up more conversation. He stammered something incomprehensible about Dante Alighieri—she was reading him at the time and the book was open on the podium in front of her at the entrance to the club—and left without saying goodbye.

'There *is* someone,' her mother said. 'The look on your face says it all.'

'There is no one.'

'I did not raise a romantic. I had one child. If I were a romantic I would have a passel of brats by now. I was relieved when your natural disposition was not to indulge in that stuff. But what has happened? You are now twenty-six and suddenly a romantic fool.'

She spoke with such emotion that Yasmine stayed her hand and looked back at her.

'Amma, there is no one.'

'Take a lover, but make sure you give less than he gives you,' her mother said finally, her beautiful face hard.

Faruq mama wandered into the garden, smiling at nothing in particular as was his way. Before he could say a word, Yasmine's mother snapped at him.

'Uff! Go now! Did I say you could interrupt us?'

'My darling, I merely wanted to know if you and Yassu moni were thirsty. I could make you nimbu pani. I came to pick some limes,' Faruq said calmly. He was used to Shirin's tempestuous moods.

As she often had been when she was a girl and her mother quarrelled with a lover, Yasmine was embarrassed. She felt her mother was a bit abusive, yet, year after year, Faruq mama held steadfast. Despite what it cost him, he would not give her mother up. Perhaps Patience was right. 'Be mean, keep them keen,' she often said. To Yasmine, this made no sense. If you loved someone, why would you emotionally abuse them? 'Men of a certain type want to be smacked about,' Patience insisted.

'What type?' Yasmine asked, genuinely hoping for insight.

'The ones with pricks,' Patience said, laughing. 'They fully expect us to be difficult. They think it's part of the great mystery that is woman. Infants, one and all, the poor dears.'

As Yasmine watched Faruq mama kow tow to her mother's whims yet again, she wondered if Patience was correct in her estimation.

When she thought of Patience lately, she felt a heaviness in her chest. She was her childhood friend, so she would not be sacked. But that was as far as Yasmine felt she could bend the rules. 'Ar kee? What else is bothering you?' her mother asked.

'Patience is with child.'

'Well, it was only a matter of time,' her mother said. She continued to braid Yasmine's hair. 'She was always a bit sloppy. Beautiful, but sloppy.'

Yasmine leaned back into her mother's lap and looked up at her.

'What have I said?' her mother asked.

'Arrey, the girls are friends, my blossom,' Faruq mama interjected. 'Your assessment is harsh.'

'My assessment is harsh? The girl is a tart, plain and simple.'

Her mother suddenly abandoned Yasmine's hair and exited the garden in a state. 'Your uncle is driving me mad,' she offered as an excuse on her way out.

Left alone, Yasmine and Faruq mama looked at one another. 'Beta,' Faruq said, 'she is worried that you will be hurt.'

Yasmine was surprised. 'This is not about me,' she said. She thought he had misunderstood.

Faruq chuckled. 'No, Yassu moni. She is worried that you will be alone, without money, and then worried that you will be heartbroken. It is a pain particular to mothers. Someday you will understand.'

Yasmine stiffened. 'I am very sensible. I will never fall in love, and I can handle Patience's problem.'

Faruq laughed then; a hearty laugh that shook his rotund body. Yasmine scowled.

'Beta, by that statement, I can tell you are in great danger of falling in love,' he said. 'I know you are a very clever girl,' he added to soothe her. 'Just like your mother. She ran the house and all the women with an iron fist, but from what I recollect, she had never been close to any one baiji, you know? She never made friends. You and Patience are very close, like sisters, so you have to be very careful what you decide to do with her life. Do you see?'

'Well, we simply cannot have a child running amok around Bombay Duck,' Yasmine said. She slapped her knees to emphasise the point and her resolve.

'All right then, your mind is made up and it is for the best, correct?'

'Yes!' Yasmine said, though she was not at all sure.

Faruq mama kissed Yasmine's head and ambled out of the garden, humming a popular tune he always did when he was in a good mood, *Tumko Mubarak Ho*, leaving her more unsure than ever. She sat silently. The sun began to set, throwing long shadows all over the fragrant garden. The air was filled with the scent of night-blooming jasmine, and she did not want to move, even as the mosquitoes began to torment her. She saw the maid walk from room to room, turning on lamps, and thought how much easier life would be if she was not so terribly ambitious. It was a man's world, after all. Maybe just surrendering to that would be simpler. She saw Faruq mama and her mother through the window, as he made her a cup of tea and handed it to her. She saw her mother smile up at him when she took the cup, and he leaned down and gently kissed her on the lips. Yasmine sighed. A mosquito stung the tip of her ear, and she hit it so hard her ear began to ring. She was finally forced to go inside. By the time she reached the end of the porch, she had made her decision about Patience.

10

'Ghosh, is your uncle still in town?' Yasmine asked the Duck's bartender.

'Which one, didi?'

'The one who helps out women who are not married,' Yasmine replied.

He nodded silently. Ghosh was a discreet man and Patience's sudden state of pregnancy required discretion. The doctor who had treated Radhika's wounds would not do.

'Well, please bring him to us.'

'Now?'

'Yes, please.'

He left at once.

Patience sat on the stage, smoking. She could not hide her melancholy. Yasmine felt guilty but was resolute.

'Is it really necessary, Yasmine?' Patience asked in a small voice.

'Yes, Patience, you agreed, please be brave. Or you can leave, but how will you live? He won't come rescue you—'

'It seems wrong,' Patience said. 'I am a Catholic, after all.'

'Since when?' Yasmine asked. 'You refused to give up anything for Lent.'

'Oh, Yassu! Why are you so … hard?'

She began to cry. Madhu and Asma heard her and immediately rushed to her side and glared at Yasmine.

'What, why can't I be devout or serious about something. Not everything is just for a lark,' Patience said. Soon, her lovely skin was mottled and her nose began to run as she worked herself into a complete state of hysteria, with the help of the others.

'We could raise it, together,' Asma said, inexplicably sobbing as well.

It must be the Japs; they had managed to rattle someone after all, Yasmine thought.

'Yes! That was how we were raised, Yasmine. In a house full of strong women, no men in sight to mess about and cause problems,' Patience cried, clinging to Asma.

'Do you really want to bring another anglo-kalo into the world, Patience?' Yasmine said, trying to reason with her. 'They would have no status, neither here nor there. You know if you don't have status, you don't exist. You can be alive and invisible. Nothing can change that, not money, not fame ... not really.'

'But things are changing!' Asma chimed in. 'Soon India will be independent, Gandhi-ji said so.'

'Well then, tell Gandhi-ji to come raise this baby and find the money for the bloody extra food it will need,' Yasmine snapped, incensed at the openly treasonous words coming out of Asma's mouth. 'If the Brits ever leave, do you know what will happen to the Anglos?' she said, pointedly to Patience. Though they had been friends since childhood, there was always that wall between them, her European blood and what it meant. 'You call England home! But guess what? They don't want you lot back there either, because back there, you are the niggers.'

The remorse was immediate, but it was too late. Yasmine hated that word and had never uttered it until then. Madhu and Asma moved away from Patience and walked upstairs.

Neither of them looked at Yasmine. The friends were left alone, both staring at the floor.

'I know you are right,' Patience finally said.

'Do you?' Yasmine said, relieved. 'I am sorry about what I said.' She put her arm around her friend, and Patience rested her head on Yasmine's shoulder.

'I know you are trying to do the right thing. You have to do all the thinking for us. Just for a moment I thought, maybe ... oh, never mind,' she trailed off.

Yasmine took a deep breath. 'I know,' she said, though she didn't fully understand. She could not imagine bringing a child into this insanity.

'I'm a dreamer,' Patience said.

'Dreams are good,' Yasmine said. 'But there is a time and a place for them.'

'Oh, Yassu, why are you so cold?'

Yasmine shrugged. 'I am not sure,' she said, meaning it. 'I have always been this way.'

Ghosh came into the room. 'My uncle is here, Yasmine didi,' he said, his face sombre.

'That was quick,' Patience said. She clutched Yasmine's hand and looked into her eyes, silently pleading with her.

Yasmine turned away from Patience's gaze and squeezed her hand.

'He was nearby, as luck would have it,' Ghosh said.

'Okay. Patience?'

She shuddered and nodded. Yasmine held her loosely. Ghosh's uncle came into the room. He was an elderly man, with rheumy eyes. The skin on his hands was thin. One could see the blue of his veins.

'I think it best to use roots and herbs to terminate,' Ghosh's uncle said, looking Patience up and down. 'No need for a messy situation. May I?' He gestured towards her belly. She nodded. He put down his bag and kneaded her belly with gentle pressure, while holding the small of her back with one hand. She flinched at one point when he pressed down hard on her lower abdomen.

'Just coaxing it out a bit. I am ready,' he said. 'I will need a mortar and pestle. I have everything else. Please rinse the mortar and pestle in boiling water first.'

Ghosh went immediately to the kitchen to retrieve the items.

'You are a bit along, I would say. Maybe three-and-a-half months?'

Patience nodded. After a few moments, Ghosh returned with the mortar and pestle.

'Rinsed?' Dr Ghosh asked.

His nephew nodded.

'Show time,' Patience said, trying to smile at Yasmine. She followed the man up the stairs.

God forgive me, Yasmine said under her breath. She called to Rahul, who was loitering close by, to boil some more water, and then poured herself a shot of whiskey. She resented the position her friend had put her in. She took another shot and grew more peevish. Patience knew the rules better than anyone. Why did she have to break them?

Yasmine sat there, staring into the mirror above the bar. She saw an old face looking back at her. Her hands shook every time she raised the glass to her lips. Her thoughts began to race. She had made it clear to every girl, even Radhika, who was so young, that pregnancy meant automatic termination, either of the baby or the job. The Bombay Duck was not a haveli but a place of business. The days of the great havelis were over.

Radhika was now barren, a thought that paradoxically hurt Yasmine to think about. She hoped that Patience would be spared that after this operation. Maybe she could have a family someday. Who knew anything? She smoothed her hair and wiped away the kohl that smudged her eyelids, and readied herself to hold Patience's hand. She went upstairs, carrying a tray with a teapot of hot water and a cup. Patience was lying on her bed as the doctor continued to knead and massage her stomach.

He placed his hands at the top of her small waist and made downward strokes, while pressing down, like he was trying to squeeze paste from a tube.

After a while, he asked her to sit up. He turned to the table where Ghosh had put the mortar and pestle and sprinkled into it the herbs he had brought with him. He saw Yasmine watching him.

'Yarrow, valerian, anjelika and birthroot,' he said as he poured water into the pestle and started to ground it into a paste.

'Wouldn't it be better as tea?' Yasmine asked. This was not the first abortion Yasmine had been privy to. In a house full of courtesans, this happened once in a while, but not as often as people would think. Yasmine's mother and her ilk were very careful and took extra precautions, some of which even involved the supernatural.

'Take a dab of paste directly on the tongue,' the doctor said. 'That's quicker.'

Yasmine heard Patience sigh.

'Birthroot is a funny name for something that does this,' she said.

'One of nature's ironies,' the doctor said.

'Will I vomit a great deal?' she asked.

'Yes,' he replied. 'And the cramping can be quite excruciating,' he added, while he measured a pinch of yarrow into the pestle. 'But it is still nothing compared to childbirth itself. It will be done within a day or two.'

'Is there anything I can do to ease her suffering?' Yasmine asked.

He looked at her over his glasses then. He held her gaze for a long while, so much so Yasmine started to get angry. He did not have to say a word. He was blaming her for what happened. She was the proprietor of an establishment that employed women who found themselves in these predicaments. He turned back to his pestle.

That night, Patience screamed in agony and lost so much water from vomiting that Yasmine thought for sure she was going to die. She vowed to Patience, as she held her hair while she threw up, that if she ever encountered the man who did this to her, she would force him to drink three big cups of tea laced with a healthy dose of birthroot and see what happened. Exhausted, Patience nodded mutely and tried to smile.

'I know you will always protect me,' she whispered.

Patience kept bleeding, more than the doctor had expected.

'She has some complications,' he said once he had stabilised her and she was asleep. 'I'm not sure there will be more babies. But she is young, who knows?'

Yasmine stroked Patience's soft cheek, wet with tears. The heaviness that she had been carrying around ever since she found out Patience was pregnant now pressed down on her. She felt old and too young, at the same time, to be making decisions that altered the course of someone's life. She knew how much Patience wanted babies.

Two days later, Patience had barely recovered, and they were back underneath the stairs at the Metro while the Japs dropped bombs.

'Why could you not predict this?' Yasmine asked Patience. 'Why always broken toes and misplaced hammers?' It was close to midnight. The attack lasted only half an hour, but they had been given two hours' notice and had been huddled under the stairs with fifty other terrified and baffled people for what seemed like an eternity. Yasmine's ears were still ringing from the explosions that six enemy planes had wrought upon them and, for years afterwards, could not help but wince when she heard a tea kettle whistle.

'The moon was waxing. I should have known,' Patience said, by way of an explanation. But she said it listlessly and did not fight back, which was not like her. Yasmine scooted over and put her arm around her.

'What nonsense,' she said, shaking her head. 'Or what happened to Radhika?' she said suddenly, after a moment's pondering. 'Why couldn't you predict that?'

It was not fair of Yasmine, she knew. Patience's face had also taken on a yellow pallor, like when she had jaundice. However, Yasmine was too out of sorts; the Japs were costing her business.

Asma, who had been silent the whole time with her hands over her ears in anticipation of the bombs that seemed to take forever to come, said, 'Steady on, Yassu.'

'No, it's true,' Yasmine insisted. She could feel herself becoming hysterical. The air under the stairs was stale and smelled of sweat. Madhu and Radhika exchanged quick glances. Adil Baboo, Rahul and the band members were together at another shelter a little further away. Radhika looked down and pulled her dupatta tighter around her.

'What was that for,' Yasmine, spoiling for a fight, asked them. 'That look,' she added when the girl shrugged. She could not push for an answer, because the all-clear was sounded and everyone practically ran into the lobby in relief. Unfortunately, the air outside was worse. It smelled of burning rubber and petrol.

The women stood around in the lobby waiting for the Air Raid Patrol to give them the okay to leave. Everyone was silent, holding handkerchiefs to their noses. Yasmine looked at a sleepy girl of about four, clutching her mother's hand and sucking her thumb, her eyes half closed. At the sound of a distant rumble, she widened her eyes and touched her mother's cheek. She did not take her eyes off her mother's face for a moment. One of the ARP tried to get her to laugh. He was an elderly Englishman, about sixty, with a waxed moustache, who knew how to fold origami animals. He would do it to entertain the children at every raid, and the women too. Many years later, Yasmine would still have a red and silver crane he folded for the little girl that night. She had dropped it as her father carried her away and Yasmine picked it up.

The ARP saw Yasmine watching him expertly fold the small square of paper into a tiny crane. He held it up when he was finished, and Yasmine smiled.

'Funny that,' he said to no one in particular and handed it to the little girl.

'What is?' Yasmine asked without thinking. She rarely made small talk with anyone under the stairs even though this was their third air raid.

'The crane is the Jap symbol for peace,' the elderly man said. 'Maybe I should make more, what do you reckon? Think that'll stop 'em?'

~

The Japanese were trying to destroy the Howrah Bridge, and they would stop at nothing. The Howrah and Sealdah stations were engulfed with people trying to flee the city. When the bombings started, Yasmine missed her mother terribly—Shirin was in Chittagong, near the ocean, with Faruq mama. The feeling of being out of control was building, and she would have welcomed her mother's guidance. It was as if she was listing and needed a push to right herself.

That night, there was a WACI there too, an Anglo-Indian woman named Sadie, who had what Patience called a 'snavely' look about her (a made-up word from their childhood, that both girls felt captured the essence of certain smug types) and who took it upon herself to tell them what to expect in the coming weeks as they stood in the lobby waiting to be released.

'There is reason to believe that several air raids such as this one are likely,' she said in a singsong Anglo lilt, not quite English, not quite Indian. She was puffed up with the importance of imparting weighty information. Asma gasped in dismay, and Sadie looked smug. Sadie had uneven, nicotine-stained teeth. Yasmine despised her at once, and the desire to smack her across her freckled self-important face was powerful. The feeling was clearly mutual, as Sadie had looked everyone up and down when they walked in and smirked when Asma shrieked as the first bomb made contact a good distance away. There was no denying the girls from Bombay Duck were the most attractive women huddled underneath those stairs. Sadie, therefore, hated them on sight. Secretly, she yearned to see the inside of the club that was gaining quite a reputation as Calcutta's top night spot, but could not afford it. She needed someone to take her—one of the GIs perhaps—but was never asked.

'As long as you all follow the rules and listen to the ARP alerts, there is no reason for worry,' she said in a patronising tone. Her eyes were closed the whole time she imparted the information and her eyelashes fluttered.

'I beg your pardon,' Patience said, raising her hand, which Yasmine thought was funny and apt, considering this chiriya was treating them like they were pigtailed schoolgirls. 'Excuse me? Can you open your eyes?' she waved her hand in front of Sadie's face. 'But the Japs are trying to kill us, are they not?'

'Well—' Sadie said, 'yes, I suppose so, but—'

'I would say then that there is a great deal to worry about,' Patience said.

'I can't stand these snavely Anglo girls who think they know something we don't,' she whispered to Yasmine.

Yasmine smiled at her. 'But you're one,' she whispered back.

Patience wrinkled her nose at Yasmine. 'I am not snavely. Bite your tongue, girl! Besides, it's plain that this one is a Presbyterian.'

'Snavely is not proper English,' Asma said. She always felt left out when Patience and Yasmine started their secret conversations in plain earshot of everyone. It seemed impudent and made Asma petulant.

'It is!' Patience said. 'Right, Yassu? Where did you read it?'

'*Mansfield Park*,' Yasmine said immediately, straight-faced. Patience's banter made her feel calm.

Asma looked sceptically from Patience's face to Yasmine's. They were both impassive.

'Jane Austen's *Mansfield Park*?' she said.

'Who else's?' Yasmine said. 'It's Regency England slang,' she added helpfully. 'Like the expression "counter coxcomb".'

'I'm not sure I believe you,' Asma said. 'Austen rarely used slang.'

'Yassu received first class first in English honours at Loreto, and you are questioning her?' Patience said in feigned outrage.

'What the bloody hell is counter coxcomb?' she whispered to Yasmine when a nonplussed Asma wandered off to look at the movie posters.

Yasmine shrugged. 'I read it in a Mills & Boon novel. But in my defence, that story was set in Regency England.'

Patience gave a low whistle and smiled.

'Since when do you read Mills & Boon, like the rest of us peasants?'

Yasmine suddenly put her arm around Patience, startling her. Yasmine was rarely demonstrative, but lately, she had been quite tactile. She gave Patience's slim shoulder a reassuring squeeze and released her.

Everyone else in the lobby, a smattering of Europeans, Sadie, and the ARP gentleman, watched Yasmine and her attractive companions curiously. Especially Yasmine and Patience, who seemed to be in their own world, laughing and whispering, like schoolgirls. It was incongruous to the situation they were all in.

Yasmine and Patience looked over at the poster that Asma was studying: Clark Gable and Lana Turner in *Somewhere I'll Find You*. In the poster, Clark Gable held Lana Turner from the back as she looked up at him, bosom heaving, her full lips slightly parted.

'Men are crummy,' Patience said, gazing at the poster sadly. She liked using the Americanisms she had picked up from the GIs.

'I thought you loved Gable,' Yasmine said.

'Yeah, but Carole would still be alive if he was not a tahnki baaj flirt.'

Patience adored Gable's wife, Carole Lombard, who had died earlier that year in a plane crash while this movie was being made. She had been selling war bonds and was rushing home—rumour had it because she had heard that Gable was having an affair with Lana Turner. Asma, Madhu and Patience were all rather put out by the whole thing as Lombard was what they thought of as a real dame, a woman's woman, unlike Lana Turner, who seemed specifically built for seduction and to betray her gender.

The all-clear was given again, and everyone was released from the lobby. Yasmine and the girls filed out silently, though Patience gave the ugly Sadie a parting smirk and saluted her.

'I heard he has bad breath,' Madhu said, of Gable, as they walked home.

'So what?' Asma sighed. 'He's a total king.'

Yasmine kept looking up at the sky, expecting it to fall.

11

Yasmine was distracted when she walked back into the Duck's foyer to find Edward standing there, with three other soldiers. After an air raid, there was always the fear the building would be damaged or someone she knew would be dead. So, she was startled to see him and remained silent, not greeting him at once. Asma, Radhika and Madhu, in no mood to be convivial to customers, filed silently past the men up to their rooms, ignoring their curious gazes. Patience greeted Edward, winked at Yasmine, and followed the others upstairs. Yasmine didn't want Patience to leave but couldn't say anything without revealing her nervousness. It had been five months since she had seen him, and he seemed different: a bit worn down, his uniform hung more loosely on him. Yet he also looked healthier. His skin was darker, the colour giving him a youthful glow and bringing out the green in his eyes.

He was awkward and did not look her in the eye at first. He had brought the soldiers he counselled and they stood behind him, looking as confused as Yasmine because he had marched them from the ARC to this club.

'How are you?' Edward asked her, finally.

'In one piece,' she replied.

'Where's your nearest shelter?' he asked as his men peered at her from behind him.

'At the Metro Cinema,' she said.

'We were in the basement of the ARC,' Edward said. 'They gave us the all-clear about an hour ago. But shut down their kitchen—as a precaution, I guess.'

When Yasmine remained silent, he said, 'We're all hankering after some food that reminds us of home, and we hear your cook has quite a reputation for making American chop suey, even better than what they have on the base.'

Yasmine smiled hearing this. It was true. Rahul had become something of an American cuisine aficionado—if there was such a thing as American cuisine—because he had been spending so much time on the base and, amazingly, advised Adil Baboo on how to improve on these dishes. Rahul insisted catsup was a main ingredient in most of them. Adil Baboo could now make chop suey as good as any served in an American diner, along with something called sloppy joe. Yasmine was annoyed by Rahul's preoccupation with all things American, but the fact was it meant more business if they adapted the menu to suit the GI palate. Everything had to be toned down. The Brits wanted their curries robust and spicy; the Americans could barely handle black pepper.

'You've heard right,' Yasmine said. 'We have surpassed Cathay. But we're not open today. We decided to remain closed because of the air raids. Things have been sixes and sevens because of the Japanese. As you must have been aware.'

'I actually wasn't,' Edward said. 'I mean, other places are open.'

'Well, we are not, I'm afraid,' Yasmine said.

Edward looked down at his feet. The truth was, he was not even particularly hungry. He had been avoiding the Duck, and Yasmine, for a reason he could not admit to himself. When the bombs had fallen that day, though, his first thought had gone to her. And when his men mentioned a craving for American food, he seemed finally to have a legitimate reason to visit the nightclub. 'It's just us four. Can we impose on your hospitality and reiterate that it is, in fact, only *your* chop suey we want?'

'Yes! Come on, ma'am.'

'Pretty please?'

Two of the other men chimed in, their pleading faces making her smile. She nodded finally and walked into the kitchen. Perhaps she could charge them double, and there were four of them. It was going to be a lucrative day for her. However, she quickly realised that there was a problem. There was hardly any food in the larder.

She came out to tell them as much but then, before she could explain, Edward smiled down at her and said, softly, 'I haven't seen you in a very long time.' He was feeling less awkward, even though his charges were curious and hardly discreet about it. Seeing her made him happy.

'No, you haven't,' she said.

'You look … well. I should have said that at the beginning.'

'Thank you.'

'Pretty sari.'

'Thank you again.'

'Business is good?'

'Yes, well, as good as can be expected but, as I said, we are not quite prepared—.'

Yasmine was brought back to the problem at hand. But now she did not want Edward to leave, given how he was gazing at her.

She asked them to wait in the bar area. Upon hearing the word 'bar', the men's faces lit up, and they looked entreatingly at Edward, who said, 'Sure thing, but I doubt you're serving drinks this early.' He looked at Yasmine, and she understood that he did not want any of these men drinking.

'Yes, unfortunately we do not have any liquor,' Yasmine said, somewhat fumbling. 'We were not expecting anyone today.'

'You got food at least, right?' a ginger-haired soldier named Sullivan asked. Edward scowled at him, and he immediately looked down.

'Yes, of course. Just wait a moment,' Yasmine said. She ducked behind the sandalwood screen separating the greeting area from the main floor, which did not hide much, and ran to the kitchen. Once inside, she started shouting for Adil Baboo and a bearer to come.

'What's the racket?' Patience enquired. She had come down to smoke.

'Ki hoicheh, Yasmine?' Adil Baboo said, walking into the kitchen. 'Did something happen?'

'No, no,' Yasmine said, staring at the abysmally empty icebox. She turned to Adil Baboo. 'Where did all the food go?'

'What food?' he asked. He was not trying to be funny. 'I didn't go to the bazaar today. We are closed.'

'Uff! So what if we are?' Yasmine cried. 'Don't we have to eat?' She was beginning to feel hysterical.

'Are you hungry?' Adil Baboo seemed genuinely baffled. 'Shall I make an omelette?'

Yasmine let out a strangled cry and plopped down on a chair. No one had ever seen her behave this way. It was alarming to Adil Baboo; like the world had suddenly turned on its head.

'Oh, she's hungry all right,' Patience said, laughing. 'But there aren't enough eggs in the world to satisfy what she's craving.' Yasmine glared at her, but Patience was not bothered.

'You need to stop reading those horrid romance novels, Patience,' Yasmine said. 'You're starting to sound like the dim-witted heroines.'

Rahul appeared a moment after that, and soon, the tiny kitchen was crowded.

'Didi? Did you call me?' he asked.

'Yes! About ten minutes ago. Why do you never come when called?'

'But I am here now,' the boy said.

'We have customers,' Yasmine said, as calmly as her racing heart would allow.

Everyone except Patience looked surprised.

'What were you planning on serving them? Roti and a single potato?' Patience asked.

'Yes, what were you planning on serving them?' Adil Baboo asked. He seemed annoyed, though his tone was characteristically respectful. For the first time in any matter concerning the club, Yasmine felt unsure of herself.

'American chop suey,' she said in a small voice.

Patience and Rahul laughed out loud then and only stopped when Yasmine glared at them.

'I don't have any of the ingredients, Yasmine,' Adil Baboo said.

'Well, what do you have?'

He went to the icebox and pulled out a skinny eggplant and three eggs and held them up.

'Also, I have ten bottles of my homemade catsup. I was planning on heading to New Market later and shopping, but just for us. The week's shopping is scheduled for tomorrow morning.'

'Right.'

'You know this, Yasmine,' Adil Baboo said gently. 'The vegetable and meat stalls are closed now, nah? After the raid.'

Yasmine's mouth went dry. She tried to swallow.

'Oh god, what have I done?'

She peeked out the kitchen door and saw Edward and his charges moving around restlessly behind the screen.

'I have an idea,' Yasmine said to the group in the kitchen. 'Patience, how much money do you have?'

'You tell me,' she said. 'Pay day's next week.'

'Tips?' Yasmine asked, ignoring what she had just said.

'Three rupees,' she said.

Yasmine looked at her intently. 'Okay, fifty rupees, eighteen annas,' Patience said eventually.

'Rahul? Adil Baboo?' Yasmine said.

'I know where you're going with this,' Patience said. 'Why can't you just take it out of the till?'

'I need to pay all the vendors this week,' Yasmine said. 'And Yadav.'

Yadav was their black-market connection, who supplied them their watered-down spirits for the bar.

'You know how he gets,' Yasmine said.

Patience glanced out at where Edward stood and then looked back at Yasmine and softened. It was the first time she had seen her friend like this, over a man. It was alarming to be sure, but also made her seem vulnerable.

Soon, they had pooled their funds for a grand total of three hundred and twenty rupees and eighteen annas. Enough to feed five people at Cathay as long as they did not order dessert. Rahul was dispatched to fetch the food.

Yasmine peeked through the kitchen door many times to see what Edward and the men were doing. They were becoming churlish, from what she could tell, and Edward was having a hard time distracting them.

Edward waited for what he felt to be a decent amount of time, but after forty-five minutes, it was becoming nearly impossible to keep his charges in check. He walked into the kitchen reluctantly to tell Yasmine they needed to leave and saw Rahul walk through the alley door with tins of food.

Yasmine looked crestfallen to be caught, and Edward hastened to assure her it didn't matter.

'I don't even care about the food,' he said.

'Aren't you going to stay and eat?' Yasmine said.

'It cost us three hundred and twenty rupees,' Adil Baboo said. Yasmine flashed him an angry look, but he just shrugged.

Edward immediately reached for his billfold.

'This should cover it,' he said, handing Yasmine six hundred rupees.

'This is too much,' she said softly, much to everyone's surprise.

Edward smiled. 'Weren't you going to charge me double anyway?' he asked.

Yasmine laughed and nodded. 'Of course.'

'Well, I wouldn't expect anything else from Calcutta's premiere businesswoman.'

Adil Baboo quietly ushered a gaping Rahul out of the kitchen, not that either Edward or Yasmine would have noticed anyone else standing next to them.

'I have to go,' he said again. 'These fools I'm babysitting are getting restless.'

'Oh, I think they're well chuffed now,' Yasmine replied.

'I don't understand half the things you say,' Edward said.

Yasmine held the door ajar. Patience's lilting voice floated into the kitchen.

'Listen,' Yasmine said. 'My general has quelled your troops.'

'You're so beautiful!' Edward blurted out. 'I'm sorry I've stayed away.'

Yasmine had her back to him and so he did not see her close her eyes and smile.

'Hello?' he said when she was silent.

She turned to face him.

'Thank you,' she said, overcome with shyness.

He stepped closer to her. 'I sent you an invitation to our New Year's Eve party. You never RSVP'd...'

'Well, that is the busiest night of the year for us,' she said. The fact was, she had ignored it. His continued absence from the club had made her feel churlish towards him.

'Come for a little while at least,' he said. 'And bring anyone you want … just, not a date.'

'Oh?'

'Well, men we have plenty of on the base, you see,' he said, nervously clearing his throat.

'Hmm, what if the Japs bomb again,' she said, 'and we are trapped somewhere?'

'Oh, the Japs aren't going to bomb again,' Edward said.

'Are you so sure?'

'Yes. They can't … we have a date.'

'Well, please let Tojo know that.'

Edward wanted to kiss her, thought better of it, and asked instead where she got the food.

'Well, Cathay, naturally,' she said, laughing. 'My main competition.'

~

On Christmas Eve, the Japanese bombed Calcutta again. In this attack, the papers reported only twenty-five casualties, two of which were cows.

Bombs were dropped indiscriminately. They gave Calcutta a three-hour alert, and back to the Metro Yasmine and the girls went, with slightly less stout hearts. As they all huddled under the stairs, Yasmine revealed that an invitation had been issued for a party at the American base.

'Do you think they will have a buffet?' Asma asked.

Radhika was sitting in the far corner, near the bottom of the stairs. Yasmine could tell she was listening. Radhika still disappeared from the club every once in a while, despite everyone's best efforts to keep track of her. That very morning she had gone missing and returned with a hamper full of rice, barley, moong daal, sugar, butter, biscuits—the tasty digestive kind, not the hard stuff everyone despised—oranges, tea, cigarettes and vegetables.

When she extracted one item after the other from the hamper and laid them out on the table, they all sighed in appreciation and stared reverently at them.

'You'd think we were witnessing the birth of Christ!' Patience said.

Yasmine shook her head but said a dua under her breath, words she had not uttered since she was a girl when her mother insisted she memorise the Koran. Even Asma was moved to put her arm around her arch nemesis. Yasmine had been hard-pressed to remain angry with the girl for disappearing. But she demanded to know where she got the hamper; she was worried Radhika had done something illegal.

'The Salvation Army gave it to me,' Radhika said.

'It's true,' Rahul said quickly, lest Yasmine demand she return the hamper, which she would never have done. It was wartime, not the time to be principled. 'I heard they gave away one thousand like this.'

The goodies in the hamper would not last more than a few days, hence the strong urge to attend the Americans' New Year's Eve party. The hamper meant there was food and necessities available in abundance somewhere in the city and, as usual, only the Yanks had it.

Yasmine caught Radhika's eye. 'Listen, beti, I think you are ready to get back on stage,' she said. 'You're certainly resourceful enough to run around Calcutta and find us food.'

Radhika seemed to shrink into herself, as she shook her head. Madhu moved next to her, pushing Asma out of the way, and put a protective arm around her.

'Yassu, steady on chap,' she said.

'No, it's time,' Yasmine said. 'Radhika, if you don't get back on stage, you never will.'

'Maybe I don't want to,' Radhika said in a barely audible voice.

'Well, then, you have a choice,' Yasmine said. 'You can stay and do your job, or you can leave.'

'Come on, Yassu!' Madhu cried. 'That's not fair. She just brought us all these things.'

'Madhu, you cannot keep mollycoddling her,' Yasmine said in English. 'It won't help her in the end.'

Later, underneath the stairs at the Metro, Yasmine watched Radhika as she chewed on a thumbnail and sneezed. She looked wan and sickly. To Yasmine, Radhika was showing all the signs of a particular melancholy that she had seen in women growing up—one that ground their lives to a halt. The girl seemed too satisfied with doing nothing.

The others huddled with the Bombay Duck girls, three English families with children of varying ages and some elderly members, refused to engage with them. They were all obviously terrified of the bombs, but they were also a bit disconcerted by Yasmine and the girls, who were constantly joking and laughing or talking of things that had nothing to do with what was happening to them at that exact moment. This made everyone around them nervous. A respectable woman would be cowering in fear, not making jokes about how small Japanese men were and speculating what else was small on them.

One of the children started to cry.

'I have nowhere to go,' Radhika, who had remained largely silent, said to Yasmine suddenly.

'Then start polishing your anklets,' Yasmine said.

'I won't dance,' she said forcefully.

Yasmine shrugged. 'Suit yourself, but it will make you feel better if you do what you love.'

'I can help you run the club,' Radhika said, her voice urgent. 'I can clean and help Adil Baboo cook. I won't talk to the customers anymore, because I don't want to talk to the filthy gorahs. They are the reason we are in this mess.' She stopped herself, but it was too late. Some of the whites were glowering at her now. Yasmine knew at least one of them understood Bangla. They started to whisper to one another. She had a feeling they would report her to the insufferable WACI Sadie, and that could mean they would all be dragged into the inspector's office and questioned.

The paranoia those days centred around the Quit India agitators and supporters of the nationalists. Neta-ji—more so than Gandhi—was considered a traitor to the Raj, and anyone who supported him was thrown in jail. Yasmine was raised to believe that Bengalis had anarchy in their blood, and this was being proven true, time and again. The British were constantly admonishing Indians to report suspicious behaviour, assemblies or pamphlets. The English looked at Neta-ji as a terrorist element inciting unrest, and his supporters were dealt with harshly. In 1857, the English had meted out punishment to the Indian mutineers by shooting them from the mouths of canons. Yasmine had no reason to believe they had become more compassionate in eighty-five years.

Radhika saw Yasmine glancing at the whites in the room and said, quickly and loudly, 'I don't like those Americans. Always causing trouble.'

This seemed to mollify the young English mother, who obviously understood what they were saying. Everyone went back to looking unhappy and terrified.

It took all of Yasmine's self-control not to shake the girl. This was the very thing she had repeatedly warned her about. Being hanged for treason, a very real possibility in that climate, did not seem to matter to her one bit. It only seemed to reinforce Asma's assertion that the girl was dangerous.

'If you don't dance, I will have to pay you less,' Yasmine said. 'And you cannot do what you want. You cannot disappear. You will have duties and chores that must be completed by the end of the day. Adil Baboo will check.'

'You'll let me quit dancing?' she said, incredulous.

'You would let her quit?' Asma demanded. 'But I thought she was our cash cow?'

Yasmine started to tell Asma to stand down, but just then, a bomb hit its mark somewhere too close. The building shook.

Asma yelped and buried her head in Patience's lap.

'Saved by the bomb,' Patience said to Yasmine, winking. 'Just in the nick of time.' Her voice shook a little as she said it.

Bombs began to drop in quick succession, and it seemed like they were falling all around the stairs they were huddled under. The building shook again, and Yasmine closed her eyes. There was nothing they could do. Nowhere safer to hide. She had not prayed since she was a child. The surahs she had been forced to memorise were still there. She held her palms up and silently mouthed the words as the building shook once more. Plaster fell onto her lap, but she continued to pray with her eyes closed. They heard glass splintering and a faint scream in the distance. She felt Asma slip next to her and clutch her arm. Patience moved to the other side and held her, as if supporting her and encouraging her to continue for all of them. Radhika brushed the plaster off and put her head in her lap, wrapping her arms around her waist. Yasmine continued praying, in a trance, until the bombs stopped falling and the building stopped shaking. Above stairs, the WACI removed the black cloth that covered the windows and front doors, letting the light in. Yasmine finally opened her eyes to see all her girls gathered around her, and the astonished faces of the others under the stairs. A beam of light from the lobby shone down on Yasmine's head, illuminating the particles of dust that had been kicked up.

To a little girl, aged about nine, it looked like stardust. She was awestruck at the sight of Yasmine sitting still, her back ramrod straight, with Patience, Asma and Radhika hanging on to her. Madhu scooted closer and put her hand on Radhika's back. The little girl whispered to her mother, 'Is she a fairy godmother, Mummy?'

Patience heard her and smiled. She looked at Yasmine. 'That sounds about right,' she said.

12

Despite the bombings, the Americans scheduled a baseball game for a few days after Christmas. Nothing seemed to dampen their spirits. The Calcutta Yankees were playing against the US–Canada team. Edward attended the game and saw Rahul. He attempted to make small talk with the boy, mainly to get more information on Yasmine. Rahul seemed unwilling to talk, though, when questioned about his boss. Edward assumed he was just being protective.

'How is she?' he asked the boy.

'Goods,' Rahul replied.

'Is business ... goods?'

The boy shrugged.

'Want some chocolate?' Edward said. He held out a Hershey bar. Rahul looked at it longingly but did not take it. He wasn't sure what to make of this American, and Yasmine's warning not to accept gifts from them too readily rang in his ears. 'Take it for her, for didi,' Edward said. Rahul nodded. The chocolate would be consumed before it could reach Yasmine, but since no one was the wiser, Rahul would not feel guilty.

'Does she ask about me?' Edward asked, knowing it was not a good idea and embarrassed that he felt the need to do so.

'Didi very, very much don't like you,' Rahul informed him, patting him on the back in what he hoped was a comforting manner. He had overheard Yasmine complaining to Patience about him a few times. They did discuss the American officer a great deal, and to his untrained teenage ears, it all sounded critical.

'I see,' Edward said, taken aback.

Rahul shrugged, smiled brightly at him and continued watching the game.

Perhaps the boy was right, Edward thought. She had been warm when he saw her last but not expressed any interest in him. Even after he had blurted out that she was beautiful. Perhaps she was just cerebral, he told himself. At the front desk of the club, he had seen her copy of Dante's *Vita Nuova*, which was about the poet's love of a young girl named Beatrice, whom he was satisfied with worshipping from afar. Under the circumstances, the book seemed poetically fitting to Edward. He had planned a number of pithy conversation starters concerning it.

'I am like Dante,' he would say, 'I admire you from a distance.' That way, Yasmine would think he was a gentleman and familiar with Dante Alighieri, a heady combination to be sure.

Recently, he had received a deeply wistful letter from Maggie that he initially wanted to read only after New Year's Eve, but guilt compelled him to read once. He had not done anything wrong—yet—he told himself. If he played it cool, he would be safe.

Many festivities were planned for the Christmas holidays on base. Edward saw them as makeshift, sorry simulations of the real thing. He was never one for baseball, preferring, funnily enough, rugby, which he had played at Wesleyan until junior year, and he could not muster up the excitement everyone else felt. The holiday preparations were all emotional stopgap measures that he found created more pain. The pathetic little palm tree with the paper chains and popcorn garlands that had been put up in the Mess hall depressed the hell out of him, and he did not participate in trimming it.

He and Maggie, being New Englanders, went all out on Christmas. She was on every committee their church had and festooned their small Victorian with the slightly lopsided porch—the result of a car taking the corner too fast and ploughing into it in 1915—with fir garlands and wreaths tied with red velvet bows. On the sill of every window, a candle burned as soon as the sun set. At the end of a long day, when it was already dark, Edward would walk up the driveway and stop and gaze at the soft glow coming from inside the house, or the smoke coming out of the chimney, and take stock of what he had. It was all familiar, predictable, safe, and warm. If he was a little bored, he did not know it. He knew Maggie had his beer ready, with a beautiful head on it, and that the house smelled of pine and cinnamon, that his family would congregate in his parents' small front parlour on Christmas Eve as they had done for generations and drink spiked eggnog, while his uncle Stash fell asleep on the couch with a dish of pirogi balanced on his protruding belly. Maggie was no great cook, but insisted on hosting Christmas dinner, much to his mother's irritation. Most of what she prepared came out of a can. Maggie had attended Smith for three semesters before dropping out and had missed the home-economics courses, she joked. She would be wearing her holiday apron with the applique snowman on each pocket and bright matte red lipstick that somehow managed not to end up on his lips. When she kissed him hello, her blue eyes danced.

'Shake out your boots on the porch, sweetheart!' she said every time, because he forgot to do it every time, and trekked snow into their pokey front hallway. The first year of their marriage, she trilled it. By the second year, there was a definite edge of annoyance present, but she rarely, if ever, snapped at him. In fact, Maggie was the most even-keeled girl he had ever met. There was nothing unpredictable about Maggie, and he really preferred that, he told himself often. In the bedroom, however, she sometimes surprised him, with the occasional request for something besides the missionary position. Maggie approached lovemaking like she did most things, in a methodical way and, as a result, hit all the marks. She was averse to blowjobs, but Edward had been told that was an inevitability of marriage, and since he had never received one that he would consider worthy of writing home about, he had nothing to compare Maggie's grudging attempts, and he resigned himself to living out his life without them.

He had taken most of his ordered life for granted and now missed it fiercely. Who would've thought that a quiet evening sitting by the fire, listening to Amos and Andy's antics on the radio or Miles Davis on the Victrola, would start to mean everything, he wondered as he watched soldiers and nurses flirt and decorate the Mess hall with paper chains and popcorn garlands. And he had not even seen sustained combat. India was such an alien environment; he was more or less comfortable on the base, but he loathed the heat, the dust, the poverty, the insects, the smell of the burning ghats that mysteriously wafted up to their rooms on still, hot afternoons, and the resignation of the inhabitants of Calcutta to their fate. He was beginning to despise the men he had to counsel and was growing more hostile towards his dour secretary.

He began to dread the prospect of being alone on New Year's Eve, getting drunk and passing out, with no one to kiss when the clock struck midnight. He thought increasingly about Yasmine, and what had happened to her dancing girl. It bothered him that Yasmine might think he was a callous person, even as he told himself repeatedly that she did not factor in his life. This was what his idle brain was doing to him, and he had enough sense to know it was not a good thing, but he simply could not control his thoughts, all of which were solidly negative.

As the New Year approached, he began to miss the snow, forgetting how much he hated chipping the ice from the windshield of his car at the crack of dawn. At the daily group sessions, his charges seemed more suicidal and bereft than usual, and in an effort to cheer them up, he obtained permission to take them on another outing. He decided to take them to the pictures. The Lighthouse was closer to the base, but he found himself taking them to the Metro, near the Bombay Duck. He remembered, though he would have denied it, that Yasmine had mentioned she went there on days the club was closed. He could not remember what days they were but decided to take a chance.

She was not there and he was so disappointed it surprised him. Louis noticed that he was antsy, and assumed he was pining for his wife. He encouraged him to go to the Duck and 'pick out one of the darkies and go to town'.

'Shut up, Deccico,' Edward said.

'What the wifey don't know won't hurt her,' Louis said.

Edward thought about that for a moment. It was true. How would Maggie ever know? The problem was, Edward did not just think about touching Yasmine, he thought about her hair, her eyes, her skin, what books she read, what she found funny, or harsh. He wanted to know about her history—she was, after all, Bengali, educated, yet not from a traditional Indian family. He was sincerely curious about her. If he could leave Yasmine in a bed and walk away, then he would not have been so conflicted. But he suspected he would linger in the bed, holding her and asking her questions, and that was dangerous. He was leaving, of that much he was certain, either on a ship or in a coffin. He was never going to stay.

13

Patience and Asma had to beg Yasmine to attend the New Year's Eve Party at the Tollygunge Camp.

'We need some good cheer,' Asma insisted. 'With the Japs trying to kill us and what not.'

'You're thinking about the food,' Yasmine said.

'And so, what if she is?' Patience said. 'We could use a little proper food, not just powdered things. It's simply not Salisbury steak if you have to add water to it to make it grow.'

Yasmine smiled. Patience rarely defended Asma, so she knew she must be keen to go. She looked a bit more closely at her friend, who seemed paler than usual, and tired. She was still lovely, but sombre and melancholy. Yasmine must have visibly reacted to this, because Patience knit her brow and said, 'What's that then? What do you see?'

'Nothing, silly.' She did not tell her that she felt responsible for any sadness Patience might be feeling. She knew her old friend did not blame her for the baby, but there were many days when Yasmine wondered if she had acted too hastily, though she would never admit this to Patience.

'Is all this about that American *lew*tenant?' Patience asked, winking.

Asma stopped munching on a biscuit and looked at Yasmine curiously.

Yasmine had been lounging with her feet up on another chair and now sat up straight and looked away, at the mirror behind the bar. She began to smooth invisible, errant tendrils of hair and pointedly refused to meet Patience and Asma's gazes. Patience elbowed Asma in the side and winked again. She started chuckling. Asma had never seen the cool-headed Yasmine so agitated. It made her nervous, and she stopped chewing altogether.

'What American lieutenant?' she asked, her mouth full of dry biscuit.

'Patience, if you used that rather sordid imagination more effectively, imagine to what heights you could climb,' Yasmine said in what Patience called her 'Loreto Convent Voice', very posh and imperious and a sure sign that a nerve had been hit.

Yasmine got up from the chair, went behind the bar and pretended to busy herself with something.

Patience's face broke into a wide grin. She hopped onto a stool, rested her chin on her hands, and stared at Yasmine, fluttering her eyelashes, until the latter, exasperated, was forced to look up.

'You are actually going to let a bloke decide whether or not you will go somewhere or do something? A bloke?' Patience said. 'Egad!'

'What American lieutenant?' Asma asked again.

'This has nothing to do with him,' Yasmine said.

Patience leaned over the bar and looked Yasmine up and down.

'What are you doing?' Yasmine said, self-consciously patting her sari.

'Checking to see if your knickers have burst into flame,' Patience replied.

'What bloody American lieutenant?' Asma cried, throwing down her half-eaten biscuit.

'Edward Lafaver,' Patience said, lighting a cigarette.

Yasmine glared at Patience. 'Enough! Have you all forgotten what happened to Radhika at the hands of these lovely Americans?' she said. For a moment, Patience was abashed as she remembered the girl's bloodied and battered body the night she was brought in.

'It was the kalo boys though, Yassu,' Patience said quietly. 'Not your lovely Lafaver.'

'We don't know who did it. And he is not my lovely Lafaver.'

'All right, all right, don't get it all bunched up.' Patience took an extra-long drag on the cigarette and looked at her friend askance. 'You won't mind then?' she said.

'Mind what?'

'If I have a go at him,' Patience said, leaning to the side to tap cigarette ash into an ashtray. 'I do so love the Yanks, as you well know.'

Patience looked up to see her girlhood friend staring at her, shocked, and was immediately contrite. She threw down the cigarette and reached across the bar and grabbed Yasmine's hands in both of hers. Yasmine was not like her or the other women they had grown up with in the haveli; she did not play the games men and women played with one another or even understand them, which was why she would never be a courtesan. Her mother always said Yasmine was unfortunate in that way. It was a disadvantage to be born into a great haveli and not understand the art of seduction. As a result, Patience felt protective of her friend.

'It was a poor joke, darling,' Patience said softly.

'If you want a go at him, you ... you should,' Yasmine stammered. 'You have so many admirers, why not add one more?'

'Oh, my darling fool!' Patience cried. 'I was just trying to make you admit you fancied him, and I did it poorly. It was cruel.'

Yasmine pulled her hands out of Patience's grasp and started to wipe down the bar.

'I do not fancy him! How can you say such a monstrous thing?' Yasmine said after a moment of energetic wiping. She threw down the towel. 'If you want him, you can have him. Have him for tea, slathered in butter and marmalade for all I care!'

'I haven't had proper marmalade in so long,' Asma said wistfully. She picked up the biscuit she had thrown down and took a bite, grimacing at its dryness and lack of flavour.

'Yassu moni?' Patience said. 'For all your books and Brontë and what not, you are still such a goose. I bet you, I could walk into his basha, wearing nothing but feathers and a smile, and he would only want you.'

Yasmine looked up. 'What?'

'He is besotted, your highness,' Patience said. 'He was yours even before he knew it. Married or not. And I admit I did notice him, but I saw...'

'What did you see?'

'The way you looked at him, and that is enough for me,' Patience said.

Yasmine began to wipe down the bar again. 'Well, I am sure you could have him Patience,' she said. 'It's no secret men find you more attractive.'

'That is not true, you fool. But Yassu, you can fancy him, just don't go falling in love, okay?' Patience said. Yasmine stopped wiping the counter but did not look up. She kept staring down at the bar.

'He will go back to Sandwich, to his wife,' Patience said.

'Norwich,' Yasmine said softly. 'I don't plan on falling into anything.'

'But have a bit of fun, take that crumpet out for an airing.'

Asma gasped. 'That's disgusting, Patience,' she said.

'I don't plan on doing anything with my crumpet,' Yasmine said.

'Good! And you can tell him that in person, at the party. That's settled then,' Patience said, hopping off the stool and bounding up the stairs two at a time, like a colt.

Asma looked at Yasmine. 'Are we going then?'

Yasmine nodded, sighing. 'Better let out your best dress. They will be serving roast beef and apple pie,' she said. 'Traditional Yankee fare.'

~

The day of the party, Yasmine tried to behave nonchalantly. She vowed not to pay too much attention to how she looked. What would be the point, she told herself. Patience and Asma decided to wear floor-length evening gowns and gussied themselves well, even though they would only stay on the base for an hour or so, since it was their busiest night at the Duck. Madhu would manage things until they came back, and they would be on stage the moment they returned, Yasmine told them.

They bathed in rose-scented water and powdered themselves so white that everyone would think they were, in fact, white. Even Asma took extra care with her appearance. Yasmine stubbornly clung to her usual costume of an understated, monochromatic sari and bodice, simple jewellery—nothing dangly—and light make-up. However, as the hour to leave for the party neared, Yasmine started to panic. She looked in the mirror and saw an aging, plain, dark hag. When Patience walked in, she was in tears on her bed.

'I look a hundred and six, not twenty-six,' Yasmine said.

'Oh, no,' Patience said. 'You just have lot on those shoulders, ducky.'

She looked at Yasmine's blotchy face, swollen eyes, wrinkled sari and smeared lipstick and laughed. 'Come on then, you goose,' she said. 'Let's get you ready to meet your prince.'

Yasmine was wounded. She knew Patience garnered enjoyment from other people's misery, and she usually joined in, but this was too much, even for her.

'He's not my prince,' Yasmine said, sniffing. 'And how can you laugh at me? I'm already miserable.'

'Don't fall in love, and you won't be, Yassu,' she said. 'Take that off.'

'No! I am wearing a sari. I am an Indian woman, not an Indian woman trying to pass for white.'

'Hmm, this is true, but you don't have to look like an ugly old Indian woman, now do you?' Patience said. She had ignored Yasmine's jab, about passing for white, which was just as well, as Yasmine was too upset to fight. Patience rifled through Yasmine's meticulously organised almirah and found a dark navy-blue sari with tiny silver beads sewn all over it, which made it shimmer, and a silver satin bodice that was cut slightly lower than her other ones. Yasmine stood, unprotesting, as Patience wound the cloth around her slim hips and waist and tucked it into her petticoat. She only protested when Patience pulled the waist of the sari down lower, so her navel was exposed and it rested lower on her hips. Yasmine tugged it back up and Patience tugged it back down; this was done silently, with both women glaring at one another, until Yasmine just gave in. She suddenly had no energy and no desire to go to the party.

'Perhaps you could escort Asma, and I can stay here with Madhu,' she suggested.

Patience shook her head. 'Madhu has mystery plans, remember? They involve a leggy redhead, I think.'

'You know I don't want to discuss what Madhu does with her free time,' Yasmine said.

Patience sat her down at her vanity and pinned Yasmine's long wavy hair into a chignon at the nape of her neck. She stood back to view her handiwork and smiled.

'Oh wait!' she said and ran into her room. She returned with her favourite blood red lipstick and ordered Yasmine to apply a thick coat on her lips.

'There, now,' Patience said. 'My god, but you look like a film star, Yassu. Look at you.'

Yasmine looked up slowly, almost shyly. She smiled. 'Well I do, don't I?'

She pushed back her shoulders and stood up. 'Let's crack on, then,' she said, with more bravado than she felt.

'We're going to a party, Yassu, not battle,' Patience said.

'Aren't we? It feels like one,' Yasmine said.

'Well, your war paint is perfect then,' Patience said, kissing Yasmine's cheek.

~

Edward dressed carefully for the evening, spending the better part of the day polishing buckles, re-pressing pants he had earlier sent out to be pressed, and grooming himself. Louis observed his actions in bemused silence, occasionally shaking his head. Edward ignored him and worked out his anxiety by taking extra care with everything he did. He was not sure what was making him so anxious, besides the prospect of seeing Yasmine again. He was concerned, he had to admit to himself, of how she and the others would be treated at the party. He expressed this as tactfully as he could to Louis and his fellow officers.

Louis smacked him heartily on the back and told him not to worry.

'We'll be on our best behaviour,' he assured Edward, which only added to the latter's anxiety. He then turned to the other men and made some remark about dark meat versus white meat, and Edward's stomach lurched. Louis was not known for his finesse with the ladies. His rough and tumble approach to courtship did not appeal at all to the nurses and WACI, but he did not notice or care. The amazing thing (to Edward) was that he had been married since he was eighteen. If his behaviour was this loutish at twenty-seven, what must it have been like at eighteen, Edward thought. He imagined Louis's wife to look aged beyond her years, a thick-ankled fish-wife, whose hair was always gnarled and dusted with flour, and who really wore the pants at home. His psychology training told him that much of Louis's personality was based on posturing and compensating for some imagined male deficiency or an overbearing mother. He would have to steer Yasmine away from Louis.

'Why do you care so much?' Louis asked him while Edward brushed and then re-brushed his hair. At that point he was already dressed and ready to go, this was just sheer nervous energy.

Edward shrugged.

'I know what you're after,' Louis continued. 'And you'll get it. Just don't get trapped by a dame looking to hitch a free ride to Norwich. Remember, you got a wife.'

'You would think that, asshole,' Edward responded and furiously started to polish the tip of his shoe with boot-black.

'You can see your face in that shit,' Louis said after a moment. When Edward remained quiet, Louis asked him if the young one, Radhika, was coming that night to the party.

Edward was surprised Louis remembered the girl's name. Edward did not recollect mentioning it to him.

'I doubt it,' he said. 'I mean, given what happened, she wouldn't feel safe.'

'Oh, she needs to lighten up!' Louis declared. He gave a short laugh. It sounded forced. 'No pun intended.'

'Are you kidding?' Edward said.

'What?' Louis said in a challenging tone. He was suddenly in a mood. His whole demeanour had changed when Edward said Radhika was not coming.

'She was raped, Louis. Plain and simple. I've thought about it, and I think that's what happened.'

'She never said that in the end, stop shit stirring.'

'Why are we arguing about this?'

'I don't know. Suddenly, you're all bent out of shape,' Louis snapped. 'What gives?'

'I am?'

'Don't do that bullshit, shrink thing, answering a question with a question.'

'Okay,' Edward said. He stared at Louis, who was now scowling and pulling at his collar.

Louis got up abruptly and left, leaving Edward and the other men shaking their heads. They were used to Louis's dark moods and sudden bursts of irritation, but given the subject matter, this seemed out of character. Louis rarely gave the Indians a passing thought, unless it was to put them down (in the name of good-natured ribbing, and 'promoting cultural exchange', he often said sarcastically). He was a virulent bigot. Everyone knew it—Louis made no bones about it. But his bigotry usually manifested itself in the form of dismissal or contempt.

Edward did not see Louis for the rest of the afternoon. By evening, the prospect of booze and women had lightened Louis's mood, and he patted Edward on the back and declared: 'No hard feelings.' As if Edward somehow owed him an apology.

Edward and his fellow officers were down at the Mess hall well before any civilian guests arrived. A young nurse from Lawrence, Kansas—Sherry Coakley—shyly walked up to Edward and offered him a glass of punch. She was barely twenty, small boned, and with a smattering of freckles across the bridge of her sunburned nose. She was sweet, and there was much speculation amongst the men about the status of her virginity. She had been harbouring a powerful crush on Edward for several months and finally, at the urging of her fellow nurses, had mustered up the courage to talk to him. He seemed distracted, however, as she tried to make small talk.

'Do you like the decorations?' she asked. 'I was on the committee.'

'Hmm? Yes! They're great!' Edward said, a bit too forcefully. Sherry was young, but she was not stupid.

'Are you expecting someone, sir?' she asked.

'Oh, no. Well, just some local pals of mine,' Edward replied. Sherry assumed it was native men Edward had befriended. He noticed the corsage pinned to her flat chest and stared at it. Sherry misunderstood and turned red. When Edward's eyes moved upwards to her face, he realised what she must have thought.

'Oh, god! Ms—Nurse Coakley. I am so sorry! I wasn't ... I wasn't—!'

'No, it's fine,' Sherry said.

'I was actually just wondering where you got that,' Edward said. 'It's pretty.'

Sherry explained that she and the other nurses had gone to the open-air bazaar early that morning and purchased flowers to make corsages for themselves. Somehow, one did not feel dressed up without a corsage, she said.

'Can I get one?' Edward asked. 'It's for a friend.'

Sherry's heart fell. She hid her disappointment and nodded. 'Oh! Of course!' she said brightly. 'Talk to Sadie. She has extras.'

'Okay.' Edward was loath to interact with Sadie more than necessary, but he wanted Yasmine to have a corsage. He thought it would be a novelty for her.

'Have you been to the Bombay Duck?' he asked, feeling the need to fill the silence.

'I've always wanted to go, but never had the chance,' Sherry said. She gave him what she hoped was a charming smile. 'We don't get out much. We need chaperones everywhere. Unless we have a date ... I heard it's ever so glamorous.'

'It's a decent place,' Edward said gruffly, clearing his throat. 'Almost like back home. The girls there sing and so on.'

'I heard the owner is a native woman,' Sherry said. 'And that she is very beautiful and gives herself airs, but can rattle off Shakespeare.'

Edward smiled at this description of Yasmine.

'Is that a fact?' he said.

'Oh. You've never seen her?'

'No, I have. I just never noticed how beautiful she is,' he said. The lie stuck in his throat, but he continued on in this banal manner, talking about Yasmine as if he hadn't noticed much about her because he had not really observed her that closely. Naturally, none of this was lost on young Sherry. 'She seemed ... very polite to me. Of course, I hardly know her,' he finished lamely. 'But some of the other fellows do, and we invited her and her girls this evening.'

'Well, of course she would be polite to you,' Sherry snorted. 'You're an American!'

'Right.' He put his glass of punch down half finished, thanked the young woman for it and started to walk away, but then stopped.

'Not everyone is in awe of us, Ms Coakley,' he said. 'India is an ancient place, far more so than where we come from. Maybe if you spent more time observing your environment, you would know that.'

'What did I say?' Sherry wondered, when he left her alone by the table.

~

Despite the red lipstick and encouragement from Patience, who wore her beauty effortlessly, Yasmine's heart was racing when they got to the camp. The guards ushered the women through quite quickly, to their surprise. The Mess hall was decorated with banners and flags (American) and every kind of tinsel imaginable. In place of a traditional Christmas tree, a palm tree was decorated with ribbons, small wreaths, garlands of popcorn and confetti. There was a long table laden with food. One traditional but scrawny turkey sat forlornly in the centre of the table, garnished with wilted parsley and a few carrots. It was surrounded, however, by fat roasted geese and duck and even a suckling pig. It was a whole pig, roasted until its skin was golden brown and glistening with fat and some kind of sweet glaze. It had an apple in its mouth and looked almost alive. Yasmine's Muslim sensibilities came to the fore and she was appalled by it; she etched the image in her mind so she could describe it to her mother later. It seemed excessive, until she remembered what these men—and women—had to go through every day, a million miles from anything familiar.

Asma was not disturbed by it. It was all she could do not to throw herself on the table and start eating her way down the length of it. Patience did not bat an eyelash as she was, as she said, 'somewhat Catholic', and was used to pigs in blankets or on tables. In her desire to be European, her mother, Daisy, had pooh-poohed eating halal when they were growing up.

Edward missed the stir the three women caused when they walked into the Mess hall. Patience's sleeveless gown was green velvet, cut on the bias and flared at the bottom. She had put her rich brown hair up and anchored it with a tortoiseshell comb in the back. She had applied jojoba oil to her bare arms and shoulders. On her ears, she wore diamond clips that she had borrowed from her mother, who had received them as a gift from an admirer twenty years ago. Even Yasmine's heart had skipped a beat when Patience came into her room. For a moment, she was wistful and wished she was that beautiful, but then shook it off. Every woman had a place. Hers was not to make men yearn for her.

Asma wore a pale-pink high-waisted gown that tied in a bow in the back. It had puffed short sleeves and a scalloped neck. It was chaste, but not frumpy, thankfully. She'd had the tailor model it after something Judy Garland wore in an Andy Hardy movie. She looked sweet.

'I want to have fun,' Asma said. 'For once. Oh! I see the buffet.'

Yasmine had walked in slowly, behind the others. Patience was confident they would be the most interesting women in the room, and she was, naturally, the most beautiful one. Almost at once, Patience and Yasmine were surrounded by men. Asma made a straight line to the buffet, where she was helped by two eager young GIs, who held her plate and cutlery while she exclaimed over every garnish as if it were a nugget of gold.

'Of course, Phil,' Patience trilled when a young man shyly asked if she remembered him from a mere eight days ago. To him, she was surreal, like a movie star stepped off the screen and into his world. He did not expect a goddess to remember the likes of him. Yasmine tried to furtively scan the room for Edward and found, instead, several pairs of resentful female eyes (Red Cross nurses) glaring at her. She was the only woman dressed in a sari, and she stood out.

Where was Edward, she wondered, and smoothed the folds of her sari down. She felt a hand on her elbow and spun around, excited, only to find a stocky man, who was decidedly not Edward, grinning at her. Almost at once, Yasmine felt revulsion. He was smiling, but his blue eyes were cold. 'We've never met, doll face, but I've been to your juke joint. Fancy place.'

'Yes, I think I would have remembered meeting you,' Yasmine replied, forcing a smile. She gently twisted her elbow from his grasp and looked out at the crowd. She thought if she did not make eye contact, he would go away.

'Wanna dance?' Louis asked.

Yasmine did not want to at all, but Edward was nowhere to be found, and she had not come just for him (so she kept telling herself), and she was a businesswoman, after all. He was a potential customer. The goal was to make Bombay Duck a regular haunt for American servicemen. She nodded and allowed Louis to lead her to the dance floor. And lead her he did. He spun her, pulled her, pushed her and all but threw her in the air. It made Yasmine laugh, in spite of the chilling feeling this man gave her.

While Yasmine was being tossed about on the dance floor by Louis, the anchal of her sari, which had been pinned to her bodice, slipped off her shoulder, with her bodice. It was only a slight slip, revealing nothing really but a thin brassiere strap, but Yasmine was not comfortable. In his clod-hopping enthusiasm, Louis stepped on the bottom of the anchal when it drooped to the floor, almost ripping it off her shoulder.

'Oh, shoot!' he said. 'Did I mess it up?'

'No, but I think I should re-pin it,' Yasmine said, relieved for an excuse to stop dancing.

'Good, I'll join you,' he said. Yasmine barely stifled a groan.

He followed her to a table that was decorated with green and gold confetti strewn on it and matching balloons tied to the backs of the chairs.

'I'm surprised those things stay up at all,' Louis said cheerfully, after Yasmine re-pinned and adjusted her sari. 'How do you keep it up?'

Just as Yasmine was about to answer him, he put two chubby fingers in the waistband of her petticoat and tugged gently, once. The feel of his fingers on the bare skin of her stomach startled her so that she froze. Her eyes darted around the room, to see if anyone was watching, if anyone would rescue her. Even as her skin crawled, she did not want to make a scene. His fingers went lower. She grabbed his wrist and met his gaze.

'Stop, please,' she said.

He pulled his fingers out, slowly, grazing her lower belly, above her pubic bone. His blue eyes never left her face. He smiled.

'I'm just messing with you. I heard that you girls didn't wear anything underneath these things. I laid a bet on you, you see? So it looks like I'm out twenty rupees. Say, where do you think I can get one of these for my wife? I doubt she'll wear it but she's always asking me junk about what women wear here. She can use it as a curtain or something,' he said.

Yasmine swallowed, trying to slow her racing heart. Bile rose up in her throat.

'Where are my manners?' Louis said. 'Want some punch?'

'No, thank you,' Yasmine said. 'Can you please tell me where the powder room is?'

'I'll show you—'

'No, please don't trouble yourself,' she said. 'Just point.'

He did so, and Yasmine walked quickly out of the Mess hall, before the tears of rage that had welled up fell. She passed Patience, who saw she was distressed. Yasmine shook her head when she saw Patience, to indicate that she should not stop dancing; she did not want to draw attention to herself. She passed a petite redheaded nurse and two others, who were standing against a wall watching Patience and Asma with barely concealed hostility. Yasmine was conscious of their rancorous gazes on her as she slowed her pace and walked by them. She nodded at them politely. Only the redheaded girl nodded back and smiled. Yasmine hoped no one had noticed the tears on her cheeks.

When she got to the bathroom, she realised she had been holding her breath. She let it out and stared at herself in the small mirror. She looked horrible, she thought. The fluorescent light overhead gave her a garish look.

When she emerged, Patience and Asma were waiting for her.

'Let's go,' Patience said. She looked grim. 'I saw that disgusting man touch you. I was about to come over.'

Yasmine nodded. Her eyes filled with tears again.

'It's good that you didn't,' she said.

'I'm so sorry, Yassu,' Asma said. 'We should not have come. We don't belong here.'

'Did you get enough to eat?' Yasmine asked her.

'Oh, more than!' Asma said. 'I have had my fun.'

While Patience and Asma headed back to the Mess hall to retrieve their wraps, Yasmine waited outside, by the entrance. There was still no sign of Edward. How could he have done this to her, she wondered. She peeked in to see Patience being accosted by another GI for a dance. She knew how much Patience loved to dance. She had been so melancholy lately that it was good to see her laugh. Asma was off to the side holding their wraps. Patience was trying—not too energetically—to extricate herself from her partner's grasp. She looked at Yasmine as if to say, what to do? Yasmine shrugged. Okay, she mouthed. And then held one finger up.

'Just one dance, you fool,' she said under her breath and smiled. She could not deny her friend this simple pleasure.

Patience nodded and began to foxtrot merrily to the other side of the Mess hall.

Yasmine lit up a cigarette. It was a cool and pleasant night. 1942 was finished. She had no real hope that 1943 would be any better. In an effort to calm her frayed nerves, she went down the list of what she had in her life that was good—a habit from childhood. She had her business, her mother, Patience and her health. But somehow, she knew none of it was quite enough. There was an ache. She felt it in her stomach. In the Chittagong dialect that her mother and grandmother spoke when they were together, the expression for being in love with someone was, literally, 'my stomach is burning'. Yasmine thought of that suddenly and smiled. She was happy when she thought of her family and her club and of course the amount of money she would be making that night. Yasmine turned around to see Tommy, smiling at her.

'Can you spare one?' he asked.

She handed him her cigarette case and matches. He was dressed in khaki pants and a sleeveless white undershirt, with an apron tied around his slim waist. His arms were sinewy and strong. Yasmine could not help noticing his beautiful skin. She looked away quickly.

'Working tonight,' he said and shrugged.

Perhaps it was his face and the sadness in his eyes that seemed to reflect what she was feeling herself. The evening's events suddenly piled on top of her. She burst into tears because of what had happened with Louis and the fact that Edward had stood her up. Tommy threw down the cigarette and started to dab at Yasmine's face with a corner of his apron, like his mother did when he was a little boy.

'I'm, I'm, s-sorry!' she sobbed, ashamed. 'But it's unfair that they make you work on New Year's Eve.'

'No, it's okay,' Tommy said. He was alarmed and moved by the sight of this beautiful woman crying. She had seemed so tough in the past, barely cracking a smile. He felt his heart speed up as he wiped the tears from her cheeks.

'I don't mind, ma'am. I'm a soldier. We do what needs getting done,' he said. He patted her head awkwardly and stopped the moment he realised what he was doing. When she had calmed down a bit, he handed her a handkerchief and told her to blow her nose.

Yasmine gave him a weak smile, took it and blew into it with all her might.

'Keep it,' Tommy said when she handed it back to him.

'I'm a fool,' Yasmine said, finally. 'I should not have come here. I don't belong here. Look at me.'

'I am looking at you, and you are the most beautiful sight I have ever seen.'

She smiled at him again, and his heart sped up even more. 'No, I am not beautiful. Patience is the gorgeous one. I'm the brains,' she said, though she was pleased with the compliment. They were standing close to one another. He smelled of soap and tobacco, like he always did. His throat was smooth and golden brown. Without thinking, Yasmine reached up and touched the pulse there with the tips of her fingers. Tommy gently placed his hand on top of hers and moved it down to his chest and held it there.

'I really want to kiss you,' he said.

'I can't,' Yasmine said, but did not protest when Tommy reached down and kissed her very softly on the mouth. His lips were warm. 'I can't,' she said against his mouth, and he stopped and pulled away from her.

'Were you invited? I don't mean any disrespect,' he added quickly when she frowned a little. She was frowning because she had recalled again that she had been stood up.

'Yes, of course. By an officer. Lt Lafaver,' Yasmine said. They both fell silent and looked out in front of them at nothing in particular.

'Are your friends out of ... jail?' she asked after a while. Her heart was racing. She could not look at him.

'No, they're still in there. Goin' on six months now,' Tommy said, trying not to think about her mouth on his. 'But now the brass are sayin' they did something else. They were accused of petty theft and so on. I think they're goin' home as no one is speaking up for them. They're disgraced, is what it is.' His face clouded over at the thought of his two friends incarcerated. 'How is the girl?'

'Fine,' Yasmine said.

'Oh, well that's good,' he said. Yasmine heard the conflict in his voice. She knew he blamed Radhika for what had happened to his friends. She could understand his anger. His friends' lives depended on this girl.

Tommy cleared his throat.

'Yes?' Yasmine said. 'Is there something you want to say to me?'

'I do. I've been ordered not to talk about the case. I trust you, though, if you care to listen.'

'I'm listening,' Yasmine said.

Tommy explained that when he was questioned by the MPs, he had said that he didn't even remember Radhika speaking. He didn't hear her voice. She had only danced for them. She did not smile once or try to talk to them. When she was finished, she bowed formally and sat on the floor, one leg tucked underneath her, another up and bent with a slender foot displayed in front of her. He remembered she wore a silver toe ring on the second toe of her right foot and that her feet were outlined with henna, and she wore silver bells on her ankles. She took one side of the sheer scarf she wore between her index and middle fingers and pulled it towards her mouth and looked down coyly.

'Yes,' Yasmine said. 'That's part of the performance.'

It was an odd, elaborate performance that Tommy guessed was some Indian flirting thing. They had thanked her and she had looked up at them then and smiled, and he did remember thinking that her smile was lovely. She was awfully young and reminded him of his kid sister. They had paid her, she had protested weakly, and then had taken the money. That was all he told the police and his CO.

'I have something more to tell you,' Tommy said now to Yasmine.

'All right,' Yasmine replied.

He hesitated.

Yasmine swallowed nervously. Was he going to confess? She hoped that he had not hurt Radhika because she liked him, more than she had realised. He did not seem capable of such violence, but with men there was always the possibility.

'The last we saw of her, she was counting the rupee notes and tucking them into her top. I felt like she had never done anything like this before, like it was her first time. I looked back when we was walking down the stairs at the Karnani Mansions and glimpsed her through the door that was still open. She was standing by a table, all business, counting the money. She did not look that young anymore. I was looking at her so deep that I nearly collided with Lt Deccico, who was coming up the stairs real fast. It was a close call. "Watch it, boy!" he hollered at me. "What the hell are you doing here? Who are you visiting?" I told him no one. Lt Deccico comes up to my chin, but he had leaned in close enough that I could smell his nasty breath. He has it in for me and all the coloureds, so I avoid him as much as I can. "You know the official army policy on consorting with prostitutes, boy!" he barks at me, like a junkyard dog. I said, "Sir, there are no prostitutes here. We was just sightseeing is all and wanted to look inside the building." It was a weak lie but he seemed to accept it. He goes, "Yeah, that's right. You better not have dipped your pen in any ink in this building, nigger. Somebody will pay for that." He looked at me, and then up at the open door. We both could see the girl still standing at the table. "No, sir," I said and left.'

Tommy paused and sighed.

He looked at Yasmine, whose eyes were glued to him. Her hands covered her mouth to keep from crying out.

'That son of a bitch is a mean drunk and always looking for trouble. He does that, he picks fights with people he knows can't fight back—enlisted men, Negros, gharry drivers, girls. I don't know how he knew we was there. But I heard he was thrown out of your establishment that night because he wanted to get near the girl. He must have waited and followed us to Karnani. He was going to get at her no matter what. I want you to know we stopped outside the building and thought about it, Miss Yasmine. All of us. We knew what he was going to do to her. We even got into a fight about it. Two of us wanted to go back on up, but we knew we was powerless. So, yes, maybe in a way we are responsible. But no one would believe us even if we ratted him out. We thought he would have his fun. We didn't know that he was going to hurt her so bad. He cut her up bad, huh?'

Yasmine nodded. 'She … she can't have any children,' she whispered. 'She's very small you know. She's just a girl.' Yasmine's voice caught in her throat.

She had started crying as she listened to Tommy but did not realise it. She seemed surprised when Tommy moved her hands gently away from her mouth and wiped her cheek again. This roused her, and she found her voice again. She held onto his arm to steady herself.

'Did you try to report it?'

'To whom, Yasmine?' He had forgotten to call her Miss. 'Who would believe three Negroes over a white officer? Plus, we would have to explain what we was doing there in the first place. I took her to the base so they could help her. That's all I could do. She told them my friends hurt her before I could say anything anyway. I don't know why she did that. We was good to her, respectful.'

Yasmine closed her eyes. As the weight of what he told her began to sink in, she felt dizzy. She reached out again for Tommy, who took her arm and steadied her.

'Why were you crying before?' Tommy asked. 'You were upset when I came out. I don't want to pry, though, so you go on and tell me to shut my mouth if I am.'

'That horrid man ...' she began.

'Deccico?' Tommy said.

'He touched me,' was all she could manage to say.

Tommy shook his head. 'Lord,' he said through gritted teeth. 'You have to tell your friend, you have to tell Lt Lafaver. They're basha mates. He has to know!'

Her hand was still on his arm and she was about to answer him when Edward walked outside. He froze when he saw Yasmine and Tommy. His eyes immediately went to Yasmine's hand on Tommy's arm. Tommy turned around when he saw Yasmine's face tense and quickly stood to attention.

He saluted Edward. 'Sir!' he said loudly.

'At ease,' Edward said. 'What's going on here?' he directed the question to Yasmine, who had clearly been crying.

'Nothing, sir. This kind young lady was just wishing me a happy new year,' Tommy answered before Yasmine could.

Edward barely glanced at Tommy. He was looking at Yasmine intently.

'Go ahead then, Private,' Edward said, turning to Tommy after a moment. 'I'm sure you have things to do.'

Tommy saluted Edward again but did not leave. To him, Edward seemed to be looking at Yasmine in a menacing way. He was glaring at her. Tommy was not sure he wouldn't be rough with her. He believed the white men here looked at Indian women as property, like they did black girls back home.

Yasmine saw that Edward held a small corsage of waxy gardenias in his hand.

'For me?' she said lightly. She wanted to give Tommy a chance to leave. She knew he was being protective—probably to his own detriment.

'What? Oh, yes,' Edward said. He handed them to her. 'You can leave, Private,' he said when he saw Tommy was lingering. 'Leave, Private!'

'Yes, sir,' Tommy said, but still did not move. His body was taut. He looked at Yasmine, who shook her head at him. Edward took a step towards him, but he held his ground, standing taller and straightening his shoulders, much to both Edward's and Yasmine's disbelief. He was taller than Edward by at least two inches.

'I promise, Tommy, I will talk to Radhika,' Yasmine said quickly. 'If your friends are innocent, they have nothing to fear.'

Tommy understood what she was doing but was still hesitant to leave. She gave him an almost imperceptible nod to say she was fine, she felt safe, and he finally, reluctantly, left.

Yasmine breathed a sigh of relief when Tommy disappeared into the Mess hall.

'What the hell was going on here?' Edward said. 'You can't be talking to him about the case. Do you understand? This is US Army business.'

He had not meant to raise his voice or cuss. It came out harsher than he had intended. He was immediately regretful when he saw Yasmine's angry expression.

'As far as I knew, this was still India!' she said.

'I'm sorry, Yasmine, really, but this is technically American soil,' he said gently. 'And this is Army business. I am just trying to protect you.'

Yasmine looked at the ground. She scooped up a handful of dirt and held it out to him.

'Aw, Yasmine, what're you doing?' Edward said. 'You'll ruin your sari!'

'This is America?' she said, feigning incomprehension. Edward sighed.

'Yes, technically it is.'

'Says who?'

'The Government of the United States of America and His Majesty, the King of England.'

He was trying to lighten the mood and tease her in what he hoped was a playful manner, but he knew he had walked in on something a moment before, something unhappy. He regretted taking so long to get to her.

'Well, we will see about that. Just give us time,' Yasmine said.

The notion that she was somehow not in India, the land of her birth and her ancestors, even though she clearly was, was absurd. She threw the dirt onto his carefully polished shoes.

'You can throw as much dirt as you want on me, but that doesn't change the fact that the dirt you're slinging is American. I don't make the rules, sweetheart.'

She walked past him, and he stopped her by grabbing her arm, which she wrenched free and kept walking.

'Come on, Yasmine, please,' he pleaded. 'I'm sorry.'

'You're all goons,' she said, stopping abruptly. 'You just take what you want, when you want it. You lot have done this, always.'

'What's wrong? I haven't been here a minute and you're already angry at me.'

'Where have you been?' she demanded. 'You invite me here and then ignore me.'

'I was getting you that,' Edward said. He turned her wrist over and pointed to the corsage. 'Did Tommy do something—'

'No!' Yasmine said quickly. 'Please don't blame him. He was comforting me, if you must know.'

'Why did you need comforting?'

'Never mind.'

Edward was still holding her wrist. 'In girl talk, that means I better mind or else. Don't get sore at me, please. I don't agree with Churchill or FDR or the king,' he said, drawing her closer to him when she did not protest. He slipped his arm around her waist, where her skin was exposed. He had never been this close to her. Her neck smelled like roses.

'As far as I'm concerned, you mussed up my spit-polished shoes with pure, grade-A Indian dirt,' he whispered, burying his face in her neck and smelling her skin.

'What are you doing?' she said nervously. She did not pull away. She allowed him to kiss her gently on the cheek. She closed her eyes as he planted small kisses on her face and neck, and only opened them when he kissed her mouth.

'Close your eyes, honey,' he said. Somehow, he knew she was watching him, even though his eyes were closed. 'And open your mouth.'

Tommy had been kissing her only a moment before, and now she was in Edward's arms. The evening had gone in a direction she would never have anticipated. But she could not kiss Edward this passionately without feeling guilty.

She gently disentangled herself. 'Can I tell you why I needed comforting?'

Minutes later, Yasmine had to run to keep up with him as he marched into the Mess hall.

'What are you going to do?' she asked Edward.

'Never mind. You stay out here,' he said. His eyes scanned the hall for his stocky basha mate.

'No, Edward,' she said. She had told him about Louis touching her, to deflect her guilt about Tommy and to distract Edward from what he had correctly surmised as being a 'moment' of sorts between them. But she was surprised by Edward's rage. 'Please forget it. There's no point. Imagine how it will seem,' she said quietly. Edward hesitated. The truth of what she said was undeniable—at least about people's perceptions. Punching Louis out in front of everyone would compromise Yasmine the most. He would deal with Louis privately and maybe even enlist the aid of a superior officer. Edward was surprised by the violence of his own reaction. What Louis had done, putting his hands on a lady, was insupportable, but his own jealousy was what gave him pause.

Suddenly, the high-pitched and excited squeals of small children could be heard echoing in the Mess hall. At the far end, where the band had set up, a group of about twelve Indian orphan children stood in three neat ascending rows of four, singing *Santa Claus is Coming to Town*, on key and with such heavy accents that the lyrics were barely intelligible. It was clear they were not entirely sure they understood what they were singing.

Yasmine was taken aback but glad the children had distracted Edward. 'I'm fine now. Can we dance later?'

'Are you up to it?'

'Yes, of course,' she said, smiling up at him. 'I came to dance with you.'

14

Only Edward was not hungover on New Year's Day. The rest of his basha mates and fellow officers groaned and yawned their way through breakfast. Louis's bed lay undisturbed. He had not come home that night, so Edward could not confront him. His mind was crystal clear, and the enormity of his infidelity was starting to hit him. When he kissed Yasmine, he had been sober. When her sari fell away and he saw up close how astoundingly lovely her breasts were, he decided to put everything and everyone out of his mind and concentrate on every curve, dip and valley of her body. Even if it was only for twenty minutes, which was all they ended up having to explore one another. This decision was also reached stone-cold sober. He did not want to forget a single detail of what she felt like in his arms. He was afraid to forget, because he had the feeling that memories of Yasmine's body and the smell of her would somehow keep him going when he needed it to.

Edward and Maggie had parted with sorrow, fear and a naiveté that all would be well. He realised that if she had an indiscretion because she was lonely, he would not hold it against her. The war made many things seem trivial. One would think that he would then forgive himself the indiscretion from the night before. Maggie was sensible, she would be hurt and angry, but then she would justify it as a result of their separation and the circumstances of war. But he could not, not just yet. It was not a straightforward case of lust, he realised, his heart heavy. Indiscretion, release, was one thing; love would be betrayal.

When Edward was growing up, his uncle Stanley, or uncle Stash as he called him, swore by pros and cons lists. 'Any problem, be it whether or not to vote for FDR or how you really feel about a girl can be figured out with one of those,' he would claim. This appealed to Edward's sense of order from a very early age. On New Year's Day, he proceeded to make a 'Yasmine pros and cons' list.

He put her name in the middle of the page with a big box around it. On one side he scribbled the word Pros, the other side, Cons. He started listing what he considered her pros to be. Smart, funny, good business sense, elegant, pretty, stable, spoke English well, and maddeningly sexy. Under cons, he paused and then wrote in all caps: 'I am married. To Maggie. I made vows.' That was all he could come up with.

Edward crumpled up the paper and threw it at the wastebasket and missed. It landed at Louis's feet. He had just walked in, with a sheepish grin on his face.

'Looks like you had quite the night, Lafaver,' he said. He loosened his tie and flopped on to his bed. 'Telling Mags all about it?'

The sarcasm was not lost on Edward. He turned slowly to look at Louis.

'I am requesting a transfer to a new basha,' he said quietly.

'Suit yourself,' Louis said. 'What do I care? We never liked each other, right?'

'I suggest you stay away from Bombay Duck.'

'Oh yeah? And what the fuck are you going to do about it if I don't?' Louis continued to undress and yawned.

'I'm going to the CO to report that you were sexually

inappropriate with a young native woman employed at Bombay Duck.'

Louis stopped undressing and turned around to slowly face Edward, who sat with his arms crossed. He shrugged when Louis turned to face him, ready to fight. 'So?' he said. 'Got anything to say?'

Louis stood up and started pacing, which surprised Edward. He had expected protests and dismissal, disdain—not nervousness. He knew in Louis's twisted psyche that touching Yasmine inappropriately did not constitute actual assault.

Louis stopped pacing and faced Edward. 'Look, Lafaver, it was a misunderstanding, is all. These Indian broads don't understand how we operate. It was one night, not even. A couple of hours. I'll stay away from the place, just cool it, okay?'

Edward sat back and looked at Louis. He was confused but he did not show it. 'I don't give a rat's ass if it was one night. Yes, you will stay away from her, you son of a bitch. If I see you anywhere near the Duck, there will be hell to pay.'

Louis shook his head. 'That little darkie is no innocent. She charged me an arm and a leg for nothing. That young thing bats her eyelashes at me, lures me, yes lures me to some crummy apartment, but not before she's fucked some niggers, which I know she did, even though she denied it, though I don't know what the hell she was saying, and then expects me to pay her after she's had coon inside her? Can you believe it?'

Louis kept on ranting and pacing as Edward stared at him, incredulous.

'You gotta help me out here, Lafaver. I know I should have said what I knew, but I mean, when I left her, she was fine. I guess they went back to finish the job. They're fucking animals, you know that.' He stopped and looked at Edward, who had gone pale. 'What's up, Lafaver?' Louis said, alarmed by Edward's pallor.

'Let me get this straight, Deccico. You were with the girl that night?'

Louis nodded. 'But like I said, when I left her she was fine. Nothing happened, because I didn't want to touch her after I saw those boys leaving the room. They musta gone back and finished the job. They musta been waiting for me to leave.'

'You swear?'

Louis nodded vigorously, putting his hand up. 'On my mother's life. It was that Tommy kid, the almost white one. You know who I'm talking about, right?'

Edward nodded. He didn't tell Louis that it was Tommy who had brought the girl to the base, and that if he had indeed raped her, it made no sense that he would have brought her back with him.

'Well, he was the one who seemed the most concerned when he saw me going in.'

'Is that a fact? Just ... just stay away from the Duck, Deccico,' Edward said.

'Whatever you want. That place is a dump anyway. Just have my back, Lafaver. There's a code, right?'

'Yes, Louis, there's a code.'

'I mean between us. Jeez. We're on the same side.'

Edward looked away. 'Are we?'

'You would sell me down the river for some—'

'Careful, Deccico,' Edward said. He stood up and took a step towards Louis, who stepped back, his hands up.

'Okay, okay!' Louis said, laughing nervously. 'I got it. You win. I know you got a soft spot for these ... people. But, *I'm* your people, Lafaver. Don't go all native on me.'

'I need you out,' Edward finally said. 'Get packed and leave. Now.'

'Fine. Just don't tell the CO or anyone else. Can I get your word on that, as an officer and a—'

'I said I would keep quiet as long as you hold up your end and stay away from the club and the women in it. Stay away from Indian women in general.'

Louis started to gather his things. Twice he paused and looked at Edward, who had his back to him. He finished gathering what he could carry in his duffel bag and left.

15

One day, a few weeks after New Year's Eve, Yasmine was given advice. 'Put the wife in a lemon,' Patience said. 'Then freeze the lemon.'

Everyone was there. Asma chewed on the ends of her hair and nodded. Yasmine shook her head and kept sorting bills. Madhu was daydreaming and smoking.

'You see, that way, you freeze all her evil influences. She can't hurt you anymore.'

'She is not evil. How is she the evil one?' Yasmine said. Try as she might, she could not bring herself to hate Maggie. Asma sighed and popped a sugar cube into her mouth. Yasmine scowled at her: sugar was hard to come by.

'I really believe in these things. This makes sense to me,' she said, nudging Yasmine in the side with a plump elbow.

'This makes sense to you?' Yasmine said, incredulous. 'But being nice to paying customers does not?'

Asma shrugged and kept sucking the cube.

From by the window, Madhu called out. 'She is the wife. He will never leave her. Not even for you, Yasmine,' she said.

Yasmine pushed back from the table and stood up. 'I never expected him to or asked him to. I suggest you all get ready. It will be a busy night.' The conversation had become far too personal. She had tried to keep things quiet, but they all lived on top of one another, and everyone had seen Edward coming and going at various times. The walls between the rooms were not thick. She would make a point of turning her ceiling fan on the highest speed because it made clicking noises she hoped would drown out conversations and intimate moments. But she also saw the genuine pleasure the others took in her love affair with him. It was not mere gossip to them. She supposed it was because there was nothing as intoxicating as the beginning of a romance. It was filled with promise. With so much violence simmering, undercurrents of agitation and rebellion, daily reports of the war and death, Edward and Yasmine's growing passion for one another was diverting and sweet. It also made Yasmine more amiable and less exacting. She was less inclined to peer over everyone's shoulders and demand they be more frugal or more industrious.

Yasmine knew what Madhu said was absolutely true, and it was also true that she would never expect Edward to leave his wife for her. She could not. It was outlandish. She knew she was not going to be chosen, however seductive her exotic charms, over a wholesome, white wife baking pies in her charming cottage in Norwich, Connecticut. She was not even sure she *wanted* to be chosen. It was not something she had come to expect. In all her years of living in the haveli and watching men come and go, men who were passionate or cold, affectionate or humble, lofty, rich, poor, sharp or dull, none had ever whisked a courtesan off to domestic respectability.

She left everyone downstairs and went up to her room for some privacy. She stood, staring down into the street, her ceiling fan whirring away, when Patience knocked softly on the door and walked in.

'I know you laugh at these things, Yassu, but there is something to them,' Patience said.

'So, I shall put Mrs Lafaver in a lemon—which by the way, are very hard to come by these days—and what will happen?'

'That I can't say, but at least she won't be tugging at him as much.'

Yasmine sighed. 'He wants to go home. He hates India.'

'I know,' Patience nodded. 'Who can blame him?'

'When you say these things, I am reminded of our differences,' Yasmine said. She did not consider herself a patriot, but whenever Patience criticised India, she bristled. It was the same when Edward said anything. The irony was that they never said a thing that was not based on some truth. India was an infuriating, horrific place at times. But it was all she knew. Everyone kept telling her how savage it was, but what place wasn't, Yasmine would argue with Patience and Edward. The world was at war. India's horror was theoretical for her, really. She grew up finding commonplace what the Europeans had trouble digesting. Yes, it was a terrible place at times, venal even, and Calcutta was its capital in many ways. She never denied that; but she felt she had the right to feel these things, as she was a complete Indian, through and through, and a Bengali, no less; whereas Patience and Edward were white. Well, mostly white, in Patience's case. Patience's fervent hope was to leave India behind forever. It did not occur to Yasmine that there were just too many bad memories for Patience here.

'I made my bed, let a Yank lie in it, and now he will leave,' Yasmine said, shrugging. She didn't want to fight about the state of the country. It was a useless argument.

'Yes, I suppose. Like our fathers did, nah, ducky?' Patience said. 'Big old circle.'

~

That night, Edward showed up to the club slightly inebriated because they had started the evening drinking at the ARC. Edward was always distant with Yasmine in front of his fellow officers. She believed it was actually a mark of his regard for her. He did not parade her around as his native mistress, like some others did. Some hapless young women, students from Asutosh College, had not been as lucky, and Calcutta was scandalised with stories of respectable college girls throwing themselves at American soldiers.

In front of his fellow officers, Edward treated Yasmine like the owner of an establishment that he frequented regularly: with jocular familiarity and courtesy. But his eyes followed her around the floor hungrily when she engaged with customers. Yasmine now always made a point of looking fetching for him, to give him pleasure, though she would never admit it to anyone. The nights that he came to the club and they performed the pantomime were exciting. The floor would be crowded with sweaty dancers, the room smoky, too smoky usually, and loud, and then suddenly, Yasmine would look up from talking to someone and see him gazing at her. That secrecy was the exciting part. A room full of people and no one could guess that a few hours before, that man had been holding her, stroking her thigh and telling her how much he wanted her.

Yasmine walked up to his table, as she did many a night, and greeted him and his fellow officers. There was a new man with them. He had the dazed look of someone newly arrived in India. He was relieved when greeted with the familiar energy of a smoke-filled dance floor crowded with only white people. 'I never expected this,' he exclaimed. 'Just like home.'

Edward ordered a round. 'The usual black-market mystery beverage for young Fisher here. He might as well get used to it,' he said, and gave Yasmine a small smile. 'On the rocks.'

She nodded. 'You look especially lovely tonight, Ms Khan,' he added.

She blushed and turned away. His new friend, Fisher, said, 'Damn, Edward, I didn't know you leaned that way.'

Yasmine, who had been about to walk away, froze. He had said it almost under his breath, but she heard it. It was not the worst remark she had ever heard. She turned around slowly and faced them. She wanted to hear what Edward would say.

'I'm sorry, can you repeat your order,' she said mildly. 'I think I missed the last one.'

He did not look at her. He looked down, like he was ashamed. That was how it seemed to her. Like he had been caught stealing.

'Whiskey, neat would be fine,' Edward said.

Yasmine nodded and walked away.

'I was just being polite,' Edward muttered. 'You know, to keep the house happy.'

'I was gonna say!' Fisher said. 'Your wife is the prettiest little girl in the world, bar none. I bet she would look even better wrapped up in one of those toga things they wear.'

'It's called a sari,' Edward muttered again. He looked up and saw Yasmine staring at him from the bar. He got up from the table. 'Excuse me,' he said to the other men at the table and began to walk towards the bar. She quickly walked away before he could reach her and sent over the drinks with a waiter.

She avoided him and his gaze the entire night, making him as miserable as possible. At the end of what had now become an interminable evening for Edward, Patience stood up to sing. She grasped the microphone and looked out at the crowd, hesitating.

'What's the matter with her?' Yasmine whispered to Adil Baboo. They stood in the back, watching. Yasmine always enjoyed Patience's last song of the evening. She was usually exhausted, but her voice was broken in and tender. She sometimes chose a mournful song to end the evening. It made the drunken soldiers cry.

'I usually don't take requests for the last song,' she said. 'But I will make an exception in this case.' She cleared her throat and looked at the bandleader, Pharaoh, and nodded. He put down his baton and instructed the musicians to do the same with their instruments.

'Huh,' Yasmine said. 'Imagine that.' Adil Baboo just shook his head, also at a loss. Patience never sang a cappella.

Her clear, throaty voice, trained for classical ghazals, poured into the microphone.

'It had to be you, it had to be you,' she sang quietly. *'I wandered around and finally found the somebody who, could make me feel blue, could make me be true, or even be glad just to be sad, thinking of you.'*

Patience made this happy song melancholy. There were tears on Yasmine's cheeks and when she looked around at the silent audience, there were quite a few people crying. Edward's eyes were dry as he gazed at her steadily. When Patience finished, it was to silence, except for a few noses being blown into handkerchiefs.

Patience looked down at the subdued audience, puzzled.

'Crikey,' she said. 'It wasn't that bad now, was it?'

Yasmine quickly walked past Edward onto the stage, gave Patience's arm a gentle squeeze and whispered in Bangla, 'That was lovely. Truly. Your mother would have been proud.'

'It was all yours,' Patience said and smiled. She nodded towards where Edward sat with his friends.

Yasmine announced the end of the evening and thanked everyone for their patronage. It was then that they applauded loudly, mollifying Patience. When she walked past Edward again, he was standing up, retrieving his cap and taking one last gulp of whiskey. Yasmine did not look at him.

~

She slipped into the alley to smoke. It was only February but already muggy. A rat scurried by and she shuddered. She half hoped Tommy would show up so they could talk and lament about how horrid the whites were in the end. He would understand, Yasmine thought.

She often thought about Tommy, and even entertained the notion of having one evening a month that she opened the club only for 'coloured folks', as Tommy called them. Adil Baboo said it was not feasible, but she argued the case of keeping up morale, and felt that if she approached the commanding officers, they might be open to it.

Edward came up behind her. She knew he would come and was determined to be cold.

'I have a half-day pass, which has already dwindled down by five hours,' he said. He took off his glasses and wiped them.

'Please don't waste it on my account,' she said, as imperiously as she could.

'When you take that tone with me, it's that thing, right? That you taught me,' he said.

She was curious in spite of herself. 'What thing?' she said, over her shoulder.

'Dhong,' he said, and chuckled. 'Being coy.'

'No, that's nakahmee, coquettish,' she said. 'Dhong is just ... bollocks.' She had been teaching him colloquial Bangla. What he learned from the guidebooks and lessons he had been taking was too formal and wooden.

Edward laughed and tried to hold her. She didn't let him.

'I don't think I'll ever get the hang of Bangla,' he said. 'Or Bengali women.'

'If you think my anger is fake, then you're wrong.'

'Look, Yasmine, what could I do?' he said. 'What could I have said?'

'Nothing, I suppose, but it's still humiliating.'

'I probably should not have said anything at all,' he said. 'I drew attention to you ... and me. I'm sorry.'

Yasmine softened. He sounded sincere.

'I don't know why I get wound up about these things,' she said. 'I'm taking it all far too seriously. You're leaving anyway. This can't last forever.'

'Is that a question?' he said. It was a statement, but she had unwittingly made it sound like a question. She nodded.

'Eventually, I have to go, yes,' he said.

'Back to Norwich,' she said.

'Yes,' he said softly.

'To your wife.'

'That, I don't know,' he said. Yasmine was surprised. 'I'm not ... well, things are a bit different now, but I also want to finish school. There are so many things that were left suspended when we got into the fight.'

'Did you request that song for me?' Yasmine asked. He nodded.

'Corny, huh?'

'Yes, very,' she said, meanly. He put his arms around her waist and kissed the tip of her ear. She let him this time and shivered.

'Can I stay with you tonight?'

She sighed and nodded. He was so hard to resist at times.

'Let me close up the shop,' she said.

She sent him up to her room and walked into the kitchen, where the bearers were cleaning up sleepily.

'Yes, madam?' one of them asked.

'Do you have any lemons left?' she said. Her face was flushed—part of the disadvantage of being light-skinned: by Indian standards, the only disadvantage—and they looked at her curiously.

One of them handed her a small, pathetic-looking lemon, slightly smaller than an egg. It was overripe and soft to the touch. The bearer asked her if she wanted it sliced. No, she said. Is it for lemonade? No, she said. Tea? Uff! she snapped. She told him to mind his bloody business and felt bad at once. He was only trying to help. She said she needed it for cosmetic purposes.

She sent everyone away and wrote out Edward's wife's full name, Margaret Ines Lafaver, in black ink on a tiny chit of paper. She cut a slit into the lemon and slid the paper into the slit. Next, she wrapped the lemon in cheesecloth and placed it at the back of the ice box, with a note in Bengali and English that read: Do not touch, at risk of amputation—The Management.

Eventually, she would tell Patience what she had done but would beg her not to tell anyone else.

'Where did you learn this anyway?' she had asked her when Patience first suggested it, expecting her to say that the old woman, Bina baji, who lived in the alley next to their haveli growing up and was a well-known neighbourhood soothsayer, had taught her.

'An American soldier told me. He said they do this all the time in Italy. And somewhere called the Bronx.'

'This is going to end badly, I think,' Yasmine had said.

Patience nodded. 'I know. But...'

'But?'

'But isn't it just a little bit worth it?'

Yasmine shook her head.

'Then get out of it,' Patience said. When Yasmine just sat there silently despondent, she put her hand on her shoulder and squeezed it. 'I'm sorry Yasmine, really. But there's no way around this one. 'Tis love.'

''Tis doomed,' Yasmine said and laughed.

'Let us see if the lemon works,' Patience had said. 'Try it. Maybe we get rid of the missus. Maybe he'll do right by you.'

And here she was, sensible Yasmine, succumbing to superstition, and not even an Indian one at that, but an American one, with Italian origins. She closed the icebox door and walked up the stairs where Edward waited.

16

'What took so long?' Edward asked when she walked in. He was already undressed, in bed and looking too expectant for Yasmine's taste.

'I had to do something,' she said.

Edward stared at her. 'Why do you look sheepish?'

'Uff, what are you talking about?' Yasmine snapped. Her face was warm. She put her hands on her cheeks.

'Are you like this with Maggie?' Yasmine said quickly, to change the subject.

He sighed. 'Oh boy, here we go.' Maggie again. Yasmine seemed to be bringing her up more frequently.

He sat up and pulled on his boxers. He lit a cigarette and handed it to her.

'Got anything to drink?' she asked.

'I liberated some gin from behind the bar,' he said. He poured her a glass. 'At least, I *think* it's gin. Are you sure you want this? It tastes like formaldehyde.'

She took the glass and finished it in one shot. He held out his hand for her cigarette and took a long drag before handing it back to her.

They sat in semi-companionable silence while she smoked. She hiccupped the gin into her throat and nearly gagged. 'Come here,' he said.

She went and sat next to him. He stroked her hair tenderly. 'I told you that stuff was lethal.'

She nodded and put her head on his shoulder. He kissed her forehead.

'I should rinse out this gin,' she said when he went for her mouth.

'I've tasted it already. It won't make a difference,' he said, laughing. She was acting skittish. He leaned back when she turned her head away again.

'Is there something on your mind?' he asked.

'You are always so eager,' she said.

'Isn't that a good thing?'

'Yes, but are you like this at home?'

Edward sighed. It could be a trick question, he thought. He was not at all sure. If he said, yes, that would indicate that he was merely a horny SOB; but it could be that Yasmine was insinuating that he was more ardent with her because he viewed her as a sexual plaything. He hesitated and thought about it. Unfortunately, in doing so, it conjured up images of Maggie in his mind, thus killing any desire he felt for Yasmine at that moment. Not that he wanted Maggie instead—it was guilt. Unable to articulate this, he cleared his throat.

Yasmine looked at him and gave a short, bitter laugh. 'You're thinking about her,' she said.

'And whose fault is that?'

'Am I a bit on the side or something?'

She had never asked him this before. They had been seeing one another for nearly two months and had only made love a handful of times. Each time was more passionate than the last. He had been careful about not pushing her. He knew she was sensitive about how she was perceived. She had explained to him, at length, the history of the courtesan in India, and he was enthralled by it, pleased to learn something that most Americans did not know. He was pretty sure there were no courtesans in the US, only hookers. Mistresses were probably the closest things to courtesans they had. But that was not what changed his perception of Yasmine as an elegant 'madam'. It was spending time with her, her sharpness and curiosity and earnest desire to better herself. She was more tender than she cared to admit, and a shrewd businesswoman. Her no-nonsense demeanour and stick-to-itiveness were reminiscent of Yankee tenacity. If anyone could make it through a harsh New England winter with one bin of coal and a field of frozen carrots, it was Yasmine Khan. She would have fit in just fine in Norwich with the other austere Yanks, he thought, if it were not for her colour. As it were, if she ever visited, she would be a creature of curiosity and derision. For the first time in his life, he viewed the people in the town he so loved as narrow-minded and unkind. What he previously admired, their fierce loyalty, would work against both him and Yasmine. If he threw Maggie over and showed up in town with Yasmine, well, he shuddered to think about the hell there would be to pay. Not so much for him, but for her and whatever kids came along. She would never be accepted as one of them, and his children would be outcasts.

'Edward? Are you listening to me?' Yasmine said. She snapped her fingers under his nose.

'I should go,' he said. 'It's late, and if this is how it's going to be, I better just leave.' He stood up and looked down at Yasmine, who seemed ready to cry.

'You wasted the time, baby, worrying about things you shouldn't.' He kissed her mouth gently. She wrapped her lithe legs around his hips and pulled him down on top of her.

~

They had both briefly fallen asleep holding one another, and Edward had only a few minutes to spare, but Yasmine—as usual after morning sex—was in a chatty mood. She lay naked on top of him and asked what he was worried about. Somehow, she could tell he was anxious about something.

'Well, dying soon for one thing,' he said and chuckled. 'The chances of that have inordinately increased since I got here.'

'They're not calling you up, though, are they?' she said. 'They don't need you to build the road. You're not an engineer.'

He sighed and stroked her dark head.

'I was talking about dysentery, but yes, they need me. They need all of us. We can't win unless we commit more troops, but the wacky thing is, it's strictly voluntary when it should be mandatory. FDR doesn't see it.'

'Does Churchill?' she asked. 'I would imagine not—his goal is to fight off the Germans. He underestimates the Japs.'

Edward smiled to himself. Yasmine was so intelligent. He kissed the top of her head.

'He's better, but myopic too.'

'I think the Japanese will be harder to beat than the Germans,' Yasmine said. She nuzzled his neck.

Edward wasn't sure and he said as much. Yasmine chuckled.

'Why? Because they're slanty eyed Asians? Don't be fooled. One thing about us Asians is that we rarely surrender. We fight until all the blood is drained from every last man, and I think the Japs are the best at it.'

'Maybe.' He was sceptical.

'Will you volunteer?' Yasmine asked.

'No plans just yet. Maybe when you finally drive me nuts.'

'That's very amusing.'

'Don't be sore. You really have to learn to laugh at yourself, Yasmine,' Edward said.

She didn't respond to that. Her heart was too heavy. 'When I asked you if you were worried, I was talking about other things,' she said eventually.

Edward groaned. They had only a few moments left together before he had to sneak back to camp, because he had overstayed his pass—something he never would have done three months ago. He did not want to spend it fighting.

He intuited—somewhat shakily—that she wanted him to say: 'I am worried what will happen when I leave here. And I love you.' Edward and most of his male acquaintances believed that was all women really ever wanted to hear anyway; that, and 'you are the most beautiful woman I have ever seen'.

So, he said: 'Listen … beautiful, I don't worry when I'm with you. In fact, that's the only time I am at peace.'

He knew that was not going to suffice. He knew she was sharp enough to see through it as an evasive tactic. The funny thing, of course, was that he had told her the truth—but it was not the truth she wanted to hear.

Sure enough, Yasmine frowned at him and said, 'That sounds like something Gable would say, only he would say "doll-face" instead of "beautiful".'

According to Patience, Clark Gable was in the doghouse because of something to do with his wife and the plane crash and Lana Turner. He had barely listened to what she had told him about the whole sad incident. He dismissed it as idle feminine chatter. Now, though, when Yasmine compared him to Gable, he knew it was bad news.

He looked at his watch, another tactical error, but he only did it because he knew she wanted to fight, and he was trying to see how much time they had to do that and make up before he had to sprint back to Tollygunge. He decided he would take rooms at the Red Cross so he would not have such a distance to travel.

She rolled off him rather roughly and deliberately jabbed him in the abdomen with her elbow as she got up.

'All these orientalists sure didn't know what they were talking about when they said the Indian woman is submissive,'

Edward called out to her as she disappeared into the adjoining bathroom. 'The joke's on those poor bastards!' he muttered when she didn't take the bait. 'And on me.'

In the bathroom, Yasmine splashed cool water on her face and gathered her thoughts. She should not have lost her temper. She knew anger made her weaker. She also needed Edward's help with something she knew he might not be amenable to, and her tantrum was not going to help matters. Patience had coached her on how to handle Edward when she wanted something from him that he may not readily give.

Edward lit a cigarette and waited for Yasmine to come out. When she hadn't, even after fifteen minutes, he started to get impatient.

The thing about Yasmine, Edward knew, was that she was not unreasonable or prone to melodramatic fits. She was less staid than Maggie, but practical all the same. Somehow, her pragmatism was more feminine than his wife's, he thought guiltily. Something was eating at her. He simply did not have the time to find out what it was and then mollify her.

He was fully dressed when she finally emerged and about to knock on the door of the room she had retreated to, ready to apologise, though as usual, he was not sure about what. She was dressed in one of those outfits that had billowy pants, with a long tunic over it and a diaphanous scarf draped around her shoulders. She looked lovely, but he was sufficiently irritated to keep this information to himself.

'I hate you,' she said, quite calmly. 'That was what I decided when I was in there.'

'You were in there for an awfully long time. That's all you came up with?'

Now he was deeply irritated. He was risking court-martial for this?

'Well, I hate you too,' he said. Two can play this game, missy, he thought.

Yasmine looked genuinely shocked, as if she had never considered the possibility.

'No,' she said, drawing out the words, as if talking to a slow-witted child. 'I hate you, you don't hate me.'

Edward smiled. 'Well, thank you for clearing that up. And on that note, I have to go.'

Yasmine watched as he put his cap on and finished tucking in his shirt. She needed his help, and now she had made him peevish, she thought. Patience was right, she did not know how to beguile a man. She was hopeless.

'I need your help with something,' she said in what she hoped was a conciliatory voice. 'Can't you stay a bit?'

It was a sudden switch. She was now smiling at him coyly. She felt awkward and was sure Edward saw right through it. 'More bees with honey' kept ringing in her ears. Patience's voice.

Edward put his head in his hands and groaned. 'Sweetheart, I really can't keep up here. One second you hate me, the next you're smiling at me all googly-eyed. I have a bruise on my stomach where you elbowed me just now—'

Yasmine waved her hand in his face to shush him. 'Edward, please stop whinging and carrying on. This is important.'

Edward looked at her and then sat down, exasperated.

'Okay. Really, only a minute, tell me what's up. Wait, oh god, you're not ...?' He looked at her stomach.

'Uff-oh, no!' Yasmine said.

'Are you sure? You're all moody and wacky and it's not like you to—'

'Edward, please! Just stop!'

'Phew, okay, go ahead. But be quick, honey.'

She hesitated, and Edward sighed and resisted glancing at his wristwatch.

'Yasmine, I have to go, please be nice,' he pleaded. 'I don't want to go, I *have* to. Do you understand the difference? I want to stay and fight and then make up, but I can't.'

'All right. I was wondering if you could direct me to the person I need to speak to, to open the club to your Negro personnel one night a month.'

Edward's surprise was visible. He did not reply at once.

'I would prefer to have it opened to them bi-monthly, but I think your "brass"—as you call them—would balk at the idea, not to mention the Brits. My god! Can you imagine? They would all faint!' she chirped away. 'What next, mate?' she said, in her best English accent. 'Gandhi as Viceroy?'

Edward looked at the ground.

'Is this about Tommy?' he asked quietly.

'Yes!' Yasmine replied sincerely, not hearing the ominous tone in her lover's voice. It *was,* after all, about him. He was the inspiration. She was plagued with guilt for turning him and his pals away that first time and wondered had she not, would Radhika have ever been hurt? She had started thinking about karmic retribution lately.

'Honey, I don't think that's a good idea,' Edward said in a measured voice. He knew he would have to tread carefully. He did not want to react at once to Yasmine's interest in Tommy, though it evoked in him a deep jealousy that he would have trouble concealing for long.

Yasmine frowned. 'Why not? Isn't it just as important to keep up the Negro soldiers' morale as it is everyone else's? Are they not part of the great Allied war machine? How are they supposed to do their jobs and fight when they are given no respite or recreation? Is that just?'

She made a valid argument.

'You're right, honey—'

'Stop calling me "honey". You do that when you disagree with me. You're trying to mollycoddle me.'

'This is not a game,' Edward said.

'No kidding!'

'Look, you're going up against something huge here,' he said.

'I know,' Yasmine said. 'You Americans are so strange. Here you are in a native woman's room, but you don't think it's right to allow your fellow soldiers into my establishment because they are black. Tommy has more character than the lot of you!'

Edward stood up, towering over her. She folded her arms and stared back at him.

'Why so much interest in Tommy, Yasmine? Is there something you need to tell me?'

Yasmine tried to keep her tone even. 'Are you mad?' She had yet to tell Edward that Tommy named his friend, Louis, as the likely rapist. She was unsure how to broach it as it was Tommy's word against Louis's, a white man. She believed, in the end, that Edward would defend Louis. Adil Baboo's words—'they all stick together'—had stayed with her.

'What? Can't imagine yourself fucking a black man?' he said, when she remained silent. 'Tell me, doesn't he deserve to have his morale boosted just as much as you boost mine regularly?'

She had never seen him like this. He looked grim.

'I don't understand you,' she said. 'I'm trying to help the war effort. These men, Negro or not, are part of that.'

'Oh, right. They raped your girl—'

'Tommy didn't, and they have still to prove that his friends did.'

'Have you asked the girl?'

'I have.'

'And?'

'And she said she's no longer sure.'

Edward's retort died in his throat. He did not expect Yasmine to say that.

'Who ... who else does she think it could be?'

'That's the problem. He hit her from the back, knocked her to the ground. She never saw his face. You know, I believe Tommy told me the truth when he said his friends were innocent. And you know in your heart it was *your* friend who did this.'

'Louis? I don't know. He was very drunk when I tucked him into bed that night you kicked him out. Can you be totally sure yourself?'

Yasmine shrugged. He lit another cigarette and handed it to her.

'I'm not sure, but I just know it wasn't Tommy.' She said this with confidence, like she knew him so well.

Edward could barely conceal his jealousy, 'And how do you know this? You talk to him a lot?'

Yasmine sighed. 'Can't you just tell about someone, Edward? Can't you just feel, in your bones, when someone is dodgy or someone is, what do you Yanks say? A stand-up guy?'

Edward glanced at his watch and did not answer her. He could not meet her eyes because he understood what she was saying. He thought of Louis's turgid face. Yes, he wanted to say. I know what you mean. He was silent.

'But you choose to think the worst of him?' she said. She knew she was pushing and should leave well enough alone. 'Because he is a Negro?'

'They're different, honey, from you and me.'

'He's paler than I am,' she said quietly. 'But we're not so different. Just go now, Edward,' she said after a moment.

'Fine by me.'

'Don't slam the door,' she said. 'I don't want anyone knowing anything.'

She heard him pounding down the stairs and slamming out the front door, and closed her eyes. His noisy departure had rattled the windows on the first floor. Now everyone would know. About five minutes later, on cue, there was a soft knock on her door.

Patience and Asma stood in the hallway. Both were sleepy.

'What's the racket?' Patience said.

'Yasmine, you have to keep it down here,' Asma admonished and yawned. 'This is not how ladies behave.' She wandered sleepily back to her room.

Yasmine sat at her vanity table and clutched her head in her hands.

'I'm coming undone,' she said.

'Yes, I can see that,' Patience said. She sat next to her on the vanity stool and put her arm around her friend's shoulder.

'I never behave this way,' Yasmine said.

'What is it about him that makes you storm about so?' Patience said.

'You heard me?' Yasmine said.

'They heard you in Bucksoddingham palace,' Patience replied, smiling. 'He is handsome, I admit, and smells nice and is polite, but so bloody what? And you never really like the dashing ones. This is the first time. You are more Spencer Tracy's girl, nah? Not Gable's.'

'I don't know what it is,' Yasmine said.

She was just as baffled as Edward about their need for one another. They discussed the war and books and the first thing they would eat when the rationing stopped and made love and danced in her room to the tinny wind-up Victrola. She had introduced him to Rabindra Sangeet, he had introduced her to Billie Holiday. Normal things. They did not dwell on what would come afterwards or what was happening to them as the war went on. They had been successful in keeping the world at bay, and this meant they kept any talk of feelings to a minimum. But she knew this was temporary.

'Be sure of what you want, Yassu. I think you can make him love you. I think he might already—but remember what our mothers told us. Love is never enough, no matter what Ghalib says. Love is hungama. Somehow, it's always us dames that get trapped.'

Yasmine nodded. She had seen what romantic love did to women like her and Patience and her mother, Daisy. It was erosive and a siren's call. It was an illusion. Because there was never any promise behind it. No weddings, no legitimacy, no constancy. It was good, she thought, that Patience reminded her of this.

'But you know, ducky,' Patience said, thoughtfully, 'he's mad with jealousy right now, so maybe you're doing just fine.'

17

When she was a young girl, Yasmine's mother told her that, during the Great War, British soldiers were fighting in the trenches and getting trounced by the Germans when a flock of angels appeared and saved them from being killed. This story was later proven to be false, but many people believed it for a long time. More bizarre was the fact that, at Christmas time, they stopped shooting at one another, came to the middle of the muddy, bloodied battlefield and exchanged tobacco and sang carols before going back to killing each other. So, Yasmine wondered, what was more absurd? Frozen lemons as talismans against abandonment or war itself?

It seemed to her that more people fell in love and more babies were made during wartime than any other. It was the survivors' way of spitting in war's eye, she surmised. Oddly, some people had more of a desperate inclination to love when a war was on.

Now that Yasmine had given in to the lemon, the floodgates were open, and when Patience urged her to go to a fortune-teller, she agreed.

Bina baji's 'office' had moved further down the alley next to the old haveli, and she seemed frozen at an indeterminate age—between fifty and one hundred fifty. She had enough patrons and goodwill that she could have moved her office indoors at some point—with maybe even a place to live—but she preferred the open, if somewhat miasmic air of Calcutta, to some stuffy little room. Her hair was pure white and fell to her shoulders in stringy, oily tendrils, was in stark contrast to her leathery, dark skin. But she was clean. How she maintained hygiene in that alley was a mystery, but she was very particular. And though she wore no bodice underneath her sari, the sari itself was always clean and even neatly hemmed.

She gave Yasmine a footstool to sit on and indicated a spot that was not wet. It had rained the night before. She squatted on her haunches, took Yasmine's hand and closed her eyes.

'Ah, yes,' she said, after a full two minutes. 'I have him in my sight.'

Yasmine's legs were cramping from sitting so low and she shifted her weight uncomfortably. Bina baji's eyes flew open, and she smiled at Yasmine. She had one tooth. It was perfectly in the centre of her bottom gum and the shape of a small tombstone, with a rounded top and straight sides.

'Yasmine, you were always very rude to me,' she lisped suddenly. 'So arrogant. A Miss Know-it-all.'

'I know,' Yasmine conceded. Growing up, Yasmine had found fortune-telling complete nonsense and scoffed at her mother and others who believed in it. She did not believe in the Sufi pir her mother swore by either. He was a distant member of their family and lived in a village in Chittagong—Mirzakhil, it was called—in a cluster of banyan and peepul trees. Her mother would visit him every once in a while when something or someone plagued her. Yasmine did not trust these types—no matter how well they quoted Hafiz. This particular pir was able to add to his bungalow in the thicket because of all his insights to her mother and was the only one in the village in possession of a radio and a bicycle, which made Yasmine suspicious of him.

'Why does he need a radio,' she asked Shirin, 'since he has a direct line to Allah? Shouldn't divine music be playing in his head constantly?'

Her mother had boxed Yasmine's ears for that.

'I know I have not been warm in the past,' Yasmine said to Bina baji, trying to mollify her. 'But I hope this in no way affects how you see my future.'

'I have no hand in your future. That's Allah's job. But your arrogance has lessened somewhat.'

'Well, that's good news then,' she said.

Bina baji frowned at her. 'Well?' she said.

'You said you have him in your sight,' Yasmine reminded her.

'Yes. He is your man, your lover, and so on.'

Yasmine tried to laugh cheerfully. 'I already know that, Bina baji.'

'His energy is scattered here and there, like leaves in the wind. Very easily pulled away from you and then pulled back. You have power over him, you know. But so does another.'

'Yes, yes,' Yasmine said, impatient. 'I put her in a lemon, so...'

Bina baji looked surprised. 'Well, good. Did you freeze the lemon?'

'Why, yes, I did.' It was Yasmine's turn to be surprised.

Bina baji popped a paan leaf into her mouth, chewed thoughtfully and then spat a long stream of rust-red betel nut juice at her bare feet. Yasmine pulled her feet under her sari.

'Who did you lemonise?' the old woman asked.

Yasmine cleared her throat.

'His wife,' she said. Her voice was barely above a whisper. She had a powerful urge to run. She was ashamed.

'Oh. Well, you didn't need to put the wife in the lemon at all,' Bina baji said matter-of-factly.

'Why not?' Yasmine said. She remembered why she had never liked the old woman. She was smug. 'Who should I have put in the lemon?' Yasmine said, scowling as Bina baji picked her teeth with a twig she had extracted from the folds of her sari.

'The wife is not the problem,' Bina baji said.

'Is it another woman, then? Besides his wife?' Yasmine said after a moment. Her voice was small. She cleared her throat, preparing for the answer.

Bina shrugged a skeletal shoulder and scoffed.

'It's not always as simple as a rival,' she said. 'He is struggling to find his way. He is fighting his weaknesses. The problem is, you are one of his weaknesses. Does he drink very much?'

Yasmine nodded yes. 'But they all do,' she said.

'Yes, but not all of them dwell in darkness.'

'What does that mean?' Yasmine said, half sobbing.

'It means that he will hurt you, but, you can avoid that.'

'By leaving him?'

'No, by not allowing him to go home. He must never leave here. He can and will leave his old life behind if you make him stay. He will soon forget ... her, the wife, and make his life with you ... only, he is not from here. I am feeling his energy is foreign. Is he Gujarati?'

'No.'

'Marathi?'

'No, he's—'

'Ah, he's Sindhi.'

'Uff, dhutt! He's American!' Yasmine cried with more force than she intended.

Bina baji's eyes widened. 'Hmm. An officer.'

'Yes.'

'Oh, my dear. Oh my.'

'Yes, yes, I know. Please don't be tiresome, Bina baji.' Yasmine twisted the anchal of her sari around her fingers.

'What do you know? You might lose him altogether to the war. Ever considered that?'

Bina baji was speaking in generalities. Nothing was revelatory. Yasmine, fed up, stood to leave. Bina baji took Yasmine's hand, stopping her. Her eyes looked past her, theatrically. 'You will raise your son alone.'

Yasmine swallowed and dabbed at the beads of sweat on her brow.

'You mean, who? Edward's son?' Her heart began to race.

'No, yours. That is all I can see now. Who his father is, has yet to be decided. It might purely be up to you.'

And then, the old woman was finished. She smiled pleasantly, flashing her single tooth, and Yasmine knew it was time to pay her.

One of the junkies who haunted the alleyways had meandered into Bina baji's 'office'. He stood, shirtless, in a filthy dhoti that was wrapped precariously low around his skinny hips, scratching a scab on his arm and staring at the two women balefully. He was so thin, Yasmine felt sorry for him. His dirty hair and beard were long and knotted. Bina baji glared at him, but he was undaunted. They had a staring contest, which Bina baji won but only because he grew interested in what Yasmine was extracting from her purse. Bina baji indicated that Yasmine should wait until he left, but he refused to go. Finally, she grew so frustrated she stood up, and in two quick strides was next to him. She grabbed his ear and led him out of the alley. He went without protest. She was strong, for an old woman.

'My youngest,' she said matter-of-factly when she returned.

Yasmine was shocked. She'd had no idea the old woman had children, let alone more than one.

'They can cause a mother more grief than she can bear,' she said. 'You'll see. Try to arrange it so your son has a father,' she said, abruptly changing the subject. 'Someone who is always with him. He will need this. He will be headstrong and as arrogant as you, but he will need his father.'

She unrolled the end of her sari and took out a tightly wrapped paan leaf, which she popped into her mouth. She replaced the paan with the money, and then tied the end of the sari into a knot.

'Why are you scowling at me?' she asked.

'Well, of course he will have a father,' Yasmine snapped. 'I am not the mother of Jesus.'

'Even he had a father,' Bina baji said.

Yasmine shook her head and smoothed down the folds of her sari. 'Barely,' she said.

'Tomar kopallay dukkoh aahcheh,' Bina said. 'You have suffering ahead of you.'

For days afterward, Yasmine wished she had not gone to see the old woman. Her words haunted her. Yet, she was inexplicably intrigued by the prospect of having a son. What would he look like, being half her and half Edward? Light-skinned, of course. Would he need spectacles? Would he inherit her love of books and his father's love of that useless sport, baseball? How does an Indian-American boy navigate the world? He would not be British. Her thoughts surprised her. Why was she even thinking about this?

PART THREE

OF MAGGOTS AND MEN

If history were taught in the form of stories, it would never be forgotten.

–Rudyard Kipling

18

Soon after New Year's Eve and Tommy's revelations, Yasmine had attempted to talk to Radhika about the night of her attack. But it had been like conversing with someone who did not speak the same language as her. In the end, Yasmine did most of the talking, while Radhika stared at her blankly.

'He hit me from the back, with his fist. I don't remember anything after that, except the burning between my legs and waking up bloodied and alone,' was all she said.

She was lying, Yasmine suspected. But what could she do? Her upbringing amongst women whose very lives depended on astutely reading situations and men's sudden shifts in mood had prepared Yasmine for life. It seemed all this empirical intelligence failed her only when it came to Edward. She was rarely able to maintain cool objectivity where he was concerned, and became hotheaded and defensive, but this was really the only time this would happen. Generally, Yasmine was the picture of calm and detachment. Nonetheless, since Patience had been a much better student at courtesanship growing up, Yasmine asked her if she thought Radhika was lying.

'Of course, she's lying,' Patience said. 'She was attacked for sure, but she is hiding something—or protecting someone.'

'Herself?'

'She's scared, Yassu,' Patience said. 'For sure.'

'Of whom?'

Patience shrugged. 'Whoever did this to her,' she said. 'The girl always looks slightly haunted anyway, so it's hard to tell. Maybe that old djinn in the tree put a curse on her,' she offered.

'That is not by any means helpful,' Yasmine said.

Radhika had been making herself useful in the kitchen; in time, she became attached to Adil Baboo and absorbed everything he had to teach. At first, when she was with him, Radhika seemed like the seventeen-year-old she was, giggling and trying to gain approval. She was not as sullen around Rahul either, and the two were flirtatious and playful under Adil Baboo's watchful eye.

That Radhika was starved for love and wanted protection tugged at Yasmine, but she was uncomfortable with neediness. She was more than happy to leave Adil Baboo to deal with the girl. He and Rahul did not find her lugubrious. They were kind to her, and patient. She grew lighter and less aloof, and more trusting of Adil Baboo first, and then Rahul. Her stripes changed around the other men in the club, easing the tension. She was more pleasant, giggly, almost dizzy at times—the kind of coquetry Asma felt was untoward. She sometimes unplaited her long hair and let it cascade around her shoulders in thick waves. Yasmine admonished her that vanity had no place in the kitchen and that her loose hair would make it harder to do her job. Before the assault, she had kept to herself. Now, she was very inquisitive with them, in a childlike way that made her disarming. Pharaoh even offered to give her piano lessons, much to Yasmine's surprise. No one but he was allowed to touch the frequently out-of-tune piano, a pre-mutiny relic that Yasmine had purchased for a song from an elderly English couple who were selling the entire contents of their bungalow and going back home to their beloved Stoke Newington after forty-three years.

Yasmine discreetly observed Radhika growing bolder with the men, asking for things—extra helpings of rice at meals from Adil Baboo, money from Rahul—and they, in turn, growing more affectionate and protective. It bothered Yasmine but she also wondered if it did so only because she was imagining it as a threat. Asma could not surrender the notion that Radhika would be everyone's undoing.

'Hoodoo, hoodoo, I am telling you, nah?' Patience said when Asma complained again. She was only half teasing. 'Some people are simply bad luck!'

'It is illogical to me,' Yasmine protested, yet again, because that seemed so unkind. 'How can a person be bad luck? In the end, the only bad luck that has occurred has happened to *her*.'

They watched Radhika as she wiped down the bar and tables one afternoon. She had filled out a little, now that she was eating more regularly, and looked healthier. Radhika stepped back to view her handiwork and caught Patience and Yasmine staring at her intently. Both women looked away quickly, but of course, it was too late.

'Okay Radhika, now do the floors!' Yasmine said gruffly. The girl started putting the chairs on top of the tables. Yasmine felt guilty.

'No one can remain a child after what happened to her,' Patience whispered.

'Yes, but surely it does not mean she is bad luck!' Yasmine said.

'She has let something into her life,' Patience insisted. 'Something dark. Maybe that djinn—'

'Please! Stop that djinn bollocks,' Yasmine said, weary of Patience's superstitions.

'Can I start at the bar?' Radhika said quietly behind them. Patience and Yasmine both jumped. Their heads had been together, and they had turned away from her to whisper.

'Uff-oh, Radhika! How many bloody times have I told you not to sneak up like that?' Yasmine said, trying not to sound guilty. The girl was silent. 'Oh, never mind. Go see if Adil Baboo needs anything in the kitchen.'

Radhika hesitated. 'I went to Karnani to make extra money,' she said, her voice barely audible. 'I was greedy, and I was punished for it.'

Patience and Yasmine looked at one another, abashed.

'No,' Yasmine said. 'You did what any one of us might have done. You saw an opportunity and took it. We are all survivors.'

Patience nodded. 'It doesn't matter if you robbed them blind, jaan, you didn't deserve what happened to you.'

'Remember that,' Yasmine said. Radhika nodded, giving them a small smile, and went into the kitchen.

~

Later, on one of her Saturday evenings in Burdwan, Yasmine sat in her mother's lush garden and asked her if she thought some people attracted misfortune. This had been weighing on her mind a great deal recently.

'Yes, I believe in that fully,' her mother said.

'Like Daisy?'

Her mother nodded. 'But Patience does not, because she is a sunny, if wayward, child. Daisy is a fool. Here she has a wonderful girl, who is the key to her salvation. All she has to do is watch how Patience conducts her life and see it is full of light and not shadow.' Yasmine nodded. She did not tell her mother that Patience would most likely never bear children.

Her mother was right. Very little cowed Patience. She always managed to smile or crack a joke no matter how dire the situation. Maybe Patience would have made a solid go of raising a baby. Yasmine wondered how much her friend resented her interference in the end. She seemed, at the moment, to not have a care in the world—with a camp full of soldiers to salivate over her.

'Why are you asking me this?' her mother said.

'I am wondering what to do with Radhika. She's very secretive.'

'Secrets are power,' her mother said. 'To keep one guessing is to keep them in a sort of stupor.'

Yasmine disagreed. Radhika made her uneasy at times, but she did not think that the girl was withholding information because she wanted control. She was doing it, Yasmine believed, because she was afraid of the consequences. Radhika had already broken many of the rules that Yasmine had laid out in the very beginning, and it was only the girl's terrible misfortune that had kept her from getting the boot. For all her strictness, Yasmine did not believe in turning her back on another female in need, unless her hand was absolutely forced.

'I don't think this is the case, Amma,' Yasmine said. 'Not telling me is hardly keeping me in thrall.'

'Not you; men. She is fragile. They would want to protect her from further assault.'

'I think she is traumatised.'

Her mother sighed and nodded. She agreed that the girl was permanently damaged by what had happened to her.

At least the men who worked at the Duck treated Radhika with tremendous gentleness and understanding. Yasmine was gratified by that as, traditionally, a girl who had been attacked would be viewed as impure. But, as she often thought and said, Bombay Duck was decidedly not India.

19

Radhika continued to insist that she remembered nothing, and Tommy's fellow soldiers were finally shipped back to America and dishonourably discharged, which, Tommy had explained bitterly, sealed their fates back home. She sent Rahul to invite him when he could get leave to come to the Duck and visit with her, so she could offer her apologies and allow Tommy to give vent to his feelings on the matter. Edward had yet to let her know if he was able to talk to his CO and others about allowing non-white soldiers, both enlisted and officers, to patronise the club one night a month, so she had taken matters into her own hands—at least where Tommy was concerned.

'They're disgraced now,' he told Yasmine the afternoon he came to see her. 'And I'm tainted by association.'

Yasmine poured him two fingers of whiskey on the house, even though he insisted on paying, and tried to comfort him.

'Miss Yasmine, I want to thank you for all the kindness you've shown me,' he said. He hesitated and laughed nervously.

'What is it?'

'Do you ever think about New Year's Eve?'

Yasmine blushed. 'Yes, of course, but so many things happened that night—'

'I see,' Tommy said quietly. He looked down at his drink.

Yasmine tried to find the right words. 'It's not what you think.'

'I don't think nothing,' he said. His handsome face was impassive.

'I was overwrought that night,' Yasmine said.

'Sure,' Tommy said, misunderstanding. 'And you got confused and kissed me.'

Yasmine shook her head. 'No, that's not it. I just, well, I don't know what to say to you because I don't understand what happened, but I was not confused.'

'What then? Are you in love with Lt Lafaver?'

The question was a surprise. Tommy felt the silence and her confusion was an opportunity to tell her the truths that he so wanted to share. His truths.

'Miss Yasmine, you're fooling yourself here. He ain't ever goin' to leave his wife. He can't marry you, he can't take you home. I've seen it before—shoot, I'm here because of it. You can tell, right? That I have at least one white parent? My mama had four children by my father, a white man, and when we would walk into town, all of us single file behind mama, high yellow ducklings, they called us, kind of like the ones you have here—' He stopped, not sure if he had gone too far. Yasmine smiled.

'I'm not sure Patience would appreciate that description, but it's very vivid. Go on, please,' she said when Tommy remained silent.

'Well, we would have to walk right past his house, and sometimes, he was on the porch with his friends or his wife, smoking his pipe, and he would look down at his feet, his hands, the dirt, anywhere but us. He never even nodded at mama, and sure, when he would come to us he was different—he was our father. He held us and bought us things and tanned us when we sassed him, but I can never forget how this same man did not even look at us when white folks was around. I was barely three and I didn't know he was not my father when we was in town, and I saw him and ran to him, wanting him to pick me up and swing me around like he did at home, and he just shoved me to the ground and left me there. When he came to us that Sunday after church where he was a deacon, he tried to explain to me why I could never do that again. He told me he was not my daddy when we was in town, and that it was for my safety. Then he kissed me, but it was never the same. He came to see me off when I enlisted. His other boys—the ones who were his sons all the time—enlisted too. One died in Italy, my brother, but he said he was proud of me especially because of what I was signing up for. Is that what you want for yourself, Yasmine? For your children? You've got schooling. My mama did not go to school past eight years old, so what choices did she have? But you're a lady. This doesn't have to be your life.'

She said nothing and poured him another shot. Her hands shook and Tommy stopped her. 'I'm sorry. I've been told I talk too much,' he said gently.

'Not that I can offer you anything better,' he said when she was still quiet. He gave a short laugh, not sure how to continue. He could not tell her how much he thought about her. 'I'm not educated like you, though I aim to change that. They have colleges for Negros, you know? If I live, I'm going to look into it. I passed the 11th grade, which is good, considering. But the life I have waiting for me back home is not for you. I just don't want to see you get thrown away,' Tommy said. 'You deserve to be treated like a lady. Too many ladies get thrown away, don't they? White people throw away precious things all the time without a second thought. My mama always called them wastrels.'

'Indian people are no better, you know?' Yasmine said.

To her horror, Yasmine felt tears prick her eyes. Lately, she had been emotional, taken to crying suddenly without warning. Things she was impervious to before—a three-legged puppy, songs sung in minor keys, a particularly brilliant shade of red—made her cry. Beauty and vulnerability affected her now.

Yasmine was about to say something more, but Radhika wandered in then, to sweep the floor, and stopped abruptly when she saw Tommy sitting at the bar. She started to leave, but Yasmine, relieved for the distraction, called her back.

Yasmine studied Radhika's face. She could not detect fear or even recognition, though she knew the girl knew him.

'Radhika, say hello, nah?'

The girl nodded. Tommy nodded back.

'Do you have something to say to him?'

Radhika looked at Yasmine. 'I'll translate,' Yasmine offered.

'No,' Radhika said after a moment. 'I have nothing to say. Please, can I go now, Yasmine di?'

'Are you sure?' Yasmine said, gently.

'I told you, Yasmine di,' she said.

Yasmine came out from behind the bar and took Radhika's hands in both of hers. 'So you tell me you don't really know who hurt you, Radhika?'

Radhika nodded but remained silent.

'Was it Campbell, the man you danced with?'

'Not him,' Radhika said quietly.

'A black man?'

Radhika hesitated. Yasmine turned to Tommy.

'I asked her if the man was white or black,' she told him. 'Radhika, please. This man's friends were shipped home in disgrace.'

The girl looked up then. 'So, they are gone?' she said.

'Yes, so?'

'Then it's over,' the girl said. 'It's done. Please leave me alone.'

'It's not done!' Yasmine said. 'What about justice?'

'Yasmine di, please!'

Yasmine looked down to see she was grasping the girl's thin wrists tightly. She released her.

'Let her be, Yasmine,' Tommy said. 'She won't talk.'

Tommy got up from the stool and walked up to Radhika. He towered over her. The girl looked up at him, but she was not frightened, Yasmine noticed at once. He smiled at her. He held out his hand. Radhika's arms hung limply at her side. Tommy dropped his hand.

'She looks like my kid sister,' he said.

Bloody hell, Yasmine thought, and decided not to fight the fresh tears that began to fall.

He turned to Yasmine. 'I want to say something to her. Can you translate for me please?'

Yasmine nodded. 'Radhika, listen,' she said.

'It's not fair, it's not right, but it is what it is for the likes of us,' Tommy said gently. 'They think they own us, and they do whatever they want. And now it's done. So you got to forget it.'

Yasmine stopped speaking. Radhika was crying. Tommy took out a handkerchief and held it out to the girl.

Radhika shook her head but gave him a wan smile.

'May I go, di?' she asked Yasmine.

Yasmine nodded and the girl left, without looking at Tommy.

'Maybe she really doesn't remember,' Yasmine said to him. She wiped her eyes with the edge of her anchal.

Tommy shook his head and chuckled, but it was humourless.

'She remembers,' he said.

Tommy suddenly stood to attention, startling Yasmine.

'At ease, Private,' Edward said, but he was looking past him. This was all too familiar to Edward: Tommy and Yasmine, alone, in the middle of some emotionally charged moment, and he, feeling like a third wheel.

Tommy grabbed his cap off the bar and put it on his head.

'I'm sorry, sir,' Tommy said. 'I know I should not be in here.'

'This is my establishment,' Yasmine said, her gaze steady on Edward. 'You can stay.'

Tommy looked from Edward to Yasmine and eased towards the door, but Yasmine stopped him.

'Why does he have to leave?' she asked Edward.

'Yasmine,' Edward said quietly.

'Why? No one's here now. It's just us.'

Edward glanced at Tommy, who suddenly became preoccupied with his feet and then gazed longingly at the door when he felt both Yasmine and Edward looking at him. He backed away from the bar.

'Lt Lafaver's right, Yas—ma'am,' he said. 'I'll be on my way, sir.'

'I think that's best, Private,' Edward said. 'No hard feelings, but you understand.'

'No,' Yasmine said. 'Edward, this is silly. Please think about it. No one is here, and this is my place and I say he can stay.'

'Yasmine, it's the law and you could be putting him in danger, do you understand?'

'What law? We're not in America. This is not American soil this time.'

'Come on!' Edward hit the bar, palm down. 'Please be reasonable.'

'The same law that keeps me out of European-only clubs, like Tollygunge and such, I guess,' Yasmine said caustically.

Edward walked up and took Yasmine in his arms. Tommy used the opportunity to slip out the door. He looked back to see Edward kissing Yasmine, trying to mollify her. He knew he would not be coming back to Bombay Duck.

'I don't want to fight anymore,' Yasmine's voice was muffled against Edward's shoulder. She watched Tommy leave. He paused at the door and raised his hand in farewell. Edward was holding her so she could not wave back.

'Yasmine di?'

Yasmine and Edward quickly let go of each other. It was Radhika, dressed in her street clothes and with a small cloth bag flung over her shoulder.

'What's this?' Yasmine said, coming out from behind the bar.

'I have to leave, di. It's no good for me here anymore,' Radhika said. 'May I have my wages for the month?'

'But ... why?'

'I cannot stay. I don't want to stay.'

'But why all of a sudden?'

Edward looked at the slim girl. They had rarely been in the same room together. She always hid away in the kitchen or her room when he came to visit. She seemed older. There were dark circles under her eyes. Her long hair was twisted into a braid that hung down her left shoulder. She was small boned, so easy to overpower. She had no hips to speak of. Edward thought about Louis writhing on top of this tiny girl, pinning her hands back behind her head, yanking her head back by her braid, prying her legs apart with his knee, putting his hand over her mouth. He thought about Radhika closing her eyes to avoid looking at his sweaty, reddened, bloated face when he came inside her. He glanced at Yasmine, who was trying to reason with the girl as far as he could make out. Radhika shook her head and kept saying the same thing over and over. Though Edward could not understand what it was, he knew the girl wanted to leave.

'Let her go,' Edward said to Yasmine.

'Edward, this is not your concern,' Yasmine said.

'I know, but she will just run away if you force her to stay,' he said. 'I can tell.'

Yasmine turned back to Radhika. 'What happened suddenly?' she asked her.

Radhika sighed. 'For me, this place is not the same. It's haunted.'

Yasmine could not argue with that; it was only too true.

'Will you go home?' she asked. 'Where will you go?'

'I have no home.'

Everyone is leaving, Yasmine thought; Tommy, who she inexplicably felt she would not see again, and now Radhika.

'Then why rush away? Where to? It makes no sense.'

Radhika shook her head again. 'I cannot stay here. I don't want to stay here.'

'No one will hurt you,' Yasmine said. Radhika looked down at her feet and would not budge. 'You will end up on the street if you leave. Here, you're protected.'

Radhika shrugged in the infuriating way she did when her mind was made up. She had been the same way when she refused to dance anything but Kathak.

'There is no place on earth now that is safe for me,' Radhika said. 'Every place is bad.'

'Surely this place is less bad than others?' Yasmine said. She held Radhika's chin. It was the first time Yasmine had ever touched the girl's face, the first tenderness she had ever shown her. Radhika began to cry, and Yasmine folded the thin girl into her arms. Radhika smelled of sweat, garlic and turmeric. She slipped her arms around Yasmine's waist and held on to her as if she was drowning. She sobbed quietly into Yasmine's shoulder.

'Hello? What's this then?' Patience had walked in and was

astonished by the extraordinary sight of Yasmine holding a tearful Radhika. 'Eddie! Is this your doing?'

Edward smiled and handed Patience a cigarette as she sat down at the bar. 'It is, I know it!' Patience said warmly. 'Now that you've made love to her, she's gone all soft! There goes the business!'

'Oh, shut your gob, for once Patience Goodwin, please,' Yasmine said, still holding on to Radhika.

'Have you grown a mother's heart then, Madam Khan?' Patience said. She grinned and leaned forward for Edward to light her cigarette.

'She wants to leave,' Edward said. 'Yasmine is trying to convince her to stay.'

'Oh darling,' Patience said to Radhika. 'Nah, tui koi jahbi? Tor basha tho aykhaneh.'

'All I understood from that was "basha",' Edward said.

'I asked her where she would go,' Patience said. 'Her home is here. You need to brush up on your Bangla, ducky!'

Yasmine gently unclasped Radhika's arms from her waist.

'For once, Patience di is right,' Yasmine said. 'Besides, Adil Baboo needs you in the kitchen.' Yasmine felt justified in allowing this small lie to escape from her lips. Radhika nodded, and Yasmine released her thinking she and Patience had convinced the girl, but Radhika picked up her tattered cloth bag and asked once again for her wages. Yasmine tried again to reason with her, as did Patience. Edward remained silent, knowing it was not his place to interfere. All he could say in the end was, sometimes people needed to run away.

20

Yasmine let her go. She gave her a little more than she owed her and sent her to the kitchen to take some bread and whatever Adil Baboo could spare. Radhika thanked her and gave her a shy kiss on the cheek. She went to leave through the back door, but Yasmine stopped her.

'You can leave through the front, Radhika,' she said. 'You are not a thief, sneaking away. You're leaving of your own volition.'

She couldn't meet the girl's eyes. Patience was silent and looked away, pensively smoking her cigarette. Edward went to comfort Yasmine, but she waved him away.

'It's fine, beti. Do as Yasmine didi says,' Adil Baboo said. He had come out from the kitchen to say goodbye. His apron was covered in grease. He wiped his hands on it and took Radhika's hand in both of his.

'But the front door is only for whites and special guests,' she said.

'Never mind all that,' Yasmine said, tearing up.

'No, it's not seemly,' Radhika said. 'I cannot walk out the front like someone special.'

'Oh, for god's sake!' Yasmine cried. 'You have nothing to be ashamed of! Nothing.'

Radhika opened the front door, squinting at the sudden sunlight flooding the small foyer. She walked through and, without a backward glance, gently closed it behind her. Everyone stared at the closed door, each lost in their own thoughts. Patience's maternal heart was filled with sadness and worry for the young girl who faced an uncertain future and more violence. Adil Baboo knew he would miss the girl's strange but comforting company in the kitchen. She was a silent and diligent helper to him. Edward was reminded again of how alien India was; people came and went, and so many had no community to protect and claim them here. It most likely meant death.

'We have to get ready for the evening,' Yasmine said quietly.

'What about Rahul?' Adil Baboo asked. 'He will be upset.'

'I will manage him,' Yasmine said. But no one looked convinced. Even Edward had his doubts. He knew how attached Rahul was to Radhika.

Rahul had been out on errands all afternoon. He returned and ran straight to the kitchen to find Radhika. The corner where she normally sat and cut vegetables and fish for Adil Baboo was empty, the stool pushed up against the wall. He slipped into the alley and threw pebbles at her window, thinking she might be ill and lying down. She did not appear at the window. Yasmine walked into the alley.

'Rahul, stop. She's not there.'

'Where is she?'

'She's gone away.'

'What?'

'She wanted to leave. It was her wish.'

Rahul stared at Yasmine slack-jawed and then ran into the club. Yasmine did not try to stop him. She knew where he was going; though he was not allowed upstairs, she knew he needed to see for himself that Radhika was truly gone.

The charpoy where the girl slept was stripped bare. What few belongings she owned, she had taken with her, except her ankle bells, which she had left on a low vanity, and a garland of dried-up jasmine draped over a warped mirror. Yasmine watched Rahul pick up the bells and take the jasmine off the mirror. He looked at her, and she nodded that he could have them. He looked very young. He sat on the floor next to the charpoy and dissolved into sobs. Asma and Patience came into the room, Madhu and Edward close on their heels. 'She finally left?' Asma asked. Yasmine nodded. Patience and Madhu picked Rahul up, each taking an arm, and escorted him downstairs. Asma loitered by the door.

'What is it, Asma?' Yasmine said, taking the handkerchief Edward handed her and wiping her eyes.

'Was it my fault? Was I too mean?'

'No, it was not your fault, but yes, you were mean to her,' Yasmine said tiredly. 'You were terribly unfair, Asma, but she was always going to run away. She was a wild, feral thing at times.'

'Yasmine, you look beat. Maybe you should lie down,' Edward said.

'I'm fine. Let me be,' she said.

In the hours that followed, Rahul shook his fist at Asma and accused her of driving Radhika away because she did not like her. Up until then, he had never so much as raised his voice to anyone, let alone his fist.

'That girl was a bad influence on you!' Asma cried, shocked at Rahul's audacity. She turned to Yasmine. 'I feel badly for her, I do, but now look, everything is upended,' she said.

'Hush!' Yasmine said. 'His heart is broken,' she added, surprising everyone, except Rahul, who did not appear to see or hear anyone anymore.

When Adil Baboo tried to restrain him, he punched his friend, twisted free and broke three glasses. He marched up to Yasmine, red-faced, and said, 'Take it out of my wages. I don't care!'

Yasmine did not react to the boy's disrespect. She merely handed him a plate to throw. Rahul took the plate, grit his teeth and threw it with all his might on the concrete floor. Yasmine jumped back as it shattered and looked at Adil Baboo, who wiped his hands on his apron and went back into the kitchen. The youngster had fallen in love and Radhika had, in his words, 'made a man out of me'.

'That's enough then,' Yasmine said to Rahul after he shattered the plate. But it wasn't enough. The boy left that night, without telling anyone.

When they discovered he had gone, Edward tried to comfort Yasmine. He had never seen her this forlorn.

'What's the matter, sweetheart?'

'What if he doesn't come back?'

'He'll be back.'

Yasmine shook her head. 'No. He's gone after her.'

'How can I help?

'Maybe someone at Tolly will have heard from him. He is a great favourite there.'

'Okay, I'll ask around,' he said, eager to help, to be indispensable somehow. 'I feel for the kid.'

Yasmine looked at him, curious. Lately, he had been so attentive and considerate. She was grateful for his support, though she did not tell him that. He was the only one who did not seem to blame her for the turn of events. She knew Adil Baboo and Patience believed she had been too harsh when it came to Radhika and Rahul's relationship, and Asma resented the disruption Radhika's initial presence and subsequent departure had caused.

'Thank you, Edward,' she said.

When she mentioned his eagerness to help to Patience, her friend said, 'It means one of two things: he loves you or he is feeling guilty about something. Or both. My money is on both.'

'What could he possibly have to feel guilty about with me?' Yasmine wondered.

'Think,' Patience said. 'He knows he will be leaving you, going back to Northfield or wherever he comes from.'

'Norwich. Yes, of course,' Yasmine said softly.

'It's okay, ducky. Let him help. Let him honour one promise at least.'

~

For one full week, Edward dedicated all his free time to locating Rahul.

What he determined was that, first, Rahul had gone looking for Radhika and, unable to find her, gone to the base to enlist the aid of his friend, Corporal Addison, who had sent two MPs looking for her. When they too could not locate her, Rahul, in despair, had fled to his village, several hundred miles away.

Edward made the arduous, two-day journey to East Bengal, with Addison in tow. His baffled CO granted him permission, on the condition that they would not delay their return.

'You'll be considered AWOL if you are not back in seventy-two hours, Lieutenant,' he was told. 'You are also responsible for Corporal Addison.'

When they finally found him, a despondent Rahul seemed to have lost weight. The sight of two dusty and weary Americans—the first they had ever seen—entering the sleepy village of Lakshmipur, which had electricity only at the police station and post office, sent shock waves through the houses. However, Rahul's young mother, a tiny, wiry woman, was relieved to see Edward and Addison. She had been praying to the goddess for something to lift her only son out of his despair and send him back to work, where he belonged, earning for his family.

Rahul refused to even look at his friends and lay listlessly with his back to them on a jute mat on the floor of his mother's one-room house, as almost every resident of Lakshmipur crowded around the entrance to her tiny dwelling, clogging up the courtyard just outside the house, peering in and at times weighing in.

'She's just a dame, like any other dame. There's more where that came from,' Addison said, in what he hoped was a soothing manner.

'I don't think that'll ease his mind,' Edward said. 'Let's go on the assumption that she was the love of his life.'

Addison scratched his head and sighed. 'Well, then he's screwed,' he said.

'Also not particularly helpful,' Edward said. He leaned down and put his hand on the boy's shoulder. 'Hey kid, your heart is broken,' he said. 'And it will always be a little bit broken where she is concerned. But if you don't get up and face it, you'll die.' He paused and looked at Rahul's family members crouched around him. 'And it looks to me like you have more than yourself to think about.'

Rahul's mother, Nandini, who was only fourteen years older than her son, somehow knew exactly what the American was saying.

'Ay! Listen to the sahib!' she cried, roughly nudging her boy. 'You will find another girl, better than this one. Why did Yasmine-ji discharge her? Because she was bad news, that's why! She might have tainted us with her bad luck if she had entered here as a bride. Thank Yasmine-ji for saving you!'

Even the insult aimed his beloved's way did not rouse Rahul.

'Listen to the Americans!' one village elder admonished, and the rest of Rahul's neighbours murmured in both agreement and disagreement.

Edward and Addison walked out of the tiny house and into the courtyard, and pondered their options. They were weary and hungry. The children and some adults crowded around them, staring at them in open curiosity. Both Americans were used to being scrutinised at close quarters. Almost without thinking, they took Hershey's bars and Wrigley's gums out of their knapsacks and handed them out to the children pressing up against them.

'We can't stay here much longer,' Addison said. 'We'll be AWOL by tomorrow night.'

'I know, but let's just give him a minute. He's young,' Edward said. 'I promised Yasmine I would bring him home,' he added, sighing. Addison grinned at him knowingly.

'Okay, I gotcha,' he said. 'You're all about the dames too, sir,'

'Easy, Corporal,' Edward said, laughing. A small girl of about three, wearing only a grimy pair of underpants, tugged on Edward's hand, and he picked her up. She had large, watery brown eyes that stared at him. They appraised one another for a bit, while she sucked her thumb.

'I think you got yourself an admirer, sir,' Addison said.

'Hmm, not sure. She doesn't seem that impressed,' Edward replied. 'One thing I have learned is that Bengali girls are hard to please.'

Both men looked towards the hut, where Rahul lay on the floor, still unwilling to emerge. Addison let out a tired sigh and lit a cigarette.

The little girl suddenly extracted her thumb from her rosebud mouth and touched Edward's cheek and grinned at him. She had exactly two minuscule teeth.

'You see?' Addison said. 'She likes you.'

'Maybe there's hope for me yet,' Edward said. 'Got any more stuff?'

Addison extracted another Hershey's bar from his knapsack and handed it to the child, who refused it and buried her face in Edward's neck.

'Aww, mouse, it's okay,' Edward said. 'Go ahead.'

The soothing tone to Edward's voice made her less shy. She held out her small, dirty hand, and Addison placed the chocolate in it.

The moment passed, and the toddler decided she'd had quite enough and wriggled to be let loose. Edward set her gently on the ground, and she ran off confidently, swollen belly protruding, holding up her sagging underpants with one hand. She seemed to know where she was going. No adult came to claim her.

'Look at that, not even a goodbye and I'll promise to write,' Addison said.

'Typical,' Edward said.

He looked around the village. Off to one side there was an enormous banyan tree; around it was a raised mound ringed by crumbling white bricks. Below the tree sat a clay statue of the goddess Lakshmi. She was pink-faced, her large, almond-shaped eyes ringed with black. A small smile played on her red lips. On her lap and strewn around her were new and old offerings of marigolds and fruits. Next to her was an earthen pitcher with a coconut on top. She also wore a garland of fresh jasmine around her neck. Incense burned at her feet.

He walked towards the statue to get a closer look.

'Not too pretty, huh?' Addison said. He, as well as several villagers, had followed Edward to the tree.

'Oh, I don't know,' Edward said. 'She's got something.'

One boy, about ten, stepped forward. 'Lokkhi,' he said, pointing to the statue.

'That her name?' Addison said.

The boy shrugged.

'I think this is Lakshmi,' Edward said. 'The goddess of wealth.'

'Her?' Addison said. He looked at Lakshmi's tranquil and somewhat garish face sceptically.

'I guess this is a Hindu village,' Edward said. He looked around at the faces peering at him and a small chill went up his back.

Addison, noticing a change in Edward's expression, said, 'What's up, sir?'

'Nothing. I got a weird feeling is all.'

'Like?'

'Not sure. I mean, they are Hindus in a predominantly Muslim area. Can't be good. They're surrounded. Things go south fast around here. One local politician calls for a strike or a protest or something and that's it. Fifty villagers have their throats slit.'

'They been living here forever, I bet,' Addison said, looking around at the villagers, some of whom smiled at him. Addison grinned back and dug around his knapsack for more candy bars.

'Sorry, plum out!'

'Things feel so fleeting sometimes,' Edward said, gazing at the idol's face.

'Sir? No disrespect, but we gotta get a move on here.'

Nandini, thinking the Americans were preparing to leave without Rahul, let out a frustrated yelp and grabbed her son by the ear, all but dragging him out of the hut, into the courtyard.

'You will be the death of us!' she cried.

This startled both Americans, and they reached out to help Rahul. They could not touch her without offending everyone in the village though.

'Easy, mom,' Addison said, when Nandini shoved him away. She was surprisingly strong for someone so small.

'Moms,' he said, shaking his head. 'Same everywhere.'

Rahul was finally on his feet. He rubbed his sore ear. Edward put his arm around the forlorn boy.

'Yasmine di needs you,' Edward said. 'I know you don't understand me, but everyone misses you. Adil Baboo, the girls. Patience said that your leaving has thrown all the planets into the fifth house or something. That sounds pretty bad.'

Though Rahul didn't fully understand, he comprehended enough, so he nodded.

Nandini glared at the blue-eyed Addison. 'You are all useless!' she said in Bengali, while Addison grinned at her. 'Stop coddling him and force him to come with you!'

'You're welcome!' Addison said slowly, putting his palms together in a namaste.

Nandini rolled her eyes, covered her head and stalked back into her house, muttering to herself. A moment later, she marched out, handed Rahul a packet with four stale chapattis and ordered all three on their way.

'Jao!' she said. She pointed to the jeep. 'Not for some low girl,' she said directly to her son, 'are you allowed to fall apart.'

21

A few days after their return to Calcutta, Edward suggested that Yasmine should leave Rahul for the time being, and not force him to work.

'Let him lick his wounds,' he said. 'He's a kid, all heart-broken, but he can't wallow forever.'

'But I need someone now!' Yasmine said. 'Business can't stop just because two teenagers fall in love! Besides, work will help him. There is nothing like work to ease a broken heart.'

'The thing is, I don't think Radhika was in love, which is why he's so upset,' Edward said. If the girl loved Rahul, he said, she would not have disappeared. She would have made him marry her or something akin to that—maybe force him to support her. She had no family, and Rahul was a goner. She could have made him do anything she wanted. She obviously did not want him.

'Rahul is young, but he isn't dumb,' Edward said. 'He sees all that clearly. It hurts.'

Yasmine was surprised at the keen interest Edward had taken in Rahul's situation, and said as much.

'Well, it's you I am more worried about,' he said.

'Me? Why?'

'You have been kind of distracted lately. I want you back to obsessing about me.'

He was only half-joking when he said this.

'I am not obsessed with you,' Yasmine said, insulted, partially because she *was* obsessed with him and was startled at being caught. But it was true; the Radhika–Rahul debacle had distracted her. She felt worn down. Edward drew her close to him and kissed her passionately. Yasmine held him closer to her and let a hand slide down between his legs.

'Oh boy,' Edward said, surprised but happy. This was unusual for Yasmine. She was uninhibited in bed but never out of it. She began to stroke him. They only moved apart when Patience walked in.

'Uff, no privacy,' Yasmine muttered.

'As you were,' Patience said, laughing. She pointedly avoided looking down at Edward's crotch. 'I am only passing through.' She started to sort through the mail and seemed in no rush.

'Ooh!' she said suddenly and held up a smudged envelope with three cancelled stamps. 'From the front! Who says I'm not doing my part?' She looked at the postmark. 'Eddie? Where is Fez?'

'Morocco.'

'Smashing! Yassu? Can I be an awful bore and snatch another ciggie? I'll give you my ration for the month.' Patience pouted and said in a babyish voice, 'Pweety pweeze, my liege?'

Yasmine frowned. She always seemed to act up around Edward and become overly silly. Patience went back to a normal voice when she saw her friend was annoyed.

'I need a ciggie to read this letter. If it's full of descriptions of wounds and what not, I get anxious.'

'Here.' Edward held out his pack. 'Take more,' he said when Patience took one and wrinkled her nose at Yasmine, who stuck her tongue out as a response. Edward smiled. They were so girlish around one another.

'We get a few more perks than you all. And that, of course, is monumentally unfair,' he added quickly when Yasmine glared at him.

Patience helped herself to three more cigarettes and ran up the stairs. Edward attempted to kiss Yasmine again, though she now looked grumpy. Eventually, she softened and even slipped her tongue in his mouth, drawing him close to her.

'Maybe we should go upstairs,' he whispered when Adil Baboo walked in a moment later, looking glum. It was true, the club was always bustling. There never seemed to be a moment of stillness. Yasmine pushed Edward away and held up a warning finger when he tried to come closer.

Yasmine smoothed her sari and looked at Adil Baboo askance.

By the time Pharaoh wandered in, two hours early, and started banging on the piano disconsolately, Yasmine had had enough.

'Why is everyone so down in the mouth?' she demanded, trying to compose herself. She glanced at Edward, who was now wearing most of her passionate plum berry lip rouge. 'Rahul is back. Everyone should be overjoyed!'

'I should get going,' Edward said.

'No!' Yasmine said, so quickly and loudly that Pharaoh smiled and Adil Baboo jumped. 'Please wait for me in the ...' she trailed off. They were in the only public room where she could receive guests. She did not want to direct him towards the office or the bedrooms.

'I am running low on cardamom,' Adil Baboo said, quickly.

'How much do you need?' Yasmine said, fishing through her purse.

Adil Baboo told her, and she handed him the money. Pharaoh continued to play a rather wistful rendition of *Smoke Gets in Your Eyes*. He ignored them.

'Wanna dance?' Edward said to break the awkwardness.

'All right.'

'Let me lead this time.'

'When have I not?' she said.

Edward chuckled and shook his head. He took her in his arms, and they danced slowly. He held her so close she had to pull away a little, laughing. She looked over at Pharaoh, embarrassed. Pharaoh started to sing softly. Yasmine closed her eyes and allowed Edward to lead her around the floor. They kept dancing even when Pharaoh stopped playing and stepped outside to smoke.

Edward let her go and looked around. 'Well, what do you know? We're finally alone.'

Yasmine smiled at him.

'What's happening in that head of yours?' he said.

'Thank you for bringing Rahul back.'

'I'm glad I could do something for you. You never need me.'

'Do you want to make love to me?' Yasmine asked him.

'I do, yes.'

'Do you have, you know?'

He shook his head. 'Damn! I didn't expect ... this, so I didn't go to the ARC.'

'We just have to be careful,' she said.

He nodded. She said that every time, and so far, they'd had no cause for alarm. Edward knew how cautious she was—about everything really. He assumed, being a worldly sort of woman, she knew what precautions to take. She took his hand and led him up the stairs.

In her bed, he took her slowly and tenderly, keeping it close.

'Give in. Let me do the work. And tell me what you want me to do.'

'Move a bit faster.'

'Yasmine, I love you.'

'Okay, you don't have to move.'

He chuckled, grabbed her hips and thrust slightly harder, making her groan.

'What is it, baby?' he whispered when she started to breathe faster. He kissed her neck and started to move again. Small, circling movements.

'It feels warm,' she moaned.

'That's all you got for me?' he said and thrust harder.

She groaned again and spread her legs farther apart so he could go deeper. He held her arms above her head and started to move faster. He kissed her neck, her clavicle and ears. He kept whispering things to her, about all the things he wanted to do to her until she was about to fully climax and then he pulled out.

'No! Please!' she begged him, nearly sobbing. She pulled his hips towards her.

'We have to be careful,' he said, teasing her.

'Oh, just a bit more,' she pleaded.

'Okay, but you have to tell me—'

'I want you to fuck me, Edward.'

'Can you be more specific?'

Yasmine looked at him, incredulous, and saw that he was toying with her.

'Do you surrender?' he said as he worked his way into her again, slowly.

'Why surrender?'

'Say fuck again. I want to see your lips when you say it.'

'I changed my mind, stop talking.'

~

'Are you sure it's okay?' he said later, yawning. They were both sleepy from their exertions and covered in each another's sweat. 'I came inside you.'

'Yes, of course,' Yasmine said, though she was not sure at all. She suddenly could not remember when her last menstruation was. But she felt it was not much of a risk. Nothing seemed to matter at that moment except what he had said to her and what she had said to him. She wondered if he would take it back or even address it.

As if reading her thoughts, he said: 'I meant it. I love you.'

He looked at her and was silent. He was trying to make her out, or he was seeing her more clearly. She did not know which one. It made her self-conscious. Edward kept looking at her. After a while, Yasmine said:

'What is it?'

'You're like the Japs, you hate to surrender,' he said and grinned.

'Yes, we Asians are not all pantywaists,' Yasmine replied.

'Sometimes, it's best to give in,' Edward said. He leaned over and kissed her left breast as he lay his head on her chest. 'Have you ever read any Rumi?' he asked her.

Yasmine ran her fingers through his damp hair. 'A white man asking me if I have ever read Jalaluddin Rumi? Hmm, fascinating.'

'Just answer the question, you snob,' Edward said.

'Of course!'

'Well, next time I fuck you—sorry, make love to you—do as Rumi says and "surrender to the wonder". Like the lusty woman you are.'

He looked up to see Yasmine staring at him, shocked, and started to laugh at her expression.

'What? You didn't know that I knew? For all your Loreto Convent airs, who wants to get flipped around in the sack? Who likes it when I growl in her ear? Who wants her pussy licked—'

'Fine! But I won't have you sullying Rumi. When he talks

of surrender, it's to divine love, you cretin, not to anything bestial.'

'And what do you think this was?' Edward asked.

'You just want to control me.'

'And what you refuse to admit is that you like being controlled, at least in bed. Come on, admit it!'

The conversation had taken an unexpected turn. After all the declarations of love, Yasmine had expected some sort of post-coital cuddling. She knew they could not discuss where the nursery should go, or if they wanted to honeymoon in Venice or Istanbul, but they could at least whisper maudlin endearments to one another and make plans to stroll along Outram Ghat at sunset.

She was starting to get angry and then looked in his face and saw what she could only describe as exhilaration. He had compared their mutual passion to divine love. It was confusing.

They had never spoken like this to one another. They were always combative, but this was different. She asked him if he was angry.

'Not at all. Why would I be? I'm not criticising you, you know,' he said. He kissed her on the mouth quickly. 'I can't talk like this to anyone. I'm hungry! Got any grub? Wait! I have a better idea, come to the ARC with me and let me feed you for a change.'

'We can't do that,' Yasmine said. She smiled, relieved. She had never seen him so energetic. Edward was a reserved man, and private.

'I don't give a damn what people think.'

Yasmine didn't believe him but was gratified by the statement. She knew that, in that moment at least, it was true.

~

While Yasmine started allowing herself the once impossible hope that they would build a life together, Edward's love for her made him more anxious—and jealous. The initial exhilaration of declaring his love led to his feeling out of control. She had not said it back, after all, something he had not noticed at once, but once he did, it began to grate on him. He was disconcerted by her independence. He was careful not to ask Yasmine about Tommy. Instead, he used his rank as an officer to keep Tommy busy on the base as much as possible. But it was impossible to avoid the subject with Yasmine indefinitely, as hard as he tried to. He knew it was inevitable that Yasmine would begin to ask questions again.

'Do you ever see Tommy?' she asked Edward one day, about a month after Rahul was retrieved. Her tone was casual.

'Sometimes, in the Mess,' he replied carefully, and returned his gaze to his newspaper.

'I think it's hard on Tommy, knowing who really attacked Radhika and not being able to say anything.'

Edward put his newspaper down and looked at Yasmine.

'The girl is gone. Does it matter now who did it?'

Yasmine frowned. 'Of course it does. How can you say that?'

Fearing that this would escalate into a fight and more probing questions, Edward remained silent. Yasmine had been more emotional than usual lately. Sometimes, however, as was the case now, remaining silent only fanned the flames.

'I suppose her life does not matter. I suppose a native girl being raped doesn't matter!' Yasmine said. Edward heard the pitch in her voice change, and his heart sank. A fight was inevitable now. Yasmine would push her point. 'If it had been me instead of Radhika, would you have given up then too? Would you have allowed my attacker to go unpunished?'

'Of course not!' Edward cried, stung that she would even consider that.

'Then why won't you help me?' Yasmine began to cry, much to Edward's alarm. 'Why are you all so horrid?'

He tried to hold her, but she shoved him away. 'Okay, okay, I'll talk to Tommy, but I don't understand why he doesn't come forward if he knows,' Edward said.

'Why do you think? Really, Edward! The attacker is white. Please do something. You can, you know; Tommy can't.'

Edward left, but not before Yasmine extracted a promise that he would pursue it. Later, during dinner at the base, he gestured to Tommy to come over to his table. Tommy silently began to clear his dishes away, dumping them into a grey bin. He did not meet Edward's eyes.

'Private?'

'Yessir?' Tommy said and stopped what he was doing and looked at Edward. He did not conceal his resentment.

'Private, Miss Khan, you know her—'

'Yessir, I do ... very well.'

Edward looked up sharply then. He had been smiling when he called Tommy over and now the smile had been wiped from his face. 'I'll let that slide, Private,' he said.

'What I meant, sir, is that she is a real lady, you know?'

Edward softened. 'Yes, I know,' he agreed. He glanced around, dropping his voice. 'She cares about you and told me that you have an idea about who attacked the girl.'

Tommy, who had been looking straight ahead of him while addressing Edward, let his eyes slide over to where Louis was sitting with other officers. Edward followed Tommy's gaze to Louis's table and quickly looked down. This was not lost on Tommy. When Edward looked up, Tommy was staring at him. 'Sir?' he said.

Edward sighed.

'Permission to speak freely, sir?' Tommy ventured when Edward remained silent, looking down at his coffee.

Edward nodded. 'Not here though,' he said.

When Tommy finished his shift, he met Edward behind the Negro barracks. Edward was waiting for him with a beer and a pack of Chesterfields. Tommy hesitated when Edward offered him the pack and the beer.

'It's okay. Consider it a gift. I know how hard you boys work for us.'

'I'm not allowed to drink, sir, I'm on duty. But I'll take the smokes.'

'Save it for later,' Edward said.

Tommy hesitated and then took the beer bottle, tucking it into his back pocket.

They both smoked silently for a moment, neither knowing how to start. Edward knew it would have to be him. Tommy could not accuse a white officer of anything outright.

'Lt Deccico has moved out of the basha I shared with him,' he said. 'We are not friends.'

Tommy nodded. Tommy was used to helping white folks absolve themselves of accountability. In his experience, they were not consistent when it came to blacks. They could not be trusted, even the polite ones. He preferred the Deccicos of the world to the well-meaning ones like Edward. He knew exactly what he was dealing with when it came to someone like Louis.

'I need proof, though.'

'The girl is the proof,' Tommy said.

'Well, the girl's gone.'

Tommy sighed and shook his head. 'Then I guess we shit out of luck, sir … unless you tell what you know. You know no one's going to listen to me. They will to you. May I be excused now?' As a rule, and for his own protection, Tommy avoided being in a white person's company longer than necessary. One never knew which way an encounter could turn.

'Private, this is a delicate matter. Please don't mention it to anyone until I know what to do. Can you give me your word on that?'

The resentment that had gone from his eyes returned, and Edward found he could not meet the man's gaze. 'I won't tell Miss Khan that you know, sir. If that's what you're worried about.'

'That's not what I meant, Private.'

'Yessir, sorry.' He saluted Edward and waited to be released.

'We're done here, Private. But one more thing.'

'Yes, sir?'

'Please stay away from Miss Khan and Bombay Duck.'

'She don't want me, sir.'

'That doesn't even come into question, Private,' Edward said. He had moved closer to Tommy without realising it and grabbed hold of the man's shirt. He looked at his hand clutching Tommy's shirt. His knuckles were white. Tommy looked straight ahead of him, over Edward's head. He was gritting his teeth. Edward released Tommy and stepped back. 'I apologise, Private. I forgot myself there.'

'I'm leaving anyway,' Tommy said as calmly as he could. He moved away from Edward. 'I volunteered to go to Burma. Please thank her for me. She was kind to me when no one else was.'

'You can go, Private. Good luck.'

Edward watched Tommy walk away, regretting the way he had handled the conversation. The soldier was irritating and insolent, to be sure, but he seemed to be honourable and intelligent as well. Edward had done as Yasmine asked. There was nothing more he could do. It was such an unpleasant and embarrassing situation—it made the army look terrible, and Americans like savages. It was best to let it go, he told himself. He was not sure how he would tell Yasmine.

22

'I wish you could see New England in the fall,' Edward said to Yasmine as they walked slowly back to the Duck from the Metro Cinema. 'The colours are even more vivid than here. If that's possible. It's like someone soaked all the trees in Holi powders.'

Yasmine nodded and smiled, but did not say anything. She was pensive. She was a quiet woman by nature, and he did most of the talking when they were together. He was used to that by now. At first it was not easy. American girls were generally more gregarious. The nurses on the base and at the ARC were chatty and gossiped a great deal. He could not recollect a moment when he heard Yasmine make a comment about another woman's choice of hair colour or her weight. When she was with her girls at the Duck, she was more like a field marshal. They were as gossipy as the girls back home, but Yasmine did not participate. It was one of the many things he admired about her.

They had just seen the movie *The Jungle Book*. He suspected her silence was a result of the bizarre two-hour odyssey the director had taken them on. If Edward had seen this film back in Norwich, he would not have thought anything of the white actors in brown-face or how the 'Indian' music was nothing like Indian music at all but just a mish-mosh of what Hollywood thought was Indian music, which was mostly the whine of a snake charmer's flute, punctuated by Middle Eastern music. The ridiculous accents and overly tropical sets would not have made an impression either. But since he now felt he knew India far better than when he had first arrived, and because he was seeing it through Yasmine's eyes, he found the film's depiction of India and Indians absurd—and embarrassing.

Going to the movies with Yasmine often made him homesick because it was so mundane, which was why he was talking about New England in the fall. The tropical weather was starting to grate on him. He longed for one cool day and trees that were not so green.

He tried again to engage her in conversation. 'The leaves turn shades you can't imagine, unless you live there and get to see it first-hand. There's a fire bush at the end of my folks' driveway that turns crimson. You can even see it in the dark.'

'Hmm, sounds nice,' Yasmine murmured.

'Do you want something to eat?'

'No, thank you.'

'Talk to me.'

'That movie was a stinker. Is that what Americans think we are like?'

He smiled. She had started using American slang and, though it didn't always sound natural coming from her, it was charming.

'Yes, it was!' he agreed. 'I guess the average Joe doesn't know enough about India.'

Yasmine stopped walking and turned to him. 'You thought so too?'

'Of course. I live here too, you know. I know what India is.'

'Do you?'

'Yup! And it's not that,' he said. 'That's just Hollywood. There's a whole room full of short, bald men thinking up ways to sell you a left-handed screwdriver. That's what Hollywood is.'

'What is a left-handed screwdriver?' Yasmine asked.

'Something that resembles something real, but just isn't ... viable.'

They started to walk again. They always left space between them so it did not seem like they were too familiar. They were careful not to touch, even accidentally. Edward had his hands in his pockets, and she would either have her arms folded across her chest or be clutching something. It did not always prevent the curious and sometimes recriminating gazes or comments, especially since Edward had the American habit of smiling at everyone who looked at them, men and women alike. He was even warmer when a pretty girl happened by.

Early on, he would try to engage people in conversation, even when they did not speak English, and demand that Yasmine translate, which she put a stop to at once.

'I'm just friendly,' he told her. 'And curious.'

'Yes, but really it's this abhorrent American need to make everyone like you.'

'We just can't help it,' he had grinned.

They walked into an alleyway that led to yet another narrow lane closer to the Bombay Duck to avoid the crush and gaze of the crowds on the main road. Edward had learned all the shortcuts and by-lanes that could get him to Bombay Duck in a hurry, and led the way. The alley was so narrow that two people could not walk comfortably abreast.

Lying in the middle of the alleyway was what appeared to be a small heap of grimy rags that stirred as they approached it. The heap of rags was a young woman, though she was so emaciated it was hard to be sure. Edward stared down at the skeletal figure, whose breastbone jutted out. He could count her ribs.

'Jesus,' he said, under his breath.

Yasmine peered around him to see.

The girl had one arm flung over her face, the other lay out, away from her side. 'We should move her,' Yasmine said quietly. 'So she doesn't get trampled.'

'You think so?'

Neither of them made a move to touch the figure. Her sunken chest and small breasts were exposed. There were open sores on her legs, which were swarmed by flies.

'We should at least cover her up.'

Yasmine bent down and drew a corner of the ragged, grimy sari over the girl's breasts.

'I think she's passed, Yasmine,' Edward said. He shoved his hands in his pockets and looked away. India still shocked him.

'No, she's breathing. Look!'

Edward leaned down for a closer look at the woman's sunken chest. He discerned a slight rise and fall. Her saw her grey tongue move.

A trolley stopped on the main road and disgorged a large, impatient group of passengers, some of whom would also want to use the alley to bypass the crowds.

Sure enough, a portly dhoti-clad man entered the alley and shoved Yasmine out of the way with his umbrella and nearly fell over the girl lying on the ground.

'Arrey!' he cried. He quickly covered his mouth with a handkerchief, as if starvation was catching, and stepped over the girl's body with some difficulty.

The man glared at them both before leaving the alley.

'Sometimes this place surprises me,' Edward said.

'Really?' Yasmine said. Her voice was weary. 'It never surprises me.'

Edward gently took the girl's thin ankles.

'You have to help me, Yasmine. I can't do it alone.'

She was light, and they lifted her easily. They gently lay her down to the side. They placed her hands on her belly so no one would step on her wrists. Yasmine removed the light shawl she was wearing around her shoulders, folded it, and placed it underneath the girl's head. For a brief moment, the figure opened her eyes, which may have once been brown, but were now covered in a milky film. She looked up at Yasmine and moved her lips.

'What's she saying?' Edward asked.

Yasmine put her ear to the girl's mouth. At first no sound was discernible, and then Yasmine swore she heard the word, 'didi'.

'What is it?' Edward said, alarmed when Yasmine jerked back. She touched the girl's hollow cheek with the tips of her fingers.

'Do you have anything to eat?' Yasmine asked Edward.

He nodded. 'Only this,' he said, and took out a small Hershey's bar from his pocket. 'It's a little melted.'

'I don't know. She's almost dead. Maybe it's too late,' she said. 'Food might kill her.'

Edward squatted down next to Yasmine and put his arm around her.

'What is it, sweetheart? You see this all the time. Why is this one different?'

'Look at her.'

'I know. She's just a kid.'

'It's Radhika.'

'No, sweetheart, it can't be.'

'It is!'

Edward looked at the hollow face, the deep, sunken eyes and dry, grey skin pulled taut over the cheekbones, and could not see Radhika.

Yasmine took the girl's head and placed it in her lap.

'I don't think she's Radhika, but I'm not sure. I do know you should not do that. She might be sick.'

'It doesn't matter,' Yasmine said.

Edward nodded. They were scared to move her again; she looked as brittle as a dried leaf. By some miracle, no one else entered the alley, allowing them to hold the dying girl.

'I don't want her to die here,' Yasmine said. 'Please go get help.'

Edward left her there, holding the girl, to fetch Adil Baboo and Patience, who could help them move her.

'Forgive me,' Yasmine whispered to the girl, who opened her eyes and stared up at Yasmine. She did not know if the girl saw her. 'Radhika?' she whispered. The girl lifted a weak hand and placed it on Yasmine's head for a moment, before it slipped down to the ground. She had died, Yasmine knew, and pulled her closer to her chest. 'Rest now,' she said. She closed the girl's sunken eyes. She wanted to cry but could not. Instead, she cradled the girl's body, all bones, to her chest, hoping it would bring tears. Still, the tears did not come.

~

'It is Radhika,' Yasmine said to Edward and the others, when they arrived in the alley.

'We can't be sure,' Edward protested. 'Her face is different.'

'It is her. I know what Radhika looks like.'

'Let's not tell the lad, then,' Patience said, referring to Rahul. 'It might kill him.'

'You look, Patience,' Yasmine said. 'Tell me that's not Radhika.'

Patience obliged her and knelt down next to the body. She looked at the face and hands.

'I'm not sure, Yassu,' she said.

People really do just disappear, Yasmine thought, as the others murmured amongst themselves. They are born, they lead an invisible life and they die in a heap of rags in an alley. And not one person misses them. Not one person wonders where they are. She wondered if that would be her fate. The thought that this soul, whether or not everyone believed it was Radhika, would be sent into the afterlife with only indifferent cremators by her side, was crushing. It meant Radhika would be erased.

The cremators, doms, were summoned to take her body away and prepare it for the burning ghats. They had all waited with the body for them to arrive. When they did—a man and his teenage son—Yasmine attempted to lie and told them Radhika was not a Dalit. The doms didn't believe her. They were experienced—their family having been in charge of the dead of Calcutta for six generations. They argued it was better she was buried at the Hindu cemetery, Topsia, and not cremated. They did not want to face the wrath of the Brahminical hierarchy down at the burning ghats.

'Who is she?' the elder dom asked. 'Who are her people, who will perform the sacred rites? I will have to explain all this to the authorities.

'She should be buried where she belongs,' he added. 'Her soul will be at peace.'

Yasmine offered them three hundred rupees to ensure Radhika would at least receive the last rites.

'Her name is Radhika,' she said, the tears that had been caught somewhere behind her eyes finally falling.

'She is a dancer,' Madhu said. 'A fine one.'

'We are her people,' Patience said.

'I will perform the rites if we cremate her,' Adil Baboo said suddenly. 'I have never done this before, but—'

'Don't be silly, dada,' Madhu said quickly. 'You've forgotten you've attended ceremonies before.' She did not want the dom to realise Adil Baboo was Muslim. He would never agree then.

The dom was sceptical, but his expression changed when Yasmine handed him a hundred rupees and assured him that she would be able to give him the rest at the ceremony. He relented.

Relieved, Yasmine and everyone else began to quietly file out of the alley. She looked back one more time to where the girl had lain, hoping now she could do right by Radhika.

They cremated Radhika that evening; the three hundred rupees were enough inducement to dispatch this quickly.

Things are sixes and sevens, Yasmine kept saying to herself, as she watched Adil Baboo, a Muslim, walk around Radhika's pyre, sprinkle her body with ghee and throw an earthen pot filled with water over his shoulder. But she also felt satisfaction. Radhika's soul would be at peace. Adil Baboo walked around the pyre and recited what Madhu had taught him, saying Lord Shiva was great, asking him to release Radhika from the mortal coil, hoping her cycle of life and death would now cease, and she would never again return to earth. And then he glanced at Yasmine, who smiled and nodded. Under their breaths, they recited in Arabic as Radhika's white-clad body was set ablaze—Inna lillahi wa inna ilayhi raji'oon, asking Allah to forgive her faults and any wrong she may have committed and to allow her a pleasant journey into the afterlife. She felt sure it was Radhika they were releasing into the arms of the Almighty, be it Shiva or Allah. She knew the others were sceptical, that they were humoring her.

'Does it matter, ducky?' Patience said, when Yasmine told her she knew the others were not sure it was Radhika and must think her a bit mad. 'This poor thing died in your arms, and you showed her some kindness and then you made sure she had a proper send-off. I hope it was Radhika, and if it wasn't, then I am happy this soul had you with her at the end. You parted with three hundred rupees on her behalf, no less. You're becoming a soft touch, Yassu. There is hope for you yet.'

Yasmine nodded, slightly comforted by the idea that in a way, every single invisible girl, every child dying of starvation, was Radhika, so in helping this girl she was doing right by her. But she knew somehow it was not quite enough.

Later that night, in her room, she lay awake listening to the clicking ceiling fan and Edward snoring gently, without a care it seemed.

She had what Patience called 'that endy feeling'. She always talked about phases and cycles ending and beginning. 'Everything must end,' Patience would say to every suitor she jilted, and she felt that was reasonable grounds to dump someone.

Yasmine put down her restlessness to the rumours of an imminent invasion by the Japanese, as well as the severe food shortages.

In October of '42, there had been a devastating cyclone that set off a chain of events. Rice crops were damaged and the peasants consumed their surplus. It was now May of '43 and too late to plant new crops. People began to hoard, and all the extra rice and grain was going to the Allied soldiers in North Africa and the Pacific. The middle class of Calcutta did not starve, but the chawls and slums of the city were filled with dead bodies, mostly children. People were abandoning their villages in the ironically lush countryside in search of food. There was no drought, but there was also no food. It made no sense.

Yasmine was not starving—Edward made sure she and the staff of the Duck had plenty to eat. Yasmine would not accept a cent of Edward's salary to buy more supplies 'just in case', but she did gratefully accept the foodstuff. Also, her club was doing good business. Somehow, it had not slowed down, except now she was not offering full meals, only appetisers and drinks. And songs. Always that. Sometimes even appetisers were not available, but no one seemed to mind as long as Patience and Asma sang, Pharaoh played and Madhu danced. Sometimes someone asked for the small girl with lightning feet but that was becoming less frequent. People were starting to forget her. Yasmine kept turning over in her head the fact that Radhika truly was gone, and when Rahul passed on, or the rest of them, there would be no one to prove she existed, that she danced and had made a life for herself, or tried to. All evidence of a girl who had been given a divine gift would be gone. This haunted Yasmine powerfully; the notion that people could walk the earth and then disappear. That she, herself, could disappear. Unless one wrote a lasting piece of music or a story or were committed to celluloid, all people were in danger of disappearing. The way people avoided that, Yasmine figured, was by having children. Children were sometimes the only proof one ever lived.

Despite being burdened by these thoughts, she tried to tuck away the image of a dying Radhika lying in her arms. She kept herself busy with the day-to-day running of the club, and the city was beginning to swelter, which was enough of a distraction at times. Edward noticed she was peaked and restless. Several times in the night she cried out and did not remember anything the next day. She told him she was having odd dreams, but she could not recollect what they were about. He dismissed his own concerns eventually, chalking up Yasmine's disturbed sleep to seeing the dying girl, whom she still insisted was Radhika, lying in the street. He did not think anyone truly recovered from seeing something like that.

Then a thought occurred to him. 'Are you giving up your rations to Rahul again?' he asked.

Yasmine nodded. Edward was angry. He suspected she felt guilty about Radhika and this was her expiation. 'But why?' Edward still demanded. 'I give you enough to spare. I thought you had lost weight.'

'A bit,' Yasmine said. 'But I don't even have an appetite lately. I can't seem to keep much down.'

'Are you pregnant?' he said and chuckled. Before answering, Yasmine searched his face for panic. He smiled at her, but he looked concerned.

'No,' she said. 'Why do you always ask me that?'

'Oh! Well, that's good!'

She nodded. She was inexplicably saddened by his reaction, but then reminded herself that a child with Edward was an absurd, impossible notion.

23

Yasmine suddenly could not stand the smell of cilantro. It made her gag immediately. When Adil Baboo served tomato soup for lunch with chopped cilantro in it, she took one whiff, ran to the alley and threw up.

Patience followed her with a wet cloth and dabbed her friend's forehead, while trying to hold her hair out of her face.

Yasmine waved her away. 'Stop, Patience.'

'Got one those nasty bugs?'

'Not sure. The soup didn't smell right. The cilantro did not smell like cilantro.'

Patience lit a cigarette.

'What did it smell like?'

Yasmine leaned back against the wall of the adjoining building. Patience held out the cigarette, which Yasmine waved away in disgust, and then held out the cloth, which she took. She dabbed her face with the cool cloth and closed her eyes. 'Like a sewer in July.'

When she opened her eyes, it was to see Patience staring at her, brimming with recrimination. Patience threw down her cigarette.

'Shall I call Ghosh's uncle?' she said. Her voice was even, but Yasmine could see she was agitated.

'Sorry?'

'The baby. You're going to have to get rid of it soon. Mustn't wait too long.'

She looked at Yasmine's flat belly. Yasmine placed one hand on her abdomen and one over her mouth. 'No,' she said softly.

'Well?'

'Patience, please! Give me a moment.'

'You can't keep it, Yassu. Remember your policy. I hope it applies to you too.' Her voice was still calm, but Yasmine knew it was only a matter of time before she exploded in anger. She would allow the possibility of Yasmine's pregnancy to stew for a day or two, she would smoke several packs of Chesterfields, paint her toenails and then decide she hated the colour and change it. She would flirt more than necessary to remind herself that she was indeed in control over some aspect of her life—men's lust for her—and then she would explode. Probably at the most inopportune moment.

Yasmine walked into the club, Patience at her heels. 'You cannot seriously consider keeping it.'

Yasmine stopped and looked at Patience. As a child, Patience would often hold her breath if she did not get her way or something upset her. Once, at age three, she had passed out from a tantrum.

Yasmine put her hand on her friend's shoulder. 'Calm yourself. It may not be that.'

Patience shook her head. 'It is, I tell you. It is! You have to do what's right, Yassu. You have to do for you, what you did for me.'

There was not a trace of irony or sarcasm in Patience's voice. And it was then that Yasmine knew that her friend had fully trusted her judgement even when she did not trust it herself. This only compounded her growing dread.

Alone in her room, Yasmine sat on her bed in a stupor. She knew Patience was right; she was pregnant. She put her hand on her belly and imagined she could feel the baby flutter.

Many women she grew up with described the moment they knew they were carrying their first child. Awe and surprise were the two most expressed emotions. Some said it made them think of God almost at once. If the child was welcome, then the joy and gratitude felt vast. If it wasn't, then the midwives sprang into action and emptied the baiji's belly. Either way, there was also fear, the sudden knowledge of pain and awareness of both the vulnerability and power of their bodies. The women in Yasmine's world knew that men, save for their initial involvement, played a very small, if not non-existent, part in their lives when they were carrying a child. The community drew their circle of women tighter around them and collectively raised the children born to courtesans, whose fathers either did not claim them or only saw them when they visited their favourite. It was not uncommon that a courtesan would bear a man's child and he would become interested in another baiji in the house—a younger, newer one—and stop visiting both the mother and the child. The one discarded would then have to silently watch as he grew distant and his favours shifted.

Yasmine felt sure her experience would be no different. Edward would leave, go back to his wife, have children with her. Until she knew what she was going to do, she would not call Edward to the club, she thought to herself. Patience's words came back to her, 'You cannot seriously consider keeping it.' And yet, that was precisely what she was doing. The realisation came as a shock to Yasmine—as if the consideration was coming from somewhere outside her. And she knew then that choice had been made a long time ago, even before the baby had been conceived. It had been made on that warm night, on the front steps of Bombay Duck, when Edward had sauntered up, looking for her club, and maybe her, as he had said to her many times after that first night. And then it had been made over and over again after that. It had been made when he brought her the corsage on New Year's Eve, when they danced even as the music had stopped. When he had gone chasing after Rahul for her. There had never really been any other choice for Yasmine. And Yasmine also knew that as she brought one more person into her life, she was going to be saying goodbye to another, for she had never wanted a baby to love the way Patience craved it. A baby would never have been a burden to her.

If it was odd that at that moment Yasmine was thinking more of what her childhood friend would feel or say about the baby than the father, it did not occur to her. Perhaps because Yasmine knew that Edward would not be raising the child and that she had never really believed that he would leave his wife for her. There would be no cottage in a Connecticut valley, with a porch swing and fireplace that was lit when the snow fell outside. She was descended from a long, distinguished line of women who prided themselves on not falling prey to such romantic notions.

As Yasmine continued to sit silently on her bed, some ancient ancestral knowledge that she had unwittingly carried around inside her started to rise up. She began to do what womenfolk had done for hundreds of years at this moment: she began to circle her wagons around the baby. Her mind was clear, and she methodically began to tick off what needed to be done. The first person she would tell would be her mother, who would advise her. The second Patience, something she already dreaded, but she owed her that much. Eventually, when she felt ready, she would tell Edward. Edward was, after all, the least important person in the equation.

~

Her mother greeted the news of the baby calmly. She was not surprised that Yasmine wanted to keep it. She knew her daughter had fallen in love, and so there was no other alternative than to keep the baby. It would be like keeping a part of Edward after he went back to his wife in America, which both women expected. Though Yasmine sometimes felt a small hope he would stay, she did not indulge it for extended periods of time.

'What will you tell Daisy's girl?' her mother asked.

Yasmine shook her head. 'I'm not sure.'

'You have created quite a conundrum for yourself,' her mother said.

'Have you no words of comfort or wisdom for me?'

Shirin drew her daughter close to her and said, 'You forced her to kill her child—you did what you thought was right and best, and now you must tell her you will not do the same to your baby because you have finally realised what love is. Tell me what words of comfort can I offer you? You have created a painful situation where someone will be badly wounded.'

'I did? Why did she go and get pregnant?' Yasmine said, and then fell silent. There was nothing she could accuse her friend of that she was not guilty of as well.

'You are going to lose Patience,' Shirin said, and kissed her daughter's head. 'She will never forgive you.'

'But I cannot lose her! She's my only friend,' Yasmine said. 'She has to help me raise this baby.'

'Who do you love more? The baby or her? Choose.'

'Surely Patience would never expect me to kill my baby.'

'Surely? Don't underestimate human bitterness, Yassu. You have created a trap for yourself. The only advice I would give you is to wait to tell her. Wait until you know you will be carrying the child to term, because it's early days and her nazar and bitterness could mar your pregnancy. Patience is a sunny, loving child, but I have seen her meanness as well, and she will not forgive you for this, not soon.'

~

Rahul was beginning to come out of his depression from Radhika's sudden departure, and Yasmine assigned him the task of keeping Edward away until she gathered her thoughts and found the courage to tell Patience she was keeping the baby. That was the least she could do for her friend. She bade Rahul to go to the base with a note telling Edward that for the next few weeks, she would be unavailable to entertain him due to some unforeseen circumstances. Rahul, who was now a friend of the American officer, felt his boss was being insensitive and told her as much.

'Uff, who asked you for your opinion?' Yasmine said.

Rahul felt that, given his recent heartbreak, he was a more wizened soul, more acquainted with the harsh realities of life and love. He had developed the habit of sharing his mostly unsolicited opinions on matters of the heart and life to the kitchen staff and sweepers, and sometimes even Adil Baboo if he could catch him, which the older man bore with equanimity and amusement. Rahul had acquired a studied air of tragedy that was starting to grate on Yasmine more than anyone else. Eventually, Adil Baboo revealed that, in fact, Rahul and Radhika had never made love in the usual sense, as she was in no emotional state to do so—but had 'lain together', with only a cloth between their bare bodies, holding one another until they both fell asleep. For Rahul, this was the same as making love. It was the first time he had held a girl so closely or kissed anyone.

'Di, after my tragedy and losing my beloved—' Rahul began.

'Dhoor! What bloody tragedy?' Yasmine cried. 'Stop talking nonsense. Radhika left because she had to; she did not mean to hurt you. Now stop moping about and do as I ask.'

'That's true,' Rahul conceded. 'Maybe someday we'll be reunited. I will marry her, you know,' he added. 'After you share passion with a person, you are connected forever—you have to marry them.'

Yasmine was silent. She had still not told him about the starving girl in the alley or the funeral. She did not have the courage. And now, she had another secret she was keeping from someone she cared for, another secret that could change their relationship forever. She decided not to chide the boy anymore.

'Please just see he gets this note,' she said.

'Di—' Rahul began.

'Rahul, I will give you a tight slap if you continue to question me.'

'Please, just hear me out! Eddie da won't accept this note, you know this. He's mad with passion for you, and as a man who has known such passion myself, I can assure you he will not stay away.'

Even though she was irritated, Yasmine suppressed a smile.

'When did you start calling him Eddie da?' she asked.

'When he saved me from myself. He's like my elder brother now.'

'Well, despite all your mad passion-tasshion, I need some time to myself, and it's not for you or Eddie da to question why.'

'Are you ill, di?' He, as well as everyone else at the Duck, had noticed Yasmine was looking peaked and worn out lately. She ate very little and spoke even less. It had not escaped anyone's notice that Patience, too, was acting differently. The two women avoided one another. When one entered a room, the other found an excuse to exit it. They were not unpleasant to each other, but they did not laugh together anymore or gang up to tease Asma. Everyone could feel a cleft growing. It was unsettling and cast a pall over the club.

Yasmine paused, which was not lost on the boy.

'No, not ill, exactly. Please just do as I say.'

'All right, but it won't work, I tell you,' Rahul said. 'He'll want to come looking for you even more.'

~

Edward read the note three times and tried to decipher the real meaning, but it held no clues. It was simple, two lines, informing him she was busy and that she would see him within a fortnight. For a moment, Edward could not remember that a fortnight was two weeks. He thought it meant a month. Rahul sat next to him, sipping on a pop and occasionally glancing at him with sympathy. He patted Edward on the back because now he felt they were friends and comrades in matters of love.

'Women, kid,' Edward said. Rahul nodded. Edward took out his English to Bangla phrasebook. 'Please tell her I understand. As long as she's okay,' Edward said in heavily accented, broken Bangla, but Rahul understood, though he was shaking his head at him.

'What? She's not okay? What?' Edward said.

He started flipping through the book, frustrated. He looked up fortnight and saw that it meant two weeks. That also seemed like a huge amount of time. Since they had become lovers, they had not been apart more than three days. After a moment, he gave up and glanced at his wristwatch. 'You and me are going to need a translator, kid,' he said. He turned the note over and scrawled a note to Patience asking for her help: *Our mutual friend is giving me the cold shoulder. Rahul seems to have an idea of what's going on, but of course, we don't understand what the other is saying. Need your enviable language skills. HELP! Yours, Edward.*

'Patience di,' Edward said, pointing to the note. 'Ami, tumi, Patience di.' He pointed to himself and Rahul.

'Yes!' Rahul jumped up. 'Cholo!' he said and pulled Edward up by the arm.

'Sorry, kid. I can't leave base now. Patience di, give this.'

Edward walked the boy to the street and summoned a gharry. He paid the driver. Rahul scrambled on board the horse-drawn carriage. He was happy he would not have to walk all the way back into town.

'I will discharge my duty most properly,' he said to Edward in Bangla and saluted him, his chest puffed out.

Edward saluted him back.

'At ease, soldier,' he said. 'I hope you survive Yasmine di's anger when she finds out you took matters into your own hands.'

'Everything a-okay!' Rahul declared. He gave Edward a toothy grin.

'Patience di,' Edward said. 'Jaldi koro.'

Rahul nodded. 'Yes! I will be very fast!'

24

Yasmine was waiting for Rahul. She had left the door to her office ajar so she would hear if the boy walked through the front door, which he was not officially allowed to do but often did. Rahul walked in as quietly as he could and closed the door slowly. He saw the door to Yasmine's office was open and turned around to walk back out and enter through the alley, but Yasmine emerged at once. She was anxious; she did not admonish him for walking through the front.

'Well?' she said.

'I gave it to him,' Rahul replied. 'As you ordered me to.'

'Okay, good. Why were you leaving again?'

'I wasn't.'

'You were!'

'Yasmine di, you look tired. You should rest. I'll fetch you some tea.'

'Did he say anything?' Yasmine asked, ignoring him.

'Yes.'

'Well, what did he say?' Yasmine said, exasperated.

'He said, okay.'

'I see.' She was disappointed. 'That's all?'

'What else can he say when the woman he loves tells him to stay away from her?'

Yasmine smiled. 'So no mad passion then? See, I told you.'

'Yes, di. May I go now? I have much work to do.'

'Since when are you so eager to work?'

'I'm a changed man, di.'

'Indeed.'

'Have you seen Patience di?'

At the mention of Patience, Yasmine became sombre.

'No, I have not. Why?'

'She needed me to run to New Market for her.'

'For what?'

'A packet of hairpins,' Rahul lied without hesitation. He had planned the answer. His quick reply worked. Yasmine did not question it.

'Well, you cannot do it now. There's too much work here. Adil Baboo needs you since Radhika—' Yasmine trailed off.

'You can say her name, Yasmine di. It causes a sharp pain in my chest, but it's a pain I can live with and it reminds me of the love we shared.'

Yasmine began to smile but stopped when she saw the look on Rahul's face. He was looking at her with an almost defiant expression, but she knew it was his way of managing the sadness he carried around always.

He aged a little in her eyes at that moment. Perhaps he was older in some ways.

'If Patience di needs you, that's quite all right. You can work later. Go and find her.'

'What's with all the cloak and dagger, love?' Patience asked Edward when she joined him for a drink at the ARC. She smiled at a young officer who had raised his glass to her when she walked in. Many eyes watched the beautiful brunette with interest as she smiled and talked with Edward. A waiter brought over two glasses of ice-cold beer, compliments of the officer at the bar.

'Oh, how lovely!' Patience said. 'I don't remember the last time I had anything ice cold.' She nodded at the young man who had sent over the drinks. 'Do you know that delicious chap standing there?'

'Yeah, he's married.'

Patience raised an eyebrow at the accusatory tone in Edward's voice.

'Yes, yes, I know. I'm a hypocrite,' Edward said, abashed.

Patience chuckled.

'Did you bring Rahul like I asked?' Edward asked.

'Yes, love. He's outside, of course. Natives not being allowed in and all.'

Patience's jovial demeanour changed when she said that. She leaned in, 'Of course, if they knew I was a bit native, I wouldn't be allowed in either now, would I?'

The absurdity of it struck Edward at once. He remembered Tommy's face when asked to leave Bombay Duck. He would not have been able to walk in here with Yasmine on his arm or sit with her like this, laughing over a glass of beer and some nuts.

'You're allowed,' Edward said. 'It's just unusual. We're not like the Brits. Negroes are a different story.'

'How?' Patience asked. She was genuinely curious. 'You know the Brits look at us the way you do Negroes.'

'It's just not the same,' Edward protested.

'Ha! Yasmine would disagree,' Patience said.

'Speaking of which...'

'Ahh yes. Giving you the brush-off, is she?'

Patience ate a nut and took a sip of beer.

'Well, I'm not sure, Patience. She doesn't seem herself lately. Have you noticed anything?'

Patience took another two nuts from the dish and ate them. She chewed slowly, swallowed and then took a large gulp of beer. Edward watched her performance in bemusement. He was used to her theatrics.

When she went to reach for more nuts, Edward stopped her.

'Okay, spill it, please! You clearly know what's going on. And so does Rahul.'

'No, the boy knows nothing. He just wants you to ignore the note and go to her. He thinks it's a bad idea to stay away. Ever since Radhika left, he's been a touch philosophical.'

'He's right. I shouldn't stay away. Something's wrong. If you know, you should tell me what it is.'

'It's not my place.'

'You're like her sister. She loves you. She knows you would never do anything to hurt her.'

Patience sighed and looked away. The officer at the bar raised a quizzical brow when she looked over at him. She gave him an absent-minded smile and turned back to Edward.

'Yasmine is pregnant, and she feels guilty because she's going to have an abortion. She's ashamed and not ready to face you. For all I know, she might have already done it.'

As Patience was talking, Edward closed his eyes. He was not completely shocked. They had not been very careful recently.

Patience stopped talking and observed Edward. His eyes were still closed.

'Oy, this is hardly the time to take a cat nap,' she said. She looked around, embarrassed, when he continued to sit with his eyes closed, and wiped the corner of her mouth with a napkin.

'I'm thinking,' he said.

'What's there to think about, poppet? Neither of you wants it.'

Edward opened his eyes and looked at Patience. Patience chuckled and took a nervous sip of beer. 'Right?' she said.

There was something in her tone he could not place. It was a surprising urgency; no, it was more than that, it was desperation, he told himself. It did not make sense to him. And because it made no sense, he ushered it out of his mind almost as quickly as it had come in.

'Did she say she didn't want it?'

'She doesn't bloody well have to. I know,' Patience said. Now she was defensive. 'And you can't want it, Eddie. How would you explain your little brown kabob back to the wife at home? Oh here, love, picked you up a few souvenirs from Calcutta, a brass spittoon and oh! A baby! He's got a touch of the tar brush, but we can trot him out for parties.'

As Edward listened to Patience, he was taken aback and then disgusted by what she was saying. His emotions were compounded by the fact she was absolutely right.

'And where there's a baby, there's a mum, now, isn't there? Will you take Yasmine over to America then—'

'I haven't thought that far ahead,' he cut her off. 'I mean, I just got this news. I need a moment to digest it.'

'Might I suggest taking her as your maid?'

Edward sat up. 'Patience, stop it!'

'Or the kabob's ayah! She can wipe his wee bum while you and your missus have cocktails at the club.'

Edward stood up. He gestured to the nearest waiter for the bill, paid and took Patience by the elbow. 'Come on,' he said and led her out, his fingers pressing into her arm. Patience waved to the officer who had sent over the beers but allowed Edward to lead her away. 'I think those beers were free,' she said, to no one in particular.

Once outside, Edward announced to Rahul and Patience that he was going to Bombay Duck, an idea Rahul now felt was not the wisest course of action, given how agitated Edward seemed.

'Tell Eddie da that Yasmine di is not expecting him, and she doesn't like surprises and will throw him out by his neck,' he said to Patience.

'Oh, hush!' Patience said, as she ran to keep up with Edward's long stride. 'You're worried about your own neck! Eddie knows what's he doing.'

At the club, Patience stopped Edward from going through the door at once. She said, 'Edward, think of Yasmine. Encourage her to make the right decision.'

'You said she didn't want it. Hasn't she made up her mind?'

'I know what I said, but she's in love and all that, and that could muddle her up. Once you leave, what will happen to the child and her?'

'None of you actually think I'm going to stay, do you?'

Patience snorted. 'Oh Eddie, please. Of course you're going to leave her. Stop talking bollocks and do the only right thing you can do.'

'I actually love her, Patience.'

'Not enough, Eddie. None of you ever love enough.'

~

Edward knocked softly on her door. There was no answer. He turned the knob and stood in the doorway. She was fast asleep on her bed, one arm thrown over her eyes. He took off his cap and sat down in a chair near the window and looked at her. He didn't want to wake her immediately—just look at her and gather his thoughts. Her bare midriff was exposed. He let his gaze linger there, imagining the baby inside. His baby. It was an unfamiliar feeling, knowing his child existed. But it made sense to him. He felt pride and protectiveness. He allowed himself to dwell on those thoughts for a few minutes. He kneeled next to the bed and let his palm hover over her belly. He touched her gently and then kissed her lips lightly. When she didn't stir, he whispered, 'Honey? Can you wake up?'

She moved her arm and opened her eyes. Startled to see Edward so close, she sat up at once, which made her dizzy.

She was overcome with nausea and ran out of the room. Edward stayed back, not knowing what to do and slightly embarrassed. When Yasmine returned, looking clammy and pale, he said, 'Gee, I don't think I ever made a girl throw up before.'

'Have you changed your aftershave?' Yasmine asked, scowling.

Edward sniffed his collar. 'No.'

'Well, it smells different. You smell different.'

She sat down on the bed and dabbed her forehead with a damp cloth. Edward started to sit next to her, but Yasmine took one whiff of him and started gagging again. Edward quickly retreated to the chair.

'Are you sick?'

'Yes,' Yasmine said. She did not look at him.

'Stomach bug?'

'Something like that.'

'That why you sent Rahul to keep me away?'

'Yes, I didn't want you to get sick.'

Edward sighed and turned his cap over in his hands.

'Please stop lying to me, Yasmine,' he said.

She looked up then.

'I don't lie.'

'No?'

'No.'

'I know, honey. Patience told me.'

At the mention of Patience's name, Yasmine stood up quickly. The movement made her dizzy again, and she almost fell. Edward was by her side instantly, to catch her.

'What did Patience tell you?' she said. Her voice was muffled. She held the cloth to her mouth in case she vomited again.

'You're pregnant.'

Yasmine was silent. Edward waited for her to deny it. He hoped a little that she would and that Patience was wrong. But when she said nothing, he knew she had been telling the truth.

'I was going to tell you,' Yasmine said.

'It's okay, honey.' Edward put his arm around her. When she went to remove the cloth from her mouth and nose, he stopped her. 'In case my smell bothers you again,' he said, smiling. 'I want to hold you.'

Yasmine looked at him. She had not expected him to be so calm. He appeared unworried.

'What?' he said.

'You're not upset?'

'Yes, but for you and what you have to go through. I'll be here. Whatever it costs or takes. Please be sensible and use a proper doctor, okay? Back home, at least two girls died doing it. One of my classmates, this poor kid named Tara, bled out in a field. The doctor had panicked and dumped her there. I'll never forget it.'

Yasmine then realised why Edward was not worried. She removed his arm from around her shoulders and sat in the chair opposite the bed.

'I'm not going to bleed out in a field,' she said. Her voice was grim.

'Yes, I know—you're too smart for that,' he said. He started to light a cigarette.

'Please don't,' Yasmine said. 'The smoke makes me gag.'

He blew out the match. She was being cold. A feeling of dread was starting to creep into him.

'Don't be angry at Patience,' he said.

'I'm not. Did she say I was going to—get rid of it?'

'Well, yeah. She assumed—'

'And did you assume that as well?'

Edward did not answer at once. He knew then he had made a terrible mistake and that if he did not say precisely the right thing, that Yasmine would retreat into her mother's garden, or into her work and worse still, into herself. He always felt that Yasmine was the kind of woman who was somewhat irretrievable once she retreated. The secret was to not cause her to run in the first place, but if it happened, if she started to step back, to block her quickly; but he felt powerless at that moment. So he said nothing and hoped she would speak first.

Yasmine watched him, knowing he was confused and apprehensive. She felt both pity and resentment. He finally looked at her. They stared at one another, both trying to work out a stratagem that would not leave them undefended, neither sure of what the other was thinking, both aware of a volatile undercurrent that could escalate into a shouting match, both hoping the other would not forsake them. She was afraid he was going to leave her; he was afraid of her coldness. It occurred to Yasmine that she had always been afraid of his inevitable departure. She did not want to hasten it. But she succumbed to her fear and decided that she was going to leave first. He was not going to measure up, and she would prove that to him and herself.

'First things first,' Yasmine said. 'Will you go to the MPs and tell them that Louis raped Radhika?'

Edward knew what she was doing, but he could not believe she was doing it now. She was spoiling for a fight and testing him. And he obliged her.

'Are you fucking kidding me?'

She smoothed down her sari and her hair. She was all business. He wasn't going to let her get away with it. His fear of her retreat was now trumped by his anger at the coldness she was using as a shield.

'I hate that kind of language,' she said.

Edward stood up. He stood in front of her chair and looked down at her. She looked away, refusing to be intimidated. Edward saw the retreat. It was heart-rending, but he was powerless against it.

'Yasmine, we have other things to discuss.'

'Such as?'

'You know what I'm talking about!'

'Don't raise your voice at me.'

This made Edward louder.

'Are you keeping the baby?'

'That's my concern.'

Edward sat back down on the bed, stunned.

'It's our concern. Our concern,' he said.

Yasmine gave a sardonic laugh. Before she could say anything, Edward launched into a tirade. Yasmine had never seen him this angry. He shouted at her, his face red.

'Spare me the "we women have done this alone for centuries" bullshit, you got me? Fathers have some goddamn rights! You can't just go making unilateral decisions. Who the hell do you think you are? You're going to have my baby and shut me out? No way!'

Yasmine did not stand up, though she wanted to. It would make her dizzy, she knew. She wanted to throw Edward out by the scruff of his neck.

'As far as I'm concerned, you're leaving, so you have no rights. Or are you staying in India, Edward? Will you divorce Maggie and come live here with me and raise a family?'

Edward was jarred at hearing his wife's name uttered out loud. It struck him that, in fact, he had not thought about her for a long time. He could not remember when he last wrote to any of his family. Maggie's letters had kept coming without fail every other week. They lay unopened in the trunk at the foot of his bed. Eleven, pale-blue envelopes that smelled lightly of her perfume. Yasmine saw his anger dissipate and knew it meant he would go now. Maggie's name was the secret word, the reminder of his sanctuary, an uncomplicated, clean place where everything was ordered and familiar. The babies Maggie gave him would be the right kind. She had uttered it to hurt him, and she had succeeded in hurting herself. Her resolve to prove how unworthy he truly was strengthened.

'I want you to do one thing for me and that is to find justice for Radhika.'

'Yasmine, Radhika never named him, and he has not confessed. There is no proof.'

'There was no proof Tommy's friends did it, yet where are they now?'

'That's different.'

'Because they're coloured.'

'Yes! What else do you want me to say?'

'I'm coloured.'

'I kicked him out of the basha. What more do you want me to do? I did take a stand!'

'So then if I had been in Tommy's position, you would have sold me down the river too? I believe that is the correct expression?'

'It's not the same.'

'And yet it is, utterly the same.'

'Why are you so obsessed with Tommy?'

'Don't obfuscate the issue.'

'That's a big word.'

Yasmine marched over to the wall and raised the speed on the fan, to attempt to drown out the yelling she suspected was going to get worse.

'And here we have it, that condescending tone,' she said, as she walked back to the bed and sat down.

'I'm sorry, I didn't mean it like that. You know how I feel about you. You know I think you're smart as a whip.'

'Yes, yes. But you're still surprised when I dare show how smart I am.'

'Who's obfuscating now?'

'I am trying to right a wrong.'

'What about the fact that you are pregnant?'

'Edward, you don't have any obligation towards me or the baby.'

'I don't doubt you can provide for the baby, Yasmine,' he said. 'But I need a minute, a moment to absorb the news. There are decisions to be made.'

'It saddens me that you need even a second to think about what is right. If one of your precious nurses had been attacked by an Indian, I can only imagine how quickly you would act. There would not have been a moment's hesitation. The hesitation here is from the fact that one of your own is the criminal, and the victim is nothing but a lowly little Indian girl who died alone in an alley. I could be Radhika,' she said.

Edward shook his head. 'No, Yasmine. You could not.'

'To you lot, I am. To you lot, there is no difference between a maharani and chakrani. To you, we're all just that in the end—servant girls.'

'Not to me,' Edward said. He knelt down. He needed to hold her. She would not allow it.

'Then prove it,' she said. She lay down on the bed and closed her eyes.

Edward sighed.

'You hesitated,' she said, her eyes still closed.

'No, just give me a minute. There are procedures and rules. If I can get Louis to confess officially, it would be better all around.'

'He will never confess, Edward. He's a snake and you know it. But you will defend him, protect him because he is your kind of snake. And you think I would let you near my child?'

'Please don't be hasty, Yasmine. Please.'

'I want to rest.'

'Let me stay a bit.'

'I want to sleep.'

'When will I see you?'

Yasmine turned on her side, away from him. She didn't answer.

'Okay,' Edward said after a moment. 'You let me know. I'll come to you.'

25

Downstairs, Patience, Asma and Madhu sat at the bar, smoking and listening to Edward and Yasmine shout at each other above stairs. Edward's voice was loudest, and then there was silence. Rahul sat on the floor, leaning against the bar, rolling a baseball back and forth between his legs. Yasmine was firm and dictatorial, but she never raised her voice to them.

'Why does it feel like my mum and dad are having a banging row?' Madhu said. Asma giggled and nibbled on a digestive biscuit. Patience was silent.

'Maybe we shouldn't be listening,' Asma said. 'Yassu would be cross if she knew.'

'We have every right to know, because what happens to Yasmine affects all of us,' Patience said. Asma looked at her curiously. She was subdued. It was not normal.

Rahul started to blame himself for what was happening between Yasmine and Edward, but Patience hushed him. 'They have to have it out,' she said.

'Why are they fighting?' the boy wanted to know. 'Because Yasmine di wants him to leave her alone?'

All three women looked at one another. Madhu started to tell him, but Patience stopped her.

'Lovers fight. Didn't you and Radhika fight?' she said.

'Never!' Rahul said. He pondered this. 'Is it bad that we didn't?'

Everyone smiled at him. 'I want to know!' he said. 'Does it mean there is no love, if there is no shouting?'

'Radhika didn't leave because you didn't shout at her enough, you silly fool,' Madhu said.

He looked down at the grimy ball in his hands, a gift from Corporal Addison. He lined up his middle and forefingers with the red stitching the way his friend had shown him. That was a curveball, he remembered. He had become a competent pitcher and often took refuge with his American friends at the base when he felt melancholy. Yasmine had been so distracted lately, she did not notice his absences. He was also running errands for the soldiers and being paid handsomely for it—more than Yasmine paid him, but he would never tell her that. She would be proud if she knew he was saving most of it. He would need it when Radhika came back and they married.

'Why did she leave me then?' he asked no one in particular.

~

Edward walked down the stairs into the main room and stood holding his cap, muttering to himself. His shoulders were slumped. He looked defeated and tired. Rahul scrambled up and went to him. Edward patted the boy's bony shoulder.

'Do I look that bad?' he said when he saw Rahul's face.

Rahul turned to the others, who were all trying to think of something appropriate to say.

'She's killed him,' he said.

Patience hopped off the bar stool and went to Edward.

'I know it seems bad, love,' she said as gently as she could. 'But it's for the best. Give her a bit of time to calm down. She'll be right as rain soon enough.'

'Hmm? What? Oh yeah. Well, I don't know what she's thinking about us,' Edward said. He had not heard anything Patience had said to him.

'We'll take care of her.'

This roused him out of his stupor. He took Patience's hands in his. 'I know. That gives me peace. I'm just trying to figure things out, you know. But knowing she and the baby will be surrounded by you all until I figure it out… You're like a family. That makes me feel better.'

Patience laughed in disbelief. 'No, no, Eddie. What I meant was, we'll take care of her after she has the procedure done.'

'She's keeping it,' Edward said. He looked down at his watch. 'I don't know how I feel about that.' When he glanced up at Patience, her smile was frozen. 'What's wrong?' he said, concerned.

Asma clapped her chubby hands. 'Oh, bravo!' she said. 'I'm so glad! A baby, here in the club!'

She ran up to Patience and hugged her. Patience, stunned, did not hug her back. Asma went to hug Edward, thought better of it and just shook his hand.

'I know this is all very improper,' Asma said, trying to strike a more sombre note, as it *was* all very untoward, 'but a baby is like a breath of fresh air. You can be sure we'll all take care of it. I'm excellent with babies. Yassu will need us. She's not very motherly.'

Edward was still looking at Patience. The comforting smile from a moment before was wiped from her face. Without a word, Patience turned and walked up the stairs to Yasmine's room.

'She's resting,' Edward called after her. Patience kept walking as if she had not heard him. They all watched as she entered the room without knocking.

Edward knew something was amiss, but he could not imagine what. The others seemed genuinely happy for Yasmine. Rahul, when he was told, grinned and slapped Edward on the back. Everyone knew he would leave to go back to America, or to the jungles to get killed, and that most likely Yasmine would be raising the baby at the club, with the family she had cobbled together, but they were all happy nonetheless. It was something different and broke up the monotony of the war and its deprivations. A baby meant new life; new life meant hope.

'I have to go,' Edward said to Asma and Madhu. 'Your boss is not feeling too well. Take care of her for me. Make sure she doesn't work too hard.'

Asma, Rahul and Madhu followed Edward to the door. 'Will you be coming back soon?' Asma asked.

'Yes, as soon as she asks for me. If she needs anything special, let me know. I'll send it.'

He put his cap on and adjusted it. He paused as if he wanted to say something more but only thanked them and left.

~

When Yasmine finally opened her eyes, the room was shrouded in darkness and smelled of tobacco. She yawned and stretched and wondered what time it was. Her conversation with Edward and the morning sickness had exhausted her, and she realised she must have slept for hours. Someone had switched on the ceiling fan but it did not lessen the smell of ash and tobacco. 'Yuck,' she said out loud. She glanced at her wristwatch but could not see the numbers on the dial. She arose and switched on the overhead light. It was well past five. Now the smell of the evening meal being prepared wafted up from the kitchen, filling her small room with too many odours. Her hand went to her mouth as the smell of onions and garlic being fried hit her nostrils. She opened the single window in the room to let some air in. It was a typical summer Calcutta breeze, neither cool nor refreshing, but the open window released some of the other smells. The muezzin's call to evening prayer started up from the nearest mosque, and without thinking, Yasmine covered her head with her sari. She sat on the wide-lipped sill and watched the busy activity on Park Street below. Usually by this time, she would be downstairs, barking orders at the kitchen staff and going over the evening's entertainment, who would go first or do what, but she was in no hurry to move.

'Allah ho akbar,' she whispered, as the muezzin sang out, summoning the faithful, the believers. She lifted her palms up and silently mouthed a dua and then ran her hands over her face. When she was small, she thought doing that anchored the prayer in place on her person. This made sense to her, though many of the practices did not.

She knew she could not hide in her room all night. She yawned again and got up to walk to her vanity. It was then that she saw the cigarette ash and butts on the floor by the chair, three of them. Yasmine pulled her handkerchief out of the neck of her bodice and swept it up. That solved the mystery of the heavy smell of stale tobacco. But who would dare to come into her room while she slept, sit in the chair and proceed to smoke one cigarette after another and then stub them out on the floor? To Yasmine, it was a sign of contempt. Yasmine walked to the window and threw the butts out into the street. Before she did that, she noted the brand, Chesterfields, covered by a smudge of red lipstick. Her heart heavy, and more than a little frightened, she went to look for Patience.

She knocked softly on Patience's door. When there was no answer, she slowly opened it. The room was dark and empty. Her vanity had been cleared of all her pots of rouge and nail polish. The necklaces that usually hung on the side of her mirror were gone. Her bed was stripped. Yasmine walked to the closet. It was nearly empty. Yasmine was a little relieved there would be no confrontation that night at least. She didn't know if she had the strength for it.

She went downstairs and asked Adil Baboo to join her in the office.

'Patience has left,' she said. She could not meet Adil Baboo's eyes.

'What has happened?'

For a moment, Yasmine considered lying. It was unheard of for a young woman to tell a man who was not a member of her family all her secrets, but everything would be revealed in due time anyway. There were very few secrets that stayed hidden at the Duck.

'I am pregnant,' Yasmine said. She said it so quietly that Adil Baboo had to strain to hear her.

'Did you tell Edward sahib?' Adil Baboo said.

Yasmine nodded. She could hear him shift his weight. He was agitated.

'And will he do what is right? He will marry you?'

Yasmine sighed. 'Of course not, Adil da.' It was the first time she had referred to him as her elder brother.

'No, of course not,' Adil Baboo said. 'Luckily, you have a family.'

Yasmine looked up. 'Yes, but not Patience. You see—'

Adil Baboo stopped her. 'I know, Yasmine. I know what you made her do.'

'Will she ever forgive me?'

'I'm not sure. You're like sisters, and in my experience, families are capable of holding grudges that last generations.'

Yasmine began to cry. 'Patience is a champion grudge holder,' she said.

'She'll come back soon, Yasmine, at least to collect her wages. You can try to speak to her then.'

She knew Adil Baboo was just being kind. Patience would not want to speak to her. Yasmine had lost her.

26

Before, when Yasmine was angry, all he had to do was crack a joke and make her smile, or even leave for a few days until she cooled down. He knew women in her state were very emotional and did not always think clearly. He was confident she would call him when she was ready. She loved him, of that he was certain, and he too needed the time to decide what to do. He knew combat was imminent. There was a part of him that almost welcomed it. It was a sight less intimidating than choosing between Maggie and Yasmine. Though he would not have readily admitted it, there were moments when he was relieved that Yasmine could, if necessary, raise the child on her own. He had wanted to tell her that he did not know of many American girls who would have the resources to do the same. In America, he had wanted to say, an unmarried girl in her condition was ostracised. Yasmine, at least, had her mother, her own money and the other women in her world to help her. He was grateful she was strong enough to raise the baby alone, because even if he chose to stay in India, he would have to travel back to the US and be away for months, maybe years before he could return a free man.

He waited, and then on the sixth day after his confrontation with Yasmine, decided to ask Louis out for a drink at the ARC, to try and gauge if he could at least trick him into a real confession. When he went to Louis's basha, he found him readying to leave for Burma and in high spirits.

'Finally, Lafaver! I'm going to get me some Japs. I've been going stir crazy in this hell hole.'

'I think Calcutta is better than the Big Green, Louis. And we're taking a beating out there.'

'Look, at this point, I need to move, you know?'

Edward studied Louis, who could not quite hold his gaze.

'What's the rush?' Edward said. 'We're all going to get called up eventually.'

'No rush. Just a change of scenery. Too many Indians start to get to a man, you know?' He gave Edward a toothy grin. 'Or maybe you don't. You love you some natives.'

Edward smiled and leaned against the doorframe. He said nothing for several seconds as he watched Louis energetically pack. After a moment, Louis threw down his duffel on the bed and turned to Edward. 'So, Lafaver, what gives?'

'Why so antsy, Deccico?'

'Who the fuck is antsy?'

'You're in an awful hurry to leave Calcutta. You think the Japs will be nicer to you?'

'Not all of us think the sun shines out of India's ass, okay? Another year here, and you'll probably turn native.'

'And that would be terrible, right?'

'Yeah, it would,' he said, turning back to his bag, 'it would be a goddamn tragedy for you to throw over your American wife for some native tail. Because you are an American officer, and you're here fighting for your country, America. Sometimes I think you forget that.'

'And as an American officer, I have certain duties to uphold. Because I am a representative in India of this great nation you so love, and that means I conduct myself in such a way that honours the fact that we are Americans.'

Louis stopped what he was doing and faced Edward. Edward could see he was trying to control himself. He continued to lean easily against the doorjamb and observe Louis.

'What are you accusing me of?' Louis demanded.

'You know what.'

'Still? Because that darkie bitch told you to?'

Edward lunged at Louis, knocking him back. He punched him twice in the face, drawing blood, before Louis managed to twist out of his grasp and pin him to the ground. Louis's face was so close to Edward's, the blood from his lip dripped on to Edward's cheek. They silently wrestled. Two officers walked by and saw them. They pulled Louis off of Edward before he could land another punch. Louis immediately put his hands up.

'A misunderstanding, guys. We're good, right, Lafaver?'

Edward was also bleeding from the mouth. Louis offered him his hand to help him up. Edward batted it away and stood up. The other officers left after determining they were not going to kill one another.

'I didn't do it, Lafaver. I don't know what she told you.' He spat blood onto the ground. Edward's punch had loosened a tooth.

'I know you want to think those boys didn't do it, but they did. And if you're going to go looking, look at that Tommy kid. How come he got off free? You know why? Because he's practically white. He could easily pass for white back East. He did some fast talking and got his own buddies thrown in the brig. Meanwhile, he's waltzing around, romancing your lady.'

Edward was not sure how Louis had deduced that, but he was not going to give him the satisfaction of knowing he was right about Tommy and Yasmine. The problem was that, now with Yasmine being in the family way, Edward had been thinking about Tommy and Yasmine, indulging thoughts that only made him feel worse.

'Maybe he's the one who got her all worked up. To take the heat off himself, he pointed at me. Ever think of that?'

It was not what Louis said, but Edward heard, 'Maybe he was the one who got her knocked up.'

'What did you say?' he said between gritted teeth.

'You heard me,' Louis replied and continued packing.

Edward shook his head. 'He didn't knock her up. You have no idea what you're saying.'

Louis was confused. 'What the fuck are you babbling about, Lafaver?'

Edward knew Tommy wanted Yasmine, and that she was attracted to him. He didn't allow himself to think beyond that. It was possible they had been alone at least once. He knew Louis was capable of hurting Radhika, but suddenly, his own jealousy pushed that notion somewhere behind the idea that Tommy was the real villain in this case. He knew he wanted him to be.

'If you want my advice ...' Louis began.

'I really don't,' Edward said.

'Fine.' Louis threw up his hands.

Edward got up gingerly and sat on the edge of Louis's bed and looked at him. 'You know I dislike you, Deccico?'

'I don't care.'

'You're not a decent man,' he said quietly, almost to himself.

Louis heard him and had no retort. He cleared his throat and finished packing. He was silent while Edward watched him, but his face had turned red. When he was done, he slung his bag over his shoulder and held out his hand to Edward, who did not take it; he looked down at it like it was a dirty thing.

Louis dropped his hand. His face took on its previous pugnacity. He grinned.

'You better pray we don't end up in the same unit, you sorry son of a bitch,' he said. 'I would watch my back if I was you.'

'Are you threatening me?' Edward said, incredulous.

For a moment, it seemed as if Louis would take another punch at him but then he backed down. 'Good luck, Lafaver. I feel for you. It's never going to happen with that darkie broad of yours. And you would be a fool to even try. You're going to ruin lives, and for what?'

~

Ten days passed, and she did not call him. Not that he expected her to, but he had hoped. He waited. Her silence eventually made him resentful. He sent her an angry note:

If you choose to call me, I shall pick up the phone. But it has to be you. I am done trying. If you come to me, come prepared to lay your heart out on the table and humble yourself. I shall accept nothing less. If you choose not to call me, then Godspeed. As ever…

He waited three days, three days that afforded him no sleep and very little appetite. He realised the note had not struck the right tone. He had typed it on a sheet of carbon paper and kept reading the copy. His heart sank. It was too harsh, dishonest. He could not stay away. He wanted to tell her he had confronted Louis—for her. That he had physically assaulted him—for her. Risking disciplinary action and maybe even a court-martial. Surely that counted for something?

When he returned to the Duck, it was to find the windows shuttered and the door barred. Both the club and Yasmine were closed for business that day as it were, so she could figure out the logistics of her confinement. He banged on the door until she let him in, but he saw it was already too late.

'I tried, sweetheart, but Louis is gone. He's halfway to Rangoon by now. He'll probably be killed. Sometimes justice is not served the way we want, Yasmine. That's the harsh reality.'

'Thank you for explaining life to me, Edward,' she said.

Yasmine looked at Edward until he turned away, embarrassed. She knew he was lying, that he had not tried hard enough and that he had allowed Louis to get away.

'How long are you going to be closed down?'

'A few days. I have some things to organise.'

'Does it have to do with the baby? Can I help—'

'I think you should leave now,' she said in a controlled voice.

'Okay, I'll be back later. Just call me, and I'll head over.'

'No, you said it was my choice.'

'Yasmine, enough of this!' Edward said. 'I'm not the guilty party here.

'Where's Patience? She'll knock some sense into you,' he said when she was silent.

At the mention of her friend's name, Yasmine's face clouded over.

'I don't think Patience will be very much help,' she said. 'Who can blame her?'

'Where is she?'

Yasmine shrugged and shook her head. 'She doesn't live here anymore. She comes in the evening to perform, and then leaves immediately after. Who can blame her?' she said again.

Edward could not understand. 'Did something happen? You two are as thick as thieves.'

Yasmine looked down at her belly, which was not yet showing. She could feel something flutter inside her once in a while, but she was not sure if she imagined it. She put a hand on her stomach.

'Nothing happened,' she said. 'Patience has grown weary of living here.'

Edward shook his head in confusion and sat down. 'I don't get it. She loves babies. You'd think she would want to be here now that she knows you're pregnant. I was hoping she would take care of you—'

'Why? So you don't have to?'

'Yasmine, you've said you don't need me. What the hell do you want?'

'Do not raise your voice at me,' Yasmine cried. 'Since Patience being gone is also your fault!'

'How? How in God's name is it my fault?' Edward was starting to think Yasmine's state was making her crazy.

Yasmine did not answer him; instead, she asked him to leave and turned her back to him.

'I'll leave for now, because I can see you're upset,' he said, as calmly as he could. 'But I'll be back tomorrow.'

'No!'

'Yasmine, don't push me, okay? I am going to be called up soon, but I'll leave early if you keep on like this.'

'I don't care.'

'Don't say that.'

'You came here to fight. Do your job.'

'Sometimes, Yasmine, you are the coldest bitch I have ever met.'

~

As the days ticked by, and he knew she was becoming even more pregnant, it began to dawn on Edward that he had lost her, somehow.

Several times he went to write to Maggie and found he could not. He finally decided to read a few of her letters. Never had he felt so much dread than when he slit open the first envelope. The guilt was almost unbearable. With each of her letters, Maggie sounded increasingly alarmed and wounded.

Never once did she accuse of him anything outright. But she knew something was amiss, in the way women know. Once, she simply wrote: *Write back to me, my love. I know you're still alive, well, I am so happy you are. Some of the girls here have not been so lucky so I am grateful, every day, that you are safe. Maybe you've been shot with Cupid's arrow instead of a Jap bullet? Just kidding. A girl can start to get a little paranoid, you know?*

Always,

Mags

Still, he could not write back. He found being idle was his worst enemy. He felt he was doing no one—neither Maggie nor Yasmine nor himself—any good by sitting around in relative comfort in Calcutta.

A directive from FDR himself ordered that a 'crack unit' of American troops be trained for jungle combat deep in Burma to engage the enemy in new and creative ways. Edward and his fellow officers joked that what the War Department really meant was they needed a 'cracked unit' of volunteers, because one had to be insane to volunteer to fight the Japs on unknown terrain during such heavy monsoon rains, when a man could not see his hand in front of his face. But, as it turned out, Washington, DC had finally heeded General Stilwell's repeated entreaties to send American Allied troops to South Asia for a deep penetration into Burma. He felt that was the only way to defeat the Japanese, who were getting closer to invading India after devastating Nanking and setting up a puppet regime in Manchuria, with the former emperor of China, the boy, Pu Yi. Because it was such a thankless task, and the jungle was a particular hardship, and possibly also because they did not place as much importance on the China–Burma–India Theatre, the army had encouraged troops deemed mentally unfit for regular service to volunteer for the mission. Amongst them were Edward's charges Sullivan, and the young Phil, who had been so enthralled with Patience.

When he learned this, Edward insisted on meeting with his CO as soon as possible to discuss volunteering earlier.

'It's a good idea, Lafaver,' the CO said, observing Edward. 'I think Calcutta's charms are waning, right? And we came here to fight; this is not a resort holiday.'

Edward blushed. 'Does everyone know?'

'Well, yes. You're in good company though. Are you friendly with Lt Williams? He was here for a while and then sent to Delhi to work in the consulate there. Real bright future.'

Edward shook his head.

'He's a kid out of, I want to say, Ohio? I think he went to Oberlin. Anyway, he goes and gets this native girl in trouble and wants to do right by her, but her parents have other ideas. So they douse her in kerosene and set her on fire. That's one way to handle the problem.'

Edward was not sure what was more shocking, what his CO had told him or the dispassionate way in which it had been said. 'Jesus Christ. Why haven't I heard about this?' he said.

His CO shrugged. 'Not sure. Probably because it was in Delhi, and the consulate kept it hushed. Point is, it's a losing proposition all around. We came here to fight and die if we have to. That is our job. End of story.'

'Did she live?'

'Who the hell knows, Lafaver?'

'Yes, sir.'

~

Two days before he left for Burma, he telephoned the club and Patience answered. She was cheery, giving him some small hope.

'I was always on your side, Eddie,' she said.

'Thanks, Patience.' He was relieved that she had been the one to answer. She was not as bright as Yasmine or as interesting, but in many ways, she was easier, softer, and warmer. Also, Patience knew how to reason with Yasmine and get around her pride.

'I'm not sure what happened here, but give Yassu a few days to cool down, ducky. She's mule-headed as you know.'

'The thing is, Patience, I don't have a few days. I leave in three days.'

'Oh no, Eddie! What have you gone and done?'

'I volunteered to go to Burma. Some of my patients were being recruited, and I volunteered with them.'

'You mean that soft-headed lot you babysit?'

'Well, yes,' Edward said. He could not help but smile at Patience's description.

'Why would they want them? Aren't they all barking?'

'That's exactly why,' Edward replied. He sighed.

'So you volunteered just because you had a little spat? That's just silly, isn't it?'

'It's not a little spat, Patience, it's been weeks. I know she thinks I won't be there for her or the baby…'

Edward kept talking, but on the other end, Patience stopped listening. When she heard 'baby', his voice faded away. Edward realised that he had not heard a single sound from Patience in nearly a minute.

'Hello?'

'I'm here, Eddie,' Patience said softly.

'I admit I was not prepared for this, but now that I have had a chance to think about it, I accept it. It's my responsibility.'

'So now what? You're all going to run off to America and set up house?'

Edward paused before answering. The hostility in her voice was unmistakable. He thought it was directed at him and his perceived unreliability. He knew Patience was protective of Yasmine.

'I'm not sure. That's why I need to talk to her ... Okay, well, thanks for listening. You've always been swell to me, Patience, and if I don't see you again, well, good luck. Maybe I'll see you on the big screen someday. What's that word you use—snogging? Snogging Clark Gable.'

'I hate him,' Patience said. 'I'd much prefer snogging Errol Flynn.'

'Can you tell Yasmine ...' he stopped.

'Yes?'

'Can you tell her I love her?'

'You can tell her yourself.'

Patience handed the phone to Yasmine, who had just walked into the room. She did not look at her. She held up the receiver until Yasmine took it and then walked out without a word. Yasmine watched her go. This was how it was now, with a barely a word, except a yes or no, exchanged between them.

'Bombay Duck.'

'It's me—don't hang up!'

'I can't talk to you now. There are too many people milling about.'

'Then meet me, please.'

Yasmine did not agree even when Edward told her he was leaving for Chittagong in three days and then on to Burma. He had hoped she would tell him not to go. He had wanted to jolt sense into her. Of course, there was no way he could get out of it even if he wanted to, and he was not entirely sure he did.

'Please talk to Patience,' Edward said. 'You listen to her, if not to me. Maybe she can explain that I am not abandoning you.'

Yasmine closed her eyes when the tears welled up at the mention of Patience. Patience, who was a mere twelve feet away in another room, yet was a world away from her now. Who didn't see her or hear her anymore.

'I have tried to talk to Patience about many things, Edward,' Yasmine said. 'We are not on speaking terms at the moment.'

Edward was confused, but Yasmine cut him off when he tried to ask why they were not speaking.

'I could die, Yasmine,' he said.

'So could I,' she replied. 'In childbirth. We all have our battles, Edward.'

27

Six months after Edward left, Yasmine travelled to her mother's house in Burdwan to give birth. She stayed for three days past her due date, but the baby did not budge. Almost every other day, she received panicked phone calls from Asma or Adil Baboo, asking her when she would return to Calcutta. At first, Adil Baboo had not wanted to worry her and assured her that the business was thriving. The truth was, without her authoritative presence, the bearers and Rahul were not quite running amok but were sloppier than usual. Because Adil Baboo had to man the front of the house every evening, he did not supervise the kitchen staff and food was left out, making it a haven for the rodents that he had managed to fight off all that time. Adil Baboo put all the orders in properly, yet there always seemed to be some discrepancy with the numbers and the accounts; something that someone on the other end had overlooked. Yasmine's eagle eye and assertiveness with suppliers had prevented that in the past. It was clear that without her at the helm, they would lose more money than usual.

Yasmine knew the only other person who could perhaps keep things running in the front whilst Adil Baboo managed the back would be Patience. She sent word, asking her to move back into the club for the duration of her confinement and run things. She said she would cut Patience fifteen per cent of the take after all bills were paid. Patience refused, stunning both Shirin and Yasmine.

Yasmine was in terrible discomfort. Both her ankles were swollen, and she could not sleep easily. Her lower back was frequently in spasms, and she could not stand or sit down without help. Her mother insisted she take vigorous walks around the garden to 'jostle the baby out'.

'This is my nightmare,' she said between sobs to her mother as she waddled around a dahlia bed. 'This is why I never wanted children, and now my business is ruined. For what?'

'You'll know for what soon enough,' Shirin soothed her daughter.

'What if it never comes out?' Yasmine said. The horrifying thought sunk in, and she began to cry again.

'Uff-oh! Enough with the whining,' Shirin snapped. 'You carry on as if you are the first woman to have a baby who would rather stay inside. Can you blame him?'

Yasmine nodded, still crying. 'How do you know it's a him?'

'Oh, it's a boy all right. Bina baji saw it, and so did I in various dreams,' Shirin said with complete confidence.

'Bina baji is a quack,' Yasmine said.

Shirin raised her eyebrows. 'Oh really? She was not so much of a quack when you consulted her about Edward, was she?'

Yasmine sighed. She forgot that her mother knew almost everything that was happening in her daughter's life. And what Yasmine did not readily volunteer, Shirin would ferret out through her various sources.

Shirin appraised her reflection in the fountain. 'I'm much too young to be a grandmother,' she said. 'Forty! I shall play the role perfectly!'

Yasmine smiled. Her mother was forty-three, but she did not bother to correct her. Shirin had always been so much more elegant and audacious than her, unapologetic as well. She was proud to be a courtesan and of her heritage. She felt sorry for all the Indian housewives chained to their roles as 'devis' of motherhood and virtue, who were discarded if their husbands passed away or were subject to the cruel whims of his mother and family. Shirin had a devoted lover, an intelligent daughter and one crore rupees in a bank account in Calcutta, gathering interest. She would leave most of it to the grandson she was secretly thrilled to be having, even at the tender age of forty-three.

'Patience, it appears, has abandoned you. I was correct then?' Shirin said.

Yasmine merely shrugged.

'And now you are in the full bloom of motherhood and you never wanted a baby, whereas Patience never wanted to be anything but a mother. Life.'

'That's not true!' Yasmine cried, stung by the notion that she had destroyed Patience's dreams. 'She was going to Hollywood, to oust Merle Oberon! We had been planning that since we were girls. You know that.'

'You planted that idea in her head. It was your ambitious nature that created that fantasy,' Shirin said. 'I remember very clearly you would cut pictures of film stars out of magazines and paste them on Patience's walls, and she just went along with you because she worshipped you. You came up with the whole idea to replace Merle Oberon. Yes, you did,' Shirin said when Yasmine bristled. 'Your memory fails you. She lacks the ambition and motivation. She is a simple girl who is extraordinarily beautiful. She has the looks the gorahs like, and you have the drive they respect. She was never going to Hollywood unless you went with her. She wants a husband

and babies. She never even wanted to be a baiji—that much you have in common—you pushed her into that too, but she plays the part well. Like me.'

Yasmine stood up with difficulty. It was more than she could bear, the thought that she had forced Patience's destiny on her. 'Who am I?' she shouted. 'To have that kind of power? I run a tiny nightclub.'

Yasmine had never raised her voice to her mother before. Shirin did not react. She beckoned to a shocked housemaid to bring her daughter some tea.

Yasmine sat back down and held her aching back.

'Power has consequences,' Shirin said. 'And you always lacked the stomach for it.'

Yasmine suddenly doubled over, clutching her lower abdomen as a sharp pain shot up her inner thighs, into her womb and radiated out to her back. 'Amma?' she whispered as her water broke.

Shirin calmly took a sip of tea. 'Good. Up you go. Let's jostle that baby out,' she said.

'I cannot walk,' Yasmine said, as a contraction hit her. Her knees buckled.

'You must. You will.'

A maid was dispatched to fetch the midwife who examined Yasmine and whispered to Shirin, 'This baby needs to be cut out of her. He's not dropping, and she is not opening up.'

Shirin shook her head. 'Reach in and help her along.'

The midwife complied. She gently massaged open Yasmine's cervix, but it hurt Yasmine a great deal, and her muscles were taut.

'If I keep doing that, we might open her up enough. But it will be a long night,' she said.

'She should squat,' Shirin said.

'It will help,' the midwife agreed, but Yasmine refused to even lift her head.

For fifteen hours, Yasmine moaned and writhed—the real pain had not hit her because the baby was not moving down. The midwife kept trying to ease it along. By the next afternoon, it was clear something was wrong.

Shirin was loath to do it but decided to summon Daisy, who had an instinctive knack for birthing babies. It was a last resort before a doctor would be called to the house.

Daisy arrived within two hours, puffed up with self-importance, and smirked at Shirin, her arch-rival since they were girls. She had forced Patience to come with her, saying she didn't trust some village midwife to assist her. She brushed the tired midwife aside and said to Shirin, 'I suppose you need me now, then?'

'Unfortunately, yes,' Shirin said. 'Would I call you if it wasn't urgent? Whatever you may think of me, you know I am practical. And I know you are the best at what you do.'

Daisy softened. Shirin was frightened, which everyone could see. She hid it from her daughter but was too exhausted to pretend in front of Daisy.

'Well, not everyone gets along, now, do they?' Daisy allowed. She kneaded Yasmine's belly, to ascertain the baby's position, while she moaned in pain.

'We were girls,' Shirin said. 'Immature, both strong-headed, wanting to be the leader. That is all.' She watched Daisy's face as she examined Yasmine, to see if she could tell how serious it was. Daisy would not say anything in front of Yasmine if it was grim.

'That is not quite all,' Daisy said, still kneading and pressing down on Yasmine's abdomen. 'You were jealous of me, but no need to get into that now,' she said quickly, to keep Shirin from responding. 'Can you fetch my daughter, please?'

Shirin held her tongue and left the room in search of Patience. Patience was in the next room, reluctant to enter the bedchamber where Yasmine lay in agony. Her resentment was plain.

'It was good of you to come,' Shirin said to her. She put her arm around the young woman's shoulders.

'I had no choice. Mum needs me.'

'Yasmine needs you.'

Patience met this with silence.

But the moment Patience entered the room and saw Yasmine, listless and pale from exhaustion, she was moved to tears and quickly started to tend to her, stroking her head and giving her sips of water.

'I think the umbilical cord is wrapped around his neck,' Daisy said, after she finished examining Yasmine. She had reached in and felt the baby's neck and the top of its head with two fingers, causing Yasmine tremendous pain because she was not fully dilated still. 'But he's dropping down. Patience, wash your hands with hot water and iodine.'

'Why?'

'I need you to put your fingers in and hold her cervix open,' Daisy said. 'Wedge the tips of your fingers between the cord and his neck, while I massage the baby down. Do it!' Daisy barked when Patience stared at her, incredulous.

Patience snaked Yasmine's arm around her neck and reached down, doing as her mother asked. Yasmine opened her eyes when she felt new fingers inside her. Patience grinned at her.

'Well, hello there, love. Fancy a pint?' she said.

Yasmine smiled wanly and kissed the top of Patience's head. 'Thank you,' she whispered.

'We have to stop meeting this way,' Patience said. Her voice was light, but her heart was thudding against her ribcage.

'Do you feel the head?' Daisy asked Patience.

'Yes.'

'Is the cord tight?'

'Not too tight.'

'Can you loosen it?'

Patience nodded.

'I can get two fingers through.'

'Ease it loose,' Daisy said. 'Be very gentle. Cradle its head however best you can with two fingers. Keep the neck supported.'

'Oh my. Bloody hell,' Patience said.

'What is it?' Yasmine whispered. 'Is it hurt?'

Patience smiled at Yasmine, her eyes filling with tears. 'No, love, it has a head full of hair, soft hair.'

'Push now, Yassu. Be a good girl,' Daisy said gently. 'Push hard.'

~

The room was dark when Yasmine finally opened her eyes. The bamboo chiks were pulled down. Her vision was blurred, her tongue and head felt heavy. She attempted to move and cried out at the sharp pain between her legs.

'Don't move,' she heard Daisy say. 'You are torn. We had to stitch you up.'

She turned her head to see Patience by the window, holding the baby.

'What is it?' Yasmine asked.

Patience walked over and placed a mewing bundle on her chest.

'It's a boy, Yassu.'

'Crikey,' Yasmine whispered. She had no spittle left in her mouth.

Patience pulled back the blanket to reveal a conical head covered in black hair that jutted straight up.

Yasmine looked down at the small creature on her chest.

He looked up at her, his new-born eyes trying to focus on his mother's bewildered face.

'His eyes are green,' Patience said.

'All new babies' eyes are like that,' Daisy said.

'What do I do now?' Yasmine said.

Her mother leaned down and pulled back her nightgown, revealing a swollen breast.

'You feed him,' she said. 'He's hungry from all his exertions.'

'All *his* exertions?' Yasmine said.

'It's not easy being born, Yassu,' Patience said.

Daisy took Yasmine's breast and thrust it into her son's tiny mouth. Both mother and son were at a loss for what to do next.

'Come on, little prince,' Daisy cooed. She turned to Shirin. 'Maybe she doesn't have milk.'

'Mum, give her a bloody minute,' Patience said.

She knelt next to Yasmine. 'Come on ducky, coax him a bit.'

'I thought this would come naturally,' Yasmine said. 'I'm so thirsty.'

Patience lifted Yasmine's head gently and gave her some water.

'Try again, Yassu,' she said.

The baby clamped down on her nipple. Yasmine cried out and nearly threw him off her from the pain. Shirin ushered a disapproving Daisy out. Patience stroked the baby's head and soon he began to suckle, his tiny fist next to his ear. It still hurt terribly, but Yasmine was relieved he was getting milk. She could see his tiny throat flexing. He made gurgling noises.

She looked up at Patience. 'I'm sorry,' she said. 'I failed you.'

This snapped Patience out of her reverie.

'Just don't fail him,' she said. She touched the baby's cheek and stood up.

'Don't go yet,' Yasmine said weakly.

'Your mum's here. I've done my bit.'

Yasmine nodded, knowing her friend was not coming back any time soon. She began to cry, alarming Shirin and the nurse, who took the baby and placed him in the cradle next to the bed.

Patience gently closed the door behind her.

'She will forgive you,' Shirin said. 'I underestimated her. She came.'

'No, she won't. This is what she wanted. I cannot even stand him suckling for too long. She knows I am not a good mother.'

'You will learn. Sleep now. He will want feeding again in an hour.'

Yasmine fell asleep, her heart heavy with regret, unable to move from the pain in her body, afraid of the task ahead of her, not sure how she was going to love this tiny thing who was now solely dependent on her. Her last thought before she fell into an exhausted sleep was to wonder where Edward was at that moment.

'I want Edward,' she said to her mother before closing her eyes. She would not remember saying that.

28

Edward realised that, ultimately, every day he survived was a miracle. Even the days that he was not shot at once or no one was killed or wounded, which were rare days, were close calls, because malaria, long slimy leeches and tigers lurked in every bamboo thicket or stagnant pool of muddy water—pools of water that Edward would be forced to drink from five days into their hilltop siege.

The Japs were everywhere, yet, were geniuses at invisibility. The jungle was as alien to them as it was to Edward, but somehow, they had learned quickly to use it to their advantage. He was now a soldier of the 5307th Composite Unit in the 2nd Battalion of Merrill's Marauders, as they were known throughout the China–Burma–India Theatre. Their main task at that moment was to hack the jungle back and entrench themselves in their hilltop fortress and keep the Japs from going over the hill and into India. It was to be a static battle, and they were on the defensive, which was problematic as they were an offensive unit. Up until then, they had engaged in fast-paced skirmishes, with minimal casualties, and undulating feints, snaking quickly around the Big Green to stymie the Japs and make them think they were being attacked from all sides.

Their most insidious enemy proved to be the jungle itself. More of his fellow soldiers had been felled by malaria and dysentery than by the enemy. Edward himself was suffering from a bout of blood dysentery. There was no potable water available, as the Japs had taken control of the spring that was the sole water supply to the village of Nhpum Ga. The few indigenous hill tribesmen in their unit, the Katchin, had shown the Americans how to suck the moisture from the joints of the bamboo trees, but they were limited to trees in the perimeter of their entrenchment, as they could not venture past that. Eventually, the trees were stripped of their moisture and the soldiers took to drinking the stagnant water left in the elephant and pig tracks in the mud. This lasted for the first five days of the siege, and by the time fresh water was parachuted down to them from Allied air drops, Edward had lost twenty pounds, on top of the previous fifteen that he had lost in the first six weeks of combat, and was nursing a steady fever of one hundred and one that refused to abate.

By the seventh day of the siege, he had lost so much fluid, his tongue and lips were grey. He was emptying his bowels every forty-five minutes or so. He had cut the seam of his already tattered pants so he could just relieve himself without stopping anything he was doing. He could not afford to be caught off guard, for even as he vomited just outside his foxhole from the stench of the rotting corpse of a Japanese marine that he had shot through the gut two days earlier, the rest of the marine's unit were steadily working their way up the hillside. By nightfall on the eighth day, their fortress would be completely surrounded, and they would have no means of escape. Before that, the Japanese started lobbing mortar fire relentlessly at the 1,100 men dug into the trenches in a 'wagon wheel' formation on the top of the hill. More than the sneaky ones who managed to scale the slopes of Nhpum Ga quickly and could be dispatched with a volley of machine gunfire from the Americans, it was the almost constant barrage of mortar fire that was eating away at the frayed, malaria-addled nerves of the troops. Then, slowly, nimble snipers, bestowed with deadly accurate marksmanship, hid in the trees and started picking off the Marauders of the 2nd Battalion one by one.

A sniper's bullet clearly meant for Edward hit a pack mule in a bamboo thicket instead. It fell with a grunt, eight feet from his foxhole. He had bent his head as he fished around his knapsack for one of the last hard biscuits he had—all he could stomach—and the bullet whizzed past his temple and hit the mule. He had felt the swish of the bullet narrowly miss him and looked up to see where it landed. Edward watched as the animal gasped a few times and then died. He shut his eyes and swallowed. He had to breathe through his mouth. It would rot there now and bake in the sun the next day, alongside the bodies of Jap Marines and Marauders who had died that week. The air was putrid with the stench of rotting corpses, human waste and vomit. It was a smell that many Marauders would not soon forget.

There were so many dead bodies of both animals and men lying around, some of the troops had started calling their hilltop fortress 'Maggot Hill'.

The world had become phantasmagoric to Edward. He was still alive but unsure of what was real and what was a hallucination. The safest bet—since he could not be sure that the fire ants crawling on him were real, even when they bit him, or the sound of someone faintly calling his name, asking him for a light, were real—was to stay as still as possible and not make sudden movements. When he saw Louis crawl into the foxhole next to him, he was sure it was a hallucination. So he ignored it.

Worse still, it was April, and the dry season was coming to an end. Now that the rains were imminent, Edward feared that he and the other Marauders would be spending their nights searching for a dry patch of earth—if they were allowed to leave their foxholes—on which to grab a few minutes' sleep. He was resigned to the fact that most likely, he would never sleep a full night again. The last time had been in Yasmine's bed.

~

The rains began, pouring down on them for twelve hours a day, seven days a week. At least it would wash away the blood, Edward thought.

When it rained, the jungle seemed to burst at the seams. For an hour or less a day, the sun showed itself and revealed how it was growing around them, fed by the rains. Every manner of insect was on parade during that time, some of them so poisonous, a single minuscule drop of venom could short-circuit a man's nervous system. Edward used to think that venomous snakes were the worst of the creatures, cobras and black mambos, but in the end, it was the non-venomous—the leeches, hanging off nearly every leaf—that brought many a Marauder to his knees. The leaves shivered from time to time, as if moved by a breeze, when actually they were crawling with writhing leeches that attached themselves to a man and set up house in any dark, moist place they could find; grey, slimy things that would become engorged with human blood. Men pulled them off so quickly that usually a small part of the head would remain embedded in the skin and fester, causing open, oozing sores that refused to heal. Edward had one such sore on his neck that trickled a steady stream of pus and fluid down his collar. He tied a bandana around it in an effort to stop the leaking, but the humidity kept everything damp.

He had managed, for the most part, to keep thoughts of Yasmine out of his mind.

His lack of lucidity now made it impossible. In the midst of a rare break in the endless barrage of machine gunfire and shelling, Edward was sure he saw her slipping in and out of the bright green bamboo trees surrounding the perimeter of their encampment. She was wearing a blue sari and silver hoops on her ears that glinted whenever they caught the light. 'Yasmine?' he whispered hoarsely.

'I am going to go away for a bit, darling,' she said. She was flippant and refused to look at him. She was so careless with him.

'Where?'

'With Tommy. We're going dancing. Don't wait up!'

'I forbid you to do that, Yasmine,' Edward cried, though, in reality, he was still whispering, now a bit more loudly. Louis, who had joined the Marauders when Edward did, watched his former basha mate from a nearby foxhole as he hissed at the air, 'Don't you let that son of a bitch near my son! You hear me, Yasmine?'

'Lafaver, shut the fuck up!' Louis whispered tensely. 'You want a Nip sniper to get you? Or me?'

Edward turned slowly to face Louis. He was real.

'Don't use that kind of foul language around my wife,' he said to him.

'Your wife's in goddamn Norwich, you asshole,' Louis whispered, and sat back down in his foxhole. Edward thought about Maggie. He tried to conjure her face but could not. Only Yasmine's face floated in front of him. Inexplicably, tears started to roll down his cheeks.

Louis peeked out when he heard the choking sobs coming from Edward's foxhole.

'Lafaver, you have to quit it,' he said, a bit more gently. Listening to Edward made tears rise up in his own throat as he imagined his mother, waiting for him at the end of the driveway when he finally returned home, folding him into a tight, warm hug.

'Okay,' Edward said. 'Sorry. It's just that I didn't say goodbye, and I'm pretty sure we're fucked here.'

'The Nips have nothing on us, Lafaver. Quit that thinking. It's sure death.'

'She hates me,' Edward said after a while. He tried to light a cigarette, but his hands shook too much. His stomach cramped from the dysentery, and his bowels emptied for the fifth time that day, running down his legs and into the foxhole. The smell was overpowering. It burned his throat and nostrils.

'Sorry,' he said again to Louis.

'Don't worry about it,' Louis replied. 'When she sees the sorry state you're in, she'll forgive you everything.'

Edward chuckled. 'You don't know Yasmine,' he said.

'What's that?' Louis said. 'Jesus, Lafaver, forget that coolie bitch. That's what you want to return to?'

Edward closed his eyes and didn't reply. Had he had the strength, Louis's remarks would have warranted a sock to the jaw.

'Why are you plaguing me, Deccico?' Edward whispered. 'Why are you here, in the next fucking foxhole over?'

'What's that?' Louis said.

'Why are you here? Why are you plaguing me? In all the shit-filled foxholes in the world, why did you have to be in the one next to mine?'

Louis chuckled. 'Just lucky, I guess.'

'I know you did it,' Edward mumbled. His throat was dry and his voice caught.

'What's that?' Louis moved closer to hear what Edward was saying.

'You raped that girl. Yasmine's girl.'

Edward was still mumbling so Louis asked him to repeat himself. Edward's eyes had been closed, and they now flew open. He turned to Louis and yelled as loud as his dehydrated, hoarse throat would allow, 'I know you raped Radhika. It was you!'

'Fucking keep your voice down, Lafaver,' Louis hissed. 'So what? So you know. What the fuck are you going to do about it now?'

Within seconds, the Japanese snipers started shooting. The air was suddenly filled with the piercing sounds of bullets discharging from every direction and whistling to their marks. A bullet glanced off Edward's helmet. He dropped deeper into his foxhole until the attack ended. He could not return fire because he could not see where the shots were coming from. He needed to save his bullets, stay out of the line of fire and wait it out. After what seemed like an eternity, the snipers stopped. He could hear other soldiers cussing him out and smelled tobacco as the survivors lit up to calm their frayed nerves. He vaguely hoped no one had been hit. He would have to wait until sunrise to find out.

Soon, he fell asleep, crouched down in his own shit.

29

It was day ten of the siege. That was the only way he knew what date it was, by counting how many days he had been on that hilltop. Not that it mattered what day it was, and if he thought too much about how long they had been up there he would go mad. The putrid stench of the corpses of Japs in their odd, yellow khaki uniforms, maggot-ridden mules and Marauders; the tigers, bamboo trees, leeches, mud, mosquitos, mortars; the moans of the wounded and dying, the retching, and Yasmine's face the last time he ever saw her all oozed together.

Edward stood, swaying in his foxhole, waiting to die. He was still there, but snipers had hit their mark after all and got Louis not once but twice, between the ears and in some other location Edward could not see. He remembered that once the bullets started to spray, he heard Louis utter a final, 'Lafaver, you son of a bitch!', and then silence. Edward had raised his voice above a rasp, and now, Louis Deccico of Hackensack, New Jersey, father of two, the son of Italian immigrants, violent, pugnacious, small-minded, rapist, was dead. Nothing seemed to fell Louis—he didn't even get the runs as bad as everyone else. Only a Jap could do the needful, thought Edward. I'm going to tell Yasmine, you got your justice in the end, but you have Hirohito to thank for it.

Someone tapped him gently on the shoulder, and he turned around to a smiling, bespectacled, Japanese face.

'I got news, sir!' Sergeant Roy Matsumoto said excitedly. He had crawled through the mud on his belly to Edward's foxhole to tell him first.

'I think this is it. I heard an Imperial commander tell two of their guys that they are coming at us—full frontal attack at sunrise.'

Edward stared at him, his eyes dull. He could not believe what he was hearing.

'Are you sure?' he said.

'Yes, sir. These troops are from Kyushu, and I understand the dialect. Two of them were talking about what they were going to do when they got back home and then—'

'Home?'

'Yes sir, well, Kyushu, where they're from, and I sat on my ass for a good hour before any of them said anything I could use—'

'What do Japs talk about?' Edward wondered.

'The same stuff we all do, sir. Their wives, what they're going to eat when they get home. These guys talked a lot about the chickens they're going to raise,' Matsumoto said, without hesitation. 'But then their commander told them the real news.'

'You want a smoke?' Edward said. He liked Sergeant Matsumoto. He had first met him at General Orde Wingate's Chindit jungle training camp and marvelled at the young man's resilience. He was also impressed that the young man did not seem to hold any grudges. His loyalties were clear. A few years earlier, Matsumoto, a Japanese-American Nisei, had been incarcerated as an 'enemy alien' and sent to a camp in California. His bank accounts had been seized, his life upended with no explanation after 7 December 1941. When the army asked for Japanese Americans willing to act as interpreters for the war effort, he volunteered at once. He had proven to be the 2nd Battalion's greatest asset, crawling into the enemy's perimeter regularly to listen to the conversations of the Imperial soldiers and report back to his commanders. He displayed no bitterness at the way his country had treated him and his family, and for that he had the respect of every member of the 2nd Battalion.

'No time, sir,' Sergeant Matsumoto said. He could see that Edward was not entirely lucid and was floating in and out of awareness. 'Do you have enough water?'

Edward shook his head and shrugged. Matsumoto unhooked his canteen and handed it to Edward, who took a thirsty gulp. He handed it back to Matsumoto with a grateful smile.

'Sir, I need you to listen to what I'm saying and pass it on. The Japs will be attacking us at sunrise. They are coming at us head on, so we can take them easily, now that we know. Do you understand what I'm saying, sir?'

It sunk in, slowly. Edward nodded.

'This is it,' Matsumoto said. 'If we lick 'em now, we can go home.'

Home. Edward heard that word clearly but was not at all sure what it meant. Where was that exactly, he wondered. Norwich? Yes, he thought, that made sense. He knew where that was, what it felt like. There was a front porch there, and a sleepy, narrow river named after a mightier one, the Thames, a main street, a textile mill by the river, built at the height of the industrial revolution where his grandmother laboured as a girl. It was derelict, if he remembered correctly. There was a woodland park that he ran through and hunted in as a boy with his Uncle Stash. There was a small, immaculate rose garden in the park with crushed stone-covered paths between the beds. His mind went back to the front porch of his small Victorian house. Wide, grey wooden slats on the floor, enclosed by a white banister with gingerbread railings. It was free-floating, not attached to a structure. Anchored by, what? He tried to remember. Anchored by a woman, a girl, with brown hair and blue eyes and a dimple in each cheek. She stood on that porch and was beckoning to him to sit with her on the porch swing. Home.

'Home,' he said aloud.

'Yeah, sir! Sorry about Lt Deccico, sir.' They both glanced over to Louis's foxhole, where he lay rotting slowly in the heat. Edward peered over to see a maggot climb out of Louis's left nostril. This struck him as funny, and he grinned at Matsumoto, who crawled back on his belly, away from Edward's foxhole, and disappeared into the darkness.

'Home,' Edward said again. This time, all he could see was a small room, and an unmade wooden frame bed, with mosquito netting draped around it. There was an old-fashioned phonograph on a low table, and one shuttered window. A ceiling fan whirled slowly. He could hear it clicking. It was a dark room, intimate. He closed his eyes and saw the bed again. It was a rickety bed, but the sheets were clean, white and crisp. The bed would break, he thought. What was holding it together? Then he saw her, Yasmine, lying supine on the bed, naked and brown. Her wavy, black hair fanned out on the white pillow under her head. She was asleep.

30

She smelled him before she saw him. Rahul came into the office, where she was working, and when he opened the door she caught the faint odour of sweat and something rotting. The boy trailed it in. Yasmine complained to him about the smell. She assumed it was the boy, who had dubious hygiene habits that she could not seem to change.

'How many times have I told you to wash first thing in the morning?' she said to Rahul. 'Behind the ears, every bloody nook and cranny. I am convinced that we lost customers this month because the gorahs are so bloody sensitive to native smells. They walk in, take one sniff and leave. If we lose one more customer, I'm docking you five annas!'

'There is a sahib standing at the bar. I think he's sick,' Rahul said.

'Yes, yes. Of course he's sick,' Yasmine said sarcastically. 'Sick with love no doubt, for Patience. Tell them she doesn't live here anymore.' After helping to deliver the baby, Patience had once again become aloof; they now barely spoke to each other.

Rahul shook his head. 'No, Yasmine di, this one is really sick. It's not love-shove. I think he just came back from the jungle. I think he was fighting.'

Rahul peered at Yasmine with concern when she did not respond. 'Yasmine di?'

She had frozen and was staring at him.

Adil Baboo walked in, holding his hand to his nose. 'A sahib is here, Yasmine,' he said. 'He is asking for you. Do you want me to tell him to leave? He looks very unkempt.'

'He's sick,' Rahul said.

'It's all right,' Yasmine said, with more bravado than she felt. 'Let me handle this.' She did not move.

'Yasmine, who is this man?' Adil Baboo asked. 'Is he a friend of yours?'

Yasmine did not answer. Instead, she remained seated at her desk, staring out the door.

'Yasmine?' Adil Baboo said again. She was still silent. When she looked up, her eyes were filled with tears, and then both Rahul and Adil Baboo understood.

Rahul went out to the main floor quickly. Adil Baboo wanted to take Yasmine's hand, but he was never that familiar with her and did not know what to do. After a moment, he went and stood next to her and placed one hand on her shoulder.

'It might not be him,' Adil Baboo said.

'It is,' Rahul said. He had come back into the office. 'Di? Please don't be cross with him any longer. I think he is dying.'

'You're sure it's him?' Yasmine said.

Rahul nodded emphatically. 'Yes. He is very different, but it is him. I asked him to be sure.'

'How is he different?' she said.

'He is sick, very sick. You can see for yourself.'

Yasmine slowly rose from her desk and walked to the door. She stopped and then quickly went back to her desk where she retrieved a small compact and smoothed her hair. She bit her lower lip to give it some colour. Her sari was an old faded cotton with ink and turmeric stains on it, but there was no time to change into something more presentable. Her hand went automatically to her still-flat belly, but now there were faint stretch marks on it. She had dutifully rubbed coconut oil into her skin every night for six months while carrying Edward's baby, but she was still scarred. Her body had changed, though more so in her own mind than in reality. She felt much older and feared she looked it.

She walked slowly into the bar. Her heart was racing.

She never would have recognised the ruined man who sat at the bar if she had passed him on the street. He had not shaved in at least a month or bathed properly in nearly a week. His dark hair was matted with sweat and dirt. The corners of his mouth were cracked and bleeding. He had been flown out of Burma, half dead from dysentery, and sent to an infirmary in Bombay, where he had stayed one month, and then, still not recovered, left to go to Yasmine. He had fought with the doctors and his commanding officers and explained he needed to get to his son. There was no convincing him to stay put.

'You'll be dead in a week, Lieutenant,' his doctor said. 'Your neck wound keeps opening up when strained.'

'Then we'll just have to amputate,' he had joked, though no one was amused.

'Is she worth it, son?' his CO had asked.

'Yes, sir, she is. She'll take care of me,' Edward had said. 'If I can get her to stop hating me.'

Yasmine and Edward looked at one another now. She stifled a cry at seeing his ravaged face.

'You should have seen me when they first brought me in,' he said.

To him, Yasmine glowed with health. He looked her up and down in awe. He had not seen anyone so healthy in a while. For so long, he had felt that death squatted somewhere nearby at all times, waiting patiently for him to slip or just give up. And there had been so many times, more than he could count, that he had wanted to oblige death. But now, looking at this beautiful, healthy young woman, he felt it retreating. His eyes rested on the dip in her clavicle and moved down to her breasts, fuller since giving birth—much to Edward's delight. Without embarrassment, he said, 'I need to sleep—there,' and pointed to her chest.

Yasmine blushed, but Edward didn't notice. 'Lots of blood-sucking leeches,' he continued. 'And fucking Japs and Louis's body rotting in the mud next to my foxhole, after a sniper got him in the head. I couldn't even get him out of the way, so I watched the maggots slowly eat him. After Nhpum Ga we were supposed to be done and they tell us the Japs invaded India, after all that, and we have to go to Myitkyina and fight them back there. We were half dead from malaria and dysentery and that bastard Stilwell tells us to get some stones and go back in! That's why it took me this long to come back. That's why I'm late.

'So we went back into the jungle and we won for the son of a bitch, didn't we? Do you understand?' Edward said again to Yasmine.

'Yes, I do,' she said.

'Phil's dead, so is Sullivan, you remember them? The boys I used to counsel.' Edward uttered the word 'counsel' and snorted. 'Fat lot of good I did them,' he said. His voice was bitter. Yasmine shook her head, wanting to be supportive. But words failed her.

'Deccico is dead and I killed him, though not on purpose. But maybe it was, who knows?' he said. 'Rats are easier to kill,' he added after a contemplative moment, 'but I did it. For you. The boys were stark raving nuts, but they were harmless, you know? I took care of them, but I couldn't there.'

'I know, Edward,' Yasmine said. 'You were good to them, when no one else was.'

He nodded. 'Everyone had written them off. But they fought so bravely, twelve, thirteen hours a day they hacked at the jungle, and they took a few Japs with them too. They were just kids. Sullivan turned twenty when we were on Maggot Hill.'

Adil Baboo and Yasmine both nodded.

'It sounds horrible, Edward. The name itself ... I can only imagine,' Yasmine said.

Edward's eyes suddenly filled with tears, further astonishing everyone; they were already speechless at his ravaged appearance. Yasmine moved towards him but then stopped.

They all watched for a while as Edward calmed himself. He looked in the mirror and attempted to tidy his hair and took out a filthy handkerchief and wiped his mouth. He stopped and shook his head at the absurdity of trying to appear presentable when he was so far gone. He smiled but his smile quickly faded when he spotted a toy fire engine with all the red paint chipped off at the far end of the bar.

'Is this his?' he asked. Everyone looked at Yasmine.

She nodded.

'Is it his favourite?'

'No. He prefers planes.'

Edward looked at the toy. He picked it up, examined it, and then quickly slipped it into his knapsack. No one stopped him. Finally, Adil Baboo went to him and clasped Edward's hand in both of his.

'Hiya,' he said softly to Adil Baboo and patted his back. The Indian had never been this friendly. 'I must be in pretty bad shape for the venerable Adil Baboo to shake my hand,' he said, smiling. Edward had respectfully removed his hat and placed it next to him on a barstool. It hurt Yasmine that he was trying to maintain his dignity when he was so clearly broken down. He was easily thirty pounds lighter than when he had left. His eyelashes had fallen out from stress. Spidery veins were visible on his eyelids, which were pink rimmed. His handsome face had degenerated into a skeletal mask. His thin neck bulged with a swollen, infected sore that would need to be drained. The left lens of his glasses had a thin crack down the side. It was a miracle he had managed not to lose them.

Eventually, Edward had to look away from Yasmine's shocked face. He covered his neck with a shaking hand.

When he spoke again, his voice was louder and raspy.

'Can a man get a drink around here?' He tried to laugh and started coughing. He took off his glasses and placed them on the bar.

Being able to see his eyes, the hazel she loved so much, roused Yasmine. She arranged her face into what she hoped was a casual smile, though it was much too late to pretend. Her voice shook slightly when she spoke.

'It depends—you have rupees, sahib?' she said.

'Oh tons and tons,' Edward replied. 'I even have Yen. Let's see, what do you suggest?'

'Saline,' Yasmine said. She nodded at Rahul, who did not move. 'Arrey!' she said. 'Jaldi saline niye ahshoh,' she said to the boy, who ran out at once to fetch water, sugar and salt.

'If by saline, you mean whiskey, then please,' he said.

'All right, but not too much,' Yasmine said.

She walked behind the bar and poured him one finger of whiskey—the good stuff—and watched him drink it. He began to cough almost immediately.

'It's probably good for your throat,' Yasmine said when he had finished coughing. 'To kill whatever is in there.'

'I hope so, because now my stomach is burning,' he chuckled.

He pushed his glass towards the bottle. 'More please.'

'No,' Yasmine said. 'It might make you worse.'

'Just a little more, Yasmine,' Adil Baboo. 'He's earned it.'

'No. He's clearly dehydrated,' she said.

Rahul returned with the saline solution, and Edward choked it down with difficulty. He wanted nothing more than to sleep in Yasmine's arms, but, though her face had softened, she was the only one who had not touched him.

'We had given you up for dead, especially with all the bad news from Burma, but not me. We missed you every day. I kept up with all the news.' Yasmine poured herself a drink but left it on the bar.

'We?' Edward said.

'Yes, all of us.' She gestured towards Adil Baboo and Rahul, and saw they had discreetly left.

'You should go to the army hospital at once, Edward,' Yasmine said.

'I know, I will,' he said. 'But I needed to see you first. It was all I could think about these past months.'

Yasmine was silent, unsure of how to respond. In truth, her heart was still racing.

'How is he?' he asked.

'Akash is very well,' she replied. 'But I cannot discuss him with you.'

Tears filled Edward's eyes again. Yasmine had never seen him cry this much. Edward wiped his eyes with the back of his hand. 'I'm sorry,' he said. 'I can't seem to control it. It happens now without warning.'

'Have you eaten?' was all Yasmine could say.

He shook his head no. 'I can't handle anything. It runs through me.'

'The ARC will have what you need,' Yasmine said.

'Have a heart, Yasmine, for pity's sake!' he said, his voice breaking. 'I always intended to come back for you, and—'

'Edward, you're weak,' Yasmine cut him off.

'You don't know the half of it,' he said and chuckled bitterly. 'Let me stay. I need to rest. I'm so tired.'

'Why didn't you go to the Red Cross?' Yasmine said.

'I wanted to see you first.'

She looked at his swollen neck.

'It's a sore. It's from a leech bite. They don't heal easily.'

'Let me see,' Yasmine said. 'Then I'll get the doctor and see what he can do.'

'You don't want to see this.'

'I need to, so I can tell the doctor what to expect.'

Edward reluctantly removed the gauze covering the sore. The dressing was already soaked with pus. The open sore was slightly smaller than it had been when Edward was first flown out of Burma, but it was still infected. It smelled putrid.

Yasmine ran out of the bar, Edward on her heels, into the office, where she threw up in the wastebasket.

Edward tried to hold her hair back as she retched into the basket. She swatted his hand away.

'I know I'm disgusting,' he said. 'But I made an appointment with a doctor to get my neck drained and sores looked at. All I need is a hot bath and a good night's sleep, and I'll be your old Edward again, I promise. I have no expectations,' he said. 'You don't have to touch me. I just need to be near you and him. I love you, Yasmine,' he ended weakly. 'I love you both.'

The effort to cram so many months of thoughts and emotions and regrets into one entreaty had left him dizzy. He sat down gingerly on the edge of a chair. He asked Rahul, who had walked in, for water.

'Kid,' he said, 'I need more jawl. Jaldi, please.'

Edward laid his head on her desk and closed his eyes to both Rahul's and her alarm.

'Yasmine di?' Rahul said. 'Eddie da is dying.'

'Dhutt! You fool! He's not dying!' Yasmine snapped at the boy. 'What a thing to say.'

They both looked at Edward, whose eyes were still closed.

'He looks half dead to me,' Rahul said.

'Well, then, you need to buy spectacles,' Yasmine said. 'Go and get the water.'

'How long are you going to punish me?' Edward whispered when Rahul left. 'I killed Louis for you, you know.'

'Hush, Edward. No more talk about killing people.'

After a moment, he stood up. His knees buckled. She caught him under the arms and dropped him as gently as she could into the chair. His thighs shook, and he steadied them with his hands. He smiled at her apologetically.

'You need the doctor,' Yasmine said. 'I'll take you.'

~

Yasmine knew instinctively how to look after people, yet when it came to Edward, she was unsure of how to proceed. She missed Patience then. Patience would have helped her take care of him and made things light-hearted.

Edward had fallen fast asleep at her desk. She sat down and looked at him and wondered what she should do. Asma ran in, excited.

'I did not believe it!' she cried.

Yasmine admonished her to lower her voice so he was not disturbed.

'Oh, poor man,' Asma whispered. 'He looks awful. Oh! He'll be so happy to see Akash! Should I bring him in after he has had his rest?'

Yasmine all but jumped out of the chair. 'No!' she said, loudly. Both women looked at Edward to see if he had stirred. He still slept and was now gently snoring.

Yasmine took Asma by the arm and pulled her out of the office.

'Are you mad?' she demanded.

'You can't keep a man from his son,' Asma said.

'This is not your affair,' Yasmine said.

'I care about the laddoo,' Asma said.

'I know you do,' Yasmine said. She smiled. All of Asma's nicknames for her son were various sweetmeats, combining her two favourite things, babies and food.

'Yasmine, he needs his father. And his father needs him.'

Yasmine nodded, thinking about what to do. She agreed with Asma but feared that Edward would take the boy away from her. Americans did whatever they wanted. She could hardly stop him if he suddenly decided that his beloved 'Mags' would be a better mother. Akash could easily pass for white, as Asma frequently pointed out, which would open up new vistas for him that Yasmine and India could not provide.

'Just think,' Asma said, after the boy was born, with green eyes, light-brown hair and almost alabaster skin, 'he would be a white man. The lord of the universe.'

Yasmine, ever the pragmatist, had to admit that to be true. No one would have to know who his mother was. So many passed as white back in England, living full lives as accepted members of European society. However, the notion of Edward's wife raising her child as a Yankee in an idyllic New England cottage was untenable.

'You also have to admit you love him, Yassu,' Asma was saying to her, as Yasmine reverted to an old childhood habit of biting her cuticles, something Asma had never seen her do. Yasmine was always in control and correct in the way she carried herself. Self-possessed, was how Asma would have described her.

'Yes, of course I love my son!' Yasmine said.

'I meant Lt Lafaver, Yassu.'

'Right.'

Rahul returned with a glass of water, and a squirming Akash balanced precariously on his bony hip. The little boy clearly loved Rahul and kept turning his face towards him if Rahul looked away. Yasmine looked at Asma, suddenly anxious.

'It's all right, Yassu,' Asma said gently. 'It's the correct thing. Imagine if you were never allowed to hold him.'

'Yes, you are right,' Yasmine conceded. 'But not now, with Edward in this state. He'll scare the baby.'

'Then make him well and let him hold his son,' Asma said.

Yasmine nodded. Asma felt satisfied that she now filled the role of Yasmine's confidante and advisor. With Patience gone, she was able to step in easily. Yasmine seemed to need her.

~

Dr Ghosh's waiting room was cramped and musty with a ceiling fan that only served to kick up dust. Yasmine had decided to let Edward be hers for a few days—that was probably all the time he had before he would be sent home—and make him as well as she could.

When he emerged from the examination room, he leaned on the much shorter and overweight Ghosh. There was a fresh bandage on his neck and his cracked lips glistened with coconut oil. Yasmine helped him into a chair, and extracted a wad of rupees from her purse.

'No, no. No need,' the doctor said. He handed her back the rupees without a hint of irony. This was a man who had once overcharged Yasmine to put three stitches in Rahul's foot when the boy stepped on broken glass. But he had been discreet about Patience, and for that, she was grateful.

'We must support our allies,' he added, not meeting her eyes. Yasmine smiled. She suddenly understood. Dr Ghosh was a known member of the Indian Nationalist Party and a devotee of Subhash Chandra Bose—the most wanted man in the British Empire; he had allied with the Germans and Italians, and wanted nothing more than to see an independent India. The doctor's son, a soldier in the Indian National Army, had fought alongside the Japanese at Imphal a month before and lost. He had surrendered to the British and was in a prison in Bombay, most likely being tortured every day, and would be hanged for treason. Now, the older man was being careful, laying low and being cooperative with the authorities, in the unlikely event his eighteen-year-old son would be shown mercy.

Dr Ghosh cleared his throat gruffly and handed Edward a tube of antiseptic salve and a prescription note.

To Yasmine, he said, 'Lieutenant sahib must not eat anything other than white rice boiled in vegetable broth, a pinch of salt, plain boiled carrots and boiled potatoes mashed, for the next seven days. After that, he may have some daal, but not with any garlic or onions. This will be a slow process. Several months of recovery, I fear. It is a miracle he survived. He must have a great need to live.'

'He will not be under my care that long, so you must write all this down for his wife, for when he returns to America,' Yasmine replied, with more coldness than she actually felt. She could not deny herself the satisfaction of seeing Edward's crestfallen face. Of course, she did not mean it. It was purely for Dr Ghosh's sake. But she was also assuming that Edward would be sent home at once, given his condition, to recover in his own country, where the facilities would be better.

Yasmine stuffed the rupees back into her purse and held out her arm so Edward could lean on it.

Dr Ghosh finished writing out the instructions and pointed to the tube of salve and cleared his throat several times in embarrassment before speaking. 'That is for the, uh, sore on his ... ahem! Anus. His haemorrhoids have suppurated.'

Edward looked away as the doctor continued to explain that the salve must be applied three times a day, in the morning after the first movement or after bathing, in the afternoon and before going to bed.

'Sometimes it is hard to see if the ointment is applied properly…' Dr Ghosh started tidying a table piled high with papers that had not been sorted since before the war. '…Therefore, it is important that, uh, whoever is taking care of him, check to see if it is applied properly—oh! I also recommend warm salt water baths at least once a day.'

'I understand,' Yasmine said. 'Anything else?'

Yasmine was embarrassed and felt a pang of resentment. Edward couldn't face his chaste, New England wife in this condition. Could not ask her lily-white, perfect hands to go anywhere near his anal abscess or his parasitic neck. Leave the dirty, humiliating work for the natives, was the English motto, after all; why not the Americans as well, Yasmine thought. I will make him whole again, she wanted to say to Dr Ghosh, so he can return to his wife less grotesque and more of the hero he has built himself up to be. Heroes do not have infected assholes or suppurating sores, she thought. These thoughts rushed at her all at once, but she managed to tamp them down when Edward smiled at her. She knew he must be grateful and embarrassed.

Yasmine hailed a rickshaw and instructed the rickshaw-wallah to help him onto the narrow seat.

She handed the rickshaw-wallah a note.

'I have money,' Edward said in a faint voice. He touched the rickshaw-wallah's skinny shoulder and indicated that he should return Yasmine's money.

'Be careful when going over the bumps,' she told the rickshaw-wallah. 'Sahib was injured protecting you from the Japanese.'

The rickshaw-wallah glanced back at Edward, who had already leaned back on the seat with his eyes closed.

Two tiny street urchins appeared out of nowhere, tugged at Yasmine's sari as she was about to get on the rickshaw, and pointed to their open mouths. Both were naked with shaven heads and a thin red string tied around their swollen bellies. There seemed to be more and more hungry children on the streets than ever before.

Snot ran down their noses. One of them turned his attention on Edward and said in a reedy voice, 'Pound sterling?'

A child's voice speaking in English made Edward open his eyes. He took some notes out of his shirt pocket and handed it to him. The small boy jumped around in glee and skipped down the street. His companion, a little girl of about four, stubbornly clung to Yasmine's sari until she acknowledged her. Yasmine tried to shoo her away, but the little girl hung on for dear life, nearly pulling her sari down. Edward's rickshaw-wallah got off his bike and tried to help Yasmine by grabbing the girl around the waist and yanking her off. He slapped her across the face and the child started to sob.

'Stop that,' Yasmine said to the rickshaw-wallah. 'She's just a baby.'

Edward had limped off the rickshaw and chastised the young man for being unduly harsh. 'Be on your way,' he said.

They were left standing on the street staring at the bawling, naked child. Finally, Yasmine knelt down and wiped the child's streaming nose with a handkerchief.

'There, stop now,' she said in a soothing voice. 'Look, I have a nice rupee note for you.'

The child stopped crying almost at once and took both the note and the handkerchief. 'Is that how much the sahib gave my brother?' she said between hiccups.

A crowd gathered quickly around the three of them. The sight of an American with an Indian woman trying to placate a street urchin was a fascinating one. Yasmine moved away from Edward instinctively, but he grabbed her hand and pulled her closer to him, much to the awe of the crowd, which now consisted of twenty gawkers of various ages and social classes. The child was still sitting on the ground, examining the rupee note and occasionally shuddering from having sobbed so hard. A red welt appeared on the cheek where the rickshaw-wallah had slapped her.

'The sahib looks like a ghost,' one spectator said.

'The lady must be his servant.'

'Maybe she tried to run away.'

'No, she's dressed too well for that. She looks like a schoolteacher.'

'She's his mistress then.'

'Arrey bhai, she's a prostitute, one of those fancy ones.'

They were oblivious to the fact that both subjects could hear them. Yasmine closed her eyes and tried to remove her hand from Edward's grasp, but he held on to it.

'Ignore them,' he said.

If Yasmine were not so mortified, she would have found the whole thing hilarious. It struck her that Patience would have enjoyed the absurd scenario most of all. Her throat tightened, as it often did when she thought of her friend. She quickly pushed the thought away and allowed Edward to hold her hand.

Edward led her through the throng and hailed a gharry. He helped her up onto the seat. When he tried to join her, she said, 'We can't.'

'Yasmine, do you think I care? Look at me.' He smiled at her and shrugged. 'So many things that mattered so much before don't anymore,' he said, simply.

The war had rendered many things unimportant and other things urgent. So Yasmine closed her eyes to the gaping onlookers who stared at the wounded American and the Bengali girl in the gharry. For the first time in the two-and-a-half years she had known and loved him, Edward held Yasmine's hand the whole way home for all the world to see.

31

Edward stayed for twelve days. He slept for a full day and a half after they returned from the doctor. Yasmine let him sleep in her bed, and boiled his tasteless meals of rice, carrots and potatoes herself. She watched over him as he ate and grew stronger after the first full day of rest. She drew the bathwater and sponged his back, and changed the dressing on his neck. Yasmine sent Rahul to purchase some clothes because it would not do to send for them from Tolly. His superiors must have known where he was but had let him be, as he had more than earned this respite.

Edward was too embarrassed to allow Yasmine anywhere near his other infection, and ignored her when she insisted she must inspect to see that the salve was applied properly.

One morning while he slept, the day after he had walked into the Duck, she smoked a cigarette and set fire to his uniform in a drum in the alley and watched it burn. That was when she realised that she was not angry at him. The jungle had punished him enough. She did not think about what would come next. Now she wanted to make him whole again, for his son and whatever time they would have together.

She did not allow anyone near the bedroom where he recovered. After a long night of running the club, she crept quietly into the room and slept on the floor next to him. Sometimes, he cried out during the night, uttering unintelligible things. Once she had to comfort him and tell him he was safe in her room and not in the mud, trapped on a hill, surrounded by Japanese snipers. He was asleep the whole time she told him this and did not recollect it when she mentioned it the next day. Some of his fellow officers came into the club and enquired after him discreetly. She assured them Edward was recovering nicely and offered them free drinks, which they gratefully accepted. She could not tell if they approved or disapproved of the situation. As Edward had told her, nothing was the same. What these men had seen and done had changed them forever. They were hardly going to care how one of them set about healing himself.

~

Yasmine hated being downstairs when he was upstairs, and longed for the night to end so she could run up and be with him. She checked in on him frequently. He was almost always asleep even though the music could be heard pounding through the floorboards. On the ninth night he was there, he awoke to relieve himself and saw Yasmine fast asleep on the floor. His sobbing woke her up.

When Yasmine heard him crying, she was alarmed and quickly took him in her arms.

'I know you think I abandoned you and our son,' he said. 'I seem to have failed everyone.'

By 'everyone', Yasmine knew he was referring to Maggie. Though her heart sped up when she thought of his wife and she felt dread, she consoled him.

'You should write to her, tell her you're safe,' Yasmine said in a halting voice. She knew it was the right thing to say to him.

The next night, they lay next to one another, touching each other's faces and kissing. She was aroused but knew he was too weak.

'I'm sorry,' he said, ashamed. 'Just give me another day. I feel stronger with every passing minute.'

'It's all right,' Yasmine whispered and lay on his chest.

They held each other the rest of the night and into the afternoon. They kissed and stroked one another for hours, falling asleep to the rhythmic clicking of the ceiling fan. It was enough for Yasmine.

He told her about Burma and what had happened to him there. It would be one of the last times he would ever discuss the war in such detail. As the days and years would go by, the horror and pain would become sharper, not duller. He knew he had the strength to recount the horror in full detail only once, and he chose Yasmine to tell.

'We were always a low priority, you see?' he said to Yasmine. 'Churchill never wanted to commit a large number of troops to the region, as they are so focused on beating the Germans back. No one has comprehended how imperative it is to re-build the road between India and China. China is cut off from aid without it, and the airdrops are proving to be too dangerous. They have to fly over the Himalayas, you see, and most of them never make it. You'd think that China would be grateful for the help and offer troops, but that gremlin Chiang Kai-shek—you know him, right?' Yasmine nodded; she had read about him in the papers. 'Well, he refuses to commit a large number of troops as well. And he's the one we're fighting for!'

He held Yasmine closer. 'I never believed in the supernatural,' he said, 'until I went there. I never believed in ghosts or monsters. They were always a part of a child's nightmare.'

'Do you now?' she wanted to know.

He nodded. Yes, he did. He told her a story. One soggy morning, when he, three of his men and a Katchin Burmese tribesman were out on patrol, they stumbled upon a tiger feeding in a clearing. The Katchin gestured to them to back up slowly. Once they were a distance away, they squatted down and watched the tiger tear away strips of flesh from the bone. Edward was the first to see the tattered yellow khaki cloth attached to one of the strips. The tiger took a mouthful and spat it out before going back to the carcass.

'Japanese soldier,' the Katchin muttered to them. Edward told Yasmine that he never found out the Katchin's name. He was a tight-lipped one, and they could never tell what he was thinking. After he told them what the tiger was feasting on, he turned and walked into the jungle. The others followed quickly, but Edward could not take his eyes off the tiger. The beast looked up at him then and stopped eating. Edward froze and someone pulled him away, saving his life. The tiger had an empty look in his eyes, and that frightened Edward the most. He said he looked back once and saw it was gnawing a human leg.

'It was the first time I felt for one of those squinty-eyed bastards,' he told her. 'They were suffering as much as we were, fighting wars for men who didn't care a lick about them, like Churchill and FDR didn't care for us. Strangely, the Japanese suffered more casualties because of the tigers than we did. Maybe because we had more Burmese working for us. They knew how to avoid them. But that changed quickly, too. The Burmese always hated us, more than you Indians ever did.'

'We never hated you,' Yasmine replied. 'We just think that your English comrades have borrowed our country long enough and now should give it back. It has nothing to do with you.'

Edward looked down at her thoughtfully. 'You're much more political than the girls back home,' he said, when she looked at him expectantly.

'Don't you mean traitorous?' she said. 'What I said qualifies as high treason.'

'Lucky for you, I'm a Yank. You know I never thought like that.'

'Yes, yes,' she said to appease him.

He sat up, annoyed. 'Please don't patronise me, Yasmine. You always did that, you know. You have something of a Catholic nun about you. Self-righteous, and a bit dour, if you ask me.'

Yasmine was wounded. She knew that she was aloof at times, and rarely shared her feelings on any given matter, but she would hardly describe herself as dour. What an awful word.

'Dour?' she said.

'Yes, like a nun,' he said. 'Even at the tender age of twenty-eight.'

Edward had mentioned several times how Louis had died. He kept telling her he left Louis to rot and that was an undignified way to die. 'I don't feel justice has been served, Edward. Louis may have died a horrid death, yes, and not given a proper burial, but he died thinking he had done nothing wrong to poor Radhika, and moreover, he died thinking that he got away with it,' she said. Adil Baboo had said to her that in the end, they always stick to their own kind. When she told him this, he fell back, his eyes closed. He did not stir for several seconds, and for a moment she thought, there you go, I finally did it. I killed him.

She shook him gently. 'Edward? Are you all right?'

She leaned in to take a look, and he pulled her into his arms and held on to her tightly.

'Please forgive me, Yasmine,' he said. 'I should have spoken up; I should have said something.'

She kissed his lips to calm him and lay her head back down on his chest. 'I knew what Louis did to Radhika,' she said slowly, 'and I did nothing for weeks. The moment Tommy told me, I should have gone to the authorities. I did the thing I abhor in Bengalis—I was resigned and fatalistic. I thought no one would care or believe me.'

'No one would have,' Edward said. 'You looked to me, and I failed you.'

'We both failed Radhika,' Yasmine said.

They talked through the rest of the night and fell asleep to the sound of the street hawkers calling out their wares.

He had not asked about their son once since that first day, and she knew it was not because he was not aching to see him. Neither of them was sure how infectious he was and he was weak, so Yasmine had sent their boy away to Burdwan, to her mother's house. After ten days, when she thought Edward was well enough, she sent for the baby.

Her mother arrived with Akash, flinty and disapproving, but she said nothing.

She reluctantly handed him over to Yasmine to take up to Edward. The baby was fast asleep, which was a miracle to Yasmine, as he was resistant to napping. Even at eight months, he was talkative and friendly, and rambunctious.

'I want to meet him,' was all her mother said about Edward.

Yasmine did not support this at all, but she had to respect her mother's wishes. The elder Khan had never met Edward, though he had asked to meet her several times. It was his small town, polite upbringing. It was absurd. He has no intention of marrying me, Yasmine thought, but he wants to go through the motions of being a proper suitor.

Her mother led the way up the stairs as Asma, Madhu, Rahul and Adil Baboo watched from the first floor. Yasmine turned to look at them, and they all smiled at her and nodded their heads encouragingly. They knew the elder Khan was a formidable woman. They were all a little in awe of her. When she came to inspect the Duck every once in a while, they did their best to impress her.

'Poor Edward da,' Rahul said. 'Boro ma is going to kill him.'

Normally, Asma and Madhu would tell Rahul to hush, but this time, they both nodded in agreement.

~

Yasmine tried to open the door before her mother walked in, to give Edward some warning, but she shot her such a stern look she shrank back to allow her to knock. But Shirin didn't knock. She opened the door.

Edward was unprepared. He did not have a shirt on and was lying in bed, smoking, an arm cushioning the back of his head. He looked like he had not a care in the world, a wholly inaccurate picture. He could not jump up and stand to attention, which, he told Yasmine later, he was inclined to do at the sight of Shirin Khan, scowling at what she perceived to be his insouciance.

He greeted her and lifted himself slowly off the bed and put on a shirt as Shirin silently watched. Yasmine stood behind her, holding the baby.

Edward and Shirin sized each other up. He noted she was beautiful, long-limbed and elegant, duskier than Yasmine and taller. She had been seventeen when Yasmine was born and did not look much older than her daughter.

Eventually, Edward spoke. 'Salaam waleikum, Mrs Khan,' he said. 'I'm Edward.'

'Hmm,' Shirin said.

Yasmine winced. She was not a Mrs by any means. No one had ever called her that. He must have forgotten that she had never been married. He held out his hand to be shaken. She ignored it and sat down on the bed, revealing Yasmine, skulking by the door. The baby stirred and drew Edward's eyes away from Shirin. His face broke into a wide smile.

'Hold him,' Shirin said tersely, forcing herself to be polite. 'Yasmine, give him the boy.'

Edward seemed nervous, but he held his arms out to be filled. Yasmine placed the still sleeping boy carefully in the crook of his arm and he held him gingerly. The baby did not wake up and rested his small face against Edward's chest and sucked his thumb.

'Don't drop him,' Yasmine said.

Edward nodded and examined his son in wonder.

'What's that?' he said softly, so as not to disturb the boy. 'On his forehead.'

'It's a birthmark,' Shirin said, defensive. 'It will fade, but it is auspicious. He was also born with the umbilical cord wrapped around his neck.'

'Uh, that's a good thing?' Edward asked.

'Of course. Buddha was born the same way,' Shirin replied. She raised her eyebrows at Yasmine as if to say, who is this philistine that he doesn't know that?

'He looks like my uncle Stash,' he said, after a while. 'Sort of. He has more hair. Most Lafaver babies are bald until they are three or four.'

'He is not just any baby,' Shirin said. 'He can talk. Well ahead of schedule.'

'I would hardly call the noises he makes talking,' Yasmine said. Her mother had no objectivity where the baby was concerned. Shirin shot her an irritated look.

'That is because you don't spend all your time with him, Yasmine,' she said. 'The other day, he pointed to a goat and distinctly said, "chagol".'

'I bet he's going to be a fast runner. Most Lafaver men are fast runners,' Edward said.

'Well, he's a fast talker,' Yasmine said. 'Most Khan women are fast talkers.'

Edward and she both laughed. Shirin remained unamused.

The boy was heavy in his sleep. Edward sat down and gazed at his son. When his little hand gripped Edward's index finger and attempted to suck it, Edward looked up at Yasmine, his eyes brimming with tears. Yasmine was relieved that the child had passed muster, though of course, there was never any doubt that he would not.

'Are you pleased with his name?' Shirin asked him.

'Sure, I suppose. I wasn't consulted, of course.'

'Akash means sky in Bangla,' Shirin said. 'You can choose his middle name.'

Edward looked at Yasmine and smiled. She had told her mother that Edward had written to request that he be allowed to choose the middle name.

'I'd like it to be Alexander, after my grandfather.'

Shirin nodded in approval. She was superstitious about names and what they meant. She believed one's name had a direct impact on one's destiny. 'Akash Alexander,' she said out loud. 'Conqueror,' she added after a moment.

'Invincible,' Edward said.

'No one is invincible,' Shirin said. 'Particularly the weaker sex.'

'Oh, I don't know about that,' Edward said. 'I wouldn't call your daughter or any of the Bombay Duck girls weak.'

Shirin raised an eyebrow. 'I was referring to men.'

'Conqueror—of the sky,' Yasmine interjected quickly before Edward could react, but it was too late.

'The weaker sex, ma'am? It was the weaker sex that beat back the Japanese so India could remain free,' he said.

'Sky's the limit,' Yasmine said, still trying to diffuse the new wave of tension that had appeared in the room.

'And it was you lot who got us into the war in the first place,' Shirin retorted. 'And it is we women who pay the highest price for it.'

Yasmine touched her mother's arm, silently pleading with her to back down.

'I hope this doesn't mean he will want to be a pilot,' Shirin said after a moment, sighing. She had let it go. Shirin had a fear of aeroplanes. She did not trust the human need to fly. It was unnatural to her. She always cited Amelia Earhart as a cautionary tale.

'I think, ma'am, he should be whatever he wants to be,' Edward said. He gave Shirin a small smile and bounced the baby up and down. He was annoyed by Shirin's imperious tone.

Yasmine indicated to him to stop bouncing the baby as he would wake up or spit up.

'Are you going to take them back to America with you?' Shirin asked. Her tone was conversational, but there was nothing casual about the question.

This was what Yasmine had dreaded. This line of futile questioning that would only serve to make him feel guilty and like a cad, and her miserable. Her mother knew he was married, and she believed that he would never leave his wife.

Yasmine knew she was asking him simply to shame him. It made her angry, but there was little she could do.

'I haven't thought all my plans through yet,' Edward said. 'I am still on duty until they tell me otherwise. The campaign is over, but it's all up in the air.'

Shirin did not question him further but got up to leave. She gestured to Edward to give Akash back to her.

'Just a bit longer?' he said.

Yasmine told her mother that they would keep Akash the whole day and night. She had never kept him all night without assistance. But this was what parents do, nah? she said to her mother. 'We'll take care of our baby together.'

'Absolutely not!' Shirin said. 'You have never minded him alone.'

'She wouldn't be alone, ma'am,' Edward said. Yasmine smiled at that.

'Uff! This is madness,' her mother said. 'What do you know about children?'

'Very little, but this is my kid. I think I can take care of him for one night.'

Yasmine could feel that her mother was going to miss her grandson and was fearful that somehow Edward would abscond with the boy in the night. He would be well within his rights, but Yasmine knew Edward was in no position to kidnap a baby. He was too weak.

Shirin left soon after, telling them she would return in the morning to collect the baby. She warned them she would be back early, but she knew she had no right to argue further with Edward.

Yasmine escorted her mother down the stairs.

'I saw the way he was looking at the baby,' Shirin said. 'He could spirit him away, and you could not stop him. He would let the white woman raise him. Akash looks like one of them. If he doesn't get any darker, no one would know the difference. You must prepare yourself for that.'

Yasmine held the door open for her.

'Will you stay in town tonight, Amma?'

Shirin looked into her daughter's eyes and held her gaze. Silent words passed between them. No one would be allowed to take this child.

'Naturally. Burdwan is too far away to travel there and back in one day. Stop making small talk with me,' she said finally.

'He's not a bad man,' Yasmine said. 'He's even brave, Amma. He fought so hard against the Japanese.'

Her mother sighed. 'Yes, brave enough to face the barrel of a gun, but not brave enough to take you as his wife. Funny, that, isn't it? This is how it is for us,' she said, almost to herself.

'Yes, yes, I know,' Yasmine said. She did not want yet another lecture on the trials of being a courtesan.

'What do you know, beti? You have become attached. You are starting to form expectations, and I can see in your face that you are hopeful—there's no use denying it. Spare yourself the pain, Yasmine.'

Yasmine looked down at her feet, her heart heavy.

'The relationship you should be most concerned about is slipping away from you with each passing day,' Shirin said, lifting Yasmine's chin so she could meet her mother's eyes. 'Patience has taken up with a Britisher, and Daisy could barely wait to gloat that there is serious talk of marriage. The man in question will be leaving India to return to England. According to Daisy, he will take Patience with him. That woman was always prone to exaggeration, but she might be telling the truth.'

'Good for her,' Yasmine said, her voice catching. 'It's what Patience always wanted.'

Shirin dropped Yasmine's chin and sucked her teeth.

'You're a fool, Yassu.'

'She hates me,' Yasmine said.

'So? What does that have to do with the apology she is owed?' Shirin said.

'Amma—' Yasmine began, stung.

'Uff-oh! You must face the double standard just like you must face the fact that this Amrikan will never do right by you.'

'Amma, please,' Yasmine said. 'This is too much for me. One painful truth at a time.'

Shirin covered her head with her shawl. 'I'll be here at seven o'clock—'

'Amma! No, please. Give us some more time, please!' Yasmine pleaded.

Shirin hesitated. 'Very well. I shall arrive at nine. But no later.'

She kissed her daughter's cheek and left.

~

Edward and Yasmine put the baby between them and lay down on the bed and looked at him, waiting for him to wake up. It was like waiting for a present to arrive or a flower to bud. Slowly, the baby opened his eyes. He looked at his mother and then at Edward and then back to his mother. His lower lip jutted out as he got ready to cry, but he did not. In this case, his young father's anxiety distracted him.

'He doesn't like me,' Edward said. He was hurt, which made Yasmine smile.

'Give him a minute,' she said. 'He doesn't know who you are. Etah tomar baba, shona moni,' she said to her son softly in Bangla.

'Didn't you show him pictures of me or something?'

'No, I burned all your pictures,' Yasmine said.

'Dammit, Yasmine!' Edward cried.

The baby's lip curled out again at the sharp rise in tone but was again distracted as he watched his parents quarrel quietly.

'How did I know you would come back?' Yasmine whispered. 'Don't yell in front of the baby.'

'I'm not yelling,' Edward whispered back. 'But how could you destroy every photo?'

'You *are* yelling and you're frightening him!' Yasmine said, raising her voice. 'Look!'

They both stopped and looked at him in concern.

He did not seem particularly disturbed by his parents' tension. He had rolled himself up to a seated position and was rubbing his eyes. With some difficulty, because he was relatively new to crawling and sitting up, he scrambled into Yasmine's lap and pulled at the neck of her dressing gown. She pulled back the dressing gown, exposing her breasts, and popped one into her son's mouth.

Edward looked shocked. 'What are you doing?'

'What does it look like I am doing?'

'Does he need this a lot?'

Yasmine shook her head at his naiveté. 'Yes, of course. But less and less lately. My milk has been drying up.'

Akash nursed but his eyes occasionally wandered back to his father, who was watching him intently. When he was done with his mother's milk, he sat in her lap where he could observe the new person from a safe distance.

The rest of the afternoon, Yasmine watched Edward watching their son, playing with him, and helping her to feed and change him. The boy was thrilled to have someone to climb all over and pull and tug. Edward asked Yasmine about the labour.

'Twenty hours,' she told him. Her hips were narrow, so it was a struggle. Edward listened intently. She didn't spare him the details, wanting, a little, to make him feel guilty. He kissed her and apologised for not being there.

Yasmine nestled into the crook of his arm, as he held the baby in the other.

'It's all right,' Yasmine said. 'Patience was there. She said the usual inappropriate things and made me laugh.'

'I'm glad she was there,' Edward said. He looked at the top of Yasmine's head and wondered if he should broach the subject of Patience. He had not done so since arriving in the Duck. No one mentioned Patience. It felt unnatural to him, but he knew better than to push Yasmine to discuss it. He watched as she closed her eyes and fell asleep. When his son stirred, restless, he gently lay Yasmine's head back on to the pillow and turned his entire attention to the baby.

After she awoke, refreshed, they changed the baby's nappy together and fed him. They spent that whole day playing with their son in the room. Edward was still weak and too much activity wore him out. Both Edward and Yasmine also thought if they ventured out into the world and its harsh sunlight with Akash, this spell they had cast around the three of them in her room would be broken. It was as if they were the only three people in the world that day. They held each other and watched their son crawl around and touch everything within his reach. He was going to walk soon; within the next three months, Yasmine was sure. Edward gazed in wonder at everything he did; every gurgle or sound he uttered was fascinating. As it grew darker, they fell asleep with the child between them. Yasmine awoke in the middle of the night to see Akash on Edward's chest, fast asleep. Before she had closed her eyes, she had warned him that they mustn't squash him while they slept.

'Don't worry, I'm on guard duty,' Edward said. 'You sleep.'

It was painful for Yasmine to see her child sound asleep on Edward's chest, and she began to cry, because she knew how temporary it was.

32

Yasmine awoke in the morning to feel Edward watching her. It was the soundest sleep she had had in a long time, even with the baby between them. Edward had pulled back the curtains, flooding the room with harsh sunlight. Akash was nowhere to be seen. For the past twenty-four hours, the room had been like a warm chrysalis for them, and the rest of the world was shut out—but now, in the bright light, the room looked bare and Edward appeared sickly and resentful.

'Your mother came and took him away,' he said in an accusatory voice. For a moment, Yasmine watched him. The affable Edward from the night before had retreated into the jungle, back with the ghosts, stuck in his foxhole, waist-deep in the mud. Or back to Norwich, with its beautiful autumns and cheery wife. It was the same old song and dance, as Patience liked to say. Yasmine's stomach felt hollow. She put on her dressing gown, then called down to the kitchen for tea and washed up. Edward sat half-dressed on the edge of the bed, dejected.

'I should leave today,' he said. 'I need to report back.'

'You should get dressed,' was all Yasmine said. She took her time getting ready—half hoping that Edward would leave before she was finished. But he was still there when she emerged from her dressing room. He had put on the hastily tailored linen suit that she had made for him. It was a nice colour but didn't fit him correctly. It was too loose. He had lost so much weight. He smiled at her, held out his arms and turned around.

'Not too impressive, I'm afraid,' he said. 'I'm not used to civvies anymore. I should wear my uniform.'

'I burned it,' Yasmine said.

'Why?' he asked.

'There was pus on the collar and on your trousers.'

'You've become a pyromaniac in my absence.'

He looked down at himself and shook his head. 'I'm all skinny,' he said. He now wore his belt three notches tighter.

'I am sure when your wife sees you, she won't mind,' Yasmine said and opened the door to leave. Edward moved quickly to block her. In his weakened state, the action was not easy.

'Don't do that,' he said. 'I will tell Maggie, and then I will come back. But I have to tell her in person. She deserves that.'

Yasmine nodded, but she didn't believe him. It was plainly written on her face. Once he left, he would never come back. Why would he?

'You know, Yasmine, a little faith in me would help greatly.'

'You don't need that. You know what is right. You just need to do it. You're acting guilty. You should have told her the moment you found out I was pregnant.'

'It's not that simple,' he said after a while. 'But, yes, I will do the right thing for both of us.'

'It *is* simple,' Yasmine said. 'Please. I need to go downstairs. I have been neglecting my duties.'

'There are laws, Yasmine. You can't keep me from my son forever.' She knew Edward was panicking now. Whenever he became afraid, he resorted to threats. Perhaps, however, her mother's instincts had been correct. Perhaps he would take the boy away to an arguably better life in America to be raised white and protected, but what if he wasn't? What if Maggie could not accept him? It was not unheard of—stepchildren being cast out into the street.

'There are few laws that concern the rights of illegitimate half-caste children of American citizens,' Yasmine said.

She nodded at the doorknob that he was holding. He let it go and put his arms around her. She let him hold her but did not hug him back. He kissed the top of her head and then her unyielding lips. Her mouth remained closed as his lingered.

After he left, she stood by the door and listened. She did not give in to the tears that were very much there. She heard him say goodbye to Rahul and Adil Baboo and thank them for taking care of him. She ran to the top of the stairs to watch him leave. He passed Madhu and Asma on his way out. Asma was polite and shook his hand. Madhu barely glanced at him. He looked back at Yasmine standing at the top of the stairs and smiled sadly.

'I'll send word as soon as I am ready. I don't care if you don't believe me,' he said. 'See you soon.'

He did not send word for three excruciating days. The only one who seemed to understand was young Rahul, who knew the pain of waiting for someone to reach out; he tried to cheer up Yasmine, making her feel more guilty about not telling him about Radhika.

'Edward da must be so busy, di,' he said to Yasmine one day. 'I heard at Nanda Lal's tea house that all the soldiers had to report to the base and have work or something. They keep them busy,' he said while wiping down the tables.

'Uff! Rahul,' Yasmine said. 'Pay attention to what you're doing. The table is still wet, and that cloth is filthy.'

He stood back and admired his rather shoddy handiwork.

'What are you looking at?' Yasmine asked.

'The clean table?' he said.

'I don't see a clean table.'

'Oh, di! It is clean…' he trailed off. 'No?'

She shook her head and suppressed a smile at the look of dismay on his face.

He started to wipe it down again—with the same filthy cloth.

'Rahul?' Yasmine said and sighed.

'Yes, di?'

'How about using a fresh cloth?'

'Oh, right!' he said cheerfully.

'Rahul?'

'Yes, di?'

'Thank you.'

'For what?'

'Oh nothing, stupid boy. Just get a fresh cloth.'

'Yasmine di, tension korben nah! Everything will be fine!'

33

Patience had been living with her mother for more than a year in the old haveli where the girls had grown up together. It no longer functioned as a place of pleasure and entertainment but housed a handful of former courtesans and their retainers, who Shirin allowed to live there cheaply, Daisy included. It was only a few streets away from the Duck, but Yasmine never ran into her friend when she was out. It was as if Calcutta and her occupants had arranged itself so they would never see one another.

For Patience, the arrangement was not ideal. Having lived so long on her own, coming and going as she pleased, she smarted under her mother's exacting scrutiny and constant comparisons with Yasmine, whom Daisy had always attempted to pit her against. Daisy had never been successful in driving the girls apart. Patience's allegiance to Yasmine had been immutable. Now, it was clear something terrible had happened, powerful enough to bring her daughter back home. Yet no matter how hard she tried, she could not coax Patience to tell her what it was. After they had helped Yasmine give birth to a healthy baby boy, Shirin had been grateful and had shown her gratitude by helping Daisy pay off all her debts and gifted her a decent sum of money. As a result, things had thawed between the older women, but their daughters seemed to grow further apart.

Besides the irritation of living with her mother, Patience discovered that being in the haveli of her childhood made her think of Yasmine constantly. Every corner held some memory. The kitchen was where they stole mangoes out of the baskets, or a clay pot of freshly made sweet yoghurt. Patience remembered a day they had managed to steal a clay pot apiece and were running down one of the long, dark hallways in the interior of the house that linked the kitchen to the main receiving area. Yasmine was right behind her but lost one of her sandals and tripped, dropping the pot. It shattered and yoghurt spilt everywhere. Patience turned around to see her friend, sitting in the mess, crying. She immediately ran back, and with one hand, dragged her down the hallway, like she was retrieving a wounded soldier from the battlefield. They ducked into a closet, just as one of the cooks and a maid found the evidence. They crouched in the pitch-black closet, stifling their giggles as they heard the cook yell at the maid for allowing this to happen. Once the coast was clear, they ran to Yasmine's room, where they proceeded to eat the remaining pot of yoghurt with relish, giggling all the while.

When there were clients in the house or one of the musical evenings going on, the girls were confined to their rooms, which were connected. By the time they were ten, Patience had managed to find a way to shimmy down the thick, gnarled trunk of an old bougainvillea tree growing up the side of house and on to the veranda adjacent to their rooms.

Soon after leaving the Duck, Patience stood in the courtyard of the haveli, gazing at the bright pink bougainvillea tree, more gnarled and solid as ever, and remembered she had to coax Yasmine down once she herself was on the ground, a distance of ten feet.

'Come *on,* Yassu!' Patience entreated. 'It's not that far.'

Yasmine had peeked over the banister, her small dark head

barely grazing the top of it. She had to stand on her toes to look over.

'I will die,' she said, simply.

Patience had not considered that possibility. She pondered for a moment and said, hands on hips and with more confidence than she felt, 'No, you won't. I will catch you if you fall.' This seemed to reassure Yasmine enough to drag a small stool from her room to the edge of the veranda and stand on it.

'Grab the big branch near you,' Patience said, trying to sound encouraging, though she was becoming less sure. Yasmine managed to hoist her small body over the bannister and clung to the tree and then refused to move an inch further.

It took several minutes of desperate pleading until Yasmine slowly, so slowly Patience was convinced it would be dawn before her friend ever made it to the ground, climbed down the tree.

Patience grabbed Yasmine's hand, and they snuck into the reception hall, tucking their little bodies behind some large, tufted floor pillows. They watched in awe as Shirin played the sitar and sang a mournful ghazal about the star-crossed lovers Laila and Majnu. She had the gathered men in thrall. Then Daisy emerged, every footfall accompanied by the sound of the bells tied to her slim ankles. As Shirin sang, she danced. The men expressed their appreciation: *wah, wah*. Their small daughters watched, clinging to one another, mesmerised by their mothers' beauty and talent and how much the audience seemed to respect them.

'Can you believe Shirin is letting her keep the child with her?' Daisy said, breaking into Patience's reverie. Patience sighed and followed her mother into the dining room, where she silently ate the food placed in front of her. 'Well, answer me,' Daisy insisted. Patience stared at her mother, who looked older than her age, and tried to find the graceful, poetic young creature from her memories. Unable to locate her, she shrugged and said, 'Yasmine does whatever she wants. She's a Nazi.'

'I never did care for the girl,' Daisy said. 'Arrogant. I wish you didn't have to work for her.'

'We need the lolly,' Patience said. 'With your extravagant habits. And she pays me well.'

Daisy ignored the reference to her spending, tearing off a piece of paratha and stuffing it into her mouth.

'Well, more than that department store at least. You're on your feet all day, having to deal with all the snooty firangi women, and they pay you a pittance,' Daisy said, licking the ghee off her fingers.

Patience had taken up working at the cosmetics counter of Whiteaway Laidlaw as her full-time job. She sang occasionally at the Duck for extra money, but that was becoming less frequent as she could not bear to see the baby and Yasmine together. However, this did not diminish Patience's love for Akash. She felt a deep affection for him that took hold the moment she saw him born. When Yasmine was not looking or out of the club, she would cuddle and hold Akash, or 'Bump' as she called him now, because he was just beginning to try to walk. He held on to furniture, pulling himself up, and would gambol drunkenly around the club, from chair to chair. Once, he knocked into the bar and an angry red knot appeared on his forehead. Before he could cry, Patience had scooped him up and distracted him while Rahul ran and fetched some ice. She put the compress on his small head and cuddled him to her.

'There now, isn't that better?' Patience said soothingly as the boy sniffled and tried bravely to hold back tears.

'That's quite a bump you have managed to get, sir,' she said. 'I think from now on, you shall be called Sir Bump.'

'Be you,' he said, extracting his thumb from his mouth.

Patience smiled. He had just started trying to say a few words. She began to sing softly and cradled him, *'It had to be you, it had to be you...'*

When she was finished, she was instructed to sing it again, and she did, gladly. From when he was very small but recognised who she was, she sang to him. Yasmine was not aware of this and the others tactfully kept it a secret. *It Had to be You* was his favourite song. He was asleep by the time she sang the last stanza, and she reluctantly handed him back to his ayah. But not before she firmly admonished the young girl to keep a better eye on the precious 'Bump'.

'I'll tan your hide if I hear he's been hurt again,' she said. The girl shrugged. She took her orders from Yasmine. Patience almost smacked her for her insolence, and decided she would alert Asma and Rahul to keep an eye on her and press Yasmine to fire the girl.

Her relationship with Yasmine continued to decline the longer they avoided facing one another. They missed each other, though. If Patience saw something funny or strange, she wanted to tell Yasmine, who shared her dark humour and appreciation for all things odd. When she felt what she called the 'Sunday scaries', the evenings before she had to go back to work at the cosmetics counter and wait on plump, rude European ladies, she sometimes found herself reaching for the telephone to call her friend but always stopped short of dialling the number. She wanted to tell Yasmine about her new beau, the nice, if somewhat dull, young man from Plymouth who was in love with her and was hinting at marriage. She wanted to hear Yasmine tell her that marriage was for bourgeois women who needed men to feel whole and lacked intellectual curiosity. She wanted to argue with her properly.

Yasmine, for her part, grew surly and even more quiet on the days she yearned for her friend. She wanted to talk to

Patience about Edward and the time he had spent with her. She wanted to sob on Patience's shoulder that it had been a month since he had left her arms. It was only to Patience that she would admit she wanted Edward to choose her, to give Akash the home and recognition the child deserved.

When they inadvertently ran into each other in the Duck, none of these longings was expressed. At most, a half-intelligible greeting would be muttered under the breath—sometimes from Patience, sometimes Yasmine—and they would scurry past one another, heads down. Any pressing communication was done through the others. Adil Baboo tried to appeal to Yasmine's rational nature and begged her to be the first to break the silence.

'Apologise to her,' he said. 'Can you not see how she feels? You have your baby. She was denied hers ... by you. I am only seeing it through her eyes,' he added quickly when Yasmine, who had been listening quietly, rose to leave. 'Not right, not wrong. Her eyes.'

'I did what I thought was right,' Yasmine said.

'I know,' Adil Baboo said, nodding. He touched her arm. He rarely touched her, so Yasmine knew this was important to him. 'But it's not fair, is it?'

Yasmine nodded. Her mother's cautionary words were now also ringing in her ears. She knew her friend was somewhere in the club. Yasmine looked in the mirror above the bar, took a deep breath and went to find her.

Patience was with Asma and the baby upstairs in Asma's room. When Yasmine walked in, she was startled. Patience was holding Akash and quickly handed him back to Asma. Yasmine snatched the confused child from Asma and glared at Patience.

'Whatever grievance you have, keep them with me. Leave my son alone!'

'Yassu, Patience would never hurt him,' Asma cried. 'She adores him.'

'Leave it, ducky,' Patience said to Asma. 'When this mule gets a notion in her head, she will not change her mind.'

'And I suppose it's a coincidence that a huge bruise appeared on his head the day you performed here,' Yasmine said. 'Explain that. The ayah told me how you were roughhousing with him, and he hit his head.'

Patience gasped. 'That little snake! She lets him run around and does not watch him. He tripped and hit his head on the bar,' she said. Tears sprung up in her eyes.

'It's true, Yassu,' Asma said.

'Were you there?' Yasmine asked Asma. Asma shook her head.

'But I know Patience loves him, like we all do.'

'Leave it,' Patience said again. 'I'm finished here.'

'Be you,' Akash said in the silence. From his mother's arms, he reached out for Patience.

Yasmine looked at Patience. 'What is that?'

'Never mind,' Patience replied. She glared at Yasmine, kissed the little boy's outstretched fingers, and left.

Asma sighed.

'Patience sings to him,' she said. '*It Had to be You*. It's his favourite. It calms him.'

Yasmine handed Akash to Asma and ran after Patience.

'Forgive me, please!' she said. Patience paused.

'I can't,' she said.

'Please try,' Yasmine said. 'I am a fool. But you're my sister—'

'I can't have babies,' Patience said. 'I'm barren, because you insisted.'

Yasmine could not meet her eyes. 'How do you know?'

'A woman knows, you fool. You also kept that bit of information to yourself, didn't you?'

'But it's not for sure. Dr Ghosh said it was not for sure. You're still so young—'

'You're a selfish cunt, Yasmine. And that's the truth.'

Not knowing what to say, Yasmine nodded lamely and watched Patience walk out the door. In her heart, she knew she would never hear from her friend again. For once, she did not think about the impact Patience's absence would have on the business. She felt only loss. A loss compounded by the fact that Edward had not called or sent word in weeks. Of the four people she loved most in the world, including her mother and Akash, Edward and Patience seemed to be slipping away or had slipped away forever. In the days following this, Yasmine plunged into a sadness she had never felt before. Not even work, always her solace, or the baby, could prevent it from invading every corner of her mind and heart. When she couldn't bear it any longer, she became hardened towards it and those who were causing it. The longer Edward went without communicating with her, the more resolved she grew to fortify her defences against him. She was the same about Patience.

~

Edward had regained almost all his strength, and with that came a measure of clarity about Maggie. He knew he could not send her a letter from India, telling her that he loved another. It would have to be done in person, and the sooner the better. There was also his family to consider. He found though, that once he had made up his mind to leave India, he felt an unwillingness to convey to Yasmine his decision. Every time he reached for the phone to dial the Duck's exchange, he found he could not. He longed to see his son but believed that doing so would weaken his resolve to leave him and Yasmine and go back to America and face Maggie. But he also knew he could not leave them without saying a proper goodbye. So he felt paralysed. After a month, he worked up the courage to do the needful, as Maggie would have put it, and called the Duck. A week before he would be shipped back to Connecticut.

Rahul answered on the second ring. Edward was taken aback—he knew the boy was not allowed to answer the phone. That should have been the first sign something was amiss.

'Hello, Southie!' Edward said. 'Yasmine di is letting you answer the phone? Do you own the club now?' He teased the boy in his broken Bangla.

Rahul was sombre. 'Di is very busy right now, Eddie da,' he said.

'I know, she always is,' Edward replied.

'Why did you wait so long to call her?' Rahul said. His tone was not accusatory. The boy sounded weary.

'Is she all right? What about choto sahib?' Edward asked.

'Choto babu is very good. Very clever,' Rahul said. He sounded more cheerful when talking about Akash.

'Can I talk to Yasmine di, please?'

'No, Eddie da. She won't speak to you.'

'Then I'll come.'

'You can come,' Rahul said, 'but she won't see you. She is very quiet and unhappy, and she won't even come down every night when the club is open. Adil Baboo and Asma di are in the front. Madhu di dances and sings sometimes, but she is not as good as Patience di. And I even serve drinks with Ghosh da sometimes. Everything is a mess.'

He didn't say it, but Edward knew the boy was thinking it. Everything was a mess because of him, because of his silence and absence.

'I'm sorry, Southie,' Edward said. 'But I can make it right.'

He heard muffled voices on the other end; Rahul was arguing with someone, a woman.

'Edward?' It was Yasmine.

'Oh, thank God, honey. Are you okay?'

Yasmine's voice faltered. 'What do you want?'

'I want to see you and the kid.'

'I should drop everything then and make time for you?'

'I know it's been a couple of weeks. But I needed to think a bit, go into a cave, you know?'

She remained silent. Edward could her breathing. 'So, honey ... I have to go back to the US ... honey?'

The line had gone dead.

~

In a last desperate attempt to get Yasmine to talk to him before he left India, Edward contacted Patience. She seemed genuinely happy to hear from Edward and agreed to meet him.

'Oh, you're alive, love! Thrilled!'

They met in Eden Gardens, a favourite haunt of his and Yasmine's. He had first suggested Freeschool Street, where he and Yasmine browsed books and argued about Kafka (he found him morbid, she, an incisive commentator on the human condition, which according to her, was inherently morbid). Patience did not agree to Freeschool Street, saying she was allergic to all the dust the books collected.

'All that information makes me squirrely,' she said, laughing.

'It's good to see you,' Edward said, kissing Patience on her cheek. 'You look gorgeous as usual.'

Patience gave a mock curtsey. 'Thank you, love. You were always generous with the compliments.' She snaked her arm through his and gave him a gentle tug. 'Now, tell me what you really want.'

'Can you tell her that I plan on coming back as soon as I can?' Edward asked.

'Why don't you tell her yourself?' Patience said, subdued.

'She won't see me.'

'That mule-headed woman,' Patience said. She shook her head. 'She'll ruin her own life just from pride.'

They were sitting under a vast banyan tree that offered ample shade. It was humid, and Edward was drenched in sweat. He was recovering steadily but still felt weak at times and needed to stop frequently when they walked and catch his breath. He looked at Patience appreciatively.

'How do you always look so cool?' he asked.

'Well, I was raised here, this is all I know,' she replied. 'I guess my body is just used to it. When I go to Blighty, I'll probably freeze to death.'

'Do you think she will ever see me?' he asked after a while.

Patience shrugged. 'I don't know, love. With Yassu, things are unpredictable right now. Being a mother now and all.'

Edward heard the change in her voice, how it became an octave or two higher. She was suddenly tense.

'Fancy a pint?' Patience suddenly said. She was cheery again.

There was nothing Edward would have wanted more at that moment, except Yasmine.

He took Patience to the ARC where one pint led to two and two led to dinner and, with dinner, came three gimlets—real ones—apiece. She ate heartily and it pleased Edward to make her happy.

It was a relief to be able to talk about Yasmine and express to someone who knew her well, maybe even better than he did, how angry he was at her. Patience explained Yasmine's need for control, which Edward knew about very well. To his own surprise, he found himself talking about Burma. He didn't share as many details as he had with Yasmine, but unlike Yasmine, Patience did not interrupt him to conjecture about politics and chastise him for his 'colonial mentality'.

Somehow, during the course of the evening, the tone of the discussion changed. It went from being an almost affectionate analysis of Yasmine's various frustrating qualities and flaws to outright criticism. They bonded over it energetically, each one failing to notice that the strength of their commiseration was in direct proportion to the amount of alcohol consumed. Both felt hurt and betrayed by Yasmine; neither felt they could talk to her about it, and this exchange was a relief. The very things that drew them to her had become galling. What they both once thought of as her regal bearing, was now arrogance; her business sense, greed; her ability to remain calm in crisis, soullessness. Patience tearfully told him that Yasmine had forced her to abort her baby. Edward's shock was gratifying to Patience.

'And now she has your baby!' she said. 'And I have nothing.'

'Maybe she thought she was doing you a favour?' Edward said. He could not imagine that the woman he loved would wilfully force someone to do this.

Patience shook her head. 'And I'm a Catholic,' she said, a little drunkenly. 'This is a sin to end all sins. Murder.'

Edward put a comforting arm around her, and she rested her head on his shoulder. She was quiet, but he could tell she was crying.

'Well, that's quite enough whinging for the evening!' she said finally, wiping her cheeks. 'We're out and about. Let's be merry, please.'

~

Patience attracted—as usual—many a male admirer and danced with a stammering, red-faced young man who kissed her hand in gratitude. With enough cajoling, she was persuaded to sing.

'Requests?' she said, and the room erupted in shouts for everything from *The Battle Hymn of the Republic* to *I've Got You Under My Skin*.

'Sorry, lads. I'm only taking requests from one man,' she said and pointed at Edward. He shrugged, embarrassed. People started wolf-whistling and teasing him.

'Come on, man! She wants you to request something!' they yelled and whistled.

'I request your hand in marriage!' someone called out. Everyone started laughing. Edward shrugged again.

'I can wait,' Patience said. 'My middle name is Patience.' Everyone except Edward laughed again, not knowing that she was telling the truth.

'Okay, you've twisted my arm,' Edward said. 'I request *At Last*—'

Patience smiled and nodded. 'Sure, soldier,' she said, holding the microphone and swaying a little.

By the time they stumbled out of the ARC, two hours later, holding one another up, singing *I Don't Want to Set the World on Fire* and getting indulgent smiles from passers-by, they were completely 'squiffy', as Patience described it. Edward tipped his hat to a European couple, who smiled at them. Even in his drunken state, he noticed that no one looked at them oddly. He turned and smiled at Patience. It was because she looked like a gorgeous white woman, he realised. Whenever he and Yasmine were out together, they were stared at, sometimes with hostility, by both Indians and Europeans. It made Yasmine tense. The thought of Yasmine suddenly made him unbearably sad, and he needed his pillow.

'I should see you home,' Edward said to Patience and dropped his cap. When both he and Patience went to pick it up, they knocked heads and dissolved into fits of laughter.

'No,' she said, after they had stopped laughing. 'My mother will see you and have a go at me. I'm not up for that tonight.'

'Well, let me get a gharry for you then,' he offered.

Patience gazed at him, listing a bit. He smiled and steadied her.

'Yasmine is a right fool,' Patience said. 'You're a keeper.'

Before he could say thank you, she leaned in and kissed him on the mouth. He was surprised and took her by both arms and held her away from him. They looked at one another intently. They kissed again, hard.

~

In the morning, she was gone—no note. He squinted and looked down at his feet. He was naked from the waist down except for his socks. There was not a trace that she had been there, save for the indentation in the pillow next to his and a single, long strand of chestnut brown hair. The gravity of what had happened sunk in. The rest of the morning, he paced in his room, smoking frantically and trying to decide if calling Patience was a good idea. A horrifying image of Patience confessing everything to Yasmine played over and over in his mind. After all, Patience's loyalties understandably lay with Yasmine. He had not yet realised that the two women rarely spoke to one another, and Patience had not told him that she no longer performed regularly at the club. The message he had given Patience to relay to Yasmine would now ring hollow, completely like a mockery. The words, meant to express his true feelings, would now actually send Yasmine further into her shell. He cancelled all his group sessions for the day. In an effort to keep himself busy, he was once again leading group sessions of soldiers newly returned from the Big Green. This morning, he thought: those nutters are going to have to fend for themselves for a change. I'm the one going crazy here.

Patience called several hours and two packs later and assured him their secret was safe. He asked her if she'd had a chance to convey the message that he would be coming back for her and their son.

She sounded quite nonchalant on the phone. 'I couldn't find her, love. I just left a note in her room. I told her what you said and when you're leaving. If you're telling me the truth, she'd be a fool not to see you off. But you know, love, Yasmine has pride, and marriage, well ... she is not too keen on it.'

'I know. You told me,' he said. 'You don't think she will ignore the note, do you?'

'I don't know, ducky,' Patience said. 'I hope not.'

'Listen, Patience, I'm sorry ... about what happened. I guess we were both a little drunk. I hope you're all right.'

He was embarrassed and grew quiet. He could hear Patience breathing at the other end.

'Yes, sure,' she said finally. 'These things happen.'

After they hung up, Edward poured himself a large glass of water and drank thirstily. He was parched. He sat down and thought about how relieved he was that Patience was being such a sport about all this. But then anger set in slowly as the day progressed and still no word from Yasmine came. His indiscretion suddenly became Yasmine's fault. Her coldness had driven him to Patience's arms. It was clear now that she would not see him before he left.

PART FOUR

AKASH/ALEXANDER

Memories are like mulligatawny soup at a cheap restaurant: they are not meant to be stirred.

–P.G. Wodehouse

34

Akash Alexander Khan '65
Clark Hall
Wesleyan University
Middletown, CT
17 April 1962

Dearest Akash,

Edward wrote to me three weeks after the Calcutta riots. That was the last time we corresponded in any meaningful way. He left India in '44, and I have not seen him since. I still have the letter he sent me in '46: 'If you are alive, please send me a wire as soon as possible and please tell me what happened. We are hearing so many conflicting reports. Some say six thousand were killed, some sixteen thousand. I am going nuts. Every day, there is some new horror story. It's like Nanking all over again, they're saying. I know you hate me, but please just let me know if you and Alec (he insisted on calling you that) are okay.' He was upset about the massacre at Lakshmipur. He had visited it once, and it made an impression on him. During the communal riots of 1946, everyone turned on each other. In Noakhali, Muslims and government-employed thugs from neighbouring villages murdered and raped Hindu women and girls, some as young as infants. Only four lived to tell the horror of the massacres to Gandhi when he came to witness the aftermath of the carnage. Edward read about it and remembered the name of Lakshmipur and a little girl he had befriended.

I wired Edward as soon as I could, when I remembered to, more than a month later. Short and not-so-sweet. 'Alive. Stop. Countless killed. Stop. Rahul amongst them. Stop. Stay well. Stop.'

As for the other information you requested, I will tell you whatever I can about those five days. It is a morbid subject to pick for your final paper in history, however.

Where to begin? They called the day of the start of the riots Direct Action Day, the politicians that is—their jaunty name for it. As if we were taking our fate into our own hands and moulding our destiny. What rubbish! You know what action came about that day? I will tell you one thing, you were almost snatched out of my arms by a crazed Hindu woman, Devika, who had just seen her fourteen-year-old son beheaded by a Muslim mob, and wanted nothing more than to do the same to someone else's child. I knew Devika, had laughed with her, bought roti and baked goods from her for the club. Patience had advised her on the best way to style her hair. She wanted to look like Mumtaz Shanti, who was Muslim, from that movie *Kismet*.

Mere days earlier, this woman was calm, even happy, maybe, but while she hummed in her kitchen and made the bread for that night's meal, Jinnah was holding court from his house on Malabar Hill in Bombay and pontificating about a place he concocted called Pakistan and putting in motion—for his own purposes—events that would render this mother a rakhosh, a monster.

The fact is, even I didn't know how many had perished. But I am getting ahead of myself. The war was over, your father was gone. You were two-and-a-half years old and growing, it seemed, every night. The Duck continued as before. Some of the characters had changed. Patience had left for England as soon as the Germans surrendered. She married a soldier and moved to Plymouth. Before she left, she came to say goodbye, but it was an embittered goodbye. I asked her to stay a bit longer, until she was sure this soldier was the right one, and she refused—partly because she was so angry at me for various reasons I don't care to discuss. Though I had my own reasons to resent her. Her beau was a clerk of some kind back in England. The way she described him to Asma and the others, he seemed besotted and a simple soul who only wanted to make her happy. She just wanted to leave India, by any means necessary, and I cannot say that I blame her. Life after Independence was unbearable for Anglo-Indians.

The British started the painstaking process of taking stock. The war had all but crippled them financially, and the agitation to end the Raj was reaching a fevered pitch. It was in this chaos that poor leadership was born, and the corruption and selfishness of the politicians seeped into the psyche of the people. But I think this is what the British wanted all along.

'Let those darkies kill each other,' they said in their parlours and European-only clubs, 'and have done with it, the ingrates, after all we have done for them.'

I know that is what Churchill thought. And the Congress and Muslim League provided much fodder. It was all some of us sensible ones could do to keep people from each other's throats. In the Duck, we were such a mish-mosh of religions, castes and rituals. Somehow, we managed. Our differences were not along religious lines, ever. It was always about personalities and living on top of one another. The usual human drama. It was during this time that all of us, Adil Baboo, Asma, Madhu, Ghosh and Rahul, understood that we had been living in a sort of dream. This was our odd little family, of which I was the matriarch. Without realising it, I had created a sort of mini-society that was almost idealistic, utopian if you will, and when the riots erupted, no one was more shocked than the staff and occupants of Bombay Duck.

On the morning of 16 August, Rahul and Adil Baboo came rushing into the club. They had gone to their usual tea stall on Harrison Street, East Bengal Cabin. It was run by a very nice gentleman by the name of Nanda Lal, whom I had known for years. He was dignified and well educated. Adil Baboo and Rahul said that Nanda Lal's tea stall had been vandalised and burnt and that he and his family were trapped in their house. Nanda Lal had been attacked as well and was wounded.

'Who attacked them?' I asked.

'Muslims,' Adil Baboo replied. 'From Mirzapore Street.' He looked crestfallen.

'I got away,' Rahul said, 'because of Adil da. He said I was his son. They would have killed me.'

Adil Baboo later told me that they had barely escaped. A crazed mob had demanded to see if Rahul was circumcised and when he refused, fell upon him with broken bottles and lathis. Adil Baboo had stood between the boy and the mob and offered to show them that he was circumcised. He told them that Rahul was his son and if a father was cut then it followed that a son would be as well. The mob did not buy this story but became momentarily distracted when Adil Baboo undid his dhoti and obligingly showed them. Somehow it worked, and he and Rahul escaped.

On the morning of 17 August, when Devika ripped you out of my arms, she did not see me anymore, and I did not see her. I saw Ma Kali at her worst. She was running down the street, a mad look in her eyes. She was covered in blood, none of it her own, I found out later. Her son's blood. She kept looking around for something to kill. Rahul had ventured out earlier to see what was happening in the Hindu sections of town and told me that her son had been killed. I was overcome with grief for her. But when she tried to get into the Duck, I shut the door on her face. She banged on the door, screaming to be let in.

'For God's sake, Yassu!' Madhu cried. 'Let her in. Her son is dead. She will be killed if we leave her to wander around.'

I thought Madhu was right. The woman was a mother like me. It was Devika. The woman who sold us roti. I opened the door. She stood on the steps, her chest heaving. She walked into the room slowly. We all parted to let her through. Her eyes were wide as she looked at all of us. No one said a word. She smelled like the streets after kurbani Eid. But this was not cow's blood. Human blood, which is what she was covered in, smells sweeter. It was nauseating.

Death had followed her into the Duck. My eyes instinctively went to where you were sleeping, in my room at the top of the stairs. Devika had been staring at me, so she saw where my eyes went, and she knew at once what I was feeling. She moved so quickly I almost did not beat her to the stairs.

I screamed and ran up the stairs, two at a time. She was on my heels. Someone, Madhu I think, tried to grab Devika's sari, but she kicked at Madhu hard and she fell back on top of Adil Baboo and Rahul, who were also trying to get up the stairs. I tried to shut the door in her face, but she was so strong, Akash. She was a small, slim woman, but she was now overcome with superhuman strength. It was adrenaline brought on by grief and rage. She pushed the door in, and I fell to the ground. She locked the door. Her movements were slow and deliberate. I grabbed her ankle and kept her from snatching you from the bed. You were awake now, sitting up and staring at me, and Devika struggle on the floor. It was a silent, eerie struggle from what I remember. I was so close to her, I could smell her sour breath. Adil Baboo, Rahul and the others were at the door, trying to break it down. I managed to shove her away and get up and grab you. You started to cry then. Devika took a fistful of your hair and tried to yank you out of my arms. You screamed, I slapped her, but she would not stop. Finally, Adil Baboo and Rahul broke down the door and pulled her off us. They held her back as she snarled at me. Like a beast. Madhu took her by the hair and threw her down the stairs. She lay at the bottom, whimpering.

Asma took you and went to her room, where she locked the door and tried to comfort you. We all stood and watched to see what Devika would do. Eventually, she got up and limped to the door and walked into the street, which was now overrun with broken bottles, dead bodies and people running around screaming. Rahul quickly ran down the stairs and slammed the door and barred it against the din.

When Asma came out of the room holding you, you jumped into my arms. You were shaking and told me that a rakhosh had come to eat you. For weeks afterwards, you could not sleep through the night without waking up to check that I was next to you. We had just managed to potty train you, and you started wetting the bed again.

Whenever I see a picture of Jinnah, or even Nehru, I want to spit at it.

He was a Shakespearean-trained actor you know, that Jinnah, so he knew how to pontificate. If he had done *Hamlet*, it would have been a Hindu skull he would have been holding. He and the Congress were the real masterminds behind all this. The history books don't mention that. He was cruel and he whipped all those Muslim Leaguers into a frenzy, and they in turn hired their goondas to exact terror. We would never have turned on one another like this—be sure to state that in your essay. Calcutta was a place where everyone was comfortable with being themselves. We were united because of our political goals and leanings. Hindu, Muslim—rarely did we judge based on such silly differences. Make no mistake, the politicians wrought this, not the people.

Jinnah was obsessed with the idea that Muslims would be systematically persecuted under a Hindu majority government. They outnumber us three to one, he declared. We will be crushed under them. We must have our own state, etc., etc. Jinnah was not even religious! His grandfather was a Hindu, for pity's sake! We were all Hindus at some point, my nanoo Pardis liked to say. Hating them was like hating ourselves. It was irrational in the extreme. She also liked to say the root of all the troubles was the cow. They worshipped them, we shish-kabobed them. She was just being tongue in cheek, but she hated the way they were allowed to lounge about on intersections and in the road, blocking up traffic and staring at us stupidly while we tried to cross the street.

'Cows are evil incarnate,' she said. 'What's that Chatgaya expression? Better to have an empty corral than naughty cows.'

Many hapless cows died in those five days, along with their owners.

All that first night, we would hear the cries of 'Allaho Akbar!' And then screaming or ominous silence. Eventually, in the distance, someone would shout 'Jai Hind!' in response, followed by bellowing or more silence. Rahul said that on the Ripon College campus, the flagpole had been flying the green, white and orange flag of the Congress in the morning, but it had been replaced by the Islamic green star and crescent of the Muslim League by the afternoon. Who had died to make that happen, I wondered. Colleges were a seething hotbed of communal strife and a perfect place for both parties to recruit pawns and henchmen. Nanda Lal would later tell us how he had witnessed a heated skirmish on the roof of the college building between the Muslim Leaguers and the Congress goondas. The Muslim Leaguers won that battle. He too heard the disparate slogans of 'Jai Hind' and 'Pakistan Zindabad' being shouted in every street and bylane. But then, and this was the terrible thing, these cries were replaced by the staccato sound of gunfire and ultimately silence.

'It came from the window of an apartment building opposite the college,' Adil Baboo said. 'Never, in all my years, have I heard gunfire in a riot.'

This, you see, had changed the stakes. On the fourth day, the street weapons changed from bottles and lathis to iron staves and knives. The killings became more brutal and frenzied. Nanda Lal's shop and home were on the corner of Harrison Street and Mirzapore Street in the Muslim section, so he had a front-row view to the mayhem when he was not cowering in the upper hallway of his house.

Since the Duck had no lower windows facing the street, we did not have much damage in the front. Someone had painted the words 'Mohammed's whores' on the side. Madhu had ventured out that afternoon to see about her family and had been attacked by Congress goondas who mistook her for Muslim when they saw her emerging from the club. They beat her so badly, she had to be hospitalised for a week. Thankfully, they did not sexually assault her. They refused to listen to her protestations that she was a Hindu. They didn't care that her real name was Padma.

On the fourth day, we thought we had somehow weathered the worst of it. The police had yet to actively intervene, and we still heard rioters from both sides thundering down the streets at all hours, but we were left alone.

'Murderers never sleep, it seems,' Adil Baboo said.

'Oh, the real ones do,' I said bitterly. I was referring to Jinnah and Suhrawady, who had tried to show his might in Calcutta and organised these goondas in the first place. You were crying incessantly because you were hungry. We had run out of food and Rahul—brave, sweet, foolish boy—insisted he go out to find some. I refused to let him, but Adil Baboo convinced me.

Rahul picked you up from where you were playing on the dusty floor and pressed his cheek to yours. You put your skinny little arms around his neck and kissed him. You loved him very much. He was like a big toy and playmate for you. Rahul was so tender with you, and far more patient than I was. He often looked at you with wonder and let you climb all over him and pull his hair. He never complained. Not even when it hurt sometimes. He would wipe down the tables with you clinging to his spindly legs.

'Choto sahib is going to break the ladies!' he would declare happily in his muddled English. He insisted on speaking English as much as possible with you because you were an 'Amrikan', and used as much slang as he could remember from his beloved Corporal Addison.

'Mashallah bolo!' I would say. I had become superstitious now that I was a mother and started believing in all the nonsense that I had been so dismissive of, like nazars and what not. Though there were many times when you were growing up when I wondered if Allah had gone AWOL, I still invoked Mashallah and Inshallah when it suited me.

'I can't see Choto sahib suffer,' Rahul said, squeezing you tightly. You let out a yelp of delight and hugged him tighter in return. 'He's so skinny now.'

He poked at your ribs, which were sticking out. In just three days, you had lost so much weight. But you were happy, even after the ordeal with Devika. You were loved, darling, by everyone in the Duck.

Rahul gave you a big kiss on your head, smiled at me winningly and walked out the door. That was the last time we saw him. We still do not know what happened to him. He just never came back, and when the riots were over, we all looked for him but he was gone. I would like to believe that he had seen his beloved Radhika, that she was somehow still alive, and they had run off together and married and had many babies. I can say now, I loved that silly boy. And I still miss him.

Your mother,
Yasmine

35

It was seventeen years since Edward had been overseas. He felt no desire to travel or curiosity about how the world had fared after the war. He trusted that things would rebuild in their time. After all, he and Maggie had managed to do that. After he returned, he went through the usual period of adjustment that all the veterans did. And she was by his side all the way. Reliable and steady, as always. They had tried to have babies without success, and Edward suggested adoption, which Maggie, being practical, seriously considered.

'We might even think about adopting from overseas,' he said one day. 'There are so many orphans from the war.'

'Hmm, yes, true,' Maggie agreed.

'So many kids abandoned by their GI dads,' he added, and waited for Maggie's reaction.

'Uh huh.'

They were in their garden in Norwich. They had bought a bigger house on the GI Bill and Edward had finished Wesleyan and joined the psych ward at Bacchus Hospital. His early patients consisted mostly of vets suffering from combat-related stress and anxieties about re-integration into civilian life. Now, he treated depressed housewives and the occasional nervous breakdown.

He watched her prune back the hydrangeas and waited.

'So Europe?' she said. 'England? France? Dare I say it—Germany?'

'What about India?'

Maggie looked at him then.

'You can't be serious.'

'Why not?'

'Well, you know why.'

'No, I don't.'

He was angry even though he knew this would be her reaction. He was always hoping that somehow things would be different. Maggie was always good to their housekeeper Adelaide, an elderly coloured woman who had worked for them for six years. She never talked about her in a denigrating way. Never referred to her race as inferior. But he also knew that this was no sign of a burgeoning race consciousness or egalitarian tendencies.

'What kind of a life would a little Indian child have in Norwich?' she said. 'Where the coloured stay on their side of town and we on ours? Where would this child fit in?'

This was not an unreasonable question.

'Somewhere between. I don't know,' Edward said. 'What if the child were a half-caste?'

'Half-caste? What's that?'

'A mixed-race kid,' Edward said slowly.

'Gosh!'

'Mags! This happens, you know? Especially during wars. Soldiers mix with the locals and, well, anything can happen. Especially when you think you're going get your head blown off at any moment. But the thing is, sometimes the kid can pass.'

'For what? For white? Good lord!'

Edward sighed. 'Why would that be an issue?' he asked. 'It's not unheard of.'

'Well, it's a lie, for one thing.'

'But only half of one.'

'Yes, a half lie equals a half-life.'

Maggie got off her knees and brushed the soil and bits of leaves from her pants. She was moving more slowly lately and complaining of aches—mostly in her neck and joints. She had always been so vital and active, it was hard to watch her slowing down, and when she was still so young, forty-two years old. She had never been sickly, but there was something bearing down on her, though she never complained or talked about it. She had become a two pack a day smoker. She had never smoked before the war, though everyone around her did. It was a newly acquired habit that had lasted over a decade.

She shook her head. 'No, Eddie. I'm a broad-minded person, but I'm not going to adopt a half, whatever it is, child from India. It's not just about what I feel. Think about the child, how they would feel ... and the child's mother. I am shocked you would even ask.'

'What if the child was an orphan?'

'Is he?'

'Sorry? Is who?'

'The child you're talking about. Is he an orphan? Is his mother still around?'

Edward shook his head. 'I'm not talking about a specific kid, Mags. War makes orphans.'

'Yes, indeed it does. All kinds.'

She looked at him and then turned and walked back to the house.

Edward had spent the past many years wondering if she knew. He had faithfully written Yasmine a letter a week since leaving India. Some he mailed, some he threw away or burned at the bottom of his garden, behind the shed. For a while, there was always a pile of leaves or twigs smouldering whenever he was at home, because he burned every letter he wrote. Burning the letters gave him a short-lived satisfaction, and he understood why Yasmine had decided to burn all the things she associated with him, the painful things, like his pictures and his old uniform. It was a way to excise the pain.

His wife never caught him—or chose not to. He could never be sure. In these letters—which were brief—he tried to show Yasmine what his life was like, in the hope that she would share the details with Alec. He had rented a post office box so she could reply to him. Once in a while, Yasmine would deign to send him a picture of Alec. But she rarely, if ever, talked about herself. It was always politics, Bombay Duck business until she left India, and the boy. In the years after the war, India began the arduous process of rebuilding—without the British at their necks. It was a violent time and Edward often worried about her and Alec. He hid his anxieties from Maggie by spending time alone as much as possible and drinking to calm his nerves.

He only felt at peace when Yasmine responded to a letter, even though he sent so few of them. It meant both she and Alec were still alive. Sometimes, Yasmine would write detailed letters on his son's progress. He was grateful for this information but was aching to know what was happening in her life, if she had met someone. He was consumed sometimes by thoughts of her with another man, but those he forced himself to control, because they made him even more reclusive and moody and Maggie couldn't understand it. It hurt her. She would ask him if he was suffering from the same depression as the other veterans, and he would say yes, because the truth was something he could not share. He knew she did not believe it to be that simple.

Finally, when Alec turned ten, he got the news he had been dreading for years. Yasmine had sent a note with a newspaper clipping, announcing her marriage to a prominent Dacca University professor of economics; a brilliant, young, handsome (and bespectacled, Edward noted with bitterness) scholar who had just won a scholarship to receive his doctorate at Columbia University in New York.

He read the note quickly and gazed at Yasmine's grainy black-and-white image in the newspaper—she was in a sari, her hair covered and jewels hanging from her ears and neck. Her new husband stood next to her, earnest in a dark suit, not touching her. Neither was smiling. Alec was not in the picture, but Asma, who was grinning ear to ear, and a more stoic Adil Baboo were. Though seeing Yasmine married was painful, he couldn't help but smile at the image of Asma and Adil Baboo. His heart skipped a beat. He was suddenly assailed with memories of the Duck, of Rahul who should have been in the photo, of Yasmine's small, safe room above the club, with the one window and the ceiling fan that clicked. Thoughts of the room led to thoughts of Yasmine's bed, which led to stirrings and longings that were almost unbearable. He could feel the panic rising up in him, and if he tried to fight it or maintain normalcy in front of Maggie, he knew he would fail.

Edward strode into the kitchen where he announced to Maggie that he was going fishing for the weekend. Alone.

He spent the next couple of days holed up in a motel in Branford, drunk and nowhere near any good fishing. He ordered takeout chop suey, vomited that up and drank some more. On Sunday, he drove home with a hangover but had enough sense to stop at a market and buy three trout, which he presented to his wife to fry up.

Maggie noted his bloodshot eyes, the stench of liquor that clung to him and the fact that the fish were already dressed, and said nothing. He had not washed in at least two days. Sometimes a man needed respite, she figured, and other women had told her how oddly their soldier husbands behaved after they returned. Civilian life was still a challenge for all of them. Many suffered from nightmares, and almost all of them drank too much. Secrecy was also not unusual. The men did not talk to one another about the war, let alone their wives or girlfriends.

'What do you do at the VFW?' she had once asked Edward.

'We shoot pool and talk crap and drink beer.'

'That's it?'

'What else is there?' He did not mention to her that there was a man who could not play pool because he had one arm, or another so badly disfigured his wife had left him. They were not stared at or shunned at the war vets organisation. The last thing any of them wanted to discuss was their injuries or how they got them.

'No one wants to talk about it? You don't swap stories like they do in the movies?'

'Sometimes, we don't say anything at all.'

She had heard much the same from other women. But Edward's secrecy continued to worry her.

~

Six months after her wedding, Yasmine wrote to Edward again, just as he was getting used to the idea that they would, in fact, never be together. It was odd, he realised; he had not known until that moment when he read the wedding announcement, that somehow, he had been holding out hope that they would find their way back to one another. This time there was no mention of weddings, only that she and Alec were leaving East Pakistan, which was what part of Bengal had been renamed to. There was no mention of a husband either. The year before, she had sold the Duck and moved to Dacca, where she had presumably met the brain trust, as Edward now referred to him.

She did not say where she and Alec were going, which Edward felt was unfair and inexcusable, even though he knew they were most likely moving to New York for her husband's fellowship. There are laws, he kept telling himself, and then remembered what Yasmine said long ago about half-caste children. He replied and found he could maintain a restrained, polite tone in the letter. He even congratulated her on her wedding. Again. He enquired after where they were planning on living and got no response. He waited one month for a response and then shot off a much less restrained letter.

Yasmine,

Enough is enough. I have a right to know where you are taking my son, and who the hell he's going to be living with. I mean, you just tell me some guy I don't even know is going to be his father, and I am supposed to just accept that crap! There ARE laws. I don't care what you say! I've looked into it. I can claim paternity at ANY time. Look it up! All we need is a blood test, that I can demand, and there you go! You are a selfish, soulless woman, who holds on to a grudge longer than anyone I know. Not even the Japanese are as vindictive as you are, and they have a lot more reason to be. If you do not respond to me within three weeks, I will take legal action. I have given you more than enough opportunities to make good on things and at least allow me some access to my kid.

Edward

Yasmine never replied to the letter and, for four interminable years, maintained a stony silence. Edward never made good on his threat. He drank excessively and spent more time away from home, always finding excuses to stay out of the house. Sometimes, it was fishing; sometimes it was camping with his childhood friend Greg Tantaquidgen.

Edward was requesting to go camping more frequently and Greg's wife was starting to resent this, but Greg ignored her complaints and explained calmly that his friend was in trouble. He didn't know what trouble, but he figured Edward would eventually tell him. This would require retreating into woods and sitting quietly by a fire drinking beer, or the side of a brook, waiting for fish to bite, and Edward to tell him what was weighing him down. The burdens were heavy as far as he could tell. It wasn't the war or it wasn't only the war, because no one talked about the war. Everyone understood it was hell on earth, and they had seen and done things they did not imagine they would have ever seen or done.

They went to the same spot every time, in Pachaug Forest, about twenty-five minutes outside of Norwich. There were now designated campgrounds there, with readymade stacked stone fire pits. It wasn't as wild or unsullied as when they were kids, but there was comfort in the familiarity of these woods that both men had hiked through as boys. They drove up silently, one or the other occasionally noting a hawk or a deer. In the fall, the colours were spectacular. Edward remembered how much he had wanted Yasmine to see this.

'I have a kid,' Edward finally said, one autumn night, their fifth visit there, as they gathered kindling for a fire.

Greg said nothing at first, letting the information sink in. 'Who's the mother? Anyone I know?' he said eventually.

Edward shook his head. 'She's Indian.'

'Is that a fact?'

'Not your kind of Indian.'

'Okay. What kind?'

'She's from India. Calcutta.'

'Where's the kid?'

'I don't know.'

'You love her.'

'Yes. But not right at this moment.'

'She's not sharing him or her?'

'Him. No. She got married.'

'You blame her for that?'

'No ... and yes.'

Greg handed Edward a beer from the cooler.

'Would you have left Maggie?'

Edward looked at his friend and smiled sadly. 'I lost the nerve. I meant to.'

'But you wanted her to wait for you? Just in case.'

'Yes.'

'Well, the way I see it, she's lost to you but the kid isn't.'

'Yeah, but I don't know where he is.'

'He's a boy. When he starts growing, he's going to go looking for his father. A half-blood? We almost always do. We're too uncomfortable, you know. Be ready for him.'

Edward drank his beer and mulled that over.

'He might get angry at his mother. Don't encourage that. She did the best she could,' Greg said into the silence. Edward knew his friend was speaking from experience. He nodded.

'I would have married her, if I could,' Edward said.

'Are you telling me that for my benefit?'

Edward was surprised. 'I didn't care she was Indian but ... What kind of a life would she have had here?'

'We'll never know now, will we?' Greg said.

~

Edward hoped his friend was right and that Alec would come looking for him to 'make sense of his skin'. At first, he had continued to write to Yasmine, even though he didn't know where to send the letters. Then he stopped. He decided to have faith in his son's need for answers. If he knew anything about Yasmine, she would have encouraged a sense of intellectual curiosity in the boy, which he hoped would inspire him to search for many things. He also realised he did not know her anymore, so he did not know what she was telling the boy about him. In her eyes, he had abandoned them. He could not defend himself. He yearned for the chance to at least explain. He would think of the boy on his birthday. Every year, he would raise a toast to Alec on that day, and recite Keats. This is how much I adored your mother, he would say out loud:

When I have fears that I may cease to be
Before my pen has glean'd my teeming brain,
Before high piled books, in charactry,
Hold like rich garners the full ripen'd grain;
When I behold, upon the night's starr'd face,
Huge cloudy symbols of a high romance,
And think that I may never live to trace
Their shadows, with the magic hand of chance;
And when I feel, fair creature of an hour,
That I shall never look upon thee more,
Never have relish in the fairy power
Of unreflecting love;—then on the shore
Of the wide world I stand alone, and think
Till love and fame to nothingness do sink.

On Alec's eighteenth birthday, he uttered the same words and wished his boy the same love he felt for his mother. 'Kid, your mother was no walk in the park, but she gave me you and she gave me joy, and knowing you're out there gives me hope.'

'Who's there with you?' Maggie said. She had knocked on the door to the den, but Edward hadn't heard her at first.

'No one,' he said, opening the door. 'Just quoting Keats.'

'Eddie, it's not even six! You're getting started earlier these days.'

He ignored the disapproval in her voice and tried to smile at her.

'Did you need me?'

She took a long drag from her cigarette.

'You have a phone call. It's not the hospital.'

'Who is it?'

'A young man. He has an accent.'

36

He had started so many times to tell her about Alec, but Maggie would change the subject or leave the house, purportedly on some errand. Finally, he stopped trying. They spent less time together: he was either working or isolated in his study, drinking, and she volunteered at the local library or was out socialising with her lady friends. She began to throw more parties and invited neighbours over for impromptu bridge nights or cocktails. She filled the space between them with activity and other people, noise and smoke. They both found it was easy for two people who lived together to never say a full sentence to one another for an entire day, if their lives were designed that way. Without realising it, they became less aware of the other's presence. They no longer ate at the dinner table, where they used to discuss their day. They ate silently, with their individual TV tray tables in front of them, watching the news or whatever programme was on that evening They would retire early, as soon as they heard the last newscast for the evening, each performing their pre-bedtime rituals at separate sinks in the small bathroom they shared. Sometimes they briefly discussed what they had seen that night.

'That Klink in *Hogan's Heroes* is a moron, it was so obvious that wasn't Hitler,' Maggie would say. Edward would nod and chuckle.

Sometimes he ventured a comment like, 'I wish the Japanese had been as dumb as the Germans.' But never elaborated on it.

'Well, surely they weren't really that dumb. It's just TV,' Maggie said.

'I wouldn't know,' Edward shrugged.

Maggie knew he would not discuss it further.

Even at night, in bed, they read silently before turning off their lamps and facing away from each another. Their lovemaking had become infrequent and more obligatory until one night, just as Edward was about to get started, Maggie said, 'Shall we try something different?' surprising him.

'Like what?' he said.

'You were in India a long time,' she said. 'Didn't you pick up anything from the *Kama Sutra*?'

Edward looked for accusation in her face and voice. But she just smiled up at him. Edward rolled off her and lay back. He stared up at the ceiling.

'What's wrong?' Maggie asked. Edward turned to look at her. Her brow was slightly furrowed and her smile uncertain, but her face appeared guileless.

'Mags, why would I know about the *Kama Sutra*?' he asked in a measured tone. His heart was racing, because he thought this was the moment he had waited for. She had given them the perfect opening. He was not fully prepared, and he was nervous, but he thought, okay, no time like the present. He sat up and faced her. 'Mags,' he began. 'Can you answer me? Why would I know about that?'

'Why are you doing your shrink stuff on me?' Maggie said. The slight furrow in her brow was now a scowl. 'I just thought we should try something new. Is that wrong?'

'Of course not. That's not what I meant.'

'Well, you're making me feel like I've done something wrong.'

'Can we try to talk?'

'About what?'

'India—'

'What, specifically? The war?'

'Not the war, no, well, partially—'

'Is this really the time to bring this up? We haven't made love in weeks. We don't spend time together.'

'Whose fault is that?' he said.

Edward watched helplessly as Maggie then got up, wrapped her naked body in her robe and locked herself in the bathroom.

After that Maggie became more laconic. They returned to their routine of pleasantries, errands, and silent dinners. Despite this, there would be more moments when Edward thought, okay, this is it, the perfect opening to face the truth. Like when Alec would call, which he started to do with some regularity. But when the boy called, she would say hello, and then hand the phone over, without a word, often to Edward's astonishment. The first time Edward visited the boy at Wesleyan, he said, 'I'm going to see Alec. He's—'

She stopped him by saying, 'Okey-dokey. Have a good time. Take a jacket. I think the temperature is going to drop.'

But the second time he visited Alec, Maggie baked oatmeal cookies and handed the cellophane-wrapped plate to Edward to take with him. She lit a cigarette, her third one in under an hour, and took a long drag.

'We'll talk when you get back,' she said. 'I guess it's time.' Edward nodded.

She gave a slight cough and cleared her throat. Edward lingered by the door.

'Do you want to come with me?' he asked.

She shook her head, unable to answer because she began to cough more.

Edward walked to the sink and filled a glass with water. He handed it to her.

'Mags, you should get that cough looked at,' he said.

She took a large sip of the water. 'I have,' she said. 'I'm waiting to hear back. They drew some blood, took an x-ray.'

Edward sat down. 'When was this?'

'Last Tuesday. You were busy.'

She started to light another cigarette, and Edward stopped her.

'Not until we know what's wrong, Mags,' he said.

She stubbed it out, took a sip of water. 'It's probably just leftover from that wicked cold I had, remember?'

Edward nodded. 'That's exactly what it is,' he said. 'But you should quit for a while anyway.'

Maggie tried to stifle a cough that rose in her throat and nodded. 'You should get on the road,' she said.

'We'll talk when I get back?'

Maggie smiled. 'Yes.'

But they never did. When Edward returned from visiting Alec, Maggie was in bed, with a fever that rose through the night. He stayed awake, watching her, giving her sips of cold water and wiping her feverish head and neck with a cool cloth. The next day, the doctor called, asking them both to come in when she was able. He didn't want to discuss anything over the phone. If her fever didn't abate by then, he said, she should be brought into the emergency room.

Two days later, she and Edward sat in their doctor's office and listened while he explained what was going to happen to her, possibly in the next six months, possibly more, possibly less. The slight, persistent cough she'd had for months came from a spot on her lung that would grow and kill her.

The feelings of guilt that had only tugged at Edward every now and again overwhelmed him. He could not hide from his failings any longer. He saw to her every need and nursed her. Once they knew the prognosis, things moved quickly. It was over much quicker than either had anticipated. By the end, the radiation therapy had weakened her so much, a mild cold could kill her. But she did not want to die in the hospital and asked to be taken back to their home.

The morning she died, a big owl flew into the cherry tree next to her bedroom window. It positioned itself on a branch that was at the same height as the windowpane. It was almost pure white, with golden-tipped feathers scattered here and there. It slept all day on that branch, unmoving, its white face tucked into its side.

'Owls are portents of death,' Maggie said, smiling weakly.

Edward started to pull the shade down. 'No, leave it up,' she said. 'It's a beautiful thing. It's come to help me along.'

Edward had never known Maggie to be superstitious. He shook his head.

'You don't believe in this mumbo jumbo, Mags,' he said.

She tried to sit up and needed assistance. He went to her side and adjusted the pillow so she could sit back.

'I'd believe in the tooth fairy if I thought she could help me die.'

'Oh, Mags.'

'Sit down.'

Edward sat next to her and put his arm around her, cradling her head. She was so thin.

'You always believed what you believed,' she said to him. 'I've had very little influence on your life.'

'What do you mean?'

'When you came back from the war, you were different—oh! I know everyone was, what I'm saying is before, I knew I could sway you one way or another.'

'About what?'

'Anything. My opinion mattered.'

'It still does, Maggie.'

'No. I have no influence on you. That is what I'm saying.

You came back, but you did not come back to me. It's like someone sapped me of my importance to you.'

It was then that Edward understood that she knew. Of course she did. She was a woman.

'I feel guilty,' she said quietly.

'God, Mags, what do you have to feel guilty about?'

'I should have met—him. I just couldn't.'

'It's okay, darling. I understand.'

'Why did you come back anyway?'

That was a good question, and one he actually knew the answer to.

'Because this is my life,' he said. 'Sometimes there isn't any great explanation. This is what I knew how to do, and this is what I wanted. End of story.'

'No, this is not what you wanted. This was what you were least afraid of.'

This was also true, and so he did not respond to it.

'Was she very beautiful?' she asked after a while. Her breath was laboured now; before, it had been even.

'Yes,' he said, and closed his eyes. There was no point in lying to her. He kissed her on the lips and she smiled up at him.

'Raven-haired? Like the girl in *Sinbad*?'

He nodded, because he did not know what else to do.

'What colour was her skin? Dark or lighter?'

'Brown. Like coffee with a little bit of milk. Sometimes it was golden.'

'Well, which was it, golden or coffee with milk?'

'Both, it depended.'

'On what?'

'The time of year, or day.'

Maggie, impressed and hurt by this intimate and poetic detail, tried to give a low whistle, but her mouth was dry.

Edward rested his chin on her head and began to cry silently.

'Why do you need to know this, Mags?' he whispered.

'You were lost to me in those years, and she took care of you, didn't she? Did you love her?'

Edward sighed and seriously considered lying to her for a moment, but then thought better of it. 'Yes, but not enough.'

'You broke her heart?'

Edward nodded. 'I think so. I'm not sure, to be honest. Yasmine was always hard to read.'

He had said her name without thinking. Saying it out loud now sent a jolt through him. Yet, it was Maggie who shuddered under his arm.

'Yasmine,' she said. 'Is that Bengali for Jasmine?'

Edward shook his head. 'It's actually Arabic, Mags,' he said gently, kissing her forehead.

'Oh,' she said. 'My favourite flower. I could never make them stick though. Jasmine is not cut out for New England weather. You should go to her and beg her to forgive you.'

'Why now?'

'I don't want you to be alone.'

He kissed her again, and she closed her eyes and slept.

37

Death Announcement
The Hartford Courant
5 November 1964

Huq, Reza Syed of Chester died on 3 November 1965 at his home. A very recent transplant to Chester from Scarsdale, NY, Dr Huq was born in Dacca, East Pakistan, and immigrated to the United States in 1954. Dr Huq, PhD, was a leading specialist in Non-Formal Education with many a publication to his credit. He served as a consultant for both the World Bank and the United Nations and taught at UConn Storrs for three years.

He is survived by his loving wife, Ruksana Yasmine Khan; his son, Akash Alexander Lafaver; and his mother, Nafisa Begum of Dacca. He also leaves behind three sisters, ten nieces and nephews and many loving friends. A memorial service will be held on Saturday, 6 November at 11 a.m. at the Old Town Hall in Chester, located on 4 Liberty Street. In keeping with Islamic tradition, Dr Huq's body was interned immediately at the Laurel Hill Cemetery. Instead of flowers, memorial donations may be made to the United Nations Children's Emergency Fund.

~

Yasmine read and re-read the note from Edward asking to meet her, and then slid it back into its envelope. It had been written a month after her husband's passing, and was deeply creased from having been unfolded and read numerous times. She tucked the envelope into a pocket in her purse and took a small sip of tea and promptly burnt her lip.

'Crikey!' she said. She could feel the blister form inside her lower lip at once.

'Are you all right?' the waitress asked.

'I burnt my lip,' Yasmine said. 'But it was my fault.' She smiled up at the young woman, who offered her some ice to put on it.

Yasmine had come in alone and sat down at the table nearest the exit for the better part of an hour. The waitress noticed her at once. She was elegant, with hair that fell just above her shoulders. She wore a light, loose green tunic dotted with dark-green paisleys over flared jeans. She wore very little jewellery, small silver hoops on her ears and no wedding ring. But her ring finger had a mark where a wedding ring used to be. The waitress was an English major at UConn with aspirations of becoming a writer. Her modern psychological novel professor told her to always be aware of people and details because one never knew where the next great story would come from. When the waitress saw Yasmine read and re-read the light-blue letter, and tuck it back into her purse, only to take it out again, she knew this was a story. There was something about the beautiful older woman that was a bit unapproachable, but her curiosity was too great.

'Are you waiting for someone?' she asked Yasmine shyly.

Yasmine nodded and took another cautious sip of tea.

'Could I have some lemon, please?'

'Oh! Of course.'

She scurried away to the counter to get the lemon. Her boss admonished her for harassing the customer.

'Ella, leave the Indian woman alone,' he whispered.

'She's so mysterious,' Ella said. 'You know she has a story.'

'Everyone does, now just give her the lemon.'

Yasmine fidgeted with her napkin and checked her watch. She had arrived forty-five minutes earlier than the time she and Edward had agreed upon to give herself the chance to gather her thoughts, and realised very quickly that with something of this magnitude, after two decades, it was virtually impossible to gather anything, except a mild form of hysteria.

How was it possible, she wondered, that after all this time, this man still has this effect on me? She looked at the wedge of lemon on her plate and thought, instead of Maggie, I should have put him in the lemon all those years ago. The thought made her smile. She shook her head.

'I hope I'm not intruding.'

Yasmine did not look up at once. Edward sat down in the chair opposite hers. When she raised her eyes to him, she saw that he was smiling at her.

'Hello, Yasmine,' he said.

'Hello.'

Her heart pounding, she tried to remember his age and decided he was fifty. One year older than her. He looked fit; his hair was still mostly brown and he had most of it, which bode well for Akash. She did not remember his eyes being so green. She always remembered them as more hazel. They looked at one another closely, each examining the other's face for all the familiar things and also the new ones; the lines around the eyes and mouth. Yasmine's skin was still flawless, Edward noted, and she had very few lines around her dark eyes even when she smiled. He realised as he looked at her that she was the same to him. She was just as he had remembered. She was still twenty-six, even though her luxuriously dark hair was now shot through with silver. Her hand went self-consciously to the small marcasite barrette that held her hair back from her face. She tucked an errant strand behind her ear. They both laughed, and that eased the awkwardness.

'Shorter,' Edward said, indicating she had cut her hair.

'And grey,' she said.

She had rehearsed their meeting in her mind so many times over the years. Sometimes she was coolly elegant, though friendly; sometimes she was neutral and nonchalant. Sometimes she gave full vent to her rage and let him have it. She would call him a cad in those instances, and when he went to beg forgiveness, she would say, 'There is nothing to forgive Edward, because I am to blame. I was the fool who allowed you into my life.' It was all very dramatic and ended with him reduced to tears while Yasmine flounced out the door. As time wore on, Yasmine allowed herself to nurse and imagine yet another possibility, one of gentleness and humour and shared nostalgia.

Now, though, as she looked at him, this older, much wearier man, none of these reactions seemed appropriate, and Yasmine just wanted to let go and see what would happen next.

'I'm sorry about your husband,' Edward said, after a moment. 'I know he was a great man.'

Yasmine nodded, unable to answer. It still affected her to hear of Reza in the past tense.

'Akash told me about ... Maggie. I hope she didn't suffer too much.'

'She did, but I don't like to think about it.'

'I understand.'

'When did you start wearing glasses?' Edward asked.

'Oh, about three years back, mostly for reading. I need them more and more though.'

'I guess all that fish oil paid off,' he said.

'Sorry?'

'Remember you used to say how Bengalis had good eyesight because they consumed so much fish?'

'You remember that?'

'I remember everything,' he said.

'I named the club after a fish,' she said and cleared her throat.

'Yes.'

'I was being ironic. Silly, now that I think of it. I always thought I was devilishly clever for that.'

'It was, you were,' he said.

He wanted to take her small hand. But Yasmine was wound tight and all scooted inward, as usual.

The waitress came over and beamed down at them.

'What can I get you?' she said. She glanced from Edward to Yasmine and thought to herself: story. They were once lovers. Why is that always so clear between two people? Was it because lovers inhabit one another, she wondered?

After they ordered, Yasmine became business-like, which from what Edward remembered, was to be expected. He almost said as much, but then thought better of it.

'Akash has decided to drop out of college,' Yasmine began.

'I know, I talked to him,' Edward said.

Yasmine's eyes narrowed. Edward's heart sank. This was a familiar feeling.

'I know what you're thinking,' he said quickly. 'He's not picking me over you. Right now, he needs … his father.'

'Hmm, I see.'

'Do you?'

'You have to forgive me, Edward, it is hard for me to reconcile how you have become his confidante in his hour of need when I have been the one all these years worried about him, loving him—'

'I have too,' Edward said.

The eager waitress came over with Edward's coffee and prevented Yasmine from shooting out a harsh retort to that.

'Well, is he still insisting on spending time in India?' she asked.

'Yes.'

'And you know this because you spoke to him or saw him?'

'Both.'

'I see.'

She played with her napkin, folding it, unfolding it. She unwound the beige chiffon scarf that hung loosely about her neck, because it was suddenly stifling her. She took a sip of tea, which was still too hot and burnt her lip again, put down the tea-cup with a clatter and looked for the eager waitress with awful timing because now she needed her, and she was nowhere to be found.

Edward watched Yasmine's agitation silently and prayed she would not get up and walk out, forcing him to run after her. Like he had so often in the past, he wished she would just explode instead of trying so hard to control her emotions.

'You're upset,' he said.

'No. I am a bit ... surprised that you saw him. Does he plan to come home before he goes off?'

'Yes, I think so.'

'That's not good enough.'

'You're awfully hard on him, you know?'

'No! What utter nonsense. I know no one has what it takes to lead the perfect life. We all just muddle through, don't we? '

'Yes.'

'Well?'

Edward was smiling at her, in that infuriating way that she suddenly remembered made her feel she was being too emotional.

'You're still pretty,' he said.

'I am? Well, what nonsense,' she said. But she was pleased, which was apparent.

'Can you leave Alec to me?' he said.

'You mean Akash? I suppose so, but I am not sure what you can do.'

'I think I understand what's happening here.'

'Yes, you would, being a shrink, nah?'

Yasmine missed Patience at that moment and her ability to distil her emotions when it came to the basics.

What would she say, wondered Yasmine, as Edward talked about how their son was in a crisis but also a period of self-discovery. Yasmine frowned slightly upon hearing the words 'self-discovery', but then her mind travelled as she tried to wrestle all the emotions she was feeling into something manageable. Patience would say, come on now, ducky! He's just a man and a Yank. Don't go falling in love. Again. Or, she would say, stop being a mule, Yassu, and hear the bloke out. This is about 'Sir Bump' after all.

'You're worried that he'll grow closer to me, or has, than you,' Edward was saying. 'Hello? Where have you wandered off to?' he added, when Yasmine looked away, seemingly lost in thought.

'Well, it's always the one who stays who is not appreciated. I was there for the nappy changes and sleepless nights and notes from deans and mumps,' Yasmine replied, snapping out of her reverie.

'There is a way to remedy that now, you know.'

'Such as?'

'Present a more united front. Be his parents … together.'

Yasmine coughed delicately into her napkin. She ignored what he said. It seemed an outrageous notion.

'Do you know where he is exactly?'

'He's on some commune in New Paltz.'

'Yes,' she nodded. 'He's a hippie.' Just saying the word made her frown. 'Suddenly everyone wants to be a fakir under a banyan tree.'

'He's one. For now.'

'I blame myself. I let him read Ginsberg when he turned seventeen.'

She was serious but Edward laughed. It was contagious, and Yasmine found herself chuckling. An awkward pause followed. Yasmine wanted the overzealous waitress to come and fuss over them and break the silence.

'Do you still hate me?' Edward asked. The question startled her.

She said, 'No, of course not. I never did.'

'That's not true,' Edward said, smiling.

'Well, it was the normal amount of hatred one associates with these sorts of things,' she allowed. 'Nothing outlandish.'

She smoothed down her hair and dabbed her clean chin with the napkin. Like she used to do when she didn't know what to say. This made Edward want to kiss her.

'That's too bad.'

'Pardon?'

'Well, if you hated me to an outlandish extent it would mean I still had a chance.'

'You are so odd,' she said to him.

Edward nodded. 'Indeed, I am.'

'Well, you left.'

'You chased me away, you never came to me that day when I—'

'You slept with Patience.'

Edward sat back. The waitress came over and asked if they needed anything else. Neither Yasmine nor Edward looked at her. She looked from one to the other.

'Okay,' she said. 'I guess you don't need anything.'

She walked back to the counter and made a face. Her boss shrugged. 'What?'

'He slept with Patience,' she whispered.

Yasmine sipped her tea.

'It was just once,' Edward said. 'And I am sorrier than you know. I still regret it.'

Yasmine shrugged. 'I always knew you found her attractive. Well, every man did. I know she fancied you a bit. But I didn't think she would do that.'

'She was angry about...' he leaned in and whispered, 'the abortion. But you must know that Yasmine, you're smart.'

Yasmine fluttered her hand in the air. 'Oh, it's all right! My god, it's so far gone. I have forgiven you and her, you know?'

'Mighty big of you.'

'Why are you miffed at me? I didn't shag your best friend and believe every blasted thing she said about me.'

'I was young, I was stupid and I was insecure. I thought you didn't love me anymore. In fact, you never told me you loved me.'

'I did!'

'Nope, never.'

'I did.'

'No, Yasmine, you never did. I told you, but you never once said it back. I knew it was all part of your stiff upper lip nonsense. You're far more English than you realise, but a guy needs to hear it once in a while.'

He looked at her expectantly. Yasmine was shocked.

'What? Now? You want me to tell you now?'

'Did you ever love me?'

'Oh, for pity's sake!'

'Well?'

'I didn't come here to ... to discuss love-shove.'

'What do you think discussing Alec is? He's our child. Yours and mine. We made him. So...'

Yasmine folded her arms across her chest. Her face was grim.

'I can wait,' Edward said. 'I waited all this time. I have an iron bladder, if you recollect. I can drink coffee and wait.'

He had her. She was softer, worn down, still a warrior and still angry with him, but softer. When he had decided to meet her, he had no intention of re-addressing his feelings for her. Until he saw her and felt young again. They had a son after all, he thought to himself, and he needed them. His lovely Maggie was gone, so was the brain trust, God rest him. It was their time. He looked up to see the waitress gazing at them wistfully. He smiled at her.

Whatever happens, Yasmine thought as she looked at Edward's smiling face, it was good to see him.

Edward cleared his throat. Yasmine remembered he used to do that when he was preparing to say something important or difficult.

'What is it?' she asked. She was not sure why she was nervous.

'I owe you an apology.'

'Well, what happened with you and Patience—'

'No, for ... for not returning.'

Yasmine looked down at her hands.

'Please look at me. This is not easy for me,' Edward said. 'I was a small town boy, who wasn't very wise or worldly. But I love my son. People don't often change, but I have.'

Yasmine nodded. 'Yes, that is true. People cling to what is familiar. Even if it proves catastrophic for them. It's good that you've changed—for the better, I think?'

'You changed me, Alec existing changed me, Maggie changed me,' Edward said. 'Her forgiveness and understanding was ... humbling. I am hoping you will forgive me too.'

Yasmine nodded, too emotional to speak. 'I didn't expect you to come back, you know,' she said, recovering.

Edward wanted to hold her but knew she would not allow it. Instead, he slid his chair slightly closer, but not so close Yasmine would feel he was taking liberties in some way.

She placed her hand over his. It was warm and soft, and the familiarity of her touch sent jolts of energy through him. He covered her hand with his. The moment he did, she slid hers out from underneath. Edward stifled a sigh and put his hands between his knees.

She looked down and began to cry. Edward took her hand.

'We can both do right by our son now,' Edward said. Yasmine blew her nose quietly and gestured for some more tea.

'I've been thinking. We should go to Calcutta together,' Edward continued, nervously. 'All of us.'

Yasmine was taken aback. 'Travel together? That would be odd.'

'Why?

'Because we are strangers now.'

Edward nodded, but that notion made him unhappy. Though he had to admit, it was somewhat true.

'Alec wants to visit Calcutta with both of us. It would be a slow ride, and we can get re-acquainted and talk about ... everything,' he said.

'What is it you really want from me?'

'Your forgiveness, your understanding. I've carried the guilt with me all these years. But what you resented me for are not the things for which I require expiation.'

'Shagging my friend and abandoning your son do not require forgiveness?'

'You pushed me away.'

'I had no choice!'

'Oh, Yasmine, you made that choice.'

'You wouldn't have left Maggie and your white-bread life. And the truth is—' her voice caught in her throat. She took a sip of tea and continued, 'And the truth is, there was a part of you that could not imagine being with someone like me.'

'A stubborn fool, well, yes—'

'No, a kalo woman.'

Edward stared at Yasmine, his shock apparent.

'Are you looking at me like that because it's true or because it isn't?'

When Edward said nothing, Yasmine motioned to the waitress for the check. She placed three crisp bills on the table, while the waitress and Edward looked on, both dismayed at how unhappy Yasmine now seemed. When she reached for more cash for a tip, the waitress said, 'No, no, that's not necessary.'

Yasmine mumbled a barely audible 'thank you' and got up to leave.

Edward placed his hand on top of Yasmine's, but she pulled it away.

'That's not true, Yasmine. I was prepared to leave Maggie. I sent word telling you that, but you never got the message because Patience never gave it to you. I think you know why.'

Yasmine sat back down.

'Is this true?'

'Of course.'

He took out a note from his pocket. Patience had written to Yasmine, telling her Edward was coming back for her and his son. She was prepared to give it to her, went to her room to do so. Yasmine wasn't there and Patience changed her mind. The note was still in pristine condition, not a crease or a stain. Patience had taken very good care of it.

'She sent it back to me last fall. She's ashamed and wants your forgiveness.'

Yasmine turned the note over in her hands.

'She has that,' Yasmine said.

Edward shrugged.

'I'm feeling so many … things,' she said, still looking down at the note. Edward knew the pain of separation had taken its toll. He knew Yasmine had longed for him at some point in their years apart, but gazing at Yasmine's face now, the most open he had ever seen it, he knew on some level that the loss of her friendship with Patience had caused her more pain than losing him. He was not jealous, only heartsore for them both.

'Call her, Yasmine.'

Yasmine looked up at him, her eyes wet. He reached for her hand. She allowed him to take it.

'Should I? Yes, I should.'

He chuckled. 'I always thought that Tommy was the main rival for my affections, but all along, it was Patience Goodwin.'

Yasmine smiled and stood up. 'I must go,' she said.

'Why?' He was disappointed. He wanted a few more moments with her. He was never certain if he was going to see her again.

'It's all a bit much for me. Twenty years to rifle through.'

'Or we put it behind us and focus on the next twenty?'

Yasmine turned pink. 'That's a bit odd, not to say utterly presumptuous.'

'Shouldn't we discuss our plans for Alec?'

'Is Akash a ploy?'

'For what?'

'For luring me back?'

'Which answer will do the trick?' Edward said, grinning.

Yasmine found herself smiling back at him.

'You're that determined?'

'Yes, suddenly I am, yes.'

'Well if you can bring Akash to his senses, you know, there's a possibility I will love you. Again. You'll be my hero.' Her smile had turned coy, and to Edward, irresistible. Despite her protestations that it was untoward, Edward kissed her hand. She had admitted she'd loved him.

'But so many years, so many things have happened. I cannot guarantee anything,' she added quickly.

Edward nodded. 'No, of course not. I'll wait. I'm pretty good at that.'

'Yes, we will sort out Akash. That is our main goal,' she said.

Edward beamed at her, his eyes filled with hope. Yasmine was, naturally, telling the truth, yet, she was also enjoying the power she had now been given.

Men are really such simple creatures, Yasmine thought. After five decades on earth, Yasmine Khan had finally learned the art of flirting.

38

Akash Khan Lafaver
34 N. Faithful Street
New Paltz, NY
10 March 1966

Dearest Akash,
I was going to write you about my hopes for what the Cal trip would accomplish. Instead, I have enclosed a more important letter from your Aunt Patience, setting the record straight. It is addressed to me but was always meant for you. My hope is that it will ease your mind, the way it has eased mine; that it will remind you that you were borne of love. In the end, I am relieved that Patience did not give me the message that your father asked her to. Even though it cost us twenty years together. Somehow, the thought of hurting Maggie, a woman I never met, is too much to bear, and things turned out as they should have. I believe that implicitly.

I'm a bit anxious about re-visiting the Duck. I know the silly little sign will be gone and the mirrors will probably be cracked. All I'll see are ghosts. Edward will insist on pointing out the room where you were conceived. Please don't indulge him. It's these types of American and wholly inappropriate exhibitions of emotion that I find unnerving. I told him the other day that visiting the Duck will remind us of our mortality because of how much time has passed. He suggested I 'lighten up and have a s'more', which is ridiculous because he knows I don't care for sweets. He is so odd. I'm not at all sure how I fell in love with him in the first place. But there it is. I still feel a great deal of affection for him. I am, however, enjoying my solitude and pursuits. I am auditing a class at UConn, Storrs, The Modern Psychological Novel, and taking swimming lessons. I don't know what will happen with your father and me. We see each other often. It's strange that we were living only a few miles apart for so long and never bumped into each other. But we are cautious around one another for the most part. As your aunt Patience said to me recently, 'The toothpaste is out of the tube, ducky, not sure you can ever go back.' Having her return to my life has made it easier and afforded me clarity. Since we were girls, she has always been the one—besides your dear late nani—who helped me sort things out. Talking to Patience helps me clarify what I think I want. She is visiting with me now and has extended her trip by a week. She'll be here until I leave for Cal. She has two boys of her own, both adopted. Her mother, Daisy, still lives with her in Plymouth. Which is probably why she decided to stay an extra week.

I am telling you this, about your father and me, not to disappoint you, but to prepare you for having both parents in your life as separate partners working for your well-being. But not necessarily together. In the traditional way. Edward and I have finally become friends, and I am enjoying his friendship. You're a hippie these days, contemplating your navel. This might make sense to you?

Good night, sweet prince. We'll all be together soon, Inshallah, under the Calcutta night sky. I am told the stars are no longer visible as they used to be. Too much progress.

Always, your mother,
Yasmine

ACKNOWLEDGEMENTS

This has been a fifteen-plus year journey and I have many people to thank. Firstly, my former, but no less beloved, agent, Rachel Mills, who patiently guided and supported this story for years and helped me find its home. Which brings me to the wonderfully energetic Kanishka Gupta of Writer's Side, who then took up the baton for me.

To Sadaf Saaz, and Tahmima Anam, founders of Hay Fest Dhaka where Rachel and I found each other. This could not have happened if you didn't create that space for Bangladeshi writers.

To my gentle but firm readers, Chaitali Sen, Frances Dorris, and Michael Kornacki, who helped me shape the story over years and multiple iterations.

I spent countless hours in the Darien Public Library working on giving Yasmine Khan life, in either a lovely, sun-filled nook, surrounded by books or next to a fireplace on those chilly New England mornings. Thank you for that sanctuary.

To Soniah Kamal, Jennifer Paddock, Rachel Paul Martin, Fariba Alam and Ihktisad Ahmed, for their abiding love, friendship, and wisdom.

Aasha Mehreen Amin, you saw me as a writer, long before I did. You are my family.

To my brilliant and patient editor Deepthi Talwar, thank you for caring about my characters as much as I did, and pulling this story to its feet.

Finally, to the men and women of the China–Burma–India Theatre of World War II, civilian and military alike, whose courage inspired and humbled me and led me to put this story down on paper. Your sacrifice will never be forgotten.